Courting
Justice

by

Robin Kruger

Published by Robin Kruger Books

ISBN: 978-0-6399865-4-8 (epub)
ISBN: 978-0-6399865-5-5 (mobi)
ISBN: 978-0-6399865-8-6 (print)

Robin Kruger Books

www.robinkrugerbooks.com

AUTHOR'S NOTES

1. Whilst Courting Justice is an original story, many incidents have been 'borrowed' from what has previously occurred on the tennis tour. This is intentional to give the reader a genuine feel for the 'real' tennis tour.

2. The Courting Justice story occurs mainly during the 1990s. Accordingly, some of the records and rules of the game that are mentioned in the book may no longer stand.

CHAPTER 1

The shrill ring of the shuddering alarm clock rudely tore into Justin's sleep at the tender hour of 4.15 a.m. The boy fumbled for the clock under his coir pillow and switched it off, but his head still throbbed. A devilish temptation to ignore the wake-up call, curl over and snuggle under the warm, cosy blankets, cried out from his aching muscles. The temptation was strong, enticingly strong.

But deep down from the depths of some irrational corner of his being, an unyielding conscience, a thorn amongst the roses of flesh, flexed its muscle and stung him with an unspoken pang of guilt. So small, yet so powerful for this unique breed.

In the face of an avalanche of reasons to succumb, Justin dutifully responded, woke into a world of slumber, wearily climbed out of bed, togged out in a tatty track suit and worn running shoes, combed his fingers through his tousled blond hair, then tiptoed past the rows of snoring bodies in his dormitory and trotted downstairs to his boarding school kitchen.

He carefully dragged an old wooden kitchen table to the pantry door. It creaked loudly in the still of the night!

Shit! Now I'm Ma Blunderbuss's din dins! lamented Justin, the hairs on the nape of his neck bristling.

He stood dead still, in trepidation of the larger than life matron bursting through her bedroom door. She slept next door, a guard dog to her pantry, and would think nothing of serving him to her 150 hungry inmates for breakfast!

The kitchen clock ticked loudly in the darkness. A long minute passed. No Ma Blunderbuss!

Justin mustered the courage to steady a dining chair on the table, and climbed the jungle gym. He delved his hand into his pocket, withdrew a jute skipping rope, then expertly threaded it through the burglar-barred fanlight above the pantry door. His hands slowly fed a loop of rope, then reeled it in until it caught a round brass knob. Drawing the rope tight, he pulled fractionally more with his left hand, the friction of the rope rotating the cylinder lock. When fully turned, he dangled his foot blindly in the dark until it located the outside door handle, pushed it down and the pantry door clicked opened.

Gotcha! Sweet dreams, Ma Blunderbuss!

Inside the forbidden territory, Justin quickly climbed the grocery shelves and selected two eggs and a stem of macaroni. With the deftness

1

of a cordon bleu chef, the boy cracked open an egg, tilted his head back and spilled its glutinous contents into his mouth.

'Yech!' he scowled.

Then the other egg. He opened the fridge, prised open the lid of a huge vat, dipped in one end of his macaroni straw and sucked deep mouthfuls of cold milk, washing the sticky egg slime down his throat. The early morning fuel of Spartans!

Now to escape!

Justin crept upstairs in ghostly silence, climbed onto his steel cupboard, bent back the loosened burglar bars, squeezed through an open window, clambered onto a rusty drainpipe and shinnied down to the ground. So accustomed was the 14 year old boy to this daily ritual, that he managed with his eyes half-glued shut with sleep.

Jumping off the creaky drainpipe into a blast of cold early morning air, Justin quickly glanced towards the front door to check on the arrival of *The Natal Mercury*, the morning newspaper.

Good! It's on time for once! he thought.

His shivering hands stuttered through the pages where his eyes roved around the print until he found what he wanted, the latest tennis news, 'SUPERCOOL CURREN TOAST OF WIMBLEDON'.

'He beat *McEnroe*!' exclaimed Justin in a misty puff of disbelief.

Folding the newspaper and about to throw it towards the front doormat, his eyes caught a word too familiar to escape him, 'tennis'. Tucked away on the bottom left corner of the front page, a story headline read, 'FAMOUS TENNIS COACH DISAPPEARS'. Curious to read further, but time not permitting, Justin's mind shrugged its shoulders.

He gazed out into the quiet dark of the morning, a time shared only by newspaper and milk delivery folk, inhaled a deep breath of cold air, then set off for the ominous ridge that brooded over the city of Durban.

There he interspersed gruelling roadwork with push-ups and sit-ups and bunny hops, hundreds of them animated on the pavement until his anguished muscles wobbled like jelly, culminating with the dreaded ascent and descent of the steepest road in the city, countless times, all run backwards.

Then he ran to the deserted beach for his favourite training, imbued with competition. The first light of dawn cast an eerie glow on the sea and the cry of a lone seagull circling overhead kept him company. Justin's bare feet sank into the cool sand and he revelled in the gritty feel between his toes, running close to the foamy water's edge, then sprinting away as the breaking waves lapped the shore and chased him.

Come on, you bastard! Catch me if you can! he taunted the sea, challenging himself to stay dry. He did this over and over again, traversing the shore from one end of the beach to the other.

Faster, Justin. Faster! he urged his body to the South Beach pier, his face grimacing with pain.

His strong, sinewy legs extracted their last ounce and his lungs reached bursting point. Then it was all over. He crumpled in a heap on the soft beach sand, taking in huge gulps of salty air.

'Gotcha!' he panted heavily. 'A new record!'

But deep inside he knew he competed against similar aspirations in the snow of Sweden, the concrete jungle of New York, and the rugged outback of Australia. Justin looked at his watch. Breaking his record bought him spare time.

Go that extra mile! he decided, his ambition torturing his body.

His feet pounded down the road on a cold winter's morning, a lonely journey through a dark tunnel of blood, sweat and tears, where the only light at the end was a dream.

§

The dream! The passion! It all started five years ago in the remote district of northern Swaziland.

Sitting level in the calm river water, dry only by a kayak, Justin Forrester, a scrawny nine year old kid, observed alone the enigmatic ways of the wild. He gazed at a large herd of impala congregated alongside the shore. Long, curly, symmetrical horns crowned a head endowed with large, resigned eyes. Below, a long slender neck joined a sleek fawn body with a white underbelly.

You beautiful creatures, you, thought Justin.

Acutely aware of him, but suspecting no danger, they nibbled juicy grass tufts, twitched their hides and swished their short, fluffy tails against their pesky foe, the fly. Some drank at the river's edge, legs spread-eagled, muzzles tickling the cool water. From time to time a buck instinctively paused, raised its head, and observed the status of alarm. A smell, a bird cry, or an unusual ripple in the water?

Suddenly a danger signal! One impala pricked up its ears, tuned in like radar antennas. It fidgeted and became jittery, its hide shaking violently to warn the others of imminent danger. Another lost courage and darted. Then panic! Pandemonium set in like popcorn exploding from a pot on a stove. One moment they were there, the next, devoured by the bush. Vanished!

What the hell have I missed? wondered Justin, suddenly alert, sniffing fear in the air.

He surveyed the terrain and listened carefully for bushveld nuances, acutely aware that if missed, death might follow. But there was only calm, a calm that belied the unseen danger. The light began to fade. It was eerie.

He navigated his dugout to the faster flowing water, past the flat, steel grey rocks, then saw the danger. Some logs slipped into the river. Justin's heartbeat quickened and his sweaty palms struggled to keep their grip on the paddle.

Uh oh! Crocodiles!

Having spent all day on their hot plates, baking in the African sun, the carnivorous, pre-historic reptiles now lurked in the dark waters below, pumping adrenalin through Justin's veins.

Home time! he decided, a cold shiver running down his spine. *Or I'm a goner!*

Leaving their domain through a channel of rapids, his kayak bumped a rock, and shuddered violently in the white water.

Great elephant balls! exclaimed Justin, an expression borrowed from his father. His boat tipping, he lamented, *Now I'm croc dinner!*

The boy fought desperately to recover, frantically prodding the water with his paddle. He toiled and sweated and panicked, then the river widened and calmed, and he restored balance.

'Phew!' Justin breathed relief, his heartbeat subsiding. Little did he know it would be a long time before he again tantalised the sinister looking creatures.

The river spewed Justin into Sand River Dam. On the western front he saw a bold ball of fire serenely sinking to the horizon in slow motion.

'You're on!' he said, accepting the challenge.

He canoed across a vast expanse of glinting water in a frantic race against darkness, against the setting sun which glistened in the spray on his tanned skin and painted magical shades of pinks and oranges between wisps of white cotton wool clouds on a darkening African sky.

'Gotcha!' Justin exclaimed, reaching the shore.

The cheery atmosphere of Mananga Yacht Club where the small farming community of Tshaneni congregated at the clubhouse every weekend, greeted an exhausted Justin.

He sought out his mother.

'Hi, Mum!' sang Justin, affectionately hugging a comfortable, dumpy lady with a pudding face sporting rosy cheeks, spectacles and a white bun. 'I'm hungry,' Justin whined above the garrulous outpouring, the aroma of sizzling venison wafting from an open fire tantalising his appetite.

After a bite to eat, he flopped down and squeezed between his maternal pillow and the side of the soft chair. Listening to the monotonous buzz of conversation, he gave a cavernous yawn and his eyes grew heavy. He was almost asleep when he saw his father and stiffened.

'Dad!' started Justin, nervous of his father's reaction.

'Stranger round here, boy!' moaned the sun-weathered, thickset, balding man with a beaky nose. He drained a large mug of cold home-made pale ale down his hot, dry throat then growled, ''Bout time you trapezed on my cat!'

Justin remained silent, his tried and tested ploy to allay his father's concern that he spent most of his time in the bushveld. *I don't ever want to lose my freedom!*

'Dad has a little something for you, darling,' Justin's mother defused the tension for her only child.

Justin quickly slipped out of the can of sardines he shared with his mother and skipped over to his father.

'Lordy! Nearly forgot. Here we are, boy!' offered Bill Forrester, handing a tennis racket to his son. 'Won the regatta today. Of all the prizes, got a darn tennis racket! Could do with a new jib, but what the heck! Anyway boy, it's yours if you want it. Blowed if I know what you'll do with it around here! Maybe keep you out of that darn bush!'

Justin's eyes lit up. 'Wow! Thanks Dad!'

Off he scooted, eager to test the gift that would change his life. He spent the rest of the evening swatting mosquitoes in the still night air.

§

The momentous day arrived, Justin's first Wimbledon!

'This tennis stuff, boy, it's gonna drive you crazy!' attacked Bill Forrester, preparing to leave for the yacht club.

Justin remained silent.

'Father and son race today. Letting me down, boy!'

'Let him stay, Bill,' rescued Justin's mother.

'You wanna stay?' Bill grudgingly relented with a ludicrous question, undeserving of an answer.

'Of course, Dad!' replied Justin firmly. *You'll have to draw and quarter me before I miss Wimbledon!*

The Forrester parents departed for Sand River Dam, routinely done each weekend, without fail, since they arrived on contract from Britain 21 years ago.

Justin watched their Land Rover disappear down a dirt track in a cloud of dust, then raced back inside, switched on the old, battered wireless and frantically searched for the BBC World Service.

'Damn! Where are you?' demanded a nervous boy, his hands shaking.

Listening to the BBC World Service on shortwave in far away places like Africa was most irritating. Over the course of a day its signal weakened on one band and suddenly popped up like a jack-in-the-box on another. So it had to be continually retuned.

And then it crackled! Crackles which drowned out vital bits of information at most inopportune moments. Even more disconcerting for Justin, these crackles seemed at their worst on Saturdays!

'Gotcha!' exclaimed an excited boy.

Justin fetched his Dunlop Maxply. Eight o'clock in the morning, seven hours to wait. For hour upon hour, Justin hit an old ball against the rickety timber garage door, rudely splitting the stillness. Thud, thud, thud! Every 10 minutes he rushed inside to monitor the time, retuned the crackling wireless and checked to see if, perhaps, the match had commenced.

Nope! Not yet! Justin looked at his watch and cursed, Damn! It's only 9.25 a.m., early still.

Then back to the old garage door, crushing petals of peeling blue paint.

Justin pretended that *he* was playing the final at Wimbledon.

I'll be Borg, he imagined. His hair was blond and his eyes icy blue, just like the Swedish Viking's. Over the course of the tournament he had come to like Björn Borg. Of course, everyone likes a winner, a hero, and Borg was both. *Yep! I'll be Borg!*

Every five shots in a row without error, Justin awarded himself a point. He battled against McEnroe and ran his weary legs ragged in his Wimbledon final. His match so engrossed him, he missed the start of the real final.

'Game and first set to McEnroe, by six games to one,' announced the umpire.

Oh no! Justin's heart sank. But he had faith in his hero. *This Borg bugger's a fighter. He's come back many times before to win. He'll do it again!*

As the match unfolded, Justin edged closer and closer to the wireless, until by the fifth set his ear rested upon the speaker, the spellbinding drama riveting him to the match.

Gripped with excitement, he heard Max Robertson commentating for the BBC.

'The 8th match point. Will Borg become, in this next moment, five times running Wimbledon champion? It seemed he would over a set ago, but not now. Will it now?'

Justin clenched his fists tightly, his knuckles turning white.

'McEnroe serves. That's right. A backhand return. McEnroe, a forehand volley. Borg, a two-hander crosscourt. He's beaten him!'

'Gotcha!' shouted Justin, jumping up and down while the wireless blared rapturous applause.

'Borg, as ever, goes down on his knees. First on his knees, then to his back, then bows forward, trudges up to the net to McEnroe, whose head is bowed.'

Justin trembled. Goose bumps flecked his arms.

'Three hours, fifty three minutes of the most gigantic, titanic, gargantuan tennis.'

The boy, all alone in the living room, screamed with delight.

'McEnroe, so sorry, so furious with himself, wanting to strike the ground and lash out because of his own fury with his own imperfections, has finally been beaten, just seven minutes under the four hours.'

Almost drowned out by the tumultuous sounds of applause, the umpire confirmed the score, *'Borg wins by three sets to two, 1-6 7-5 6-3 6-7 8-6.'*

Justin gazed out of the window to his Wimbledon Centre Court, the garage door. Drowned in emotion, lost in thought, he pictured the emotional scenes unfolding before his eyes.

Peter Jones, his voice steeped in drama, continued for the BBC.

'Oh, my word! What a match! What a match! What else can you say? Absolutely superlative stuff!

'But despite all the drama, and the tension and the superlative skills shown by both men in that memorable final, the ground staff and the organizers here haven't time to dwell on that. They've their own part to play. Very quick and very efficient, everything's organized, the green carpet, the table and the Union Jack. And in the next few seconds, indeed as I speak, so the Duke of Kent, President of the All England Club, and the Duchess, again looking lovely, despite the cloudy sky looks like sunshine, and walks down that green carpet past the rows of ballboys – crackle ...

'And away to our left at the umpire's chair, John McEnroe, at 21, sits with his head in his hands. He came so near, so near to being the king of Wimbledon. But in fact it's the five times king now, behind him, who's shown no sign of emotion at all.

'The Duke and Duchess stand in the middle of this Centre Court, one of the great arenas in the world. And that gold cup, the Challenge Cup, which in fact Björn Borg is used to, he'll go back again for a record fifth time, a record that may never be equalled in the history of lawn tennis. He receives the cup from the Duke of Kent. And in a moment you will know that the cup has gone back to Sweden. The cup has gone back to the champion of champions. That's the man standing there now on Centre Court which rises, all 14,000 people, to Björn Borg!'

Justin shook his head in utter disbelief!

'And now it'll be the turn of the challenger, who's made so many friends

here today. He's going to be a champion, surely in the future. Listen to this, for John McEnroe – crackle …

'John McEnroe having a few words with the Duke and while the umpire – crackle – who's umpired superbly in this emotional final, will now shake hands with the Duchess and the Duke. McEnroe stands, the great competitor that he is, disappointed to be second best. He's in fact only got a silver medal, and for McEnroe that won't be enough. But his behaviour today on court, impeccable. And Björn Borg standing nonchalantly, holding the biggest prize in tennis in the world in his hands, frankly as if it's just a cup and saucer.

'A marvellous performance by Björn Borg then. And a remarkable and unique atmosphere on this Centre Court as the arena for a great final. A stillness of a cathedral during play, and the explosions of a bullring at winning points. Quite, quite remarkable! And when the final presentations are over, then will come the moment when Björn Borg must go to a forest of photographers. And he'll now do that. And they'll ask him to stand and they'll ask him to smile. He might just allow a little smile. And he holds up the Challenge Cup. And it belongs to Björn Borg again. As Gerrie Williams was saying, Björn Borg has bought an island off the Swedish coast where he swims and he fishes and they tell me he finds peace. At the moment he won't mind the noise, because the noise here on Centre Court means that he's king again. Cool, apparently showing no emotion, but as we heard when we spoke to him yesterday, beneath that, a steely determination to be the best in the world. He's the best in the world yet again, and he knows it.

'And again, a little moment for the ballboys as the Duke of Kent stops to speak to one or two of them – crackle …

'And in the middle of it all John McEnroe stands looking relaxed, but looking also bitterly disappointed because that's John McEnroe. Pugnacious, brash, we've called him all that. But a fierce competitor, volatile, highly self-critical and I'm quite certain that when he leaves this court he'll go and talk to his father and he'll find out exactly what went wrong. The cheers are for Björn Borg, but John McEnroe, I'm quite certain, will be planning the revenge.

'As the cheers ring round Centre Court – crackle – the clouds grey above us. And when people like David Lloyd and Fred Perry and Bob Howe and, indeed, Max Robertson, who have seen so many finals, when they say this will go among the great ones, believe them!

'So they stop for photographs. They walk slowly towards us. They bow, almost forget to bow. And McEnroe, at 21, in his first final, has made a lot of friends and played some superlative tennis, and been a very important part of a great final. Björn Borg sits away just a few feet below us. Chris Gorringe, the new secretary of the All England Club carries the trophy, and although it will stay here, of course, at the All England Club, it doesn't make any difference – crackle – Björn Borg who's now being collared away to my right by television* *all over the world – crackle – American television, our old friend Bud Collins is there, not unnaturally he's going to John McEnroe first, the Irish American from New York. And so all round the world at this moment they're seeing first of all, why not, the face of the loser, John McEnroe.*

'And then they'll see the face of the champion yet again. Björn Borg, a quite remarkable young man. Five consecutive Wimbledon titles. He's certainly written a new record that we feel will never be equalled. He's also five times French champion. He's lost only two matches since last Wimbledon. He was the official world champion for the past two years and he's proved it again this afternoon. But, my word, what a fight John McEnroe gave him.

'So at this stage then … it's almost difficult to find your breath here, it was such a marvellous match, but at this stage we're going to say goodbye to all our many listeners overseas, wherever you may be, at the end of a great, great singles final that we're going to remember forever. And at the end of it all the king still reigns, it's Björn Borg! … As a man once said, 'Follow that!''

Lost in thought, Justin carved his initials into the laminated wooden shaft of his Dunlop Maxply racket. Scouring the final touches, his pocket knife slipped, nicking his thumb, but the young boy did not feel the pain. Staring vacuously at his thumb bleeding copiously onto his racket, he smeared the blood over his initials, his life soaking into the timber.

Drained of emotion, he walked listlessly to his bedroom, oblivious of the wireless melodizing ABBA's *The Winner Takes It All*. He was numb, punch-drunk with drama, and remained quiet the rest of the day. Nor did he speak to his soul. The Justin of old withdrew into himself, stunned into a vacuum. He lay in bed a long while, staring inwardly at emptiness.

At some stage of the night his breathing quickened and grew heavy, and with a great sigh he broke from his cocoon, the metamorphosis over, the new Justin born.

'I'm going to win!' he cried out passionately with the heart of a lion. 'All I want is to win Wimbledon!'

He sat up, reached down to the floor, and in the darkness his hand found leather. Drawing his racket up to his chest, he caressed it, breathing in the mellow fragrances of varnished wood, gut and leather. He held it close to his chest and fantasised under the covers with the lights out so nobody would know, and fell asleep with one word on his lips, 'Wimbledon!'

Justin woke at the crack of dawn, brimming with excitement. Suddenly his heart plunged in despair.

Damn! I've no place to practise. The garage door had long exhausted its useful purpose and was driving his mother mad. A shard of fear thrust into his heart, *How can I win Wimbledon?*

Aah! The bush! resolved Justin, looking at his playground, a vast tract of virgin bushveld abutting his yard, a haven of open grassland punctuated by umbrella thorns, a living paradise of wildlife and birds.

He immediately began laying the foundations for his quest. Day after day, under a scorching sun, he toiled in the bushveld next to his home, chopping down some acacia trees. His scrawny body and a spade cleared away a patch of veld, and with his black stallion, Mamba, he dragged in a ton of ochre anthill gravel.

Wielding an axe in blistered hands, Justin split young marula trees down the middle, sending a cold crack across the bushveld plain, then nailed them together to make his tennis wall. An excruciating pain seared from the flesh of his torn hands, but the motivation to win Wimbledon numbed the agony. Finally, the finishing touches. He and Mamba dragged a rusty 44 gallon drum filled with sand across his Centre Court, rolling the anthill gravel hard and flat, and with a bundle of veld grass tied together he swept the patch clean.

Weeks later, after much blood, sweat and tears, Justin stood on his court, eager to christen his practice wall. *Centre Court!* he beamed proudly.

'Here goes!' The first ball flew over the top. 'Oops!'

Undeterred he tried again and again, scuttling back for the ball as fast as he could, not wanting to miss one moment of his tennis. And so the rigours of hard work became a way of life. The uneven split poles returned the dirty, scruffy, old white ball in random patterns, much like an opponent would, and the gravel provided a sound base to build a bedrock of solid strokes and toughen the mind.

In this bushveld court, Justin learned how a ball spun, how spin increased his range of shots, and he discovered how to use this to his advantage. He practised the art of sliding, and he always tried hard. He was crazy, like a madman, and played with fire. Each time he missed, his legs grew in strength, scurrying after the fleeing ball. No time to be wasted.

Justin always played competitive games against his opponent, the wall. Five shots in a row without error earned him a point. This increased to 10 and then 20. In the following months he played passionately, and single-handedly won the Davis Cup and all the major titles around the world, including, of course, Tshaneni! Only when the light faded did Justin go inside. Washing his hands, he imagined himself a tennis professional doing the same after a hard match.

'Must practise and practise,' the panting, sweaty kid reminded himself. 'I want to win Wimbledon!'

At the first light of dawn, Justin eagerly returned to his practice court carved out of the bushveld. On scampering after a ball prised loose from a rally, his vigilant eyes caught sight of specks spiralling in the blue morning sky.

'Vultures!' he exclaimed. His eyes lit up. *Lions?*

The curious Justin quickly mounted Mamba and closed in to view the kill, hoping to find a big cat feasting at the end of the rainbow.

The pot of gold horrified the boy. It was no ordinary kill. Nature could not be so cruel. A crude wire snare trapped Justin's friend, a young impala, in a life and death struggle. He dismounted Mamba and guardedly edged closer to the stricken animal. A lump filled his throat.

Damn! Her leg's all cut up! cried a distraught Justin, noticing the rusty wire cutting through her sinews, deep into her hindquarter. *I must set her free!*

He stalked closer, but with each step forward the frightened doe pulled against the snare, the wire tearing the flesh to the bone.

Damn it! cursed the helpless Justin, haunted by her wide, terrified eyes. *She'll die a lingering death if I leave her, but she won't let me get close!*

The frantic boy was beside himself, mired in a trap of helplessness.

'I *have* to save her!' he cried aloud and took the plunge, rushing to the young impala.

In the baby's frantic struggle to wrench herself free, in fear of the approaching boy, her mangled limb severed from her body. She staggered forward on three legs and collapsed.

'Noooo!' screamed Justin, rushing to her aid. He cradled the frightened baby in his arms, comforting her but to no avail. Her natural instinct for survival would not allow solace from a human.

Justin looked at the ruptured leg, broken flesh minced with white sinews, blood gushing out of a crudely torn hole. Tears welled up in his eyes.

She's going to die, wailed Justin, staring at the stark truth. Still the impala struggled to break free.

Justin took the doe's head in his hands, swallowed against the lump in his throat, and with tears streaming down his face, twisted her neck, closing her windpipe. He fell over the baby impala and lay on her, sobbing until the struggling movement against his belly died.

A noise caught Justin's attention. He looked up and through tear-blurred eyes saw a huge vulture swooping down 20 paces away. Justin rose, drenched in blood, and looked around, searching for his unseen enemy, the poacher.

'Where are you bastards?' he cried out. 'How can you be so cruel? I'll hunt you down. I promise!'

§

At last my day has come! thought an excited Justin. *My first tournament!*

He mounted Mamba, and with wooden racket replacing rifle in his scabbard, set off for the Mhlume Tennis Club championships. Mhlume was a small town, nine miles away from Tshaneni, but a hundred-fold bigger.

Justin took the shorter route through the bushveld where he came across a herd of impala. It was the end of summer and little ones abounded, springing into the air as if treading on a hot tin roof. Justin lost himself in thought, remembering the days of old, tinged with a little sadness of nostalgia. He saw less of them now.

Wimbledon! His mind jolted back to the present. 'Wish me luck, you buggers!'

Justin's first opponent in tournament play was a middle-aged man who chopped the ball off both wings. Barry Lester returned ball after ball with the interest of underspin, the 'wear your opponent down' syndrome he had employed all his life to perform well in tournaments of this ilk. He was champion of Mhlume five years ago and a finalist last year.

Great elephant balls! He's steadier than my practice wall! exclaimed Justin, surprised. He soon learned one telling fact, *Damn! I don't win the point after hitting 10 balls in a row!*

He tried hard, using his strong legs to run down everything that came his side of the black asphalt court, but in little time he went down 6-0 and 5-0.

Facing a humiliating defeat in his first ever competitive match, Justin pursed his lips, gritted his teeth and spilled his guts to get on the scoreboard.

First point to Lester, love-15. Second point against the youngster, love-30. An exhausting rally and Justin's ball clipped the net and fell good, 15-30. A point here, a point there, meagre pickings, some gained on good luck too, but not enough!

Then it was 15-40. Match point! Justin served, but before long he pulled the ball wide. Match to Lester, 6-0 6-0. Justin forlornly walked up to the net to offer the customary shake of hands.

'Bad luck, boy. Better luck next time.'

Justin wanted to say something like, 'Well played!' but his mouth glued tight with disappointment and offered no help.

A lost boy, feeling small in a huge world, Justin headed to the locker-room, placed his head under a tap and drowned his face in cold water.

Damn! Damn! Damn! I didn't win a game! he cried.

Minutes later, alone, so he thought, he switched off the tap, dried his face, and on peeling away the towel found himself looking at an elderly man.

The man was short, slightly stocky, with close-cropped, grey hair and a moustache attached to a reddish face with crease lines. Above sat a straw basher, adorned with a small feather sprouting from a band. Below, baggy long pants suspended over a white shirt with sleeves half rolled up, and a maroon silk scarf concealed his neck. If nothing else, his shoes, sporting speck holes, gave away his age. In his right hand, he swung a cane.

'Where did you learn your game, son?' asked the man.

'At home, sir!' Justin replied, surprised that anyone would be interested in him, the loser.

'You've got it all wrong, son!'

The blood in Justin's face drained away. *Damn! First I lose, now this bugger tells me I've wasted the last eight months!*

'Your technique is up the pole! Discard it. Here, let me show you,' offered the man, reaching for Justin's racket. He mimicked a forehand.

'You *swing* your ground strokes.'

He shadow stroked a backhand.

'Remember, you swing your ground strokes.'

Justin nodded, digesting his first advice.

The man then asked Justin to clench his right fist, and put it to his shoulder, then held up his own wrinkled hand in front of the boy.

'Punch my hand!'

Justin did.

'Again!'

Justin repeated.

'That's how you execute the volley, son. You *punch* it!'

Justin nodded, absorbed.

'What about the serve, sir?'

'Follow me!'

Justin shadowed the man to the back of the clubhouse.

'Pick up a stone and throw it as far as you can.'

'That's easy!' he responded, complying. Many a time a well thrown stone had relieved him from danger or brought him an ace in the bushveld.

'That's a very good throw, son. One day you'll have a fine serve, too! You *throw* the serve!'

'Gee, thanks a ton, sir!'

'What's your name, son?'

'Justin.'

'That's a good name. And you can be a fine player, too! You run like a gazelle and you have spirit, the heart of a lion. Speed and heart. That makes a champion. Of course you must have a good technique. Remember, you swing your ground strokes, punch your volleys and throw your serve! Work on that and you'll win here next year!'

'A mighty big thank you, sir!'

'It's my pleasure!' smiled the old man, patting Justin on the back. 'The name's Morris. Charlie Morris.'

Justin mounted Mamba, and headed home, almost as pleased as if he had won his match.

'Swing your ground strokes! Punch your volleys! Throw your serves!' he sang over and over, in rhythm to the three step waltz of the canter, all the way home.

§

Inextricably bound in the leopard cubs' play, is the instinct to hunt. As they frolic in the long grass, chase after crinkled wind-blown leaves, or attack one another's swishing tails, they learn the essential skills of stalking and pouncing. If it moves, they will investigate, with a view to kill.

While mother is away, now is the time to explore. One cub in particular, is inquisitive. He notices fuchsia branches swaying in the still air. Monkeys! Red flowers shower in bloom and their abundant sweet nectar attracts a troop. The cub is curious and watches alone from the concealment of a nearby tree. So engrossed are the vervets in their feast that one foolishly strays. The cub pounces, but in his inexperience he bites into the back of the neck, his canines not long enough to inflict the fatal wound. Sucking onto a mouthful of monkey bewilders the cub. What to do? Aah, of course! Climb a tree, just like Mum! As the cub attempts the hoist, he errs. Too many paws for his own good! For a fleeting moment he releases his grip, and the monkey escapes to live another day, with only his pride hurt. While the monkey screams abuse, the leopard cub contemplates a lesson he will never forget. Such is the way the self-taught leopard acquires its skills.

§

A year later, Justin discovered the advice of Charlie Morris paying dividends. The young boy progressed through to the final of the Mhlume Tennis Club championships with consummate ease, causing a turning of heads and a raising of eyebrows. He was hot news at the quaint tennis club.

Across the net on the other side, he found his conqueror of a year ago, Barry Lester.

I have *to beat him!* exhorted Justin, yearning to cleanse the bitter after-taste of his whitewash at the hands of his foe. That defeat solely motivated 12 months of solid training devoted exclusively to putting it to rest.

This past year, Justin immersed himself in tennis, voraciously digesting a wealth of tennis information, gained from books, magazines and newspapers lodged in Mhlume's library. He learned how to play the game and about his future life on the professional circuit.

Justin found Coach to be a wonderful source of knowledge and spent plentiful time in his company, listening to rambling, vivid tales about the great Rod Laver, the evergreen Ken Rosewall, the Davis Cup and Wimbledon. Charlie Morris found the boy a pleasure to teach, a quick learner. This give and take and give back relationship forged a friendship between the two, who adopted each other with a mutual interest.

'What's the greatest tournament in the world?' asked Justin eagerly.

'Oh, that's an easy one, son,' smiled Charlie Morris, patting the boy's shoulder. 'Wimbledon, of course!'

'Who won the first Wimbledon?'

Charlie Morris would tell him it was a gentleman by the name of Spencer Gore. He would go on to tell the interested boy how Spencer Gore beat someone, who beat someone else, who beat someone else, and so it went on, until finally someone beat Borg, the champion of today.

'Are you saying this Gore bugger is the best of them all?' asked a suspicious Justin.

'No! It works the other way too! A tree of results shows that Borg beat someone, who beat someone, and so on, until eventually the first Wimbledon champ gets beaten.'

'Who then is the best player of all-time?'

'Well, Rod Laver has always been my choice. They called him the 'Rocket', fast and furious. He won two Grand Slams, and he came from Australia. But I think your fellow Borg may have pipped him to the post, now. Five Wimbledons in a row is stupendous. They seem to get better all the time!'

'What's the Grand Slam?'

'That's the Mount Everest of tennis, son. A player achieves the Grand Slam when he wins the four major championships of Australia, France, Wimbledon and the United States, all in the same year! It's well nigh impossible these days.'

'*I* want to win Wimbledon! *And* the Grand Slam! I want to be the

15

best. Maybe the best ever. Yep, I want to be the best player of all-time. But please don't tell anyone, Coach. That's *my* dream. Only *I* want to know it. And you, too, of course!'

Charlie Morris placed a hand on the lad's shoulder. 'Don't think too heavily about tomorrow, son. Keep your dream in the back of your mind. Concentrate on your next match, the next ball you hit. Hit that one to the best of your ability and you put one more piece of your Wimbledon dream jigsaw puzzle into place. Your time will come!'

Like a sponge, Justin absorbed every word from his beloved Coach.

'But I must warn you, son, the tennis tour is a dog-eat-dog world. Survival of the fittest.'

Justin's eyes lit up. He knew all about survival of the fittest. He saw it every day in the bushveld, the predatorial hierarchy, where all life supports the big cats. *I like that. I want to be like them, king of the hill!*

'Back to your game, now. You lean forward into the volley. Make believe you are stepping down a stair. Lean forward!'

Justin lost the first set to Barry Lester, 6-2.

Damn! This can't be happening! thought Justin, disbelieving of his predicament. He had played with authority coming into the final, yet here he stared down a barrel of doom, watching a replay of last year's match.

Justin delivered another high, looping topspin drive. His opponent sliced the ball back low, gnawing away at Justin's backhand, exposing his Achilles' heel, a struggle to dig out low balls sliding away from his two-hander.

One-love became 2-0, then 3-0. Tears welled up in the boy's eyes, his dream shattered. He could barely see the ball!

Biting his lip to restrain his face from melting in despair, Justin walked to the umpire's chair to towel off during the changeover.

He caught a glimpse of Charlie Morris, and a lone piece of his advice, from months back, rang a bell. 'You're a natural!'

Head buried in his towel, he quickly searched his mind for the most natural panacea to his dilemma.

My high top spin is cannon fodder for him. That's for sure! thought Justin. Maybe I'll give him some of his own medicine, slice! Better still I'll just try to hit the best shot each occasion demands. 'Yep, I'll give that a shot!' he said aloud, unintentionally.

'What's that, boy?' asked a puzzled Barry Lester.

Justin just shook his head and remained quiet. *You'll find out!*

Heeding the advice he read in a coaching manual of his idol, Björn Borg, not to copy others, Justin cut the umbilical cord and broke the shackles that held his game in check. Courageously, he forsook his two-handed backhand. Even his manic topspin disappeared. He entered the realm of variety.

Justin countered with slice. With his one dimensional chop action, Barry could only pop up the ball. Food for a hungry man! Justin gorged, following his ground strokes in to the net, and cutting off the high returns on the volley.

He won the next game to be down 1-3. The fifth game of the second set went the way of his opponent, 1-4.

That's okay, thought Justin, shrugging it off to experiment.

There followed a succession of plays and ploys rich in subtle effects. The boy displayed the speed and skills that would plague all others for years to come. Flat drives, drop-shots, topspin lobs, and acutely angled forehands and backhands ran his ageing opponent ragged. Such was the nullifying effect on Barry Lester that he never won another game.

Justin Forrester won his first ever tournament, the Mhlume Tennis Club championships, and for the joy he showed, it may well have been Wimbledon. He ran up to the net, jumped it, but tangled his foot in the webbing and fell flat on his face on the rough asphalt. He rose sheepishly with a bloodied nose.

I'll never do that again! reprimanded Justin. *That's for bloody show-offs!*

Justin garnered more than a tournament that day. He laid a foundation that might allow him his dream of playing and winning on the most famous Centre Court of all. A courageous improvisation to break free from his idol, purging self-inflicted constraint and forsaking the purely topspin game to play what comes naturally, enabled Justin to find his avenue to walk down and find triumph at the end. No longer would he be a clone. Instead, he would follow the advice of his hero. 'Be yourself! Recognise your own strengths and build on them, and don't be afraid to experiment. Use whatever suits you, reject what doesn't.'

After a second Mhlume title under his belt, whilst Justin walked forward to receive the trophy, Charlie Morris, the pedlar of tennis wisdom, confronted Justin's parents.

'It's time for the boy to move on,' whispered Charlie. 'He's got talent, bundles of it. It oozes out of him. Staying here will stunt him. He must broaden his horizon.'

Justin knew it too, and hated it. He mounted Mamba and rode out into the bushveld. For hours he roamed the land, communing with the wild, the animals, his friends.

To win Wimbledon I have to leave all this.

Justin sat on a rock, picked a piece of veld grass and nibbled its stem.

'But how can I?' he asked himself, almost expecting an answer to echo from the land.

He left Mamba and climbed a koppie, rising to its peak where he overlooked the bushveld. Coveting his land, tears welled up in his eyes. He knew it so well. He understood the ways of the wild. But like the leopard he so admired, that prince of predators, Justin too, instinctively felt the need to fight to the death to become king of the hill.

'I *have* to,' he said out aloud. 'I have to leave you. I've got to win Wimbledon. I'll show you. But I'll be back. I promise you, I'll be back!'

Later that evening, dusk setting in over the dam, Justin and his father stood at the water's edge.

'Boy, this tennis thing. Really what you wanna do?' Bill asked his son, gruffly.

Caught for a moment by the surprise of his father's interest, Justin looked up with wide eyes, hoping, and replied with passion. 'It's my *life*, Dad. My ambition is to play professional tennis.'

'Know the risks involved? Chances are blow-all you'll make it. Only one king of the castle.'

'I believe in myself, Dad!'

'So be it!'

Justin's heart pumped, anticipating a punch-line.

'You can go to a boarding school in Durban, if that's what you want. At least it will get you out of that darn bush!'

'What I want? You bet it is!' exclaimed an incredulous Justin. 'I can't believe it!'

'Hang tight, boy! I'll ring the school in the morning and check if they've got room. Call the tune from there. But you gotta promise you'll finish your schooling.'

'I promise! I promise!' responded Justin, anything to play competitive tennis. 'Thanks, Dad! You don't know how happy you've made me!' *I'll show you one day! I'll show you!*

§

The Forresters' car crested Durban's ridge overlooking the city, a spread of skyscrapers, the sea, the traffic, and all the people!

Great elephant balls! exclaimed Justin, eyes widening. This country bumpkin had never seen anything bigger than the village of Mhlume!

A roar emanated from above, shuddering the ground. Suddenly he saw it. A Boeing 747, low overhead, majestically rising into the blue sky.

It excited Justin. Adrenalin pumped inside him.

'My tennis is going to blossom here. Soon I'll be on that jet, flying to the great tennis tournaments of the world!'

CHAPTER 2

Three months later, Vich dragged profusely on his brown, homemade cheroot. Intent on wasting precious little, he quickly drew its life to an end and stubbed out the charred butt underfoot. The smoking habit died at this door.

A knock on the ornately carved wooden door reaped the inevitable wait.

'Open the fucking door!' Vich growled under his breath.

He tolerated temporary cold turkey, but nothing riled him more than this pecking order game played at his expense. In the pregnant pause a fly buzzed frantically around his large, rotund head with close-cropped, brown hair thinning on the crown, atop a surly bear with a barrel chest encased in a matted rug.

Finally the inner sanctum, a stately wooden-panelled office suite in a mansion in Greenwich, Connecticut, opened its doors to Vich. Here stood a large, oak desk, behind which sat his boss, Amos Creighton.

'I trust you bring me profitable news?' enquired Creighton brusquely, a man in his early forties, with dark hair greying at the temples, boasting a trim body, albeit slight.

'Hmmph!' the messenger replied, standing uncomfortably in front of the seated Creighton. Vich always felt ill at ease in the presence of his employer. His large, puffy hands fondled a Donnay Allwood tennis racket.

'Where?'

'Prague.'

'Czechoslovakia!' Creighton exclaimed, his interest aroused. 'That bodes well. What of his progenitors?'

A muffled grunt emanating from a droopy moustache begged clarification.

'What is his pedigree?'

'What you asked for,' spat Vich, his accent betraying Eastern European ancestry.

'Then execute my Grand Plan,' instructed Creighton, rising from his leather upholstered chair.

Their meeting was brief. They always were. Creighton ushered his right-hand man out of his office.

'Don't foul up!' he ordered, closing the door.

'I deliver,' grumbled Vich indignantly, glaring menacingly at the closed door. 'Don't ever doubt!'

He reached into his breast pocket, fumbled for and found another crude cheroot, struck a match on the wall, lit up and walked out into *his* world where *he* was boss.

Vich had played henchman to Creighton for several years, although their scant dialogue revealed little of his indispensability to Creighton. They served each other's needs. Creighton needed a job to be done, Vich needed a job to do. How he did it, mattered not. No questions were asked, no answers were given. Their relationship abruptly ended there.

At their introduction, a face bearing dark rings round sunken eyes, eerily expressionless, befitting a dark and sinister role in a spy movie, confronted Creighton. Very little issued from underneath his droopy moustache. Only garlic breath and utterances of necessity, the chaff of superfluous chatter non-existent, each word spat, definite and to the point.

All that Creighton extracted from a garbled foreign sounding name was 'Vich', and so he became known. That was all he needed to know about him. Nobody knew where Vich hailed from, though they suspected the Carpathian neighbourhood of Dracula, and nobody asked! What mattered, was that each and every cog of the Grand Plan slotted into place, and the wheels of machinery set in motion. Creighton planned, and Vich drove.

§

'Darling, your father and I are going to divorce.'

Amos Creighton's boyhood body paralysed with fear, but his mind flashed an array of images of future fright. He had suspected this moment for a long time, always dreaded it, but nothing had prepared him for the dawning of reality. Now an ordeal loomed large. Divorce would shatter his protective third party shield and give his father indisputable dominion over him.

Amos returned from his fortnightly weekend with his father, dropped off like baggage.

'What's the matter, darling?' Mrs Creighton asked of her eight year old son.

No response, just a vacant stare.

'Darling?'

'Nothing,' Amos forlornly replied, barely audible from within his shell.

'Come on,' she pressed him, growing impatient. 'This is nonsense.

Each time you return from Greenwich you're not yourself.'

'There's nothing wrong!'

'Damn it, Amos!' Mrs Creighton shouted, starting a spasm of coughing. 'You're killing me. Tell me what's going on!' she demanded, throwing up her hands in frustration.

'Why don't you believe me?'

'Because he did something to you!' she cried. She approached Amos to put an arm round him. 'And I want to help you! But you just won't let me!'

'Leave me alone!' he shouted, throwing off her arms and running to the bathroom, repeating a fortnightly ritual.

'Damn you, Arnold!' Mrs Creighton cursed her husband, slumping her frail body into a sofa. Her hands shaking, she lit up a cigarette, inhaled, dropped her head forward onto her chest and covered her ears with her hands to block out the sobs that tormented her. 'Damn, damn, da ...,' she spluttered and coughed in a cloud of smoke.

'I can't stand this!' she cried out and stormed into the bathroom to wrench the truth from Amos.

And suddenly the reality stunned her. Disrobed before her eyes, she saw blood smears on her son's buttocks. She had suspected, but the reality jolted.

'My baby, why haven't you told me?' she said painfully.

'I couldn't, Mum. I don't know why, but I couldn't. Please don't be mad at me, Mum!'

'I promise you, darling, he will never have you again!'

Amos ran into his mother's arms. He was naked, but this did not matter. *She* was loving.

Three months later, enjoying a spell of bliss in the shelter of a maternal web, Amos jumped off the school bus, and ran into the house.

'I'm back,' he sang, skipping into the living room.

Slumped in a chair, Mrs Creighton's ashen body lay lifeless, a charred bullet hole invading her temple, and a revolver dangling from the end of her limp hand.

'But you promised me, Mum! You promised me!' Amos wailed, fearful and confused, unaware of a letter lying on the coffee table.

The letter confirmed conclusive test results that Mrs Creighton, suffering from emphysema, had terminal cancer and the end was near.

'Amos Creighton will be placed in the custody of his natural father,' deemed the judge.

'I believed you, Mum. But you betrayed me. I hate you!' A deep resentment festered in young Amos. 'Women! Dirtbags! I hate you all! You'll never get me again!'

He never married, preferring to pay for merchandise in seedy districts frequented by prostitutes, discovering riches could buy power over women.

'I will become richer, and more powerful than any dirtbag on earth!' vowed Amos Creighton.

§

Vich geared down his olive green VW Caravelle full of pre-teen tennis players to a snail's pace. Ahead snaked a queue of two dozen vehicles. Not that leaving West Germany was in vogue. Rather, this border post strained the normal realms of patience, especially that of someone with a mission.

One of Creighton's several operations involved subtle dealings in the rich sport of tennis. In the early eighties he saw the future in West German tennis, and through his subsidiary, Tennis Pro International, bought and sold tennis in any form a buyer or seller wished it packaged.

A formidable tennis talent in his youth, but a dispensable pawn in the Eastern bloc political power game, Vich frustratingly saw the Iron Curtain draw closed on his tennis career. Now as head of Tennis Pro International, he vented an anger that festered out of lost opportunities.

Every 20 minutes the queue of tortoise shells edged one car closer to inspection at the cold and sinister border post. Emanating from each side stretched two parallel fences as far as the eye could see, six paces apart, constructed of concrete posts threaded with rusty barbed wire, and punctuated with wooden miradors, housing soldiers armed to kill.

'Wow!' exclaimed Boris Bauer in response to his first glimpse of the real Iron Curtain. 'These commies mean business!'

Subdued, but intent, Vich surveyed the setting with hawk eyes. Having originated from the other side, he always grew edgy when entering the cold. He had not defected, not officially, nor had he remained. Nobody knew where he came from, none knew where he headed. Now this threatening border post severely tested his independence.

'Put your foot on it and buck jump the fence, Mr V,' Boris suggested impishly.

The other 11 kids laughed, breaking the tension. They felt lucky in the company of their mascot, the round-spectacled Boris with the flaxen, pudding bowl hair, joker of the pack, an orphan whom Tennis Pro

International had taken under its wing. Somehow a tour across that ominous border post would be a whole lot more fun with him on board.

Vich remained quiet, immune to the laughter behind him.

A young soldier, sub-machine-gun slung over his shoulder, drove a pair of farm horses harnessed to a set of harrows in the corridor between the fences. This turned the earth between the fences every day so that police hounds that loped up and down the passage could pick up fresh scent of anyone passing through.

Boris rolled down the Caravelle window, leant out, put two fingers to his lips, whistled loudly and beckoned the soldier.

'Come here, comrade,' he shouted, then glanced round mischievously and whispered back to his friends, 'Hope he'll touch the fence and fry!'

A glare from the most menacing visage outside a horror movie abruptly arrested the laughter. Vich did not need trouble now, not with what he had to do. He restored discipline immediately and effectively without a word slipping through that droopy moustache. Nobody ever dared to explore what might come after a Vich glare!

Entering the first of two wooden booms, a prickly silence enveloped the minibus. Two soldiers, sub-machine-guns at the waist, patrolled around the vehicle. The air was tense, and fear reached deep inside the nostrils. Then a customs official emerged from his crude office and pushed a mirrored trolley underneath the VW Caravelle.

'Hey!' cried Boris. 'They're stealing our car technology secrets—'

'Hmmph!' spat Vich, terminating Boris's complaint.

'Remove the tarpaulin,' the official ordered curtly.

Vich stepped out of the Caravelle, and untied the canvas sheet protecting their luggage on the roof-rack. The soldiers opened containers, even removed rackets from their covers, and expertly scrutinised the baggage before crudely dumping it, to be neatly repacked by its owners.

'Everybody out!'

The West German kids stepped apprehensively from their secure box. The stench of fear tainted the air. The soldiers pulled up the seats of the vehicle and combed the inside.

'Passports!' demanded an unfriendly inspector.

He paired off each person with a matching passport before allowing him to return to the vehicle.

The customs officer turned to Vich and beckoned him to his office.

'Come with me.'

What the fuck has he found? speculated Vich, standing dead still.

His heart thumped but his head knew he must dutifully respond. He followed the man to the office hutch clutching his Donnay Allwood.

The official brusquely peppered him with questions. 'How much money?'

He noted the amount, to be compared with the residual amount on exit reflected against contents purchased.

'Where are you going?'

'Prague.' Vich was equal to trimming the excesses.

'How long?'

What bloody hell business is it of yours? Vich thought. But he knew better than to rebel against this system. 'Six days.'

'Why?'

Vich briefly explained that he was taking a dozen tennis playing kids on a tour at the invitation of some tennis clubs in and around the capital.

Suddenly the official's attitude grew a touch more conciliatory, since sport was the state's medium of communication about the righteousness of their system, a way of keeping the mind off unpleasant things at home.

The Caravelle passed through the second boom and entered Czechoslovakia. An eerie silence born at the border post lingered, and grew even deeper when the kids, accustomed to the lush and beautiful scenery of West Germany, witnessed the astonishing contrast of the bleak and cold terrain of Czechoslovakia. Barracks and barbed wire, and gasworks and blast-furnaces, scarred the barren land that once flourished with romantic hilltop castles brooding over lush forests of firs, beeches and oaks.

The number of cars diminished except those of patrolling police. And what strange cars! These odd box shapes on wheels tempted the kids to laugh, but something inside stopped them. They suffered from *litost*, sharing with the Czech people a sense of loss, of dispossession, felt at the core of their souls. Carrying a memory of what was, living a sombre reality of what is.

They reached Pilsen, wound through the Berounka valley, entered Prague and quickly made for Hotel International to catch a breath of relief. Eastern Europe was indeed dark and drab, shaped by the dead hand of communist oppression.

But suppressed beneath the layer of gloom smouldered a majesty, a majesty that could not be contained forever, and surely someday, like a bud bursting into springtime bloom, would break the shackles of communism.

Baroque churches with bulbous spires and palaces with pink tiled roofs, shady medieval cloisters and drowsy courtyards, all embraced the majestic River Vltava, winding northwards through the city. And dominating the dramatic skyline along the crest of the great natural ridge of Hradčany stood Prague Castle, crowned by the lofty Gothic Cathedral of St Vitus. The soulful magnificence of Prague, a jewel of old Europe prophesied by the legendary medieval Princess Libuše who stood upon a high rock and looked down on the River Vltava and exclaimed, 'I see a city whose glory shall reach the stars!'

Vich stood at the edge of the gigantic concrete Spartakiade stadium, and gazed at a sea of young bodies rhythmically gyrating in time to music, polishing up for the great national gymnastic display that captivates Prague every five years. He quickly spotted his prey. The fearless one, the silent one, the loner.

'Martin Madl!'

One brief observation and Vich knew with absolute surety the 11 year old boy was the right choice.

Vich leant against the Old Town Hall's eastern wall, devouring a *horky parky* hustled from a street vendor, all the while observing. Uniformed soldiers milled about and communist banners, some turned backwards in protest, festooned neighbouring buildings in Old Town Square. Above him a procession of iron figures, the Twelve Apostles, emerged from an astronomical clock, break-danced, then retreated. The cock crowed and the clock struck three times.

It is time! declared Vich.

He climbed into a black Škoda sedan, and hugging the Vltava, coughed his way south, crossing the river at the first point after the statue fortified Charles Bridge, then snaked through ancient cobblestoned serpentine streets into the red roof district of Malá Strana. He quickly sought out an old tenement, home of Jiří Madl and Renata Madlova.

Great things were expected from Jiří, an ex-Olympic skier, but a freak accident crushed his and Czechoslovakia's dreams. His wife was more fortunate as a champion ice-skater, but their refusal to support the Czech Communist Party quashed hopes for a better lifestyle afforded sports champions.

Vich again stubbed out a cheroot butt before knocking on a door, but on this occasion the surroundings sharply contrasted with Amos Creighton's stately home in Greenwich.

'What may I do for you?' enquired Renata, tentatively peering through the crack in the door, her long Slavonic face framed by lank, dark hair.

'I wish to speak to you about your boy, Martin,' Vich replied with authority. Using the Madl son's name lent credibility and sowed the seed of curiosity that might allow entry.

Renata, dressed in black with grey trimmings, looked back enquiringly, and having obtained authority, smiled at Vich and said, 'Please come in.'

Vich entered, took one look at the pitifully small, dank and musty lodging. He was in a single room apartment, a nook for a kitchen, another for a bedroom.

Hmmph! he shuddered, thinking of what might have been for him.

Vich came straight to the point, addressing Jiří, the presumed decision-maker, a black-rim bespectacled man with short, dark hair.

'Now listen good. What I have to say will change your lives dramatically,' growled Vich, sitting on the edge of the seat and leaning forward to emphasise importance.

The Madls listened in anticipation.

'Your son's athletic prowess has come to my notice, and—'

'You are?' asked Jiří, confined to his wheelchair.

'Tennis Pro International. I have granted your son an all-expenses paid scholarship at my tennis club in Munich. We will groom your boy to be a champion. I want your approval.'

Jiří looked at Renata and then back to Vich. 'What guarantees can you offer?'

'I deliver! I have an exchange program with Sparta. Check it out.'

The name dropping of the famous Sparta sports club of Prague set Jiří and Renata at ease.

The carrot of the trappings of wealth in tennis was tempting. Jiří asked, 'What's in it for us?'

Vich looked around the apartment and shuddered, wondering why they asked such foolish questions.

'Listen good. I *said* your lives will change. You will be rich,' promised Vich. *You'd also be out of this fucking hole!*

Czechs had a choice, work in a bleak factory or see the world through sport.

Vich handed Jiří a wad of American dollars, equivalent to a handful of gold in Czechoslovakia.

Clutching his newfound wealth, Jiří asked, 'What good is money to us when the state confiscates all and only pays out meagre expenses?'

'Their policy is changing. The Navratilova defection embarrassed them. They don't want a repeat. You'll keep 80 percent.'

Jiří looked enquiringly to Renata, but without waiting for her nod, said simply, 'We have a deal!' and put out his hand to shake on the arrangement.

'Sign!' commanded Vich, shoving a contract in front of Jiří.

He did.

'Witness,' he ordered Renata, noticing she wrote with her left hand.

'May I get you some coffee and gingerbread. It's freshly made,' offered Renata, having become ever more domesticated in the Czech way of life, mother spending her time in the warmth of the kitchen with a fire in the stove and everybody bustling about.

Vich nodded acceptance and Renata disappeared around the corner into the kitchen nook lying at the end of the living room.

Vich stood up and patted his fly-zip, suggesting an urge.

'Opposite the kitchen,' said the voice from the wheelchair.

Instead of turning right to the bathroom, Vich entered the kitchen. His finger plucked the main string of his trusty Donnay Allwood racket, releasing the handle from its shaft that masqueraded as a sheath for a gleaming jagged-edged hunting blade.

Despite his barrel body, in one swift move born out of natural athleticism, Vich silently smothered Renata's mouth with his left hand, reached round with his right, and with the deftness of a well-practised surgical operation, plunged the knife into her neck. The blade pegged into her spine, and with one sharp crank, Vich swivelled the sharp steel through her throat, severing her head as one lops off the top of a pineapple and she dropped to the floor with a dull thud. The headless woman gurgled, arteries and windpipe frothing in confusion, while the iron smell of blood permeated the air.

Unmoved, Vich calmly clamped his modified knife under the Czech woman's hairy armpit and dragged the blade clean of blood, much as one would wipe a knife of excess butter on a slice of bread.

A shuffling noise caught Vich's attention. He swung round to see Jiří wheel himself into the doorway. A moment of stunned silence split into a shriek.

'You bastard!' screamed the stricken Jiří.

Suddenly Vich saw Jiří furiously work his wheelchair and come charging forward, lunge at him with flailing arms, and taken by surprise, felt the desperate clamp of the man's vice-like grip. The paraplegic may have lost his legs, but his strong, athletic hands compensated, and Vich fell victim to a frenzied attack from a man desperate to avenge his wife's death and prevent his own.

In the heat of the battle they sweated, and Jiří's hand slipped. Vich quickly drew the blade through Jiří's clenched fist, cutting his flesh to the bone. A painful withdrawal reflex and a momentary loss of concentration proved fatal. Vich was free.

Suddenly the man held captive by the wheelchair lay at the mercy of the mutant grizzly. Vich slowly walked round, cradled Jiří's abject head in his bare hands, administered a chiropractic adjustment *à la* Vich style, and broke his neck. Jiří's body slumped forward in the wheelchair to meet all else that was dead.

Vich recovered his money and quickly rifled the apartment, discovered a family photograph, cut the face of Martin away from his parents, placed it in his pocket and left for the car.

He opened the boot of the stolen black Škoda sedan, procured two cans of petrol, slumped a body bag over his shoulder and returned to the apartment. He slit the bag open and rolled out a dead body between Jiří Madl and Renata Madlova. Vich hastily drenched the apartment with petrol and upon leaving, put to the torch the volatile liquid.

'Get in!' Vich ordered Martin Madl sharply.

Vich meandered the box car from the Spartakiade stadium and stopped a block away from the Madl's gutted apartment.

The brown eyes of the dark-haired boy grew wide. He started to point ahead to smoke billowing out of his parent's home, now swarming with officials from the militia, but said nothing.

'They're dead! Kaput!' spat Vich, swiping his finger across his thick neck, the universal cutthroat sign transcending all languages to indicate someone is dead. 'Listen good. Come with me or you go with the authorities.'

The frozen Martin offered no response.

Vich shrewdly forced the issue. 'If you wish to go with the authorities, then nod your head,' explained Vich, animating a nod of his head. 'Otherwise you come with me.'

Again, there was no response.

'Hmmph!' growled Vich, handing over a West German passport to the boy. 'Your name will be Boris Bauer.'

CHAPTER 3

Sitting in the school hall for morning assembly, Justin glanced up at the wooden honours boards where embossed in gold on the roll extolling sports glories of pupils past, the name Kevin Curren stood proud.

I can't believe the bugger beat McEnroe! thought Justin, still shaking his head in disbelief at the humiliating demise of the defending champion on the Centre Court of Wimbledon less than 24 hours earlier.

Someday I'll stand on the grass of Wimbledon, victorious, he imagined. *Someday I'll become the number one player in the world. And then maybe, just maybe, my name will stand with the legends, Don Budge, Rod Laver and Björn Borg.*

Dreams of the young!

But first the school championships final this afternoon!

He reached into the pocket of his grey flannels, found a squash ball and kneaded furiously.

Need the forearms of a bloody crab! he exhorted himself.

The bell rang, class was out, so Justin, armed with a racket and a water bottle, headed straight for the tennis courts. He discovered his opponent, Nigel Blanchard, already warming up with his brother Solomon.

Hmm, something's fishy, surmised Justin, walking onto court pinching his nose!

Nigel and Solomon formed a most unlikely pair of siblings, Nigel, the dumb jock with impressive athletic deeds, masterminded by the brain of Solomon. Nigel won these championships a year ago, so had all the pressure on him to put Justin, three years his junior and with nothing to lose, firmly in his place. Peer group pressure dictated nothing less.

Little did anyone realise that the ambitious Justin also suffered enormous pressure to win, self-imposed pressure.

'Focus all your energies of concentration and effort on the ball *now*, then your dream will come true,' Charlie Morris once told his protégé.

Yep, Coach is right. To win Wimbledon I'll have to become a pro, so I must be successful in junior years. Each year is made up of matches, comprising sets, and games, and points. Each point consists of shots. Play my best shot now and I'll lay a foundation brick in the house of Wimbledon! I have to win today. I believe in my tennis, so I pray the buggers don't get up to their usual skulduggery, especially since there're no spectators!

'You're late!' asserted the lanky Nigel. 'Should we scratch him, Solly?'

Justin quickly glanced at his watch and noted he was 10 minutes early. *Solomon's obviously put him up to this. It's too much for Nigel to concoct alone!*

'Yeah! Let's scratch him.'

Justin's knuckles turned white where he clutched his Dunlop Maxply like a club.

'Cluck, clu, clu, clu, *cluck!*' Justin yodelled, flapping his arms, enacting a fine rendition of a cackling chicken, hoping to goad Nigel out of his brother's spell by daring him to rise to the challenge. He strode to the baseline, bounced a ball and stood challengingly for the duel.

'You think you can beat him, you cocky little runt! He'll wipe you off the court!' sniggered Solomon. Snapping his fingers he shouted, 'Go get him, Nigel!'

Climbing into the lofty umpire's chair, the podgy Solomon shouted to Justin, 'You were late, so I tossed for choice before you came. Nigel has first option.'

You mean I didn't bunk classes like you did! thought Justin angrily, marching towards Solomon. 'What do you mean *you* tossed?'

'*I'm* your umpire!' Solomon answered smugly.

The school adhered to a pecking order, and according to all yardsticks, except possibly tennis talent, Justin ranked lower than both Nigel and Solomon, both his seniors.

As Justin walked back to his side, Solomon caught Nigel's attention and nodded to him, signalling a cue to effect the next stage of his plan.

'I choose *your* side,' declared Nigel with a vapid grin, pointing across the net. Solomon planned to disrupt Justin's flow and rattle him.

Shit! I'll have to use all my wits to avert being out-psyched, Justin quickly surmised.

Once a player has elected side, only the more discerning of amateurs are aware that the opponent may then choose to receive, forcing the toss winner to serve. At just that moment, the headmaster strolled past the courts on his way to watch a rugby match. Justin exploited the fortuitous timing.

'I'll *receive* serve!'

'You've got to—' started Nigel indignantly.

Solomon hastily raised his hand to shut up the jock, not wanting to attract the attention of greater authority.

'But Solly, now I'm serving into the sun!' moaned a flummoxed Nigel.

Serve you right, you bastard!

Nigel's first serve sailed out, but Justin intentionally returned it into play. He did so again and again.

'Solly?' whined an infuriated Nigel, looking up to his brother.

Solomon shrugged his shoulders.

That should help get my eye in, felt Justin. *Go some way to compensate the loss of warming up!*

Nigel's brittle game embellished by Solomon's chicanery matched the class of Justin game for game, so the first set demanded a tiebreaker. The first person to win seven points with a two point margin would win the set.

At 0-1, a delivery from Justin split the centre line for an ace.

'Out! Two-love, Nigel,' announced the umpire triumphantly.

Lines obviously don't count with this bloody cheat! fumed Justin, but shrugged it off with discipline.

His next serve was good but returned wildly over the baseline. Justin retreated to pick up and pass the ball when umpire Solomon surprised with a most imaginative but absurdly late verdict.

'Foot-fault! Second serve!'

Justin bit his tongue and consoled himself, *Someday, someday I'll compete on the professional tour under a system judged fairly and competently by impartial umpires.*

Meanwhile, eked out of Nigel's two service points, Justin went down 0-5.

Shit! I'm in quicksand, Blanchard bog! I need a lifeline or this first set is history!

Justin marshalled his defence resources, injecting massive margins of safety into his play to obviate close linecalls. He hustled every point with the tenacity of a bull-terrier tucked into a leg of trousers.

That's it! Examine his ability purely on tennis terms, decided Justin, forcing the issue. *How good are you now? Suffer, you bastard, suffer!*

It worked! Nigel's technically moody game self-destructed. The deficit slow-dripped away, and with much relief, Justin broke the Blanchard back and stole the tiebreaker by 8-6.

As quick as ever to change sides, Justin turned round to witness his opponent sipping from his yellow, plastic water bottle. His tap of patience rapidly trickled dry.

'Hey, get your mangy mouth off my water bottle,' ordered an infuriated Justin, stalking closer to Nigel at the umpire's chair. 'Nobody messes with my tennis stuff!'

Nigel turned to Justin but ignored him, tilting his head back for another swig.

'You bastard!' shouted Justin.

In a cathartic outburst, he broke into a run, jumped up and flew at Nigel, sending a right hook packed with an afternoon's anger to the jaw. His fist deflected off the moist bottle, plumb onto his nose. Nigel went over like a ninepin, sprawled after a strike, his nose bloodied and broken, out for the count. The bottle leaked water from his limp hand onto the pea green hardcourt.

Panting heavily, Justin surveyed his antagonist, picked up the bottle and directed the spilling contents into Nigel's face. He recovered his racket, looked up at the dumbstruck umpire with piercing blue eyes and walked off without uttering a word.

'The taste of Wimbledon glory the day before yesterday is soured today,' the headmaster sounded sternly from his rostrum in morning assembly. 'Forrester saw fit to rewrite Rudyard Kipling's exhortation to be a man in the face of triumph or disaster. For him, it mattered if he won or lost, when he was losing. Unable to triumph, he wrought disaster on the name of the school.'

'Wha …? You've got it all wrong!' protested Justin, feeling a thousand pairs of eyes turn and stare at him. He desperately wished to skulk out but the occasion trapped him.

'The school board has ratified a suspension from tennis for the remainder of the year as suitable punishment, with immediate effect.'

No! You can't do that. I'll die! mourned Justin, his world caving into the gloom of a black hole.

To starve him of tennis would be to kill him. As a terminally ill patient is rationed life before death, so diametrically opposite, Justin was dosed with death before life.

Locked in a crucible of loneliness, starved of the sport he loved, a seething anger baked a layered façade emotionless as enamel on his face. And out of this adversity his tennis career was reborn, fortified with a promise learned out of lesson never again to let an opponent's antics phase him.

Let the system take care of a crisis, resolved Justin. *Avoid risks like breath after a garlic meal!*

Such resolve rewarded him the following year with a magical Christmas present delivered from the public courts of Flamingo Park in Miami Beach, Florida. He won the Rolex Orange Bowl International Tennis Championships, considered by most to be the junior championship of the world. Who was this blond mystery boy from Africa?

§

After his schooldays, Justin mentally mapped out his career and knew immediately he must base himself abroad.

'What you gonna do with this tennis thing, boy?' asked Bill Forrester disparagingly. 'Settle down and get a job!'

'But I'm a tennis player,' pleaded Justin, beside himself for parental understanding.

'Education!' countered Justin's father. 'They do everything these days with these, these calculator things. You need an education to use them.'

'Bill, if the boy promises to study overseas, let him go,' counselled Charlie Morris.

'I promise. I promise, Dad. Just let me go!'

'I'll hold you to it, boy.'

Great Britain! Home of the greatest tennis tournament in the world, Wimbledon! Justin happily pondered in anticipation of his new home. *My game will flourish there. How can it not, right next to Wimbledon!*

No sooner had Justin arrived at Aunt Hilda's in London, when he went to Dunlop's plant in Yorkshire, in search of some desperately needed racket equipment.

'I'm looking for some Maxply's. These have given up the ghost,' announced Justin, dumping his old, warped frames in front of Richard Collins, Dunlop's public relations officer.

'Lad,' laughed Richard, shaking his head. 'The only Maxply frames we have are collectors' items in our museum!'

'But—'

'Follow me,' invited Richard Collins. 'I'll show you what we do now.'

Traipsing around the plant, Richard proudly demonstrated the manufacture of their blue-chip baby, the Dunlop Max 800i.

'What's the recipe?' Justin asked curiously.

Richard held up a handful of dark chips. 'These are short graphic fibres in a matrix of nylon. They're heated until molten and injected under pressure into this press around a low melting die-casted mould,' informed Richard. 'That done, we fry the frame in hot oil until the core melts out. This hollow frame is our patented injection moulding technology, the premier shock-protection system available. Lad, if you're used to a wooden frame, then I think you'll like this.'

'Uh huh!'

They carried on round the plant.

'We consistently monitor all the frames for weight, straightness, wall thickness and stiffness,' enlightened the PRO. 'I think you'll agree that we take pride in offering a high quality piece of equipment.'

Justin nodded his head.

'Here we polish the frames in a bath of ceramic chips and then paint them with our Dunlop insignia. Then we add the handle.'

Liquid polyurethane bubbled out of the frame to the required size.

'Wow! That reminds me of when I blew up the school fish-tank with a chunk of sodium!' exclaimed Justin, amused.

'Before the final test, these ladies wrap the handles with leather grips and string the frames. Finally, a gun fires a tennis ball against the strings to test for rebound speed and to establish the size of the sweet spot. A jolly fine frame, if you ask me!'

Justin grudgingly swapped his trusty wooden frames and a whole lot of paper bearing the queen's head for some high technology, carefully selecting the master's instruments.

Armed with his new widebody weapon, Justin went in search of Queens Club to audition for the British tennis squad.

He quickly sniffed out the indoor polished-wood court and introduced himself to two tennis-looking people.

'Hi, I'm Justin Forrester. I'm here to try out for the team.'

'Byron Belvedere is the name. I'm a baron!' said the red-head, flicking back his quiff. In his lofty voice, 'You from down under?'

'Huh?'

'From Australia?'

'Oh no. I'm a Swazi.'

'Oh, really. I'd expect you to be black.'

Great elephant balls! You're the whitest bugger I've ever laid eyes on, thought Justin, staring intently at his lily white complexion. He plucked up the courage to ask Byron, 'Are you some kind of albino?'

'Oh, tit for tat. Jolly good!'

Justin turned his attention to the other light complexioned player standing next to Byron. 'Are you brothers?'

'Jasper Ogilvy. Do they play much tennis down there?'

'Not really!'

'And you're here to test for our training squad?'

'Uh huh. Is a Mr Heathcote around?'

'He'll be in shortly. Presently at tea.'

Justin had never seen such pale people before and had to stop himself from staring.

'Wanna hit?' asked Justin.

'Splendid.'

'I'll take that side. You buggers stay here,' arranged Justin.

The ball skidded through on the polished wood like a flat stone skims on mirrored water, lightning fast and low. Justin had never experienced such extreme speed.

This is like playing on ice, he thought, finding himself hitting fractionally late for the first few minutes.

'Care for us to hold back?' asked Byron.

But Justin implemented his exceptional raw qualities of dazzling speed of foot and catlike reflexes, and adapted to the pace of the court. He shortened his backswing and used the pace of the ball to generate cutting drives to the far reaches of each corner. Twenty minutes elapsed.

'Time up!' gasped Byron, raising his hand with a white handkerchief, which Justin had difficulty seeing at first.

'I feel like I've been to hell and back. Where, may I ask, did you learn such imposing skills?' asked a drenched Jasper.

'Oh, a couple of tribal buggers and I would bang a ball about,' joked Justin, having barely broken a sweat.

'Forrester?' bellowed a sergeant-major's voice.

Justin turned round to see Albert Heathcote returning from tea. The British tennis coach stood tall, erect like a telegraph pole, without a strand of his shorn, steel grey hair daring to stray from his fastidious habits.

Also a bloody albino! thought Justin, nodding his head with a lowered gaze and offering his hand, but in vain.

'Your togs are out of line,' accused Heathcote, then with lofty contempt informed, 'White is *de rigueur* in my squad.'

'I'm sure it is!' responded Justin, looking at the pale faces around him. The World Wildlife Fund panda bear insignia emblazoned Justin's otherwise white T-shirt.

'I see Byron and Jasper have warmed up,' said Heathcote, observing them dripping with sweat. 'Byron, play a set with the new lad so I may see if he's any good. Don't be afraid to knock him off the court. And Byron, get some backbone!'

'Yes, Mr Heathcote!' Byron meekly succumbed. Then he turned to Justin and offered, 'Serve or receive?'

'Spin your racket! I'll take rough,' advised Justin, incredulous that an opponent would *offer* a choice.

'Rough it is!'

'I'll serve!'

Departing to take up opposite sides, Justin whispered to Byron, 'Is this bugger for real?'

'Afraid so, old chap!'

Justin served and volleyed, and chipped and charged the net on every occasion to win the set 6-2.

'You won, but a dearth of ground strokes in your repertoire,' criticised Heathcote.

Byron looked incredulous, remembering his rigorous warm-up.

'What grips do you use?' demanded Albert Heathcote.

Justin remained silent. He did not even know the names of the grips.

'Cat got your tongue, lad? Show me your forehand grip,' ordered Heathcote.

Justin complied.

Heathcote shook his head in amazement. 'Backhand?'

Justin showed him the same grip.

'No wonder you don't hit any ground strokes,' Heathcote said scornfully. 'Some idiot back home throw some bones and teach you to play all your shots with the same grip?'

Justin seethed inside, annoyed that someone should call Charlie Morris an idiot.

'I attacked the net because of the fast pace of the court,' countered Justin.

'How do you expect me to assess your game if I can't see forehands and backhands?' sneered Heathcote.

'Do you ever play on clay?'

'How big is a hole? Spit it out, lad.'

'*Then* I'll stay back and you can rate my groundies.'

'You pompous clown. We're here aren't we?'

'You don't get it, do you?' asserted Justin derisively, then spelled out his point, 'If I play a set, I play to win. Put me on polished wood, you see serve and volley.'

'If I tell you to stay back I expect you to comply, Forrester,' shot Heathcote superciliously. 'We don't have places on the team for know-it-alls like you.'

'Well, stick it up your clay pipe!' spat Justin vehemently, not believing his ears. Fuming, he stormed off court.

Tennis is an individual game. No coach, not anyone, will ever force me to change my style of play and compromise a chance to win.

'I'm sorry Aunt Hilda, but this is no place for a tennis player to grow. Everything is too stiff here. I'd be better off back in Swaziland where you just go out and hit a ball. No *de rigueur* rubbish!'

'I was so looking forward to having you stay, dear.'

'I'll be back. But on my terms.'

Within a week, Justin received two dozen full scholarship offers at prime American colleges. He accepted Stanford. In return for the fine opportunity to mature as a tennis player, Justin bagged two consecutive NCAA titles for Stanford to wallow in. After a three year absence, he felt ready to turn professional and make an assault on the tour. With the shift of the power base of tennis to Europe, he returned to London.

'Justin, your return is well-timed,' remarked Aunt Hilda, relieved. 'A Mr Heathcote has been beside himself trying to get in touch with you. Going on like a constipated glutton! Something about Barcelona.'

'Barcelona! Great elephant b – ballet! He's talking about the Olympic Games!' Justin thought out loud, his heart thumping with excitement. 'Could it be that he wants me to play?'

Justin wasted no time in contacting Byron Belvedere.

'Give me the split on Heathcote's team selection for Barcelona.'

'Jasper and me,' answered Byron. 'Why do you ask?'

'Singles *and* doubles?'

'As far as I know, old chap.'

'I suspect Heathcote is going to dump one of you,' Justin informed, aware that only two players per nation had direct acceptances.

Justin held the matter abeyance for two days, allowing Albert Heathcote to stew before phoning him.

'Aah, Justin! The prodigal son returns!'

'Uh huh!' *But not in need!*

'Do you do the Flamenco? There's a party in Barcelona. We leave in four weeks.'

'It's not my style to gatecrash,' responded Justin indignantly.

'But I've RSVP'd on your behalf,' countered Heathcote.

'What beast are you sacrificing?' accused Justin. 'Byron or Jasper?'

'Uh, how did …?' started Heathcote before lapsing into silence. 'You pompous idiot! This is the Olympic Games!'

'It could mean your demise, but I play according to the rules.'

'Don't get on your high horse with me, Forrester!'

Justin assumed a deliberate tone of voice. '*If* I play it'll be as a wild card, and for singles only. Tamper with Byron or Jasper and I'm a party-pooper.'

'Dammit Forrester! You're being awfully difficult,' remonstrated Heathcote, but then he remembered losing Justin once before. 'You leave me no option. A wild card it is. Be sure to turn up for training in a fortnight.'

'I'll consider the offer and confirm my decision tomorrow,' replied Justin, assuming control.

'You *what*? Who do you think you are, pussyfooting your way into the team? Your selection is tenuous, you pompous idiot!'

'It's terminated, unless I have a stay of acceptance until tomorrow.'

Justin slammed down the receiver, but stood there waiting for the telephone to ring. It did.

'Tomorrow?' enquired Justin, confidently.

'As you wish.'

Justin put down the receiver, grabbed a blushing Aunt Hilda and pranced around the room. 'The Olympic Games! Wow!'

The Boeing 747 lost height on its final approach.

'Ladies and gentlemen, in a few minutes we'll be landing. Please fasten your seat-belts.'

As wheels met tarmac in screeching pain, the Iberian hostess added the magic words, 'Welcome to Barcelona. Let the Games begin!'

The morning after his arrival, Justin headed to a training field to run the cobwebs of travel out of his legs. After 20 laps he noticed the British athletics team arriving.

I'd better scoot, he decided, not wanting to impose.

'Wait up there, son,' hailed a man clad in a white British track suit.

Justin glanced around to see if he was addressing anyone else, but there was no one. 'Me?'

'A blimmin' fine running style you have, lad,' Sam Sneadon, the short, stocky, elderly British athletics coach praised Justin. 'Wish m'lad Herbie would take note. He splays his feet, you know, like a blimmin' duck. Loses half a bloody second. Could mean the difference between gold or feathers.'

'If he's a duck, he's a pretty fast duck!' Justin spoke well of the famed Herb Johnson, latest in a production line of superb middle distance runners born out of Great Britain.

'Could be faster if he ran like you!'

'Mr Sneadon, please!' responded Justin, embarrassed that he should be made an example for Herb Johnson.

'Care to show him?'

'No!'

'Then I challenge you against m'boy!'

'You're on,' accepted Justin, his reticence melting to a confident bearing, belying his medium height.

Squaring off on the track, Justin nodded acknowledgement to the brown, curly-haired Herb.

'Four laps. Mind you take a good look at his gait, Herbie! No pronation. Off you go.'

Herb quickly opened a gap.

What a bloody ugly duck waddle! mocked Justin.

Not caring much for it, he tried desperately to catch Herb. For Justin, the pace was fast, like nothing he had ever experienced. The last time he ran track was way back at high school.

Shit! Four laps at this pace! Is this for real?

Justin tagged his countryman for three laps but with great difficulty.

Damn! I'm a bloody fool! he suddenly questioned the race. *Herb Johnson, the great miler, playing cat and mouse with me. And the British athletics coach advised him to observe me! Of all the blundering fools to be suckered into this farce.* To save face, Justin decided, *I'll give him a run for his laughter!*

Already in fifth gear, Justin found another in his remarkable body machinery and slowly inched ahead of Herb going into the final lap, throwing down the gauntlet. The race was on. Herb Johnson, the fastest miler in the world, versus the barefoot 21 year old Justin Forrester, his lean and wiry body tanned golden brown, straight flaxen hair flowing in the wind, a man driven by the chase.

They surged down the back-straight. Coming round the bend, Justin's icy blue eyes blazed in a planed face glistening with sweat, the straight nose breathed fire, lips pursed in a rage of determination, and his lungs expressed like a steam engine.

Shit! They're pumping blood! he thought. *How much more can they take?*

But challenge steeled his mind and these were the sleek legs that tracked animals on the African plains. He pushed and groped and surged forward, but as he cut the imaginary tape he felt a shadow at his side equal to him.

Both athletes bowed their heads between their knees to catch their breath.

'Fine race,' offered Herb putting out his hand.

Justin accepted, but seethed inside, *Damn! Damn! Damn! Why didn't I break the dead heat, even if the bugger* had *followed orders to hang back and observe!*

'Not much chance to see his fluent style, eh Herbie!'

'No chance!'

'Who's your coach, lad?' Sam asked Justin.

'I don't really have one,' answered Justin. *Except, of course, Charlie Morris.*

Sam's left eyebrow raised in surprise. 'You from the Aussie team?'

'No, I'm on the British team … the tennis team.'

'You're a *tennis player!*' expressed Sam, stunned. 'What on earth for?'

'It's my sport. I love it!'

'You've just run a sub three fifty-five mile and you tell me you're a blimmin' *tennis player!* Have you any idea how—'

'Fast?'

'Come with me and you'll run faster than Seb Coe or Steve Ovett or Steve Cram or—'

'Thanks Mr Sneadon, but no thanks,' smiled Justin. 'I'm a tennis player!'

An amateur amongst professionals in a changing Olympic Charter, Justin hurdled over formidable seasoned players as Jasper Ogilvy and the Hamilton twins, Tugboat and Terrier. Many top players opted not to contest, some preparing for the upcoming United States Open championships, others not comfortable with the marriage between the Olympic Games and professionalism.

Fortuitously, perhaps, Justin progressed to the semifinals, where surprisingly he was to meet a fellow Brit, Byron Belvedere. Surprising, because Britain's top player ranked low in world tennis. He had talent in abundance but no skeleton to hold it. But inspired by the toilsome work ethic of Justin, the British team, buoyed in spirit, trained for four weeks and now it paid dividends.

'Come, Byron, let's catch an early night. We have a match tomorrow,' encouraged Justin.

'You go ahead, old chap. I'll stay up awhile.'

Awhile meant all night. Byron suffered so much from nerves, he intentionally stayed awake before a big match to be sleepy and relaxed on court.

Thrust into the spotlight of an Olympic Games semifinal, the occasion suddenly dawned on Byron and his cocktail of complexes returned.

Justin won the toss. *Hmm! Let's test the bugger's nerve.* He decided, 'I'll receive serve.'

Serving, Byron distorted into a spastic jerk. Propelling the racket forward from the backscratch position, it thumped him on the head. Thwack! He fell to the floor.

Great elephant balls! Has he lost his bloody marbles? wondered Justin, flabbergasted. *He's got the elbow!* chuckled Justin, the elbow being a tennis colloquialism for a wretched dose of nerves.

And that was not the only time Byron received a lump on the head. Justin decimated the luckless Byron Belvedere without the loss of a game and beyond his wildest expectations sailed through to the final to meet the Spaniard, Manolo Gonzales.

Back at the Olympic Village a bewildered Justin asked of a nonchalant Byron, 'You don't seem to mind losing?'

41

'Not really!' Byron hesitated before confiding in Justin, 'To climb the social ladder at the All England Club, father hired a coach to come to our estate every day to teach me to play the ruddy game. He hoped I'd win The Championships, being British and all that. Dare I say I've failed him. ... I fear losing, Justin. But when I lose, I feel smug inside, as if I'm getting back at the old chap for all those tedious years.'

'You can overcome those nerves,' Justin advised an embarrassed Byron.

'Consult a psychiatrist?' asked Byron ruefully.

'I don't doubt you need some head shrinking right now,' chuckled Justin, looking at the lumps on his friend's red head. 'But I was thinking more of building up your body. Work like a crazy man and get as fit and strong and—'

'A trifle odd, dare I say?'

'Not at all. Somehow it gives one psychological overspill. You'll get confident. Stick around with me. I need someone to train with.'

Byron wore a worried look. Which was worse? To play like an idiot or train with that madman, Justin Forrester.

What little interest British tennis enjoyed at the Olympic Games, ceased with the demise of Byron Belvedere. No one had expected him to proceed so far. 'Jolly good show, old chap!' But everyone expected him to lose. 'Jolly bad luck, fellow!' After all, British tennis players just did not do well in tennis!

Bewilderingly, the country that gave tennis to the world and was host to the greatest tennis tournament in the sport, could not produce a tennis player worthy of playing on the Centre Court of Wimbledon. British tennis was in despair. Unknown to the media back in Britain, a player by the name of Justin Forrester played under the Union Jack.

The copper-skinned Manolo Gonzales, with a mop of shiny, black hair, fast approached the twilight of a career that started out as a ballboy. Living just a block away from the Real Club in Barcelona, the champagne cork popping sound emanating from the clay courts attracted the young Manolo. Hanging around, he soon collected the odd pesetas scrambling for balls, and between matches he borrowed a racket and fooled around with other ballboys.

But this was no ordinary niño with a racket. He was a born maestro, blessed with the sublime gift of ball control. A prodigious talent, an artist supreme whose racket resembled a paint brush and the court his canvas upon which he painted masterpieces for the angels. Such flair extraordinaire took this genial man to the French Open title only a year ago.

Justin warmed up with Byron in the seclusion of the Club Esportivos Hispano-Frances, hoping to avoid the mayhem of nationalistic fervour bubbling at the seams.

'Shit! Manolo's got the same idea!' bemoaned Justin, seeing his opponent leading droves of worshipping Spanish fans to the courts.

After his warm-up, the genial Spaniard, as friendly and affable as a dachshund, approached Justin. *'Buenas tardes,* Justin. We go play our match, *si.'*

Together they led a swarm of worshipping Spaniards across a footbridge to the picturesque La Teixonera and onto the centre court, nestled into the wooded hillside like a Roman amphitheatre.

The first set bewildered Justin.

This is weird! he thought. *As if I've woken into a misty dreamland and impossible things are unfolding in slow motion.*

The dream was all Manolo's, the nightmare Justin's. In awe, he watched the maestro conjure up magic with his loosely strung racket. A touch player artist supreme, without a hint of power to his game. Such crude strategy was anathema to his gift. Instead, Manolo's talent scorned the big hitters of the modern game, cushioning their power in the soft strings of his wand held by a floppy wrist, the dampened ball trampolining with an assortment of spins.

Manolo mesmerised, he hypnotised. The locals have a saying, 'A Catalan can make bread out of stone.' They appreciated Manolo's ability to carve winning placements out of seemingly nothing. 'I can't figure him out!' was the oft lamented cry of despair after a dizzy jerk around defeat by Manolo.

This bugger plays like ... well, like nobody else on earth! mourned the hapless Justin. *He's thrown away the textbook of tennis and written his own, a bloody mystery! Predictable only in his unpredictability!*

'Olé! Olé! Olé!' screamed the Spanish crowd, worshipping their hero, their adulation a spectacle second only to the enchantment on the court. Gold was coming home. Manolo won the first two sets by 6-1 6-1 and led 2-1 in the third with little Justin could do to stop the flow. He gored the Brit and the crowd settled in for a quick kill.

Damn it! I want to win gold. I must *win. But what the hell can I do?* worried a distraught Justin, the gold medal he coveted tarnishing to silver.

A lump choked his throat. *I feel so helpless. I don't even know where to begin to impose. This is so bizarre!* thought Justin, an impression that would one day play a gigantic role in his fate.

Then suddenly the magic stopped, and the music of Manolo's talent sounded a muted note. As had happened so often before, especially before his home crowd, he went walkabout, from dominant to dormant. A genius on the verge of his biggest home-grown victory, suddenly started losing. But more extraordinary, he seemingly lacked concern, for win or lose, the same toothy grin flashed across his face.

With the match oozing out of the Spaniard like sand from an egg-timer, the once raucous crowd subdued to silence. Quite amazingly, a match Justin had no chance of winning, was suddenly his for the taking.

Manolo ballooned another ball over the baseline and Justin won a most bizarre match. The Spaniard ran round the netpost and threw his arms round Justin for a huge hug.

Justin sat in his chair, his head still reeling in puzzlement.

I'm losing badly, then suddenly I'm winning. I had no control. Eerie. What the hell happened?

Justin had to shake his head free of bewilderment before appreciating the joy of winning the Olympic gold medal. Then his heart filled with unfettered joy.

Gold! What a coming out party! thought Justin, surprised.

After all, he had served no apprenticeship. He felt a quaint bond with the inaugural Olympic Games. Then, an Englishman, John Pius Boland, touring Greece in 1896, came upon a sports festival. Having left his tennis racket behind in Oxford, Boland bought a new one, entered the tennis tournament and won it. So the Olympic Games crowned the first tennis gold medallist!

With the Union Jack rising in step to 'God Save The Queen', Justin climbed atop the tiered podium, an amateur towering over professionals, fondling the glittering gold medal he found at the end of the rainbow. As the national anthem reached a crescendo, he felt hot and cold waves flushing through his body and tears misted his eyes.

Nothing beats winning!

'That was spiffing, old chap!' radiated Byron aboard a British Airways Jumbo headed towards London.

'Yep. Not just the gold medal, but the team spirit,' added Justin. 'Pretty infectious!'

'It helped Jasper and me to play better,' beamed Byron, clutching his bronze medal. 'I hope we can do well in Davis Cup tennis.'

'Mmm. ... Did you see that German girl with the legs?' asked Justin, changing the subject. 'Bit of a beaut! Instead of Davis Cup we should have a mixed team event. I'd like to play doubles with those legs!'

'Wrong nationality, I'm afraid, old chap!'

'Yep! Pity!' commiserated Justin. After a moment's thought, 'You know, we should have a World Cup like they do in soccer. Yep, a bloody team event … men and women … maybe annual. … Hmm! … Gotcha! World Cup Tennis to decide which country is best. I'll see what I can do!'

Meantime I have a more pressing engagement. This gold medal will always be special to me. It's my first. But tennis is the tour and the Grand Slam tournaments, and the US Open is only a moment away. My first tournament as a pro. My first Grand Slam tournament. I wait with relish.

Gold in Barcelona counted nothing for tennis rankings, so Justin's status merited no more than a chance to qualify for the United States Open championships. On the tour they call them 'quallies', a pre-tournament tournament that enables 16 players from 128 to enter the main draw. The rabble play three rounds over the three days prior to the tournament. But before they say hello, most have said goodbye.

In the jet set tennis world of high living, qualifiers are the squatters. Players room together to make ends meet or sleep in the car park. In the depressing dog-eat-dog world of the quallies, the pressure to win works against winning. A whole strain of self-perpetuating, downward spiralling, hard luck stories and false confidence permeate the locker-room. 'My strings were too tight. If only I had a better racket I could beat him!' laments a hapless qualifying competitor who lost 6-0 6-0 6-0. Theirs is a world where 'Did you make it?' refers to the lifeline of getting into the main draw and not into bed with a draw card of the fairer sex!

Justin won his first two matches. Whilst waiting in the locker-room, he took one look around him and decided, *I don't belong here. These buggers are a bunch of losers. I've got to get out of here! It might be catchy!*

Then the bubble burst. Justin Forrester crashed out of the US Open, not having made it to the main draw. He bit his lip to hide the abject disappointment that seethed inside him.

Olympic gold medallist, now I blow it in the bloody quallies!

'Justin, some good news. We've drafted you into the main draw as a lucky loser,' a US Open official told Justin. A lucky loser replaces a withdrawal from the main draw. 'The bad news is that you have to play the 16th seed, Tugboat Hamilton.'

Play Tugboat? Justin responded, then confidently proclaimed, *That's no problem. I beat the bugger in Barcelona!*

He extracted the most from his fortuitous reprieve, beating the 16th seed and another two professionals before reaching the fourth round.

Now for the acid test.

The draw matched Justin against the grand old man of American tennis and 5th seed for the tournament, Larry King.

Sitting in the locker-room before his match with Larry, Justin felt in awe of the tennis aristocracy around him.

The tennis gods! Roland Drechsler, the Wimbledon champion, stood only a few paces away. So did Sern Stenmark, Swedish, but French Open champion. And swatting his racket with nervous energy like a man after flies, was the inimitable Tyrone Summers, the number one player in the world.

Players I've dreamed of playing, thought Justin, reverently. *Now I'm rubbing shoulders with them. Still unnoticed, but only time away.*

Larry King held out his hand and nodded his head, 'Hi, I'm Larry.'

'Justin Forrester,' replied Justin with a lowered gaze, in respect for the man with the shock of white hair.

When they took the Stadium Court, Justin gazed absolutely agog at the steep-walled stadium that rose into the heavens. And the noise, the throbbing noise!

This is it! Justin announced to himself, his blood bubbling. *I've arrived.*

In no time, Justin went down 3-0, then 5-2, and suddenly the first set disappeared.

He resorted to his master weapon, his legs. Arousing the Flushing Meadows crowd with his spill-your-guts attitude, he battled the leonine maverick of the tour to a fourth set tiebreaker, but lost.

'Where've you been hiding?' asked Larry after their match, intrigued. 'You play tough!'

What a compliment! And from Larry King! marvelled Justin. He could have doled out no greater praise to Justin, who prided himself in his ability to tough out a match. *But I lost. I must never lose! It sucks to play well and lose! There's no place for losers where I'm going.*

Justin followed Larry King into the locker-room like a dog after its master, plucking up the courage to confront him.

'Uh, Mister King?' called Justin.

'Call me Hoss, it's my nickname. They think I'm the old war horse around here. What's up?'

Justin lowered his gaze. 'I was wondering if you knew anything about the ATP Council.'

'I should. I'm vice-president.'

Justin felt embarrassed, but hitched his wagon to Larry King in the hope of hot-wiring the ATP Council. 'I was wondering if I could address the council.'

'Be my pleasure!'

'Who's the decision-maker?'

'Guys, I've taken the liberty of allowing Justin Forrester to address the meeting. He has an idea to share with us.'

'Gentlemen, I believe Tyrone Summers's refusal to commit to playing a full quota of tournaments can be overcome.'

'What magic wand do you wave?' the president asked sarcastically. He had had his fill with the enigmatic Summers. 'If he doesn't stick to the rules, he'll be punished!'

What's the point of rules if they don't work! Justin wished to say, but knew not to tread on toes. 'Would he ever give up playing Wimbledon?'

'Not likely!'

'Why not?'

'Prestige, dummy. *You* know players would pay to play Wimbledon.'

'Hmm,' thought Justin aloud. 'Wouldn't it be wonderful if our tour had that same compulsive pull.'

'What do you mean?' asked the president.

'I'm not sure. You're the brains. ... But some sort of carrot dangling at the end of the tour to motivate the players to want to support it.'

'A big money prize?' suggested the president.

'Sure. But something more. Wimbledon doesn't pay the best.'

'No, it's prestige,' answered the president. Then the penny dropped. 'Holy shit! That's what we need. Some dominating goal, something so attractive they'll overlook the hassles.'

'Quite!' Justin pampered the president before prompting him, 'Something a champion desires.'

'Recognition! That's it! Any ideas?' asked the president.

'Honour the player who tops the year-end ranking with some sort of title,' answered Justin. He feigned thought. 'Hmm ... what do other sports have?'

There was a long silence.

Come on, spit it out. Just say the bloody words, 'World Champion'. Justin could hardly bear the sounds of silence, but he had to keep quiet. He knew the idea must come from the president.

'Holy shit! I think I've got it,' the president snapped his fingers with delight. 'He will be World Champion! ... That's it! A player's goal on the tour will be to become World Champion. Provided we couch the title in prestige, the players will *want* to support the tour in a desire to become World Champion. ... Abracadabra! All other problems fall away. No need for rules! No more rules for designations, exhibitions and guaranteed payments. The World Champion carrot automatically takes care of that. That will make our job easier!'

'And no more minimum tournament rule!' interjected Justin, a great believer in free market competitive forces.

'Thank you, Justin, for bringing this to our attention. If you could leave now, we'll take it from here.'

'The Council unanimously accepted the idea of the ATP Tour being a world championship tour, but we stopped short of eliminating the minimum tournament rule,' informed the president.

'Why?' asked Justin, indignantly.

'Until our idea guarantees success, we want the backup of the rule.'

'You'll be sorry. There'll come a time when you'll regret the minimum tournament rule.'

After the meeting, Larry took Justin aside. 'I want you to know that I'm fully behind you on scrapping the minimum tournament rule. It's an indictment on our ability to deliver the goods. The Council wants the honour of introducing *your* concept of the ATP Tour being a world championship tour, but they're shit scared to put their balls where their mouths are, their teeth chatter so much.' Larry looked at the newcomer to the tour. 'Why are you so concerned?'

The aspirant to fame replied, 'I want to control my destiny!'

CHAPTER 4

'The boy has suffered from some severe trauma,' diagnosed Dr Skarstein. 'Not speaking is his way of shutting out his grief.'

'Will he ever speak again?' asked an anxious Amos Creighton about Boris Bauer.

'He could well speak again,' nodded the doctor. 'If he comes to terms with the root cause from which the trauma stems, his mute defence wall can come tumbling down. But the problem—'

'How long will this take?' demanded Creighton.

'Recovery is totally unpredictable,' answered Dr Skarstein. 'As I was about to say, the problem is to penetrate the defence mechanism and gain his confidence. But there are no guarantees. Sometimes they miraculously snap out of it as quickly as the trauma triggered it. Usually another form of shock releases them from this self-inflicted captivity.'

'It's a miracle!' exclaimed an astounded Amos Creighton, sitting in his leather chair behind the large oak desk. Vich stood opposite, ill at ease in the smokeless zone. 'The boy not talking is a great asset. He will be relieved from the pressure of the press curse. You deal with them. Talk for the boy.'

'Hmmph!' mumbled Vich.

'Just make sure he never talks again!'

Creighton ushered Vich out of the inner sanctum. Returning to sit at his desk, he proudly pondered his well thought out Grand Plan. The bloodline. Czechoslovakia.

The kid will obey me! He's Czechoslovakian. The Russians have oppressed them. Toeing the line has become their way. They're subservient, amenable to control. Yes, the kid will obey me! Creighton reassured himself. *Good for you, communists!*

At his rolling property in Greenwich, Amos Creighton owned a major tennis complex, the nerve-centre of his Grand Plan. The first meeting took place.

'I have the results you ordered,' announced Professor Von Trapp, holding up an X-ray of Boris Bauer's wrist to his audience of Vich and the accompanying Bob Wallace, a player who once knocked on the door of the great Australian tennis dynasty. He found fame, instead, as a tennis coach before his sudden disappearance.

'How tall?' growled Vich from under his droopy moustache.

'Based on the size of his wrist at his current age of 11, I believe—'

'How tall?' Vich reiterated his demand, increasing his tone of growl.

'Six foot three! Just as you predicted.'

'Hmmph!'

'Now for the final test before we can begin training,' announced Professor Von Trapp.

The short, slim, beady-eyed professor with shiny, black hair connected electrodes over the temporal and parietal lobes on both sides of Boris Bauer's brain.

'I want you to draw this figure eight for me, over and over again in the same place.'

The left-handed Boris Bauer complied.

The professor assessed the electroencephalograph. 'Hmm! Definite high-voltage slow alpha waves emanating from the left hemisphere of his brain.'

The professor then gave Boris Bauer a series of simple arithmetic problems.

'Eureka! Exactly the reverse.' Professor Von Trapp turned to Vich and pronounced, 'You're absolutely right! His mother was indeed left-handed.'

Vich said nothing, but merely fondled his Donnay Allwood.

'Quit bein' a lug punisher. What ya tryin' to say, mate?' asked a puzzled Bob Wallace, a tall angular faced, tawny-haired man, tanned rich brown and sporting a beer paunch.

'The kid *must* play right-handed.'

'Bloody 'ell 'e won't!' snapped Bob Wallace. ''Ave you any idea the benefit o' playin' tennis left-handed? Ut's a boon to be a southpaw. At least a bloody 10 percent advantage! Their spins—'

'Let me explain.'

'Ya're on borrowed time, mate.'

'The brain divides into two halves that control the opposite sides of the body. Normally, the right-brain is the creative side whereas the left segment relates to logic. I suspect there have been several great left-handed players with a penchant for creativity?'

'Bloody right, mate!' Bob Wallace replied. 'Laver, McEnroe, Navratilova—'

'It could well be that as left-handers their right-brain controlled them. The creative side! There is a saying that left-handers are in their right brain!' Professor Von Trapp laughed at his own joke.

'Then why the bloody 'ell do you want the little bastard to play right-handed?' demanded Bob Wallace.

'Don't you see? Left-handers who have left-handed mothers tend to have reversed specialisation. The electroencephalograph confirms this for the boy. *Ipso facto*, the boy plays right-handed.'

The look on Bob Wallace's face did not buy the professor's idea.

'Is there any record of tennis players born left-handed but forced to play right-handed?' asked the professor.

'Righto!' Bob Wallace recalled. 'Donkey's years ago, society forced lefties to change. Ken Rosewall. And, o' course, those Grand Slammer beauts, Margaret Court and Little Mo.'

'Don't you find that odd?' asked Professor Von Trapp patiently.

'I guess so, mate.'

'Quite possibly these players playing right-handed tapped into their left-brain, their creative brain! It's imperative the kid must do the same.'

'You'd better be right, mate,' glared Bob Wallace, not convinced. 'I'm buggered if I'm goin' to waste a left-hander!'

Vich addressed them both. Taking care of the quotidian details of the Grand Plan was his responsibility.

'Nine years. Nine years and he's unbeatable. Don't screw up,' warned Vich, fondling the centre main string of his Donnay Allwood tennis racket, the Vich bargaining tool!

They had no choice but to comply. Simply, Bob had cheated on his wife Daphne, and Professor Von Trapp had embezzled funds at Georgetown University School of Medicine to further his private work on the brain's learning process. Creighton had surreptitiously discovered the skeletons in their closets, but instead of blackmail, he offered them the grand opportunity to exercise their skills and paid them a handsome sum to boot.

Amos Creighton wanted Bob Wallace and Professor Von Trapp to devise a method of coaching Boris Bauer into a perfect tennis player. Essentially, the plan was to draw on the seat-of-the-pants know-how of the great Australian tennis coach, and optimise Boris Bauer's learning by utilising the professor's expertise on the brain.

In September 1985 whilst Ivan Lendl overpowered the artistic John McEnroe in the US Open final at Flushing Meadows, only 40 minutes away at his tennis court complex in Greenwich, Creighton held a meeting of his players. He called on Vich, Professor Von Trapp and Bob Wallace to mobilize another stage of his Grand Plan.

'I want you to build me the perfect player,' instructed Creighton.

Bob Wallace drained a can of Foster's Lager into his raw-boned, craggy face and belched. 'Bloody good drop o' piss, that!' Keeping the others waiting in anticipation, he slowly wiped the froth from his mouth on his shirt sleeve before issuing, 'Bloody impossible!'

'The kid has ideal genes, and we have unlimited resources. I *want* the perfect player,' demanded Creighton.

'Not on! Tennis is a bloody difficult sport to master. Too many interrelated bits,' Bob Wallace enlightened in his Strine twang.

'More than other sports?' enquired Creighton, peeved at being told what he could not have.

''Ell, yes! They got ut easy, the bastards,' informed the coach. He extended four fingers on his right hand to count.

'Ya got the physical, ...'

Unlike one-dimensional sports, tennis makes enormous demands on that triumvirate of stamina, speed and strength. Not bulk strength, but resilient strength to wield a light weight over and over again. Fitness to play up to 5 hour matches 7 times in 14 days to win a Grand Slam tournament, with on-court temperatures of up to 65°C. The tour goes on week after week, year after year, with hardly a break. And that magical quality of mercurial speed, a tennis player needs it in spades. Dazzling speed of 10 paces here and 5 paces there, always twisting and turning, and pushing and stopping and reflexing.

'... the technical, ...'

In reality, no one tennis shot is alike. Players hit backhands and forehands with different amounts of topspin or sidespin or backspin or no spin, when the ball is anything from shoulder height to scraping the floor, from deep behind the baseline to close in the forecourt, to be got back over a net and down again within the baseline, generally with great speed. Add to this complex equation of physics the enigma of a moving ball, and suddenly the demands of fine-motor skill technique are exacting!

Just consider that when returning serve, once the server strikes the ball from anything up to 220 kilometres per hour, the receiver must assess whether it is going to his backhand or forehand, change the grip on the racket accordingly, take the racket back, run to the ball, judge through sight and sound the incoming ball's spin, inhibited by innuendos of disguise, which not only can be sliced wide, swerved into the body or kicked out high, but also bounces and is rising like a deranged slinky. The receiver must simultaneously keep one eye on the opponent to decide what type of a plethora of possible shots to return, execute the shot with timing to be struck in a precise position, in the dead centre of a racket, which, if out of alignment by a fraction of one degree, spells the difference between perfection or disaster, all in the space of half a second!

'... the mental ...'

Tennis is won and lost in the mind. This weapon is subtle, the ability to read and spot weaknesses, and exploit them, converting opportunities into reward. This requires intense concentration in a time frame that defies human ability, necessitating ebb and flow, and the intuition to use patience or strike quickly and accurately at the right moment, to win.

'... and the intangibles.'

Champions have that special something, absolute fire. The spark of desire, the belief in ability, the ambition to want it all, the competitiveness to fight, the killer instinct to dominate, and the nerve, courage and heart for the ultimate test of the self, all bound in an invisible aura that is champion.

Like golf but not running, tennis requires a high degree of fine motor-skill, a stringent test of the nerve. But in common with running and unlike boxing, there is no coaching during tennis contests. Tennis and boxing revel in close rapport with the crowd, wearing your heart on your sleeve for all to see, unlike in swimming. In concert with most water sports, however, tennis is an individual sport without recourse to bail out by a team, as in baseball. In common with baseball, but not snooker, tennis has to deal with the enigma of a moving ball. Frame by frame for snooker and set by set for tennis, a contestant has to go for the kill to win a championship at its final hurdle, a huge test of mettle, while a soccer team may take a winning lead, then crawl into a defensive shell and wait for the whistle. But in contrast with golf, which plays over a course, both tennis and soccer contests are dynamic, where opponents have direct interaction with each other. Yes, tennis goes full circle. It has it all!

'Sorry, chief!' disappointed Bob Wallace, rubbing his hawk nose. 'But ut's bloody impossible for any bloke to come close to the perfect tennis player. And that's dinkum. Bit of a bugger, ain't ut?'

'This does not sound encouraging! I *want* this Boris Bauer to be unbeatable!' demanded an irate Creighton.

'*That* can be done!' defused Bob Wallace, to the sudden surprise of Creighton. 'A perfect player, 'ell no! An unbeatable player, maybe!'

'What do you mean?'

'Most players try to master the game o' tennis. Except they're bloody human. Ut's impossible. Too many variables in tennis. So the bastards wind up two bob short in a pound of the ideal tennis player. A jack o' all trades, master at none. But there may be another way. I 'ave this trick up my sleeve, but ut's a gamble.'

'Out with it!'

'Power!'

'Power?'

'Yeah, mate! Bludgeonin' power! You simplify the bloody game into five basic strokes. Serve. Forehand and backhand ground strokes. Forehand and backhand volleys. These pretty much cover most o' the game. Add a mule kick o' power and you 'ave a bloody one dimensional robot so dominant, there's no need for that fancy crap. Drop-shots. Lobs. Spins. No cat and mouse. 'Is opponent'll be so bloody shit scared, 'e'll spend most of the match kangarooin' the dyke!'

'A powerful shot draws a weak reply, negating the need for exceptional speed?' queried Amos Creighton astutely.

'Ya wisin' up, chief! But above all, brute power gets rid o' the mind. You can teach a galah with a 'ead full of standard mix concrete to play tennis!'

'But isn't the mind a major weapon, where you win or lose matches?' asked Creighton, concerned.

'Yeah, but mostly ut's a lousy bastard. Only the champs use their minds to win matches. For the other bastards ut's like a bloody sieve. Match goes right through for a dirty big loss.'

'But power replaces the mind?'

'It makes the block redundant. Stills the mind. Like a bloody robot, 'e just thinks power. On the critical points 'e can't freeze, just wham bang! Besides, this mug will be so like King Kong, 'is matches won't test the mind.'

'Which is good news,' interrupted Professor Von Trapp, 'because mental strength will be extraordinarily difficult to teach.'

'Spot on, mate! We mustn't allow the little bastard to think on court!'

'And this does not make a perfect tennis player?' queried Creighton.

'Nah! There's always a chance some bugger might come along with equal power, but also 'ave that fancy crap o' spins and touch. Bloody unlikely if you ask me, mate. Let's leave ut at unbeatable.'

'The scenario is perfect for controlled learning,' interjected Professor Von Trapp, having absorbed everything with zest. 'Reducing tennis to such simplistic terms will enhance the benefits of controlled learning. What does worry me are the intangibles.'

'*I* am his master!' emphasized Creighton. '*My* ambition is his! *His* drive will be controlled by *me!*'

'If the kid rebels, nothin' this side of the black stump will make 'im win a bloody tennis match!' countered Bob Wallace.

'The kid will *not* rebel! Now let it be,' ordered Creighton. He addressed the professor. 'Your enthusiasm excites me. Explain yourself.'

'For several years, now, we have known that the brain controls the physical learning process through nerve pathways. Imagine the brain as a computer, with billions of nerve cells connected to the nervous system in complex circuits,' elucidated the professor. He pinched himself on the arm. 'When I pinch myself, a series of electrical impulses travel along the nerve pathways to the brain, where it interprets them as pain. They return to the spot pinched, where a synapse releases an excitatory chemical to stimulate the sensation of pain.'

'Cut the drivel, mate, and get on with ut,' demanded an irritated Bob Wallace.

'Well, the same thing happens with a tennis stroke. Every movement and feeling behaves the same way. The problem with natural learning is the inordinate time a person spends developing and becoming trapped in a bad habit.'

'Righto, mate! A jackaroo spends more time groovin' a buggered shot. Ut's bloody difficult to noose the lousy habit.'

'It is! You see, each impulse burns, if you like, a neural pathway between the arm and the brain. If the technique is incorrect, which is most likely for a beginner, then bad habit pathways etch into the nervous system. The obstacle arises in unburning these pathways.'

'It takes a mule kick in the backside to unlearn a bad tennis 'abit. Rather give me a good ol' bastard who 'as never played tennis, than a prize wanker with lousy technique.'

'Hmm! It can be done,' assured the professor. 'They can be unburned. The secret lies in relearning correct technique. The more recently etched pathways are more dominant. But you're right. It's extremely difficult to teach an old dog new tricks.'

'Where ya headin', mate?' demanded an impatient Bob Wallace.

'Mr Wallace, am I right in saying that, even with your famed expertise, teaching a beginner is extracting good technique out of a glut of bad? After a long time and many frayed nerves, few will emerge as tennis players, the others will forever remain hackers. Not so?'

'You got ut, mate! I'll kiss your bloody arse if you can tell me why?'

'Simply, at the embryonic stage, a player will only hit, say, one good ball for every nine bad ones. In essence, they practice and etch far more bad habit neural pathways than good. The result is a perpetual downward spiral in the learning process—'

'Go get rooted, mate!' cursed the Australian, offended.

'Unless there is intervention,' pacified Professor Von Trapp. 'Mr Wallace, you have to sweat blood and tears to sway the balance in favour of more good neural pathways than bad. Not so?'

'Bloody right!'

'This is where we will use biomechanic feedback into the brain to short-circuit the learning process.'

'Ya bloody bull artist!' accused a sceptical Bob Wallace. 'This I wanna see!'

'Recently, the Japanese connected some electrodes to a subject, and wired him up to a computer to monitor the electrical processes during sexual intercourse. They stored these impulses. Later they fed them back into the brain, and astonishingly, the subject experienced the same sexual excitement to the point of orgasm!'

'Hooly-dooly! Sounds like a bit o' fun. But 'ow the bloody 'ell is this goin' to help in tennis?'

'Instead of using the hit and miss process of natural learning and risking a poor recording, view the kid as a blank audio cassette and we will burn neural pathways of correct technique from the outset.'

The professor connected Boris Bauer to a series of electrodes, which measured the current at the synapses. Under Bob Wallace's guidance, he shadowed forehands, that is, without actually hitting a ball, until on the nineteenth attempt, he produced one to the satisfaction of the coach.

'Stop, mate!' shouted Bob Wallace. 'That one's a beaut!'

The professor stored the impulses of this stroke. Over the next hour he relayed them back into Boris Bauer's brain, equivalent to over 300 forehands.

'The moment of truth, Mr Wallace,' an excited professor announced, discabling the boy to test a shadow stroke by himself.

Boris Bauer perfectly imitated the recorded forehand, and could do it again and again with little deviation.

'Hooly-dooly! That's bloody amazin', mate! The chief is right. 'E *will* be a robot!' exclaimed Bob Wallace. 'Who said Ned Kelly was dead?'

Over the next three months under counsel of the coach, the professor repeatedly wired up Boris Bauer and fed his brain, each time refining his strokes, until finally, they emulated the simulated strokes optimally designed by computer modelling for his projected body size.

CHAPTER 5

Another one bites the dust
Another one bites the dust
And another one gone, and another one gone
Another one bites the dust
Hey, I'm gonna' get you too
Another one bites the dust

The mournful drum roll struck a sombre note and presaged revolution, but the rumble of the tumbrel barely hushed the clickety-clack of knitting needles. The 'Black Widow', *la guillotine*, resurrected, and one by one distinguished heads rolled. The Parisian public shrugged their shoulders. After all, they had witnessed such scenes all too often before, to be overly concerned.

This is Roland Garros, crucible of revolution, home of the Dirtkickers' Ball, where they bounce out the gatecrashing exponents of the fast court and return their impotent serves across the channel to their beloved grass in England. Brought up on a diet of the explosive, quick-kill of serve and volley, the demands on patience, control and guile exacted by clay, torment grass-courters. It's tennis on the red clay courts of Europe! It's *Les Internationaux De France!* It's Paris in the springtime!

Justin entered the picturesque grounds of Roland Garros and tasted an ambience of the enchanting city of Paris. He strolled the promenade and sat on a marble plinth, Roland Garros's own 'Arc de Triomphe'.

'The French Musketeers!' he whispered to himself, gazing at bronze statues of the fabled four on each avenue radiating from a central fountain, immortalising memories of French tennis past. René Lacoste, Jean Borotra, Henri Cochet and Jacques Brugnon, for whom they built Roland Garros to provide a home for their glory days, stood proud.

'And there's that ballerina dame!' he spoke of Suzanne Lenglen, goddess of the game.

This French Open, as always, breathed a festive and deliciously Gallic air, a reflection of France's deepest way of life. Culture, couture and cuisine created the unmistakable ambience of elegance.

Around Justin milled spectators, foreigners mixed with Gauls, permeating the air with a *mélange* of polyglot chatter. Pretty ladies, elegant and chic, Frenchmen, suave and debonair, the odd one puffing on the end of a cigar. The aroma of strong brewed coffee and baskets of freshly baked baguettes and gourmet cheese platters from the food stalls and roaming vendors, wafted through the spring air. Here and there, birds chirped in the stately chestnut trees that cascaded a fine mist of bloom on the morning dew. People emerged from hibernation and gazed at the freshness. Outdoor cafés bustled with people watching people watching people. And everywhere lovers held hands. A time when Paris was most *vivant*. Spring was in the air!

Mmm! Roland Garros is very beautiful, thought Justin, *and very special!*

'Quinze-trente!' announced an umpire from an outside court.

'Quinze-quarante!'

'Jeu, Gonzales!'

'Jeu, Summers!' echoed in the boulevard.

Justin gazed at the surroundings of Roland Garros. The crushed red bricks of the courts and the grey concrete façades of the stadium, washed with every imaginable shade of green from mint to bottle green.

He looked up towards *Court Central* and found the names of former champions engraved on the stone rim surrounding the stadium, a testimony to their victories. Two names, Björn Borg and Chris Evert stood out like colossi, the greatest champions of this venerable tournament, the acknowledged *grande dame* of clay court tennis.

One day my name will be engraved on that stadium! he imagined. *Champion of France!*

'Damn!' cursed Justin at the sight of the draw, an opening encounter with the tall, strawberry blond-haired German, Roland Drechsler. *My first match against the reigning Wimbledon champ. That's tough!* Then turning bad into good, *But great, it's on* Court Central. *I like that!*

The moment Justin took the red clay court brought back memories of training on an anthill dust patch in the middle of the African bushveld.

Those crazy days, sliding and gliding and braking in the gravel, he remembered. *Dreaming of playing the finals of Roland Garros! All those years of training, now I'm here. I love it. It's a dream come true!*

The match began. Justin crouched, ready to face the biggest serve in the game. Roland's body cocked like a gun, then triggered, uncoiling in an upward spiral, transferring lethal power through a pronating wrist into the suspended ball, imparting astonishing pace to the projectile, hurtling the ball wide to the deuce court.

Hubba hubba! exclaimed Justin, startled at the speed of the oncoming serve.

He ran and ran, stuck out his racket and hoisted the ball back into play. Suddenly, they stood on level terms. The German's delivery counted for nought. The reason?

Red clay is *terre battue,* crushed brick, a terrifying battle in the mind of the serve and volleyer. The big players who live and die by the big shot, get buried in the clay. With their catapulting balls biting into the soft bed of calcined clay, the power dampened by the cushion, hitting winners is no different from cracking a macadamia nut on a bed of soft feathers, even if armed with a mighty sledgehammer. Clay is tennis's great equaliser. One has to probe before the kill, play cat and mouse, gradually build up a superior position, then exploit the weakness.

Gotcha! exclaimed Justin, sending a lifted backhand and his opponent scampering off into oblivion.

With Roland's serve disabled by the clay, Justin discovered technical flaws in the Germans's game, flaws concealed in the cut and thrust style that served him so well on fast grass. He preyed on them, exploiting their vulnerability until they exposed like a tooth's raw nerve-end, then he pulled and prodded, and inflicted pain.

'*Jeu*, Forrester,' announced the umpire, Justin winning the first game.

As his serve went, so went the game of the German. On début day, one the press labelled 'BLACK MONDAY', out crashed the world number two, gone before the championship's first sunset, sent packing to England for grass court practice he did not want. Out, too, went a sachet of top seeds that failed to germinate, withered in the dust-bowl of Roland Garros, squeezed lifeless by the weeds of clay, the dirtkickers. The big guns showed at Roland Garros out of a sense of curiosity or pride. If they won it once, they would never come back. But until they did, they would always come back.

Wow! I can't believe it! I beat the number two player in the world and on the centre stage of Stade Roland Garros! exclaimed Justin, his mind swirling as he shook hands with a dejected Drechsler. *And these French buggers love it!*

The crowd stood to their feet, hailing a new hero. The French love new blood, and Justin bled fresh life.

Leaving the court, an official immediately ushered Justin right and into an interview room decorated with a thousand or more yellow tennis balls, each stamped with Roland Garros.

'You speak French, no?' asked the French television interviewer.

'Is this going public?'

'Yes, of course!'

'Then no. You don't want to hear *my* French!' answered the fresh-faced Justin tongue-in-cheek, wired up to an earpiece that magically transcended language barriers.

'Before you went on court, did you think you'd win today?' asked the surprised Frenchman.

'Nope! Never!' Justin answered flatly, sipping from a bottle of Perrier water.

'Does it surprise you?'

'Sure!' replied Justin, towelling off the water he drank, as sweat from his face. He shook his head and thought, *I can't believe it!*

Would Justin go the way of the other giant killers? Flushed with a hangover from the success of yesterday, his guard down, and be killed off himself? Hero today, gone tomorrow?

It seemed not! Destiny ruled he would take another scalp, and another.

'Can you win this tournament?'

Nope! No way! I'm just killing time! Justin relished to reply, but opted for restraint. 'Anyone still in has a chance. I'll take it one match at a time.'

'You don't seem very happy when you win, no?' asked an intrigued interviewer.

'I'm happy!' answered Justin, allowing just a little smile. 'If you gloat over your win today, you might forget what you have to do tomorrow.'

Incredibly, Justin survived into the second week with 16 others, led by the world's number one player whose half of the draw resembled a bunch of sultana grapes, seedless. On the other hand, Justin had a minefield to soft step through. First assignment, solve the riddle of Naresh Singh's Indian rope trick.

Together, in a match of real spice, they sculptured a masterpiece out of clay. Two lovely movers. Justin glided along the court, head still for eagle-eye vision. Naresh, so stylish, so graceful, not a hair out of place.

A living testimony to the efficacy of Brylcream, chuckled Justin.

The Indian's tennis flowed like a sari in the wind, at times strangling Justin with the silken strands of his gossamer touch. But the man with the charming manner born out of Madras could not apply the killer blow. When the dust settled in the Greek styled amphitheatre of Court 1, the slither of shoes on the shale carved a Rosetta stone narrating a story in hieroglyphics. It was a success tale for Justin.

This brought an eagerly awaited quarter-final showdown against the defending champion, Sern Stenmark of Sweden.

§

The leopard, beautiful, elusive, and silent, the instinctive hunter. She walks alone with a characteristic aloofness. For three and a half months she carried

60

them inside her. Now suckling three growing and demanding cubs, she must eat regularly to sustain herself.

From the vantage of a dead tree, hearing, sight and scent, fused in perfection, locates her prey. With endless patience, the cunning predator plots her hunt. Ever the professional killer, she utilises every nuance to her advantage, instinctively stalking her dappled black rosette coat in sunlight filtering through leaves of thick riverine bush. As she moves, her chin whiskers and tufts on her forelegs relay information of her surrounds in an instant, allowing this amazing athlete to keep her eyes fixed on the prey in total concentration. And her hind feet, designed to walk exactly in the tracks of the forefeet, let her glide in ghostly silence. Such stealth and camouflage brings her ever closer for the ambush. Should the prey show any signs of suspicion, she will stop dead in her tracks and wait until the intended victim relaxes once again. Instinctively, she knows it is time.

She crouches, contracting her muscles, belly almost touching the ground, her eerie, deadly pale eyes fixed on the prey. All is peaceful. Then suddenly, without warning, the leopard explodes into a swift spurt that blurs in the eye. The predator pounces, quickly sinking her canine teeth into the throat, severing the main artery to cut off blood to the brain and blocking the windpipe to prevent the distress call. For the leopard hunts alone, so must kill silently and efficiently to prevent other predators from stealing her kill.

Immediately after throttling, she is tense and alert. Intuitively, she moves the quarry under cover and out of sight from the prying eyes of vultures who would signal to all others the position of the kill. She expends enormous energy during the hunt, so she rests awhile, panting. Then she feeds to gain strength, meticulously covering the intestines to prevent the smell from spreading.

Suddenly the wind changes and betrays her. Danger is in the air. Scavengers start moving in. She senses this. Quickly, she invokes her remarkable adaptability and hauls her kill, as much as her own weight, high up into the tree, gripping the bark with her retractable claws, clutching the prey in her teeth, and counter-balancing with her long tail. There she can feed at leisure, a sleek silhouette stretched out on the branch of an acacia. Below, the scavengers must be content with meagre scraps dropped from her kill. Again she has diffused a confrontation with an age-old competitor, that great opportunist, the hyena, asserting her status in the inter-predator hierarchy. She is arguably Africa's most complete killing machine.

But all the while she knows she must get back to her vulnerable young. The three cubs play and are oblivious of the danger.

§

Justin followed the champion down the steps that led to *Court Central*, an innocuous-looking red sand pit housed in a chiaroscuro border backdrop of green and black billboards, that belied a torture chamber upon which players traversed marathons in pursuit of triumph.

Flowing locks of blond hair rose out of a headband like a rising loaf of bread. A two-handed backhand stamped his trade mark, and of course, topspin. Born out of the womb of clay, Sern Stenmark came from a school of tennis players spawned in the afterglow of their native hero. So a Björn Borg clone, but a paler model. Sern had taken the strategy of a rock-like defence to its zenith, but lacked the flourish of his master. A Swedish brick wall, but constructed of stock bricks, not facings.

Nevertheless, Justin quickly discovered that in his natural habitat of clay, the Swede played unlike anything he had encountered in his fledgling career.

He's a human backboard! Everything I deliver, he refunds with huge doses of manic topspin!

Justin found himself engaged in a torturous match against the interminable retrieving of Mr Patience, punctuated between points with the twitching and spitting of an opponent bundled with nervous excess energy. On that balmy day in spring, each stamina-sapping-point told a story, an epic, something like *War and Peace*.

After a half hour journey in the valley of dirt, Justin called for his towel and wiped his face and racket handle dry. With damp hair clinging to his neck, he looked up at the Seiko scoreboard, and thought despairingly, *Shit! It's only 3-all!*

As the sun baked the court, it speeded up, so officials hosed it. Clay court tennis, the lifeblood of French tennis demands rallies to last forever. The Gauls delight in slow drip torture. Unlike plebeian spectators, drawn only by the stab-and-draw-blood brand dished up on fast courts, they understand the subtle ploys of the mind game at work in the arduously patterned beauty of rallies on clay. Another long rally, but this time boos and whistles replaced applause.

What have we done? wondered Justin, bemused.

Oh, the irony! Without a touch of drama in the long rallies, they punctuate them with derisive whistles.

Sern delivered a three-quarter pace serve, conserving energy for his war of attrition, forcing Justin into another of those interminable rallies that hauled him through the slow-burning fires of hell, trapping him in a web of topspin, dragging him from side to side in a gruelling *guerre* on grit.

Shit! Justin lamented. *No wonder this bugger's won the French! He's a maniac! He's immovable! What can one do to beat him?*

A short ball. Justin hit out on the backhand, but netted. Another unforced backhand error.

Hmm! Something's wrong with my backhand, thought Justin, a nerve of doubt niggling.

Sern quickly launched a barrage of topspin haymakers to that wing. A hairline crack appeared in Justin's armour and his effectiveness leaked.

Damn! I can't hit a backhand. I'm losing because I can't hit a bloody backhand! It's all shaky! he panicked. Then he reminded himself, *Keep calm. It's only the first set. Early days still, in a best of five set match on clay. Anything can happen.*

More backhand errors. The crack widened. The metronome drilled away at this cavity, eroding the enamel of Justin's game, exposing the flaw like sugar attacking a raw nerve. His confidence oozed out, and fear pervaded his being like a cancer.

'*Set,* Stenmark, 7-5,' called the umpire.

Justin desperately tried to plug the cavity. He went back to the basics, the building blocks of the game, technique.

Turn the shoulders. Keep the eye on the ball. Hit through the ball.

But the pattern exacerbated. Tennis portrays as a physical game, a pastime of placing a ball into a geometrical pattern. That belies the truth. Enter the element of competition and the visible chess board moves become an outward expression of a battle of the minds, and the story of the match, an unfolding narrative of the mental game. When a stroke stutters, it reveals evidence of a troubled mind.

Unwittingly, Justin fell victim to the oldest trap in the book. Unable to quieten the demon of fear, he panicked, and instead of dealing with the cause, he foolishly tried to treat the symptom of unforced errors, by analysing his technique. In tennis parlance, he got the elbow.

So who was Justin Forrester that he could not play badly? Who said Justin Forrester could not lose? After all, he was playing the champion. Nobody expected him to win, they only hoped. The French public had tasted new blood in tennis, but now it congealed to a scab. He was human, they shrugged their shoulders. Reality stepped in.

Not for Justin. *He* expected to win. He always did. Feeling sucked into quicksand, he swallowed back a lump in his parched throat. *Why? Why is this happening to me?* he cried inside, secretly harbouring designs on winning this championship. *I'm only three matches away from a Grand Slam title. I have to win.*

Such desperation bred fear. His heart thumped remorselessly, anxiety tightened his muscles and floundered his technique. His hand wobbled on execution, exaggerating another backhand error.

What the hell is going on? Justin panicked deep inside. *This is crazy. I hit my backhand with deadly precision just a day ago. Now I can't get a bloody ball in court.* He felt 15,000 pairs of eyes staring into his window of vulnerability, his mind. *Shit! They're looking at me, laughing at me. They can see I'm hurting. I feel naked. What are they thinking? That I'm just a hacker! I wish I could run away!*

Trapped in his troubled mind, he lost the second set 6-2 and went a break down in the third.

Whilst a groundsman dressed in mint green calmly swept the white plastic lines clean of dust, a nervous man sat at the changeover and wrestled with his plight, his confidence whittled away.

Damn it! Damn it! Damn it! This is ridiculous! I'm acting like a bloody dribbler! Get a grip on it, now! ... Handling this pressure is what separates the champs, and I am a champion. The pathway to the mind is through the eyes, so seal it. I will not be read! No one *will peek into my most important weapon! I will not be controlled!* declared Justin, radiating a piercing glare with his icy blue eyes set in an impenetrable veil, locking out all clues to his emotion. *Now I must deal with the evidence, those bloody unforced errors!*

Justin took a deep breath. *Okay, I've got no backhand. If I carry on this way, I'm out!* Justin came to terms with the crisis, forcing himself to view it objectively. *Just have to win with what I've got. Improvise! Make up for my backhand. I still have that great weapon of mine, my legs. If I can nullify his game with my running, I can turn this crisis into an opportunity,* he resolved.

Down 1-2 in the third set, Justin emerged to face his torturer with a tactic born out of a tried and tested axiom, 'when losing badly, take a risk'.

Predictably, Sern served to Justin's backhand, but on this occasion, Justin ran around his Achilles' heel with lightning pace and returned on the forehand. Instead of positioning himself in the bisected angle of extreme returns, he camped in the backhand corner, baiting Sern to hit to his forehand. There followed an interminable rally, Justin playing every ball off his forehand wing, arcing the ball with topspin, the extra flight path giving him the split second he needed to recover. He lost that one.

That's okay, felt Justin, unperturbed. *I'm confident my legs will compensate the loss of my backhand.*

Instead of filling the cavity, he extracted his ailing weapon and bridged the gap, compromising between the tennis he wanted to play and the tennis he needed to play, to win.

It worked, shattering Sern's cosy world of simple routine, his metronomic game lacking the flexibility to deal with the unpredictable.

The spectators abruptly woke from their sorrow. Games went with serve, and each time Justin captured his, they jumped to their feet and cheered him to an echo. Justin's courageous gamble reinstated him on an even keel, in terms of effectiveness, if not in score.

At 5-4, Sern served for the match, a do-or-die game for Justin. Would he have the courage of his conviction and continue his newfound ploy, however absurd?

The bugger's got to be feeling the pressure. The match was his on a plate. Anxiety must be creeping in. My defence must be impregnable, willed Justin.

It was. It confused Sern. He tried playing to his opponent's backhand, but Justin ran and ran his heart out, hoisting everything back, high and deep off his forehand. His power of retrieval was like some mythical force. Somehow he was always there. He stuck to the Swede like a leech and Sern could not shake him loose.

'Zéro-quinze.' Love-fifteen.

The Swede switched tactics. With Justin out of court, Sern, duped into a cocoon of security, attacked the gap down the line. But he had not counted on Justin's dazzling speed.

'Zéro-trente.' Love-thirty.

Having absorbed all the punishment Sern inflicted, and contained him, Justin audaciously played to the Swede's strength, his backhand.

Twitch, you bugger! Spit! he chuckled.

Then at a critical moment he switched to the Swede's forehand, and won the point at will.

'Zéro-quarante.' Love-forty.

Three break points for Justin. The crowd murmured like a waterfall.

First serve, fault, verified by the beep of Cyclops. The Roland Garros crowd grew restless in anticipation. Sern settled down to serve, but the unruly spectators bayed for blood. The Swede spat, then looked up to the umpire in desperation, appealing for quiet.

'Shssh!' hushed half the crowd in the stadium, making a big noise.

'Shssh!' responded the other half to quieten the first hush, making even more noise!

The Swede twitched.

'Silence!' called the umpire.

Twitch, you bugger! Spit! urged Justin gleefully.

The ball barely made the net.

Gotcha! exclaimed Justin, breaking serve to level at 5-all. A shiver ran down his spine. *I live!*

The crowd jumped up as one in a crescendo of applause. The match was alive! Justin Forrester was back! Like the great Houdini, he picked his way out to mastermind the great escape. Appreciating his remarkable courage, an infectious love for this man spread like wildfire through the crowd.

Hmm! This crisis has presented an interesting edge! Despite my buggered backhand, I've kept on even terms with the doomsday stroking machine of tennis. And he only plays one way, no other game to inflict damage. I cannot lose! bubbled Justin.

But his comeback, although mentally refreshing, was physically exhausting. *How can I win? I can't last this gruelling match running around my backhand!*

Justin's elation spilled over into confidence. *It's time to take another risk. I can do it! My backhand will work. I'll play the game my way.*

Justin threw all caution to the wind, recasting his tennis into another dimension. The play of two giants of the game characterises the extreme ends of the continuum of style, Björn Borg's impenetrable baseline defence and John McEnroe's scything serve and volley assault. Their ability to adapt augmented their greatness, Borg to venture from his castle, and McEnroe to sneak round and slip in the back door.

With holistic awareness, uninhibited by those two impostors, safety and risk, Justin's sublime talent bridged the gulf in a symbiotic scaling up and down the keyboard of this diverse range of style, searching for the game plan that best befitted his goal to win, striking the chord that offered the sweetest taste of success. The guile of his serrated cutting edge made beautiful by its classical fluency, harmonised with Africa's most efficient fighting machine, that prince of predators, the leopard, whose striking rosette coat camouflages a cunning cocktail of stealth and style.

Having blown away all the chaff that is extraneous about swinging a racket, Justin relied on invention and reflex to inflict subtle pressures, constantly testing the fringes, looking for a slight edge here, an imperceptible edge there, perpetually reshuffling the cards and adapting, ever vigilant of changing situations to outmanoeuvre his opponent whilst holding onto every inch of terrain he gained for himself, until he spotted an opening. Then with his opponent locked out of rhythm, Justin would seize the initiative. Whoosh! A sudden change of pace and he would strike for the jugular with frightening speed and precision.

With such an armoury of skills, he decimated the Swede's defence, employing an endless mix of random spins with his sliced backhand, a cut here, a nick there, twisting and turning the Scandinavian's legs, asphyxiating their life like two washerwomen squeezing water out of a towel. Always the point ended by drawing Sern out of his shell with short angles, Justin following his ploy in to win on the volley, or enticing the herring out of the Baltic Sea and into the net with a smorgasbord of drop-shots laced with poison.

With his pronounced western forehand grip, the racket face almost parallel to the ground, the Swede seemed unable to taste the venom, and one after the other, he netted the ball. No volley lay beyond Justin's skill, but every jaunt to the net for Sern became a nosebleed nightmare. By choice, he would only come to the net twice, once to toss the coin, the other to shake hands after the match!

Set point to Justin. He conjured a drop-shot and the Swede came in on a wing and a prayer. A lob. Sern dumped it meekly back into play. Another lob. Another ineffectual reply. Sern twitched, cowering for another lob.

Hubba hubba! He doesn't have an overhead! exclaimed Justin, preying on signals. *Losing the overhead is a sure sign of loss of confidence.*

Justin projected another ball deep into the blue Parisian sky, and Sern, arms groping and flailing, tangled and hit an air shot.

'*Set*, Forrester, 7-6.'

This was clay court tennis at its very best. Probing, discovering and exploiting weaknesses, suffocating the mind with self-doubt. Before long, the match squared at two sets all.

Justin kept a high tempo, wasting no time between points, playing as if double parked. At 4-all in the fifth, before serving, he briefly looked across the net at his opponent. Sern's head hung loosely, his racket wearily trailing furrows in the red clay, toiling under the Forrester yoke. A matter of time before the end.

The bugger looks as if he's not wearing socks! chuckled Justin.

Red dust glued to the Swede's sweaty socks, making them so pink and flesh-like they camouflaged against his legs.

Come in to the net, Justin invited his opponent with a drop shot. *I want a closer look.*

No sooner had the sick-looking dog arrived, when Justin threw in his *coup de grâce*, hurling the stick over his head with a killing topspin lob.

Go fetch! the master chuckled.

Sern's legs would not move. They were like bags of sand, lifeless, without feeling, their blood bled dry, stained on the clay.

He never won another point. Justin had the temerity to unseat the defending champion, without a backhand! As he ran forward to shake hands with his broken opponent, the French fans hailed their new hero with deafening applause.

Now, I know I can do it! exclaimed Justin, utterly convinced after this match that he had arrived.

If you can win on clay at the highest level, you are a master craftsman at the most exacting art in the wide and varied game of tennis. In Paris you have to show more of what is in you because of the surface. Clay prolongs the drama. The matches are cat and mouse affairs. You have to reach deep inside for all your stuff. Justin had.

Justin temporarily excused himself from a television interview. Sern took his place in the chair.

'You had the match in your hands, no? Now you're out of the tournament!' exclaimed the interviewer, animating surprise.

'For sure, he's tough!' replied Sern, resignedly.

'Without a *backhand?*'

'For sure, he's fast!' answered the Swede, shaking his head.

'Have you ever seen something like this before?'

'No!'

'Was there anything you could do?'

'I kept telling myself to hit to his backhand, but he suckered me into his forehand. Like a fool I succumbed. He knew what I was going to do before I did. That was rough. He's very fast.'

'Did you get tired?'

'I was sucking air, even in the first set. I wanted to die!'

'He plays at a high tempo, no?'

'I felt rushed. During points, between points. Always,' lamented the laconic Swede. 'It just feels like he's all over you.'

'He hits hard?' asked the interviewer, intrigued by Justin's play.

'No. He doesn't hit that hard,' replied Sern, bemused. 'But he cuts you up. His shots feel heavy. For sure, he's fast.'

'Will he win the tournament?'

Sern shrugged his shoulders. 'For sure, we'll see a lot more of this guy. He's for real.'

Justin limped straight to the locker-room, slumped down on a chair and removed his clay encrusted shoes.

Aagh! he grimaced, gingerly peeling away his sweaty, red-stained socks, from feet smeared with blood.

Blood blisters had formed and burst sometime during that four and a half hour endurance epic. He washed his feet clean, had the ATP trainer, Norrie Bowden, tape the broken skin, then grabbed two rackets, and barefoot, headed straight for a practice court.

'Backhands only, please Manolo. Float them,' Justin asked of the gifted Spaniard, desperate to correct his offending shot.

Playing Manolo's floating cotton wool balls will demand that I provide the character for each shot. Emerging unscathed will be the ultimate test for my backhand.

A throng of fans gathered round to gawk at their barefoot hero. Bone weary, Justin battled hard to keep his concentration in the din, but stroked backhand after backhand with deadly precision. There was nothing wrong with his technique. The restoration of the cavity in his game was more a reaffirmation of confidence in the mind.

I'm happy! Justin pronounced after half an hour.

Leaving the court, autograph hunters suddenly mobbed him. He duly obliged. Then they started to touch him and pull his hair.

'Justin! Justin! Justin!' they screamed vociferously.

Shit! What's happening? Justin feared, his heart thumping. *I can't breathe!* Gasping for air, he tried to wrestle himself from the mob and panicked, *I must get out of here!*

But without success. The frenzied mass reached out and in no time lifted their hero up in the air, waving him around like a bobbing flying carpet above a seething mass of bodies. Gendarmes entered and blew whistles. Pandemonium broke loose with people scuttling everywhere. Justin crashed to the ground, trodden on in the stampede. Curled like a foetus, cowering in the forest of fleeing legs, he smelled the animal scent of their bodies and had to cram a fist into his mouth to stop himself from screaming.

Eventually, an official rescued him and helped the battered and bruised man to his feet.

'Phew!' exclaimed Justin, his face white with fear, not for his life, but injury. *Those buggers nearly spoiled the fairy tale!*

He headed for the sanctuary of the television interview room to regain his composure.

'Congratulations, Justin, beating the defending champion. What can you tell us about this extraordinary match?' asked a curious interviewer.

'Tough! Very tough! The most difficult match I've ever played!'

'Yes, most find the long rallies on clay tiring. But you looked stronger at the end, no?'

'It was hard physically, but mostly it drained me mentally.'

'No backhand, but you won!' exclaimed the interviewer, throwing up his hands. 'This is the talk at Roland Garros. What made you decide to discard your backhand?'

'I had no choice. I was about to lose.'

'Can you tell me, uh, can you tell the French public how you beat Sern Stenmark without a backhand?' asked a bewildered interviewer.

'I'm not sure. I took a risk and it turned out fine this time. It was not easy for him. My plan worked, and I'm sure he didn't expect it to, so he tried to exploit a weakness that didn't exist. Lucky for me it knocked him off track!'

'There has been some dissension amongst the press corps. What is your best stroke? Your forehand or your backhand?'

Justin answered with a smile, 'My legs and my mind.'

'I think nobody would argue with that,' the interviewer nodded in agreement, but looked puzzled. 'And I'm told you only use one grip.

Something like Ilie Nastase and John McEnroe, no?'

'Uh huh.'

'Were you taught this way?'

'Um, I just picked it up,' Justin answered soberly. 'It's natural for me.'

'Have you a coach? We don't see one.'

'Yep. He's back in Swaziland.'

'Remarkable!' commented the television interviewer, looking mystified. 'You look so calm, even in bizarre circumstances. What is going on inside you?'

'A fire burns brightly—'

'You get nervous?' asked the interviewer, taken aback.

'Yep! But not so much nerves. Huge waves of passion to win!'

'*Merci*, Justin.'

Justin asked the referee, 'Please would you excuse me from the press conference. I'm very tired. I need sleep.'

'I'm afraid that is not possible. Post-match conferences are regulation.'

Justin stared at the man, disbelieving his ears. 'I cannot attend.'

'It will cost you $1,000.'

'An expensive sleep, but so be it!'

After a remarkable day of high drama, Justin left Stade Roland Garros and headed to his youth hostel. Like a big cat after a kill, he urgently needed sleep. This way, he replenished the cells of his batteries, not so much physically, but mentally. The very nature of Justin's game, searching and probing, testing for weaknesses whilst exerting strength, demanded intense concentration of the highest order. The Sern Stenmark epic had exhausted him. He flopped on his bed, buried his head in a pillow and put his mind to sleep.

Deep in slumber, Justin felt someone pulling at his shoulder, but a throbbing headache quelled an attempt to ignore it and returned him to reality.

Shit! What's this? griped Justin, focusing his bloodshot eyes.

'Ted Parsen of the *London Daily News*. Sleeping on the job! The readers back home will riot if I don't give them a story. Mind if I ask you a few questions? What—'

'You saw the match?' shot Justin.

'Uh, yes.'

'Then you have your bloody story,' he said hotly. 'And I'd like some privacy. So if you don't—'

'The way you played today. Not very British is it?' accused Parsen.

'Nope! I would say not,' replied Justin sarcastically, thinking of spineless British tennis.

'Is that cheating? Running around your backhand?'

'*Cheating?*' enquired an incredulous Justin, raising his voice.

'Uh, bad sportsmanship!'

'The only bad sport is you, you bastard!' attacked Justin, rising from the bed and walking forward. 'I desperately need rest and you're not giving me a chance. Now get out!'

'But—'

'Out!' ordered Justin pointing to the door.

'You'll regret this, I promise!' threatened the tabloid newshound, backing away.

'Not as much as you will if you don't stay away!'

Half an hour later, another tug woke Justin. Word had spilled out where he lived and a procession of paparazzi led to his door.

'I'm out of here!' Justin declared, irritated.

He quickly packed his bags, hailed a taxi and searched for a sanctuary. With his semifinals showing, and the concomitant winnings, he could now afford a hotel. As the taxi rolled down Avenue des Champs-Élysées from the Arc de Triomphe, Justin grilled the driver about hotels, but a divide of language inhibited mutual understanding.

Passing the Place de la Concorde, a highly fashionable area of boutiques, luxury hotels and palatial buildings, Justin shouted, 'Stop! That one should do the trick!'

He retrieved his bags and entered the revolving door to an elegant palace hotel with eighteenth century decor. Above, a sign read, 'Hotel De Crillon'.

Justin made a beeline for the concierge. 'Is this joint quiet?'

'Most certainly, Monsieur Forrester!' the concierge replied loftily.

Shit! How does the bugger know my name? wondered Justin, taken aback. 'Got a bed for me?'

'Let me call the manager.'

While Justin waited, a familiar sight caught his eye and his heart pounded.

I'd recognise those legs anywhere!

The legs entered an elevator, and on turning round behind closing doors, their owner gave Justin a smile.

Heidi Schültz!

'We *have* room, Monsieur,' the manager assured, waking Justin from his daydream. Then lowering his voice the manager continued, 'But there's the little matter of affordability.'

He was not joking considering the daily tariff of 4,000F.

'I've made a few bucks so far, I think. I need a place until Monday morning.'

'You're very confident,' the manager commented with a friendly smile. 'For you, Monsieur Forrester, only the best!'

Justin followed a porter through the lobby of butterscotch marble pillars and gilt-framed mirrors, up to a magnificent royal suite overlooking the Place de la Concorde.

'A bit of okay!' exclaimed Justin, absorbing the oozing prestige. Then looking out on the Place de la Concorde, he queried, 'But how quiet?'

'Double glazing, Monsieur. Perfectly quiet,' bragged the proud porter.

'*Merci!*'

At last I'm safe, felt Justin, protected from the growing army of supporters who meant no harm, but unwittingly scared him as they pawed for a piece of him. *I've also escaped the talons of those vultures, the gutter press!*

Justin woke up to find his face splashed in colour across the front page of L'Équipe. His heart pounded as it does when passing traffic police, even when innocent.

Shit! What have I done?

Then suddenly he realised. The headline screamed, '*C'est Magnifique*'. He was in the French Open semifinal, and the press had made a big deal of it.

Friday of the second week, men's semifinals day of the marathon tournament. On opening point Justin served a double fault and the crowd roared and clapped their approval.

Hero two days ago, villain today! puzzled Justin, bemused at the cruel sound. But he showed nothing.

It was not that the French crowd had turned on Justin, but on the other side of the net stood a Frenchman, the suave dark-haired Jean-Pierre Perrot.

In a city that exerts a timeless appeal, in a tournament that develops slowly and lingers, sensuously seducing the senses, almost like an afterthought as though you are sipping cognac, Jean-Pierre raced through their hearts like a shooting star. They adored this man who loved fast cars, fast music, and lived in the fast lane. He played his tennis fast, too, with the reckless cut and thrust flair of a Gallic fencer.

Like the ephemeral cherry blossom, Jean-Pierre Perrot had bloomed early, then quickly withered. Only now after a long journey in the wilderness was his fruit beginning to mature.

With each passing match the spectators sat nearer to the edge of their seats, striving to get a closer look, nervous at what they saw. For years he had hauled the French public through the fires of hope, only to deceive them. Each time he resurged they forgave him. Now he titillated again, dangling the tempting thought, after a long drought, that a Frenchman might win at Roland Garros. The crowd sat in their seats with a look of glee, relegating Justin to a mere prop upon which the designs of French tennis could unfold.

Damn! I'm up shit street without a paddle! moaned Justin, down two sets to one and 4-5 in the fourth.

He struggled more against this wildly partisan crowd than his opponent. *I can't concentrate in this din. And he's so flashy I can't find a weakness. One game to go. ... But I'm not out yet. Keep looking, keep looking.*

Justin served and the man from France returned with a rapier thrust.

'*Zéro-quinze,*' Love-fifteen.

The crowd howled.

Damn it! Where is that soft spot?

Another reckless winner.

'*Zéro-trente.*' Love-thirty.

The crowd went wild. Jean-Pierre mimicked a fencer's stance, and dancing, stabbed his racket forward for the kill, orchestrating the packed court's response.

'Jean-Pierre! Jean-Pierre! Jean-Pierre!' they screamed.

Shit! They're a bloody madhouse! lamented a distraught Justin, feeling the loneliest man on earth in front of 15,000 onlookers, cornered by the fervent support of their French hero. As waves of the baying crowd inexorably lapped and undermined the foundation of his game, he felt it on his skin, the hairs on the nape of his neck stood out and his vision blurred. His throat tight, he anguished, *They're getting to me! Drowning my mind!*

The crowd sentenced him to death. Now he faced the executioner.

Toiling under mass hysteria, he sought a way to escape the blade. *My only hope is to invade his mind. Convert his crowd weapon into a handicap. ... Hmm! The burden of expectation.*

Egged on by his supporters, Jean-Pierre thrust an attack at the net. Right out of court, without a hope of winning the point, Justin raced across the baseline like a madman, using his racket for balance like a leopard's tail, and parried with the highest lob in memory, shrewdly seeking to test the mettle of Jean-Pierre Perrot at this most critical moment.

Think, you bugger! You've got all the time in the world. Time to doubt, time to freeze with fright! hoped Justin, offering the Frenchman enough rope to hang himself.

Everyone waited and waited, and the crowd's groans of expectation seeped into the Gaul's mind.

Jean-Pierre overhit the smash.

'Oo-là-là!' sighed the crowd.

Under the ultimate test, scaling the last peak of the mountain, Jean-Pierre slipped again, falling victim to the demons of his fragile temperament. Only the true champion has the nerve and the guts to go over the horns for the kill. Jean-Pierre failed, gored by his doubt.

He puffed up his cheeks, looked wide-eyed at the spot he missed and shrugged his shoulders, as only the French can. *Hausser les épaules,* they call it. His Parisian fans animated much *haussement d'épaules* in return.

Gotcha! exclaimed Justin, escaping.

It had been difficult. A small fish drowning in the near hysteria of the French connection, he suddenly switched roles. Like a fisherman fighting the big fish, reeling in and letting line out, Justin ran the full gamut, testing, pacing, constantly assessing the percentages of this dynamic one-on-one sport, running the risk of five sets if that were necessary to win, patient to the point of near-extinction to find the edge. Eventually it surfaced.

Now I have your balls in the palm of my hands, thought Justin with smug satisfaction. *Get ready for the big squeeze!*

With Jean-Pierre's inner mettle cracked for all to see, he had dug himself a hole, and Justin proceeded to bury him. The set, poised on a knife-edge, effectively ended right there. The Frenchman, inhibited by a sudden affliction of nerves, won no more points.

Jean-Pierre would bemoan that it is sometimes more difficult to win in front of your own supporters. Do the slightest thing wrong and you change from hero to villain in a flicker.

He was right! Justin, the man the French press dubbed *'Le Chat'*, had escaped again. He delighted with his comeback from the brink of defeat, and the fickle French crowd, who could change allegiance on a questionable linecall, possibly the fault of a linejudge, switched support to their new hero.

'Justin! Justin! Justin!' they screamed.

Drawing on the gift of crowd support, like a hungry man devouring French fries, Justin surged to a 4-2 lead in the fifth set as the juggling act of Jean-Pierre deflated like a circus tent.

At 30-all on Justin's serve, the Frenchman ran down a Forrester lob, and with his back to the court tried the nutcracker, the 'ouch shot' swatted between his legs, lobbing the ball over Justin's head for a clean winner. Break point to the Gaul.

'*Bravo! Bravo! Bravo!*' the spectators roared, standing as one.

They came alive! Was it possible? Could Jean-Pierre confound his past and hold the tricolour aloft? On the strength of one spectacular shot, the Frenchman prised open the coffin.

Uh oh! lamented Justin, his heart sinking. *Flashy players feeding on adulation are dangerous. One burst of the spectacular and I'm out of the tournament!* He exhorted himself, *Tie the bugger down. Play boring tennis, if that's what's necessary!*

He did just that, trying desperately hard to subdue the Frenchman and nail the coffin shut. In a heartfelt passion to win, Justin played his shots deep and with heavy topspin, the bland brand of a tennis ball machine, to quench the fire Jean-Pierre's game thrived on.

It worked! He lulled his opponent's attack back to sleep. The nutcracker was the Frenchman's last gasp and in the dying stages of the match he frittered away aimlessly like a tadpole and croaked in falsetto. Game, set and match to Justin Forrester.

As always, Justin waited for his opponent to join him to exit the arena. Jean-Pierre slumped in his chair, looking glum. Then suddenly he shrugged his shoulders and never gave it another thought. For Jean-Pierre, a case of *c'est la vie.* For Justin, the final of Roland Garros.

'Justin!' exclaimed a flabbergasted interviewer. 'The crowd was hysterical. And you're not even a Frenchman!'

'It was strange today. At times I felt so alone. I don't understand,' replied Justin, his eyes resigned.

'Back from the dead again. Incredible!' bubbled the incredulous interviewer, shaking his head. 'Now you're in the final. Can you believe this?'

'Nope! What an extraordinary fortnight! Just don't pinch me, I might wake up!'

'What are they saying back home about an Englishman doing so well in France?'

Justin shrugged his shoulders. *Buggered if I know!*

'Do you think about what you have done?'

'Nope! It might get to me. I don't want to interfere,' enlightened Justin, munching a banana. 'So if you don't mind calling it a day.'

'Last question. The French public saw this as the final, no? For you—'

'Nope! Before now is history. All depends on the next match.'

'Jean-Pierre, can he win the tournament?' asked the French television interviewer.

'He can win!' answered the Frenchman in Gallic animation. 'Justin knows he can beat us. When a player knows that, he's arrived.'

'Who is this man Justin Forrester?' asked an intrigued interviewer.

'He's silent, you know. From Africa. He has animal instincts. And he gets to you. You don't know if he's crying or laughing inside. It gets to you.'

'What is it?'

'Something special, you know. *Savoir faire*. You can't teach anybody. You either have it or you don't.'

A porter at Hotel De Crillon knocked on the door of a royal suite.

'Yes?' enquired the occupant, disentangling her shapely body into a black, satin negligeé.

'Mademoiselle Schültz. Your room service.'

'Oh yes! Please come in.'

The haughty porter snapped his fingers and two waiters wheeled in a dining trolley, and masterfully set up a candlelit dinner.

'Why places for two?' enquired Heidi, intrigued.

'Compliments of Monsieur Forrester!'

Her eyes lit up. 'Is he coming?'

'Of course!'

Again the porter snapped his fingers and the two waiters dissolved out of the suite. To Heidi's utter astonishment, he peeled off his waxed moustache and tilted back his pillbox porter cap, revealing a mischievous face.

'Justin Forrester!' cried Heidi. 'Of all the sneaky tricks. I …,' she started, expressions on her face fluctuating from mock horror to surprise, before continuing, 'I love it!'

Justin presented Heidi with a red rose, escorted her to a seat at the dining table and lit the candle, perfectly timed for a violinist who entered and serenaded them. They smiled, almost embarrassed. Then tired of the wail, Justin snapped his fingers for privacy.

'I hope this is not intruding on your final tomorrow,' queried a concerned Justin. The attractive Heidi Schültz from Germany reigned as the undisputed best woman tennis player in the world.

'Well, I haven't eaten yet,' Heidi replied with a twinkle in her eye. 'But I'm just not dressed for the occasion!'

'*You're* not dressed!' exclaimed Justin, glancing ruefully at his dishevelled porter attire.

Whilst Heidi feasted on *canard à l'orange*, Justin tucked into lean beef and potatoes, and glanced across the table at the 22 year old blonde. Long, silky hair, cascaded away from a pretty face with blue eyes and a firm chin, a face that showed the fierce determination with which she ruled her sport.

I like that! She's like me, he thought. He also liked her looks, especially those long, sleek legs, legendary in the glamour pages of glossy fashion magazines.

'Mmm, that was delicious, Justin,' smiled Heidi when she finished eating, stretching like a cat.

In the glow of the candlelight, two people who yearned to dominate their sport, momentarily lost themselves in each other.

'Are you East or West German?' Justin queried.

'Ich bin ein Deutsch!' Heidi answered with a hint of indignation. 'But, yes, I'm originally from East Germany.'

'Is there a difference?'

'Well, yes and no. We're all Germans. But that wall, it made a big difference. It trapped East Germany in a laboratory experiment, and failed! You can't believe the poverty ... the pollution ... the starkness. But it's more than that. It took away the soul. That's why my parents decided we should all escape.'

'Escape!' exclaimed Justin, stunned. 'You *escaped* from East Germany?'

'Yes,' Heidi replied softly with little emotion.

'Climbed over the Berlin wall?' Justin asked, astounded.

'Not exactly. We left from Köpenick in a hot-air balloon.'

'That's incredible! How? Tell me about it,' asked Justin, fascinated.

'I was eight years old and my parents did not want for Eva – that's my younger sister – and me to live our lives there. ... For many years Papa and my Uncle Carl built two balloons. Not these fancy colour ones you see floating in the sky. No, they made them from scraps—'

'Did the, um, police, army or whatever, did they not suspect?'

'The *Stasi*. No. Of course there was always the possibility. Papa and my uncle made them in a secret underground basement. We lived next door to my uncle and had a tunnel joining our simple homes, so little was seen of our collusion.'

'How long did all this take?'

'Many years, ever since I can remember. It was always a part of my life. A family friend from West Berlin forged West German passports and posted them to us from inside the GDR. She also gave us labels from western-made garments. Mama stitched them onto our clothes so that if we were caught we would stand a better chance. ... Suddenly it was time to leave.'

Heidi spoke softly.

'Everybody was quiet. We set off just before daybreak. I went with Uncle Carl and his daughter, and Mama, Papa and Eva went in the other. It was all planned according to weight. We left—'

'Your aunt?'

'She passed away many years ago. ... We left first, and, and as we,' started Heidi, her voice faltering, 'as we baled sandbags out of the gondola to ascend I could see something was wrong with the other balloon. ... I shouted after my family, but my uncle covered my face.'

'Your parents and your sister? They never made it?' queried Justin, aghast.

Heidi shook her head.

'What happened to you?'

'I went to stay with Uncle Fritz in Hamburg. He worked at a tennis halle. So I learnt to play tennis. ... I've never told anyone, but when the Czech authorities allowed Martina's mother to go and see her daughter win Wimbledon, I saw tennis as a way to see my parents again. I *had* to become a champion. *Nothing* would stop me!'

'And? Did you see your parents again?'

Heidi remained silent. Her eyes moistened.

'Shh,' hushed Justin, holding her hand. 'Don't talk about it if you're uncomfortable.'

'No, it's okay. I want to tell you,' Heidi said, swallowing. 'When the wall came down, I discovered they, the *Grenztruppen*, they shot them. ... Shot them in cold blood. And all we wanted to do was live in the West.'

'Why haven't we heard this tragic story before?'

'The wall came down before I came to prominence. There's no point in telling my story now. It's too painful.'

Both sat in silence for a moment. Then Heidi's eyes grew resigned. 'I'm lonely, Justin. For years I missed my parents and sister and tried to reunite with them through tennis. Now tennis has cast me into a vacuum of loneliness. I'm probably the most famous woman athlete in the world, but, but people won't get close. Somehow men are always unnerved by my stature.' Then Heidi managed a smile. 'Until you.'

'Why don't you give up tennis?'

'Justin! *You* should know better. Winning is a drug. It's in my blood!'

Sensing her need, Justin led her by the hand to the sitting-room. Against a background of soft music, he bowed in his porter's suit and asked, 'Would Mademoiselle Heidi care to dance?'

In a subdued light, he took her in his arms and they swayed in time to the music. When all went quiet, Justin brushed Heidi's long hair out of her face with his hand. They stared intently into each other's eyes, longing. Justin leant forward and touched his lips against hers, softly, probing her desire. She responded, and they melted into an embrace, kissing passionately, exploring through moist, tender lips the taste of warmth. Two athletic bodies, lean and firm, found softness.

Justin led Heidi to a sofa, sank into it and gently laid her on his lap, looking into her blue eyes. He tenderly blew kisses up her arms, breathing in the scent of her warm flesh through a sweet perfume fragrance, until he pressed his lips against hers. His hand explored her body, sensuously arousing the smooth skin on her firm tummy, before rising up the cleft to caress the softness of her breasts. She grew hard in his hand as he did below her. His tongue entwined round her rosy nipple while his hand slipped under her panties, through a forest to a crevice. She was already moist. Whilst caressing her, massaging up and down the gorge, her hand joined his, urging him along. Justin felt Heidi tighten, her bottom thrusting up and down against him.

She writhed her tortured body and cried out, 'Justin! Justin! Oh, Justin! What are you doing to me!' before flooding with relief.

'The same I'd like done to me!' he smiled.

Heidi obliged with delight, opening his porter trousers to release a spring-loaded penis. Justin felt her hands clutch him, and gently massage him as he undressed. He shuddered, a tension gnawing in his groin.

Heidi looked up to Justin from below, her eyes almost betraying an innocence. She whispered softly, 'Make love to me.'

Justin quickly slipped on top of Heidi who guided him between her long, shapely legs. He entered her, slowly and deliberately, savouring the journey in virgin territory. Gripped by strong legs in an oasis of sensitive sensations, Justin twisted and squirmed to a fever pitch. Suddenly he clutched tightly onto his lover and throbbed deep inside, echoing with a loud cry that ebbed away to a whimper.

In the afterglow, they lay in each other's arms, kissing lightly, tenderly, without speaking, mutually relishing the tranquillity. After an eternity of treasured moments, Justin woke from his absorption with a jolt.

'Heidi, you have your final tomorrow!' exclaimed Justin.

There was no response. He looked at her. She lay asleep, cradled in his arms. He carried her to the bedroom, and carefully slipped her under silk sheets. Then he scribbled a note, 'Good luck, today! JF', and quietly left the room.

The evening before his final, Justin carefully folded and methodically packed into his tennis bag, five changes of shirts and shorts, an equal quantity of pairs of tennis shoes and 20 pairs of socks, to cater for his habit of donning a fresh pair at each ball change.

The maestro carefully inspected an array of equipment, swinging each racket to test its balance, grip size and feel. He was exacting about his rackets. If each Dunlop MAX 800i did not weigh exactly 362 grams and measure 10 mm head heavy, with a cowhide grip 4⅝ of an inch in circumference, Justin felt it in an instant and tossed it out like a piece of trash. Like a violinist tuning up for a concert, he plucked at and listened to the singing strings. Each racket used Bow Brand strings made from the stomach gut of four cows, 17L in gauge, and tensioned precisely as if tied to a rafter and a weight of 55 pounds dangled on the end.

After he found 12 rackets that felt and sounded identical, Justin packed them into his voluminous bag, with a paraphernalia of plasters, scissors and a floppy hat. Such was his pre-match ritual to acquire poise and calmness of mind, a built-in mechanism to minimize nervousness, a superstition to pre-empt question. There could be no reproach or doubt, never a case of, 'If only I had …'

After an amazing fortnight beyond his wildest imagination, Justin stood on the threshold of contesting a Grand Slam final, a chance to etch his name into the annals of the sport he loved so dearly. He thrived on the big occasion and the pressure it generated. The bigger the occasion, the more his victory would be worth. Shivers ran down his spine as he contemplated the day ahead.

'Roland Garros!' he whispered, laying his head on the pillow, eagerly looking forward to his dream of a match destined to rank amongst the finest in the history of Roland Garros.

Satiated with a leisurely buffet lunch from Les Ambassadeurs in the courtyard of the Hotel De Crillon, Justin retired to his suite. He drew a curtain open to overlook Paris. Below him bustled Place de la Concorde.

Hmm! That's where they chopped off the head of that Louis bugger during the French Revolution. A revolution that ignited on a tennis court! Then Justin smiled, Now two centuries later, another revolution is taking place!

A revolution on the red clay courts of Roland Garros, with a bloody execution of the tennis aristocracy. But just when it seemed everything had changed, paradoxically, in the end little had changed at all. When the carnage ceased, the shouting died down, and the dust settled, it was not the anarchists at the helm, but the king of tennis, challenged by none other than an heir apparent of pure pedigree.

They say a revolution has seven stages. A Grand Slam tournament has seven rounds! The final round, the finale messieurs is about to begin!

Almost unnoticed, Justin quietly gathered his tennis gear and fearlessly headed off to the battlefront on the west side of Paris, Roland Garros.

His car entered the park grounds of the Bois de Boulogne, and the stadium suddenly emerged upon him out of the leafy green foliage. No longer could Justin stroll the promenade and absorb the deep culture of

France as a fortnight ago. Stardom locked him inside a goldfish bowl, into which everyone stared, but could not touch.

§

The cheetah is built totally for speed. Unlike other cats, its slight body has an amazing backbone that arches up as the wiry hind legs come forward, and provides impetus to each stride. Even its claws cannot retract, acting like running spikes to aid traction.

Guided by its mother in its youth, the spotted cat often hunts in pairs, usually in the open grass plains where it can employ its dazzling speed. For better sight in long distance, it mostly hunts during the day, at dawn or dusk when temperatures are cooler. Tear-drop lines cut the glare of daylight and help to break its facial pattern. After sighting its prey, usually one that is slightly apart from the rest of the herd, the cheetah lowers its head, but the legs remain straight. Suddenly the fastest animal in the world bounds with startling speed, a breathtaking sight when in full flight, adroitly using its tail like a rudder to change direction of its long, lithe body.

Predator and prey disappear in a cloud of dust and an uproar of hooves that signals death. The kill must be over quickly or the cheetah gives up, for its body temperature soars dangerously high. If successful, the cat seldom eats straight away, having to rest to restore the strength to eat, panting hard to cool itself, nervously glancing about. In this weakened state, the cheetah is vulnerable. Then it bolts down its food, never enjoying its meal at a leisurely pace, lest a lion or a leopard or some scavenger like a hyena or vulture, asserts its superior strength and steals the quarry.

§

In the locker-room, Justin sat waiting, butterflies running amok inside him. Not nerves, adrenalin. He was eager, excited and the blood pumped.

At three o'clock in the afternoon, Justin met his opponent and nodded as a mark of respect, but without reciprocation. The two adversaries carried with them their voluminous tennis bags and in Justin's opponent's case, as always, a brown paper packet.

What's in the packet?

Nobody knew! The truth may have lain somewhere in his winning an important match whilst in possession of a brown paper packet. Now he could not be without one!

Suddenly *Court Central* came into view. As the protagonists walked out onto the red clay, a rousing round of applause greeted them. Shivers of excitement bubbled in Justin's blood like spring water. He quickly

81

looked around, absorbing every minute detail about his battleground. Very little escaped the vigilance of Justin Forrester. He was exacting about his domain, conscious of the discerning role of extraneous elements on his fate.

Justin looked across the other side of the net at the menacing spectre of Tyrone Summers, the number one player in the world. His slender frame of medium height walked in a confident and cocky gait, with just a trace of pigeon toes. Yes, tennis rewards pigeons more than ducks! And big beaks too! In Tyrone, the snout spoiled a pixie face sporting a page-boy style of straight, dark brown hair, tinged with red when caught in the sun, legacy of Irish ancestry, which might explain how a small man in tennis could square off to anyone in the game.

Highly strung and controversial, this vibrantly confident lefthander with a double-fisted backhand, ruled the game tempestuously, a colourful renegade from the tennis establishment. Over the years, he dragged his fans through the most awful rollercoaster of emotions. They wanted to laugh at him, cry with him, defend him and kill him, all in one match!

Hailing from Lookout Mountain, Tennessee, home of the fastest tennis gun in the west, Tyrone, without anyone to play against, learned the game from his mother. Essentially, he played what was considered a woman's game, a baseline style with little or no spin, but with a difference.

Tyrone Summers hurled the full weight of his body into every shot he played, generating blinding speed to wreak devastation on all that stood in his path. His game went for the kill at all times, shattering from almost any point at any given time. Very rarely would he go quiet, unless he chose to pause and take a deep breath. Such ferocity of pace set fear into his opponents.

His irascible temper, born out of an acute sensitivity to supposed injustice, set fear into the umpires, or anyone who dared to differ. In return, umpires treated the *enfant terrible* like the troublesome relative who insisted on coming to stay every year. They were a red rag to the bull in Tyrone, who charged with the self-destruct temper of a grenade with a rusty pin. In an instant his private demons sizzled with spontaneous combustion and all attempts to douse the fire met virulent diatribes and tirades of spewed expletives and invectives. Deeply suspicious of authority, absurdly sure of himself, he relied only on *his* judgement.

He was especially exacting with Tyrone Summers, pitilessly deriding his shortcomings when he craved utter perfection.

Territorial like all tennis champions, the player, nicknamed Terror by the tennis world, possessed a gunslinger mentality, utter disdain for opponents on a court only big enough for one fast gun.

The *arbitre de chaise* read out the 'road to the final', where in a grim weeding out Darwinism 'survival of the fittest' process, 128 competitors whittled down to 64, and then 32, and halved again and again, inexorably determining the food chain hierarchy, until finally there were just two, the super predators.

'…, unseeded, Justin Forrester!'

The crowd cheered. The French would adopt one player and cheer him to an echo.

'On my right, the number one seed, the number one player in the world, Tyrone Summers!'

Whistles and jeers droned.

A buzz of expectation seeped through the crowd. The plot contained every ingredient of a human story. Like a western movie, Justin portrayed the goodie, Tyrone, the baddie. All it needed, was the happy ending.

As in a boxing duel, the protagonists felt each other out in the first few games. Then from Tyrone's Wilson Hammer, all hell broke loose. The pace of his game, even on the slow clay courts of Roland Garros, clearly startled Justin.

Like a true Brit, he took it on the chin, but like British tennis players of late, he was losing. First set to Tyrone Summers, 6-4.

Tyrone pumped his fists and unleashed a primal scream, 'Yeah!'

It did not seem possible, but he stepped up the pace in the second set, and took an early break of serve, whilst Justin could only play second fiddle.

Stick to the bugger! Justin consoled himself. *Be patient. My time will come.*

Dashing from side to side like an elastic band stretching and slackening, the rampant Tyrone played with exuberance, unleashing all his weight into forehands and double-fisted backhands, struck with no intentional spin to gain maximum speed through the air. With such daring play, majestic and breathtakingly beautiful in full flight, hardly a hint of margin for error with the ball skimming the net and penetrating deep, the pace sparkled.

Hubba hubba! His speed of shot is extraordinary, thought a surprised Justin.

But he adjusted, quickening his preparation and deploying his remarkable speed of foot.

This rebuttal equally surprised Tyrone. Outright winners against other players, somehow returned. The pace of the rallies grew and crackled with electricity, each exerting heart and mind into every point.

As the business end of the set neared, the battle rose to a crescendo. Each point grew in significance with Tyrone pressing to stave off a break of serve, and Justin now confident he could match Tyrone, having solved the riddle of the Summers pace of shot, desperate to level before the set reached its conclusion.

Tyrone looked across at Justin, surprise creasing his face. His page-boy hair acted like a wick, syphoning sweat progressively from the bottom, rising in dampness until after a gruelling match only a dry tuft radiated from the crown. The level of wetness of Tyrone's hair duplicated as a barometer, measuring the difficulty of a match. Very little was dry now!

After 90 minutes, Tyrone Summers led Justin Forrester by a set and 5-4. A referee whistle blown now would be the sweetest music Tyrone's ear could hear. He would be declared the winner based upon his lead at that moment. But in tennis it is not like that. You cannot lose simply by running out of time. Taking a winning lead, then crawling into a defensive shell and waiting for full time or the bell, is not an option. No, you have to go for the kill and win by a knockout. As someone once said, 'It ain't over 'til it's over!'

Fighting toe to toe, matching blow for blow, the crowd on the edge, Tyrone crossed the tape in the race for the winning-post of the second set with a super-charged shot of naked aggression. He took it 6-4.

'You moron!' Tyrone rebuked himself for hitting a low percentage shot, though he won the set with it!

Shit! cursed Justin, livid, but like all true champions, he immediately injected a positive attitude. *The bloody match will simply have to go the distance!* he firmly believed, without a hint of doubt. *I must break serve early in the third set!* exhorted a desperate Justin.

At 30-all in the first game, in an attempt to discover a weakness in the Summers game, he stepped in early and sliced an off-paced backhand, floating the ball wide to Tyrone's forehand. His adversary netted.

Is Terror tiring? an alarm bell sounded in the Forrester brain.

Tyrone retreated to the baseline with his inimitable cocky walk and bounced like a ball of energy before serving.

Perhaps not. Let's test. Make the bugger sweat!

Probing the forehand again with low, angled slice, netted another point.

'Jeu, Forrester!'

Great! Maybe a factor of fatigue has crept into Terror's game, caused by over-leverage in the first two sets of a match that demands he wins three, thought Justin hopefully, walking to the chair. *The bugger's not huffing or puffing. Nope! He'll be suffering from subtle fatigue, that hidden enemy that betrays the clarity of mind, not the legs. The brain is simply not sending messages efficiently any more. That's got to be why the bugger netted those two crucial forehands.*

Tyrone was first to the seat, in a frenzied search for the bottle to wash the sticky slime down his throat. His sweat so drenched him, he would not be out of place in a nightclub wet T-shirt competition. He shed his soaking shirt and climbed into a fresh one, then went back to the bottle.

Justin's game could not match the power of his opponent, so he relied on reading the signals, subtle changes in body language, looking for soft spots to exploit. He found what he was looking for. Passing his protagonist at the change-over confirmed his suspicions. He detected the glint in Tyrone's eyes had evaporated.

Gotcha! Yep, his finely tuned and fragile body is paying the price for the way he plays. The bugger's clutching the prey in his claws, but hasn't the strength to feed. He's vulnerable, unable to protect his meal from being stolen, and I'm hungry!

A weakness detected, Justin pounced like a predator and stole the quarry, versatilely hoisting the match into his lair. He strode ahead and broke again for a 3-0 lead. His fangs sank deep into the jugular and tasted blood.

'I'm losing to a pale wog! A nobody!' screamed Tyrone. 'I can't believe it. A nobody!'

Great! Terror's rattled! discovered Justin with the verve of sucking on a sachet of mental energy booster.

With Justin serving for a 4-love lead, Tyrone gambled his last gas to push the game to advantage. Justin delivered a vicious serve, wide to the American's forehand. He followed the weak reply with a topspin forehand to the open court. Tyrone groped. The short ball presented Justin with the perfect opportunity for the drop-shot, not so much to win the point, but to exploit the depth and breadth of the court to expire his opponent's life.

Tyrone scurried forward. In a desperate attempt to keep in the point, he dived for the ball, scooped it back into play, but his recovery was futile. Justin guided the ball with a majestic Rosewallian sliced backhand down the line for an exquisite pass, landing just inside the sideline. The linesman put both hands together, palms down to signal the ball was good.

'Égalité' announced the umpire. Deuce.

Tyrone stood akimbo, sucking air. Then shaking his head, he slowly ambled to the spot where the ball landed, looked up at the umpire and glared.

'How did *you* see it?'

The umpire pursed his lips, not wanting to enter the fray.

'Hey, I'm talking to you,' continued Tyrone, waving his hands like a windscreen wiper, trying to catch the attention of the man in the hot seat.

The umpire leant forward and again uttered into his microphone, *'Égalité!'* Then he sat erect in his high chair, looking smug with his fait accompli.

Tyrone scowled at the umpire, stared at the mark, then marched to the *arbitre de chaise*.

'Naughty! Naughty!' said Tyrone, wagging his finger at the umpire. 'Didn't your mommy tell you, you might go blind! How could you not see the ball was out?'

Justin walked back to the baseline and stood his ground ready to serve to the deuce court. Whilst hitting the pass, he looked down the sideline, the best seat in the house to judge. Tyrone assessed across the flight of the ball.

No way was the ball out! Terror must know that, surmised Justin. The outburst confirmed his initial suspicions of Tyrone. The bugger's tired … stalling, buying time for his cut to heal to stay in the fight.

When a tennis player is winning, he will do everything in his power not to tilt the status quo. But losing can cause the mind to play tricks, deceiving one into believing what is not.

Tyrone Summers, remarkably poised so far in the match whilst winning, slipped into the dark side of his personality with which he waged his biggest battles.

'Ask him to check the mark,' Tyrone instructed the umpire, referring to the linesman.

Silent defiance shrouded the umpire.

'Come on, you loony tune, all I ask is that he checks the mark,' pleaded Tyrone in a raised tone.

'Égalité!' the umpire called, stubbornly refusing to budge.

'The fucking ball was out, you moronic jerk,' Tyrone screamed, his elastic jowls opening and closing like a high-speed shutter on a motor drive camera. 'Where'd they get you. Pick you out of a hat! I want the referee. *Now!'* demanded Tyrone belligerently, the issue no longer about the questionable linecall, but an all consuming distrust of authority that seethed in him like a demon.

'I'm the referee,' replied the umpire, unable to resist. It was the referee's privilege to umpire the men's final at Roland Garros. Laughter broke the whistles and jeers, and rippled through the crowd.

Hold steady. Don't get involved, Justin cautioned himself, having never experienced the tetchy mood of Tyrone Summers. He pondered the ramifications of this outburst. *Surely this can't help Terror's concentration. He must be a very worried bugger. Good! That'll be to my advantage. The longer it continues the better for me. Unless, of course, the bloody umpire reverses his decision. But how can he? The linesman called the ball good and the ump has called the score three times. Shit! How can he let this go on and on? … Hush, Justin. Keep calm. Let Terror hang himself.*

The umpire looked at his stopwatch and announced, 'Time warning, Mr Summers.' This, after a four and a half minute hiatus from play when the rules permitted only 25 seconds between points.

'Damn you, you fucking frog!' responded Tyrone and vented his rage by smashing his Wilson Hammer racket to splinters on the netpost.

Had the umpire played according to the book, he should now have disqualified Tyrone Summers, giving warnings for time delay, swearing and abuse of equipment. The procedure is to warn, award a penalty point, and thirdly, disqualify.

Come on, Terror. Let's play the game and see who's the better tennis player, urged Justin mentally.

'I demand the supervisor!' ordered Tyrone.

The umpire suddenly wore a startled expression, looked to the linesman and nodded his head. The linesman got down from his Lacoste platform to inspect the mark. He confirmed his original call, palms down.

Tyrone glared at the umpire and beckoned him with his arm to go and check the mark. He did. After a cursory glance, to everyone's astonishment, he held his arm out parallel to the ground, finger pointing.

The stadium echoed in boos. Tyrone scowled, he always did. The linesman needed the skin of the Lacoste crocodile he sat on, not to feel a fool. And Justin was stunned.

Bloody hell! From deuce, I lose the game, my serve! How can the umpire stoop to checking the mark. That's absurd! Bloody coward!

'*Jeu*, Summers,' announced the umpire to a cacophony of taunts. Justin led 3-1 in the third set.

I'm still a break up, thought Justin, feeling peeved. *Just don't let this bugger back in the match. Terror's got to have lost concentration after that vitriolic outburst, so take advantage.*

Justin quickly reached love-40 on his opponent's serve, giving him triple break point. During the next point, Justin raced to his left, and glided into a slide to execute a sidespin crosscourt backhand, sharply dragging the racket from high to low across the outside face of the ball. As he turned, lowered to a crouch to spring off again, a sharp pain seared in his thigh muscle and a reflex reaction caused him to plop gracelessly on his *derrière*. A collective gasp sounded from the crowd.

Justin immediately clutched his thigh. It knotted into the size of a tennis ball and he cried out in agony. Cramp!

Shit! What's happening? anguished Justin, the blood draining from his face. *My body is my great weapon, my ally. It's deceiving me. Why now?*

He quickly massaged out the knot.

As he rose to recover, the umpire called, 'Time warning, Mr Forrester!' Twenty five seconds had elapsed on the Seiko clock.

Now the umpire plays by the book! spat Justin, hardly believing his ears.

The rules deem cramp, not an injury, but a failure of the body to cope with the tough demands of the game, so a player may not take the single three minute injury time out allowed per match.

Come on! Get back into this game. Fast! Justin exhorted himself, fighting the pain. *No way I'll lose by default! Not having come this far! Never! Never! Never!*

Justin hobbled to the deuce court to receive serve. Still a pair of breakers at 15-40.

Tyrone had remained quiet throughout the incident. If an opponent was slipping off the cliff, he would be more apt to grease the edge than hold out a hand. He would take the title he lusted for any way it came, even by default.

He served wide to Justin's forehand, then attacked with a sharply angled crosscourt shot to Justin's backhand side.

Aagh! grimaced Justin, his legs faltering underneath. *Damn! The bugger's tactic is obvious!*

Make Justin run and exploit the weakness, exacerbate the cramp, and when the Brit was cowering in a disabled heap, sink in the fangs. This was fair game in tennis where 'survival of the fittest' was lore. Justin knew it. He just wished it were not him on the receiving end.

Don't show the bugger I'm hurting, counselled Justin, gritting his teeth beneath his glacial mask.

But his body would not respond. Top level tennis requires bountiful parts to work in perfect harmony to effect the meticulous precision it requires. Years of training hone the cogs into a delicate balance. Put a spanner in the works and the mechanism becomes eccentric. Justin reeled from the pain in his leg, and trying to compensate, his technique infinitesimally altered, and the effectiveness of his game diminished.

It was not that he suddenly made a host of unforced errors, but he hit a little shorter, or with slightly less pace, or he did not get to the ball quite in time to execute perfect precision. Winning a point in tennis, especially on clay, is about a death fight to transfer a rally from a state of equilibrium to one of domination through minute but mounting pressures. Taking the ball earlier or hitting with a touch more pace exerts subliminal pressure on the opponent, whose efficacy correspondingly ebbs, putting the aggressor in a more favourable position to apply further pressure. The defender tries to extract all his powers to sway the balance. A mind game of playing the percentages, balancing the see-saw of risk and patience, continues until an opening arises, whereupon the aggressor will gamble going for the winner.

Justin's impairment took the edge off his game, immediately distorting the equilibrium, loading the odds in Tyrone's favour. Almost at will, Tyrone created openings to hit winners, while his opponent, racked in agonizing pain, could do nothing.

Justin's 3-1 lead whittled away to a deficit, the vice squeezing in on him like a python. At the change-over, oblivious that Antenne 2 beamed a montage of the 6-4 6-4 4-3 score superimposed on his backside, Justin refrained from sitting, choosing to stand and jiggle his legs against the stiffening pain, fearing they would freeze.

Energy! Justin gasped to himself, munching on a banana, unaware he was tightening his noose! *I need it! I've got to win this bloody set, then anything can happen. Maybe I'll recover in the fourth.*

Justin gritted his teeth and ran his heart out, fighting tooth and nail to stay alive in this third set, his mind furiously trying to quieten the pain screaming from his shaking legs, *Get out! Get out! Get out!*

It was no use. He lost his serve to go down 3-5.

Damn it! My cramp has given Terror a new lease of mind, discovered Justin despondently, looking across at his opponent. *He doesn't look tired, he's sharpened his concentration. His face looks eager and hungry.*

The whiff of victory filled the air and Tyrone's chops salivated at the prospect of winning the French Open he craved, now only a game away.

Dark clouds brewed in the sky to cast a gloomy pall across the stadium. This served to deepen Justin's despair. The spectators wrapped up in coats and huddled together, lugubrious of their hero's chances.

With his back against a cold, hard wall, the hunter closing in, Justin reminded himself, *A wounded animal is most dangerous when cornered.*

He came to terms with his plight. *It's fatal to assume this injury will cause me to lose. Only the mind can lose a match. So I've lost my legs, but I've still got my head. Get my mind over that net! Play the match around my injury. Avoid long rallies, they're killing me. My only option is to nullify his game tactically.*

At the first opportunity, with Tyrone still at the back of the court, Justin hoisted a lob deep into his opponent's less effective forehand court. As Tyrone retreated five metres behind the baseline to deal with this new species, Justin snuck into the net and cut off the reply for a winner.

'*Zéro-quinze.*' Love-fifteen.

A buzz permeated the stadium atmosphere. In close rapport with the players and every shift in the pattern of play, the French crowd absorbed the excitement like a sponge.

Justin repeated the sequence and scored another winner with an angled, punched volley.

'*Zéro-trente.*' Love-thirty.

The crowd could hardly contain their excitement. They wanted to see five sets of these two gladiators waging war, and of course, they wanted their hero to win.

Justin continued hitting moonballs, high lofted shots with topspin, which seemingly buried into the clay each time before rebounding slowly and deep, lulling Tyrone into parabolic hypnosis. Buying time, the huge arcs gained Justin leverage to limp into the net. The slow balls pinned Tyrone so far back they fleeced him of the power to generate effective passing shots.

Great! The bugger hasn't detected the invisible pressure, Justin assessed of his incessant net-storming. Amazingly, he broke Tyrone's serve to stay alive.

Another series of ozone unfriendly moonballs, and again Justin gobbled up the proffered fare with relish, holding serve to square the set at 5-all, which with a little more difficulty, since the surprise element grew stale, progressed to 6-all. *Jeu décisif* to settle the third set.

Damn! There's still a whole tiebreaker to go. It's too long. My moonball tactic won't last, Justin realised, fearful his tactic would grow stale. *It's foolish to moonball again. But what else can I do?* questioned Justin, trapped in his broken body. *I'm in Terror's hands, now. How good a player is he?*

Still Justin pressed with his lofted approaches to the net.

Down 2-3, expecting the moonball, Tyrone suddenly changed tactics, rushed forward and struck the ball on the volley, precipitating a wild mêlée of rapid-fire rat-a-tat volleys that rewarded the American's more able body.

He did it again. Roland Garros was agog. Home of the long, 'bring your lunch for sustenance' rallies, they saw Justin and Tyrone at the net, simultaneously duelling for vital tiebreaker points.

Uh oh! Terror's discovered the antidote! mourned Justin, feeling sick in the gut. *And I've no more cards to play!*

Inevitably, with Justin's hampered agility, Tyrone pulled away from his opponent, and at 6-3 in the tiebreaker had triple match point.

My last chance! sighed Justin with a deep breath, clinging to the edge, teetering on the brink of extinction. *I'm not dead yet! Keep looking. Go with the gut!*

The crowd stirred restlessly in their seats. A kaleidoscope of cameras from the dugout pits at the rear of the court trained on Tyrone Summers, man of the moment. He was about to become French Open champion.

Whilst all settled for the death knell, an unexpected squall blew up and a cloud of dust swarmed the stadium. The spectators scurried for cover and buried their faces in their flailing arms to protect their eyes from the stinging dust. Paper cups and *haute couture* millinery flew wildly throughout the stadium.

Great! A reprieve! exclaimed Justin.

Racked with cramp, he hobbled to his seat, held his breath and braced himself, then pressed his thumb deep into his aching thigh muscle, massaging out the knots.

Aagh! he flinched, misty eyed. *Don't give up the ghost! Not now!*

He returned to the service line, took a deep breath and prepared to serve. Then something dramatic happened. The squall had blown the surface clear of loose dust and immediately increased the pace of the court, rendering an ideal opportunity for attack. Justin reacted on cue.

He served wide to the left-handed forehand in the ad-court, and with instinct drawn from innuendoes rooted in the spirit of the wilds of Africa and sublimated into tennis, threw caution to the wind, fearlessly break-danced in on splintered legs, and hurled his body forward to volley a meek return for a winner.

Gotcha! exclaimed Justin.

The crowd screamed their approval.

Aagh! he grimaced, walking back to the service line, pain from his legs screaming at his brain for its foolishness, but missing the mark. It was Justin's heart, the heart of a lion that spurred him to gamble.

I'll do it again! he decided, desperate to extricate himself from his quandary.

He did, crying out aloud on execution, playing on the heartstrings of the gallery, giving the last ounce of his superb athleticism. The onlookers went wild, thriving on these propitious serve and volley forays to the net.

Two match points saved, one to go! urged Justin. He looked across at Tyrone. *Hmm! The surprise element of that sudden change of tactics has caught the bugger off guard. Terror looks bemused, but at 6-5 ahead, he now serves for the match.*

Justin crouched, ready to pounce his prey. His body rocked from side to side, slowly edging forward in anticipation, but his piercing blue eyes locked still on the ball, his face a study of intense concentration.

Tyrone went through his extraordinary fastidious preparation of serve. He got a ball from the ballboy, inspected it, then returned it for another. Superstition? Then his hand went into the pocket and withdrew a handful of sawdust. He wiped it on his racket handle, snapped up his head and served. A fault. He knew it, but he looked at the mark long and hard, just to let the umpire know he could have called it good.

Second serve, a let. Tyrone turned round to the ballboy and got the same ball he had rejected earlier. He did not flicker an eyelid. What was wrong with it first time round? Who knew! He served, straight as an arrow down the centre.

Pumping adrenalin numbing his body of pain, the scent of his prey in his nostrils, Justin stalked the incoming ball, met it on the rise with a truncated forehand, briefly assessed the opportunity, and suddenly charged into the net for the kill. He marauded the whimpering counter and purged his slate clean.

'*Six-à.*' Six points all.

'You stay out of this!' Tyrone shouted, looking to the sky. Then he coughed. Was he talking to the wind? With Tyrone, who knew!

'*Bravo*, Justin!' screamed the delirious Roland Garros crowd.

Amid the deafening noise Justin's blood pumped, his breathing quickened and goose bumps flecked his skin.

Keep calm, keep a level head, Justin reminded himself. Desperate to gain the sanctuary of the beginning of a set, where a match cannot be won or lost, he drummed into his brain, *Two more points! I need time, time to heal. Just two more points!*

Amid euphoric scenes, he continued his absurd net-rushing tactics and won the third set.

'*Set*, Forrester, 7-6.' Tyrone led 6-4 6-4 6-7.

A visceral triumph this, for Justin, when desperation drove him into deep communion with his wild nurturing. For someone so inexperienced in big time tennis, he miraculously demonstrated an innate sense of timing, instinctively harnessing the elements to his advantage in a moment of severe crisis, to engineer, tactically, a dramatic turnaround. Justin's phenomenal resource of mental strength kept him alive.

'Chocolate! Gimme some chocolate!' Tyrone ordered a ballboy, knowing a long battle could ensue.

Roland Garros erupted. They had a match on their hands. Whilst Tyrone plied himself with chocolate and Justin wolfed down a banana, officials dragged sacking over the court, spreading back the menacing soft cushion of dust.

As the clouds darkened to enhance the mounting gloom, Justin's legs cried in pain and ground to a halt, hobbled by the ravages of cramp. He tried and he cried and his heart lunged, but his feet remained buried in the quicksand, his body crushed and broken on the infamous red clay, a soakaway that sponged up the blood, sweat and the tears of joy and sorrow of the warriors who dared to wage war on this battleground.

Going down 0-4, the match slipped from his grasp.

My body has cheated me! mourned a dejected and forlorn man, choking back a lump in his throat. His senses grew numb and tears blinded his eyes. Perhaps this accounted for his not noticing the rain drops.

The crowd went mad, whistling at the umpire to call off the match.

'Ladies and gentlemen, please let the officials make the decisions,' rebuked the umpire. He immediately looked up at the sky and announced, 'Play will be suspended because of rain.'

What a bumbling buffoon! thought Justin, flabbergasted, but after a moment he realised the umpire had rolled the dice in his favour, answering his supplications.

Saved by the rain! he sighed with relief, eagerly grasping his *deus ex machina* lifeline. A rain break always favours the losing player!

Justin asked a ballboy to collect his belongings, then limped off court. Blooded by *Les Internationaux De France* into professional tennis in a baptism of fire, limbs on the rack, mind on trial, he went straight to the infirmary and lay on a bed.

Within a minute Larry King joined him.

'Hi, Hoss,' Justin whispered, barely moving his parched lips.

'Cut the monkey food,' bellowed Larry, coming straight to the point.

'The bananas?'

'Damn right! And no chocolate. It's full of fat.'

'I ate the bananas for energy,' defended Justin. 'Buggers didn't seem to help.'

'Bloody hell they won't. They're *causing* your cramp.'

'Wha—?'

'Bananas are full of potassium,' elucidated Larry. 'An imbalance of potassium dehydrates and—'

'And dehydration causes cramps!' continued Justin, slamming his fist in frustration as the realisation dawned. 'Damn!'

'You got it.'

'Bit late now,' lamented Justin bitterly.

'Get rid of it!'

Justin looked enquiringly at Larry.

'Yeah!'

Justin hobbled to the toilet, stuck his finger down his throat and retched banana puree, loads of it. Drawn and pale and clutching his stomach, he returned and slumped on the bed.

'And now?' whispered Justin.

'Adam's ale!'

'Water?'

'Long sips of pure cool water, pal,' advised Larry, passing the ailing Justin a decanter. 'Sip on this.'

Justin clutched the glass bottle and slowly washed acidic vomit down his throat.

Larry's advice sustained him. He looked to his friend and asked, 'Why're you doing this for me?'

'Let's just say I'm settling an old score.'

Hmm! That's right! The errant genius has supplanted Hoss at the summit of American tennis.

After a hot shower and a deep muscle massage, Justin announced to Larry, 'I want some shut eye. Would you—'

'You crazy? You going to sleep in the middle of this match?'

'I need to recharge my batteries. Care to act as a bouncer and give me some peace?'

'Sure!' assured Larry, then offered some parting advice, 'Give it all you've got, pal. Hang in there.'

'If I lose they'll have to carry me out on my bloody shield!' reassured Justin wearily.

Forty minutes later the two protagonists returned to the court with the score reading 6-4 6-4 6-7 4-0 in Tyrone's favour. As the old balls rolled out, so the atmosphere returned.

Damn! My legs are still bloody sore! grimaced Justin, the knotting having bruised the muscles. But psychologically the rain break was a great fillip. *I can deal with that. At least the cramping's gone. I will not lose! I will die out here today before losing!*

With his back to the wall, at 0-4 down, he gritted his teeth and set about like a madman cut loose from the noose. For each nail driven into the coffin, his hand crept out somewhere else, clawing his way back to life like some modern day Lazarus. He had been to hell and back. Reincarnated, would he haunt Tyrone?

Would Tyrone have the conviction to force the pace that had generated his present lead? Resting on the laurels of a 4-0 buffer, never one to temper his game, he recklessly tested the old tennis adage, 'never change a winning game'. Reckless, because the balls picked up moisture and grit from the wet clay, making them heavy, robbing him of his most penetrating shots.

Hmm! Just as a cheetah needs its prey in flight to attack, so Terror's slight body needs pace from me to generate his own power. I'll anaesthetize that pace.

With the cunning feigns and subtleties of a leopard, Justin lured his prey from the open plains into the bush, exposed the panicking prey and silently and efficiently inflicted the killer blow.

So close to finishing off the match for the second time, Tyrone's game, pigheadedly unaltered, was found wanting. He panicked.

'You choking moron!' screamed Tyrone, putting his hand to his throat, miming self-strangulation.

On set point in the fourth set tiebreaker, Justin feathered a backhand drop-volley off the American's attempted pass, a shot that had the same effect as a shaft of sunlight piercing an angry sky.

And the sun did! To celebrate the revival, on a day for all seasons, the wind died down, the flags that decorated the stadium like candles on a birthday cake stood limp at their stations, and quite appropriately, the sun came out and bathed Roland Garros in glorious sunshine.

Counter-balanced at two sets all, the scoreboard reading 6-4 6-4 6-7 6-7, the match, destined to be ranked amongst the finest in the memories of Roland Garros, entered the crux, a fifth set. All before, 4 hours and 50 minutes of drama, was a titillating foreplay for the climax that lay ahead.

Stung by the loss of his fourth set, Tyrone dug deep into his resources and regrouped. Suddenly, his vibrancy back, he stalked his domain with his inimitable rule-the-roost peacock strut.

Locked in a memorable duel, point and counter-point played like a major crisis, they swapped blow for blow, battling it out in a timeless fifteenth round. Inevitably, as the set progressed, the legs grew weary and the mind numb, punch-drunk. But what never lacked was the colossal obstinacy of these two warriors. So bull-headed were their wills, fused like kudus in a hornlock, that game after game it appeared neither could yield even if they so wished. Late in the Parisian evening, the match still hung in the balance, the issue well and truly drawn at 4-all. Who would win?

Ultimately, in the lottery of a fifth set, victory often goes to the player who manages to extract just the finest edge of mental sharpness out of the humdrum maze.

This bugger's no Roland Drechsler, no Sern Stenmark, thought Justin, suddenly looking at his opponent with new respect. *Terror's like me. It's going to be a case of who dares, wins!*

Justin and Tyrone, each desperate to win the French Open for their personal reasons, wore their hearts on their sleeves, their pumped up passion naked for all to see. It had the spillover effect of driving them on, transcending the tennis into another realm. With death-defying athleticism, Justin finally broke through the Summers's serve.

Jeu, Forrester.' He led 5-4.

The crowd stood to their feet, absolutely abuzz, struggling to contain their exuberance. Goose bump time!

One game! Just one game! exclaimed Justin, his heart pumping hard in his chest at his sudden chance to win a bizarre encounter. *A chance to live my dream, to become French Open champion. But Terror will fight tooth and claw to wake me. Hang tough!*

The two fierce rivals, united only by a desire to win, marauded like two madmen armed with buzz-saws. At deuce, Justin whipped a topspin lob over a weary opponent.

'*Avantage,* Forrester.'

Match point! gasped Justin, tingling inside.

The crowd hushed. Tyrone coughed.

Justin paused, then served. Tyrone's return dumped into the net and the crowd screamed. Justin had won!

'*Premier service!*' called the umpire. A service let!

'Not over! Not over!' Tyrone hushed the groaning crowd, wagging his finger. Only when it was dead quiet did he allow the match to resume.

But for Justin, the drama continued.

Damn! Not now, he lamented. A string had broken in his racket.

He collected a new racket from his stockpile, then asked for a ball from a nearby ballboy. As he walked back to serve, he profusely bounced the ball on the ground, desperate to get the feel of his new racket. He then swapped the ball with the one in his pocket, its nap slightly flattened. *Should travel fractionally faster!*

Ripples of tension washed over the red clay of Roland Garros. What now?

Suddenly the pugilistic Tyrone gambled, sized up his slender body for a final desperate blow to usurp the match. A quick shuffle, he stepped in closer to take the ball on the rise and unleashed his feared two-hander. The ball smacked straight into the tape, popped up and argued with the shaking net as if wagging its finger, then plopped for a dead netcord winner with the aplomb of a lump of soggy dough. The crowd gasped.

'Yeah!' Tyrone cried out, arching his back and pumping his fists until the veins bulged in his neck. 'I practice that shot!'

He dashed up to the net, kissed the tape and bowed like a matador who had just plunged the sword. Then looking across at Justin, he held up his hand for the customary acknowledgement to suggest he was sorry, but he was not. He would take it anyway it came. So would any tennis player.

Shit! Shit! Shit! Justin burned inside, but outwardly appeared the most unconcerned person in the stadium.

The cruel blow rivalled the most memorable dead netcord in tennis history, struck by Boris Becker on match point to wrench the 1988 Masters crown from Ivan Lendl after 37 strokes!

Forget it! Justin urged. *That point's history. Focus all energies on the ball now!*

Touched by the magic honouring the proudest traditions of this tournament, Tyrone broke through Justin's service game to level at 6-6. There are no tiebreakers in the fifth set at Roland Garros, no easy way out. You have to break serve to win. So the drama built, the tension heightened. The tennis gods in the sky, choreographers of the match, deliberately tightened the keys to fever pitch.

Tyrone held serve. At 7-6 in his favour, and 30-all on Justin's serve, suddenly a point of immense significance, a 'big point' in tennis parlance. The clock ticked closer to nine o'clock in the evening with the light beginning to fade, the drama highlighted by the golden hues. Drained of emotion, the spectators drew on their own reserves of adrenalin. Now they were uneasy, their hero only two points away from defeat.

Tyrone gambled all, unleashing a humdinger down the line for a complete winner. A moment ago Justin served for the match. Now he served to stay alive, down match point. Stunned silence.

Tyrone looked to his mother sitting incognito in the stands, who radiated vibes of support to her son. She stuck up a finger to impart a pearl of wisdom, just one more point! As if Tyrone did not know! Strutting back to receive serve, he pointed his own index finger to the sky. Yes, just one more point.

Shit! Only a few points away from the title but I'm looking down the barrel of a gun again! moaned Justin, tension straining. *So close, so elusive!*

Justin started to serve when Tyrone held up his racket, halting play. The fastest mouth in the game had the unmitigated gall to insist the spectators were church quiet. He gave Justin time to think, time to tighten up.

It was the ultimate pressure point, one that demanded to be won without recourse to correction. Justin swallowed, took a deep breath and served. An ace!

Phew! That saved my backside! thought a relieved Justin.

The crowd screamed and jumped to their feet as if Justin had won the match.

'Faute!' overruled the umpire, almost drowned by the din.

Startled, Justin looked straight to the umpire who nodded his head in confirmation. Another cruel blow! Justin felt like a child who had a birthday present confiscated.

The screaming crowd crossed the great divide of Gallic mood, and swung into solemn silence, holding their breath.

As Justin prepared for his second serve, he caught a glimpse of an odd sight behind Tyrone. He arrested his serve motion and attracted the attention of the umpire. 'Looks like the lineslady's fallen asleep!'

The crowd broke their quiet and a round of suppressed giggles reverberated through the stadium. Tyrone walked up to the lady perched on her Lacoste crocodile platform.

'Hey, wake up, lady!' spat a belligerent Tyrone. On closer examination of the slumped woman he turned to the umpire, and shaking his head, declared, 'She's wasted!'

The crowd grew solemn again. Officials laid the poor lady on a stretcher, covered her top to toe with a blanket and whisked her off court.

With the interruption of play, Justin was awarded the chance of another first serve, but another ace was overruled by the umpire. Steeling his mind as he prepared for a second serve, Justin heard a sudden crescendo of cheers, jeers and whistles.

What now? he wondered, looking up to discover why. *I'll be damned!*

The championship in the palm of his hands, his nostrils smelling the scent of victory, Tyrone had trotted right up to the service line. So much closer, he loomed large and menacing, an act of aggression, taunting Justin to double fault, daring him to come up with something spectacular, or die.

This has never happened to me before! Now the bugger does it, on a second serve at match point! Crisis time! What the hell do I do? wondered Justin, the incident sending a flurry of thoughts through his mind. With raw nerve and gambling instinct he resolved, *This is my last chance. Rise to the challenge. Be strong! Muster up something special!*

The crowd hushed and focused all eyes on Justin. Even the trees peeping over the lip of the stadium seemed to bow a little closer to catch a glimpse of the drama.

Justin reached into his pocket and retrieved a ball. He paused for a moment, suspending the match at fever pitch. In the hushed silence, a trickle of perspiration sent a shiver down his spine. He looked at Tyrone with his steely glare, flames of fire dancing in his eyes, lips determined, then took a deep breath and proceeded to serve. Like a man teetering and tottering as he lifts a heavy stone, finally holding it overhead with fully stretched arms, body trembling with every muscle bulging before plunging it to the ground, the poker-faced Justin drew on atavistic instinct, mustered all his strength and propelled his delivery. Thwack!

'Gotcha!' Justin exclaimed aloud.

Voilà! Right on target. The ball soared through the air as straight as an arrow and buried into Tyrone's belly, doubling him over, smashing his grand opportunity to filch the trophy. Point to Justin!

Serve Terror right! thought Justin, hot and cold waves of excitement surging through his body. *I* will *not,* will *not lose!*

Roland Garros went berserk.

Shit! What's the buzz? wondered Justin, before seeing the approaching horde.

Delirious fans swarmed onto the court, screaming and shouting and pawing Justin. He panicked and ran for cover, tearing off court and into the refuge of the television interview room. A frightened-looking Tyrone joined him.

There was mayhem on court. Officials fought with fans who fought with officials. The umpire tried to command order, but in vain. And each person in the stand vocally animated *his* way to restore sanity.

Eventually reason prevailed and the Parisian traffic jam unlocked and dissipated. Gingerly, Justin and Tyrone entered the *Court Central* crucible for the third time that afternoon.

Suddenly the spunk in Tyrone ran dry. He had climaxed and his weapons grew flaccid. Exploiting the lull, Justin exerted pressure, held serve and broke his opponent's to lead 8-7.

Again, Justin earned the chance to serve for the match, a moment every tennis player dreams of, but a game that tests the nerve to the limit. He took it by the throat, played like a true champion and had three match points.

Balle de match! exclaimed Justin, his heart fluttering in his chest like a caged bird. But nobody would have known. *Revel in the battle,* he reminded himself, trying to deaden the nerves.

The bugger's returned serve crosscourt for most of the match, Justin analysed. Tapping his tennis shoes with his racket to loosen the grit to aid traction, Justin mentally took a step back to view the larger perspective before committing to his battle plan. *All the facts suggest he should do it again.* But a niggling doubt gnawed at Justin. *This Terror is something else!*

Tyrone coughed, his bark always more prevalent under pressure. Justin aided and abetted his cause by serving wide to Tyrone's forehand in the advantage court and tore in, intuitively blanketing the down-the-line return. With relief he guided the volley into a wide expanse of court for a winner. He had iced the fire!

When the dust cleared, Justin's arms raised high in triumph. The noise was deafening, almost frightening, but when the umpire read the score in Justin's favour, 4-6 4-6 7-6 7-6 9-7, he knew his ordeal was over.

The two combatants, looking drawn and weary, trudged up to the net, almost limping, and shook hands. Justin nodded his head. Tyrone said nothing.

Justin had shown that unfathomable champion quality to raise the level of his game in a moment of crisis. For Tyrone, his pride hurt. He allowed himself to fail by that one point at the end. Such is the ecstasy and the agony, the beauty and pathos that is Roland Garros.

A sea of cameramen flooded around the champion, who felt gawked at by a multitude of one-eyed monsters, clicking their shutter tongues against a background of whirring motor drives. Justin's head swirled in the claustrophobic hive of activity.

Suddenly a man thrust a microphone in Justin's face as he tried to sip some water. A very untidy interview toggled back and forth in French and English, conducted courtside amid the hustle and bustle.

'Champion of Roland Garros! Can you believe what you have done?'

Justin shook his head. He tried to towel himself down.

'When did you think you had the match won?'

Justin stared at the man with incredulity, but remained silent.

The world had just witnessed a most bizarre match, a drama filled encounter that bristled with incident. Justin Forrester and Tyrone Summers gave them a match that drank deeply from the finest vintage of Roland Garros, to be talked and written about and long remembered. One thought of Björn Borg and Ivan Lendl, both having to come back from two sets down to win their début Grand Slam titles, also on the red clay courts of Roland Garros. In the end, after carving a special niche for himself in the annals of tennis history with one of the bravest matches ever played, it was Justin who triumphed!

Victor and vanquished ascended up the red carpet as battle-scarred Homeric giants to the President's Box. A jubilant Justin Forrester juxtaposed against a devastated Tyrone Summers. Justin received the trophy, and as he turned around to hold it aloft, a thunderous applause greeted him. Tennis paid him its warmest tribute and he smiled for the first time.

Champion of France! he said to himself, a warm tingling feeling flushing his skin.

As dusk drew closer to night, Justin honoured the gallant loser in a victory speech peppered with applause. 'My heart goes out to Tyrone. He fought to the death. That's my kind of tennis player. ... A match like this should have no losers? Some people say that. I disagree! If tennis were like that, our match would never have curdled your blood! Nope! Tennis demands a winner, and with loads of luck I'm glad it was me today.'

Justin looked to Tyrone and promised, 'One thing is for sure, there's a long road ahead with lots more of these duels!' This brought a smile of acknowledgement to Tyrone's gloomy face.

'When I think that so many great champions of the past are French virgins, and now I have this little lady in my back pocket, sweet dreams are made of this!'

'*Bravo*, Justin!'

'These two extraordinary weeks will stay with me for the rest of my life. Thanks for sharing it with me. As that bugger Roland Garros himself once said, 'If you weren't present, you don't know how splendid it was!''

Whilst Tyrone spoke, Justin looked at the trophy he caressed in his hands. In calligraphy engraved, *'Coupe des Mousquetaires'* and on the base plate *'Roland Garros – Simple Messieurs'*.

I can't believe it! he exclaimed, shaking his head. Punch drunk with emotion, he held up his trophy, the toast of the tennis world.

While a sick-looking Tyrone slunk off from Roland Garros, Justin walked straight into a shower, fully togged. Sighing, he felt the warm water wash over his aching body, below he saw bloodstained water drain from him, a river of red clay and sweat flowing out of his socks.

'Phew!' he sighed, two weeks of exhaustion purging from his body and mind.

Refreshed, he headed to a press conference and sat in a room that hummed with anticipation from the capacity media. He faced an octopus of microphone tentacles, each eager to capture every nuance of the new champion of France. Journalists fired questions at him.

'If someone told you two weeks ago that you would win at Roland Garros, what would you have replied?' a reporter asked.

'Put it in writing! ... Then see a bloody shrink!' laughed the champion.

'Has it sunk in yet?'

'Nope! I don't think so,' replied Justin, still stunned. 'I tried not to let it get to me that I was playing Tyrone for the French Open.'

'Did playing him for the first time worry you?'

'I've played him many times in my dreams!'

'How did you fare?'

'Oh, I win every time, 10-8 in the fifth!' Justin shot with an impish grin. 'This was a shade easier.'

'Do you like these long matches?'

'Only if I knew I was going to win like this. Otherwise love, love and love.'

'Have you thought about the money?'

'No,' answered Justin, then grinned, 'only that I hope it covers my whopping hotel bill!'

'Why were the French crowd so for you today?'

'I guess I was the underdog. If Tyrone hasn't won it when he's older, they'll support him.'

'Have you heard what he said?'

'Nope!'

'He said he got bored with the long rallies.'

'Be interesting to know what excites the bugger!'

'Did your injury affect him?'

'Ask him.'

'I did, but he just complained that his shoes were too small!'

The press corps giggled.

'Perhaps the bugger's too big for his shoes!'

The pressmen roared with laughter.

Bloody arse creepers! Justin continued, 'It shouldn't affect him, but you never know. A lion is most dangerous when wounded.'

'But he's the number one player in the world. Why didn't he drop-shot you?'

'It's hard to play an injured opponent. The pressure is suddenly on you to win. If you change your game and it falters, you get criticised for not sticking with your usual game that you know to work. But if you stick with your game, the critics haul you over the coals for not exploiting the injury. It's very difficult. I wouldn't get on his case. He spilled his guts, and that's good enough for me!'

'How do you explain *your* extraordinary play when injured?'

'Well, the reverse is true. Suddenly there was no pressure on me to win, so I took chances and hit out, and escaped the hook of pressure. In a perverse way my injury gave me freedom.'

'So would you rather play injured?'

Justin never answered.

'Justin, I'm sure everyone here wants to know about the amazing way you staved off defeat when down match point.'

The pressmen eagerly leant forward, hanging onto every word Justin uttered.

He shrugged his shoulders and said prosaically, 'I just decided I couldn't be cautious at match point. It seemed the most natural thing to do.'

'What went through your mind when he came up to the service line?'

'It was kind of scary. Suddenly I was out of my groove. I lose this point, I'm out of the tournament. It forced the extraordinary.'

'What did you think of him daring you to double fault?'

'I answered that on court!' shot Justin.

'In the end, the last two games, it was all rather easy. Why do you think the fight suddenly went out of him?'

'It certainly wasn't easy for me!' replied Justin, indignant. 'I shook like a mating jellyfish out there! Almost couldn't hold my racket!'

The press corps seemed staggered, bewildered that beneath the impassive mask there existed a person with human frailties.

'French Open champion. What now?'

'Whatever happens the rest of the year is icing on the cake, but I look forward to Wimbledon,' answered Justin, treating his first Grand Slam title merely as a crumb that meagrely satisfied an insatiable appetite to win them all.

'No celebration?'

'You can get drunk with success, and then the tennis world passes you by,' answered Justin, assuming the experience of a seasoned campaigner. 'But tonight I will celebrate. And to do so, I must leave now.'

Departing from Stade Roland Garros, Justin pinched himself to believe he was champion of France. He thought back to Sunday June 21st in 1891, where at the Racing Club in Paris in the Bois de Boulogne, another Englishman, a man by the name of Henry Briggs, won the first French Championships. Said the organiser, 'We really hope that next year we will be able to sell more than 50 tickets.' Now Justin shook his head in disbelief at the magnitude of his win. Tonight he would party.

It was party time! A date with the blonde German wonder girl of tennis, Heidi Schültz, the new king and queen of France did Paris. From dining *haute cuisine*, a master chef creation for royalty at Le Bistrot de Paris, to dancing the waltz to an orchestra in the glitter of gleaming mirrors and chandeliers at Maxim's, to tits and feathers at the Crazy Horse Saloon, erotic temple of the night. A night that never seemed to end.

In the sweet aftermath of their famous victories, their cup of joy overflowing, they boarded a boat on the Seine. Leaning over the railing, staring into the light reflecting water, bursting with contentment, Justin hummed the tune, 'I love Paris in the springtime, I love ...'

They sailed off into the night.

Au Revoir!

CHAPTER 6

'*Acht!* This is vot I call a racket!' exclaimed Otto Weiner, proudly revealing his masterpiece. 'Not those vooden things the boy has been playing vit.'

The frail, white-haired German scientist, with a penchant for inventiveness and unrivalled skill in computer technology, held up his black, prototype space-age racket to the inspecting eye of Creighton's brains trust, Team BB. Until then, Bob Wallace had purposely honed Boris Bauer's game using a wooden racket, to develop control.

'The racket is extremely strong. It is a ceramic compound iced vit aluminium and baked into a material called 'Cermet'. The same vot they use for the bullet proof vests. Also, this racket is aerodynamically shaped. I placed the racket in a vind-tunnel and connected it to a computer. Then I fed into the computer the projected frequency and importance of each shot and homed in on the optimum frame that yields the least vind resistance for the kid's style of play.'

Bob Wallace burst the German's bubble. 'Vot's so, uh, what's so bloody special about that? They make all rackets that way!'

'*Acht!* Now for my ingenious plot. This is not von single string as is the case of the conventional rackets vot you talk about. Each main string and cross string you see in my racket is separate. The strings near the perimeter of the frame are strung progressively more loosely. This thing vot you call the sveet spot is so big it vill make cavities in the opponent's game,' chuckled Otto Weiner.

'Dinkum! How the bloody 'ell do you connect the floss?'

'*Himmel!* Each string is threaded and pulled through a self-clamping grommet and tightened. Ven released, the tension of the string pulls on the grommet that holds the string in check.' Otto raised his finger. 'But, vot's more, each grommet duals as a vibration damper and also muffles the sound of the ball striking the racket, making it difficult for the opponent to use the sense of hearing. Of course, the strings are superfine to decrease the drag.'

§

'Shield the boy from events in Wenceslas Square,' Creighton ordered Vich, referring to the winds of change sweeping across Europe. 'Under no circumstances must he know about the demonstrations.'

'The time 'as come to teach the little bastard to play a competitive match,' Bob Wallace informed the rest of Team BB, comprising Amos Creighton, Vich, Professor Von Trapp and the latest addition, Otto Weiner.

Both Bob Wallace and Professor Von Trapp beamed with unbridled pride, as they demonstrated the 15 year old Boris Bauer relentlessly hitting the ball with clinical precision and bludgeoning power.

For the past four years, hour upon hour, day after day, he had hit against a ball machine to a specified target. Flush in the butt of his racket sat an electronic counter connected to a built-in microscopic strain gauge to measure the number of hits in a row. Each time Boris Bauer missed the target, the counter reset to zero. Each time he reached the specified goal of 200 consecutive bull's eyes, the target imperceptibly reduced. When the target diminished to a square metre, the ball machine fractionally increased its speed and the target area expanded to full size, and the whole process repeated.

Inexorably, the ever slowly increasing pressures honed Boris Bauer's game to clinical precision. The subject had reached his maximum potential.

Over the past year the coaching duo introduced another variable, point sequences. Again, they incremented the number of shots per rally and their severity. Enter Otto Weiner.

'*Acht!* Vot I aim to do is connect this ball machine to this computer and replicate a tennis player,' explained Otto Weiner.

Alive with 'fuzzy logic', the computerised OTTO ball machine could move forwards and backwards, and from side to side, and shoot a ball from a variety of heights with an assortment of trajectories, spins and speed.

'I have stored the point sequences of the video tape matches you gave me in the memory bank of the computer,' explained the scientist. 'You know, matches of these fellows Connors, Borg, Edberg and so on, whomever they are.'

'Demonstrate, mate?' queried a very suspicious Bob Wallace.

'*Himmel!* Now let's see,' puzzled Otto Weiner, stroking his long white goatee. 'Hmm! Aah, ve take Wilander's perspective against McEnroe at the French Open of 1985. He's 6-1 7-5 1-2 and the score is advantage to Wilander.'

The scientist keyed in a sequence of data and pressed an execute button.

Quite extraordinarily, the futuristic ball machine roared to life like a crab performing a mating dance, projecting a pattern of shots to the other side of the court. First, the machine blasted a ball from the baseline, swerving to the far corner of the service box. Then it raced forwards and fired a ball sharply angled crosscourt.

'Now from McEnroe's point of view!' beamed Otto Weiner.

Amazingly, the ball machine reciprocated, this time offering only the return of serve up the line.

'Ya a bloody bull artist, aren't ya? Tryin' to put one over me with a ringer! I ain't no mug, mate!' defended Bob Wallace, sceptical of the system's efficacy. He challenged the scientist. 'Becker's play at match point against Lendl, Master's final, 1988?'

There followed a long sequence of balls emanating from the robotic monster and on the equivalent of the 37th stroke, the ball hit the tape of the net and died lifelessly on the opposite side.

'Bloody strewth!' Bob Wallace looked wide-eyed and stunned. 'No flies on ya, feller! That's a perfect replica!'

'*Acht!* That's not all,' beamed the scientist. 'If you so vish, ve can shift the goalposts and increase the speed and the spins.'

There are two schools of thought on training. Some believe in running uphill with weighted shoes or swinging a heavier racket so that the perception is lighter and faster in competition. Others prefer specific training, claiming it impossible to discover the true angles by practising snooker on an uneven table.

'Ultimately ve can have the boy playing against match patterns much sterner than those guys vot you call McEnroe and Becker.'

'Dinkum! Vot, uh, what next?'

'And vot's more,' continued the scientist, wagging his finger, 'I have used artificial intelligence expert systems to discover the best vay of beating Connors and Lendl and so on.'

Vich addressed Team BB. 'Five years. Five years and he's unbeatable. Don't screw up,' he warned, fondling the centre main string of his Donnay Allwood tennis racket.

CHAPTER 7

'Justin! Justin! Justin!' screamed thousands of success-starved locals who flocked to Heathrow to greet an unsuspecting Justin Forrester on his return from France, giving him a hero's welcome befitting the Duke of Wellington. They adopted him as their own, paying homage to their idol. Banners bearing Justin's name draped buildings, Union Jacks swayed in the breeze and newspaper headlines screamed superlatives.

This is embarrassing! thought the new French champion of this tumultuous welcome. *I wish I could hide.*

Without being asked, a helpless Justin found himself caught up in the heaving mass, and pushed and shoved about like a piece of airport baggage, channelled to a conference room where he faced the media horde, reporters from Fleet Street of old, and television and radio moguls.

'Justin Forrester. Who are you?'

Justin shrugged his shoulders, bemused at this sudden interest, and uncertain how to answer. 'Just a tennis player. A bugger who likes to win, and lucky enough to do just that.'

Of course, unaccustomed to local lads winning, even with luck, the British media salivated at the prospect of having a British champion.

'You conquered France for Britain,' remarked a reporter from *The Times*. Then desperate for an affirmative answer, asked, 'Are you British?'

'Well, yes––'

A rally of happy applause interrupted him, and relief descended upon the conference room.

Justin continued while they hung onto every word he uttered. 'I was born in Swaziland, but my parents are British and work there under contract. So I have a British passport. When I'm in Swaziland, I'm an African. While I'm playing tennis and live here in Britain, I'm British!'

That was good enough for the flock. British tennis emerged out of the doldrums and the party began.

For Justin, the party was over.

'Wimbledon!' he whispered, hankering after the coveted title on the eve of the premier tennis event. *I'll shake the French red clay out of my feet and play the Wimbledon warm-up tournament, Queens. There I'll turn a few screws and tighten a few bolts to tune my game for grass!*

Damn! cursed Justin on arrival at Queen's Club in a Victorian corner of South-West London near Baron's Court tube station.

An avalanche of screaming schoolgirls besieged him, clamouring for his autograph. Fighting his way through the starry-eyed teenybopper brigade to the clubhouse, he felt shoved and bumped, pawed and pulled at. They touched him, as if to be healed. Justin dutifully signed a ream of autographs, lest he cause a riot.

'Phew!' he uttered with great relief as he walked up the steps and into the seclusion of the clubhouse.

An agitated tournament director confronted him.

'We're assigning police protection to you, Justin,' advised the director, worried that he could lose his star attraction. 'Goodness knows what it's going to be like during The Fortnight. For your safety you'd better not win the bloody tournament!'

The Fortnight! thought Justin. Wimbledon!

To escape the stresses and strains of living under a constant, ever probing spotlight, Justin went on a pilgrimage to Wimbledon, and immersed himself in the mists of time, to that sweet summer of 1980 when the dream began.

Time for the memories …

Southfields tube station disgorges an army of eager tennis fans, some boarding a red bus to take them to the Church Road ticket queue, others, like Justin, preferring to stroll the picturesque, meandering walk past the yacht-speckled Wimbledon Park Lake.

Quite suddenly, out of her nestled camouflage in the loveliest and leafiest suburb of London, Wimbledon, she appears in view.

'The Centre Court stadium!' gasps Justin. 'Standing proud like a hen brooding over her chicks, the outside tennis courts!'

'She is the landmark of SW19,' resonates an ethereal voice, 'a looming presence as if she has stood there a thousand years and more!'

'Huh? Who are you?'

'Oh, let's just say I'm the Spirit of Wimbledon!'

'Spirit of Wimbledon?' asks Justin, fascinated.

'Indeed! Where else to rest my weary bones!' replies the Spirit, then looking in the distance, he goes into raptures, 'Synonymous with Mount Everest or the Mona Lisa, Wimbledon is a paragon in her niche, transcended into the upper realm of universal reverence. They are one of a kind!'

'Who are all these buggers?' asks Justin.

'Aah! That's the famed Wimbledon queue!'

Ahead stretches a human chain, snaking its way from the golf course car park, onto the huge footbridge over the traffic, and along the pavement to the entrance gate, all of two kilometres long. Armed with a sense of humour and loads of patience, dressed in the ubiquitous Wimbledon uniform of anoraks, jeans and trainers, their blankets and sleeping bags rolled up, they sit in folding chairs reading books or newspapers whilst drinking coffee or tea from their Thermoses and nibbling from picnic hampers. They listen to Walkmans or radios, catching snippets from the BBC commentary, and mark their cards for the matches they hope to see.

'Does everybody who comes to Wimbledon have to queue?' wonders Justin.

'Oh no, the legend of the Wimbledon queue is not for all,' reassures the Spirit. 'The currency of Wimbledon is the Centre Court ticket. Demanded a hundred fold or more, Wimbledon sells these tickets by ballot some five months earlier. So this queuing fetish is a sprinkling of the unfortunate unable to win a ticket in the lottery, but with a great longing to be a part of it all.'

'Tired of the waiting? Walk right in, mate, cheapest tickets in town!' tempts a sinister tout, lurking in the shadows.

'Who's that bugger?' asks Justin. 'And what's all that noise on the golf course?'

'Bothersome touts,' replies the Spirit disparagingly. 'Haggling down their grossly inflated prices resembles an Indian market, but counts for nought against the seedy merchants, hardened by years of foul weather and conniving deals. Only the rich succumb.'

'Letter for a Mr Gareth Travers,' broadcasts a Wimbledon official. 'And one for Diana Perkins.'

Justin raises his eyebrows questioningly.

'Aah! The morning mail call. Yes, so famous is the Wimbledon queue that the British Royal Mail timeously delivers epistles addressed, 'c/o The Overnight Queue, Church Road, Wimbledon'!'

'Keep my place?' asks a young man with three day's growth. Nature calls.

Another fan hauls out a gas stove. Soon the smell of bacon and eggs frying in butter, soaked up by bread, permeates the morning air.

'Some say they are the unlucky ones,' the Spirit tells Justin. 'But even if rain tumbles out of an indigo sky with no imaginable prospect of tennis, their spirits are dry and sparky.'

'I could stay at home and catch the tennis on telly,' explains a lady wringing yesterday's rain out of her socks, 'but being here is something very special.'

'All this and there is the very real possibility of queuing and not seeing any tennis,' informs the Spirit, 'because Wimbledon shuts its gates when the numbers reach 28,000. But there are ways around this dilemma.'

'We're sharing a ticket,' explains a couple. 'After each set, one of us will come out and the other goes in!'

'You see,' beams the Spirit, 'the queue is all part of the Wimbledon adventure. Indeed, the true Wimbledon fan would not have it any other way!'

'All this for tennis?'

'Goodness, no! Wimbledon is not only about tennis. It's an occasion! Come with me and experience it!'

At eleven o'clock the gates open, and like a dam wall bursting, a sea of people with only a grounds pass gush forward to book their favourite lookout spots. Those with Centre Court tickets take a more leisurely stroll. Their seats are reserved.

'I'll try the museum,' says a young man, heading to a faintly musty set filled with splendid antiques and Wimbledon memorabilia. 'Care to join me?'

'Oh, do go on without me. I'll mill around here,' replies his partner, joining the common multitude at the Member's Entrance.

'What the heck for?' asks Justin.

'To gape at the Rolls and Bentleys ushering in royalty!' replies the Spirit.

'Royalty?'

'Indeed! Wimbledon treats all competitors royally, chauffeuring them in stately limousines. Here's one now!'

The throng gathers round to ogle a pretty chauffeur ferrying a player in a limousine flying the Wimbledon colours of mauve and green on a small pennon from its bonnet.

'Who's that bugger?'

'Not sure!' dismisses the Spirit loftily. 'Must come from the Gloucester!'

'Huh?'

'That's the official players' hotel. The stars, indicated by not staying there, converge from the plush hotels of London. Here you can also catch a fleeting glimpse of kings and queens, presidents and prime ministers, and film stars, pop stars, and sports stars, because anybody who is somebody makes a trip to Wimbledon!'

Other spectators indulge in delicacies from the Food Village or Wimbledon souvenirs.

'Ice lollies. Keep cool on court.'

'Brollies. Keep dry on court.'

'Programmes. Keep informed on court.'

'Of course, coming to Wimbledon would not be complete without sampling strawberries and cream and a glass of Pimms. But be warned, if you're a nobody, expect your fare dished up in polystyrene and plastic.'

'And the somebodies?' asks Justin, savouring a juicy Kent berry.

'Oh, they repose on lawns in the Member's Enclosure under white parasols, and delight in lobster and best-end-of-lamb salad, and strawberries in Devonshire cream washed down with champagne.'

'Hmm! Class distinction at Wimbledon!' comments Justin, feigning snootiness.

'Indeed! And not only for the spectators but for the players, too! Wimbledon divides locker-rooms into 1 and 2, the former for the seeded players and past champions, housed in the clubhouse, the latter for the plebeians, way out over there in the field courts.'

Borg and McEnroe are both in locker-room 1. Like violinists before a concert they tune their equipment. Borg tests his rackets, checking the tension, his harpsichord session all part of his meticulous striving for perfection. McEnroe swats the air with his weapon. He has excess nervous energy to dissipate, and winds down his temper.

'Who runs this tournament?' asks Justin.

'Oh, it's offered by The All England Lawn Tennis & Croquet Club, a most exclusive society, I might say! Becoming a member is more rare than knighthood, and probably more coveted, too!'

'Hmm! Perhaps the easiest way to become a member is to win their bloody tournament!' chuckles Justin, aware that the club traditionally bestows honourary membership upon the singles champions.

'Perhaps!' agrees the Spirit. 'But whatever their exclusivity, the fellows do a jolly fine job of running The Championships. That's what the hoity-toity insiders call it, as if no other tournament exists! To us *hoi polloi*, of course, the greatest tennis tournament in the world is simply, 'Wimbledon'.'

They enter the Member's Entrance, and in the foyer near the case that holds the perpetual trophies, Justin quickly discovers large green and gold plaques of burnished mahogany inscribed with the names of Wimbledon winners.

Perry won it three times. McEnroe, too! Laver won it four times. Borg five, successively. Justin Forrester?

'Come!' whispers the Spirit. 'Let's sneak a look at the Royal Box!'

'Is that allowed?'

'Oh, no! Invitation is by decree of the Royal family or the approval of the committee. They have this large blue book, you know, embossed with Royal Box in letters of gold, which records such privileged visits, and includes dignitaries from King George and Queen Mary to Queen

Elizabeth and her daughters-in-law Princess Di and Princess Fergie, and, of course, the Duke and Duchess of Kent. But we'll just nip in!'

After a journey through the narrow, twisting corridors in the bowels of the three storey dodecagon, climbing stairs to new decks, they emerge into the Royal Box.

'Wow!' gasps Justin, as the mystical, often unfathomable Centre Court casts its spell on him, cutting the clamour and seething crush outside its walls, creating a sudden stunning silence like closing a door on a crowded room.

The Spirit of Wimbledon says nothing, just smiles. He knows the magic is born.

'Mmm!' sighs Justin, his eyes quickly surveying the hallowed Centre Court, soaking up the antiquated elegance and charm of this special place. Staring, mesmerised by the celebrated prospect, he reflects, 'A place I've read and fantasised about since I was a boy. ... To think this is where the great champions of the past have graced the game of tennis.'

'Indeed!' replies the Spirit, inhaling a deep breath. 'If I'm not mistaken I can feel the giddy charm of Evonne and almost smell the perfume of Chris left after their battle of British ma'ams here yesterday.'

Justin sits quietly, totally absorbed.

'Oh, Charlton Heston is here today,' discovers the Spirit. 'What do you think of this Centre Court?'

'It's like the gladiators, you know. Like an amphitheatre. The Centre Court is the Palladium, the Mecca of anything you care to name of any sport, of any profession. Every tennis player in the world dreams of playing on that court. And, you know, soccer has the World Cup in different places. The same with American World Series and the Super Bowl. And boxing championships are held in different places. But the most important tournament in tennis is played in this club, and the most important match is played on that court!'

'And that match is about to be played!' relishes Justin, eagerly awaiting the finalists in a Centre Court mood of great expectation. 'Borg versus McEnroe!'

Justin's mind reflects back to his first Wimbledon, listening to the BBC World Service at his home in Tshaneni.

'A very good afternoon to you. This is Peter Jones at Wimbledon, the final day of the 1980 championships. The clouds are high, but it's dry and bright and the forecast is good for the men's singles final. Can Björn Borg, at 24, win his fifth consecutive title this afternoon, and so write a new record that might never be equalled? Or will the Irish-American, John McEnroe, win the title in his very first final?

'And the two men couldn't be more different in temperament and in style. Björn Borg, the classic Swede, blond, lean and ice-cool, but burning with ambition.

'Yesterday when we spoke with Björn Borg, he has this to say, 'I've been winning Wimbledon now for four times, so I know how it feels to hold that trophy up on the last day. And that's a wonderful feeling. You're probably the most happiest guy in the world at that moment, because that was my dream when I started to play, is to win Wimbledon, and I think it's everybody's dream, just to have that pleasure to win that last point in the final, and then 5 or 10 minutes afterwards to hold up that cup. I mean that's the most wonderful feeling you can ever have."

Peter Jones continues, 'John McEnroe, the number two seed, the brash Irish-American, pugnacious, highly self-critical and a fierce competitor. When he contested a linecall in the early stages of his match with Connors, the roof fell in.'

Umpire: 'Well no, no! The call came before the ball was played and—'
McEnroe: 'He never even called it.'
Umpire: 'Well, no, yes he called—'
McEnroe: 'No. He never said anything.'
Umpire: 'He called a fault. '
McEnroe: 'He didn't call a fault. He just went like that.'
Umpire: 'And he called a fault!'
McEnroe: 'He—'
Umpire: 'Play a let, please!'
McEnroe: 'Can I have the referee, please?'
Umpire: 'No, no, not, not, no, no—'
McEnroe: 'I'd like the referee.'
Umpire: 'You must play on.'
McEnroe: 'I feel I have the right to get the referee.'
Umpire: 'Mr McEnroe, you are getting a public warning. Now please play on.'

Peter Jones continues, 'Well you can be sure that the volcano of John McEnroe could well erupt if things go wrong against the iceberg of Björn Borg. But it could be a great final.

'… So as the minutes tick away here at Wimbledon, we come closer to the high point of any championships, the men's singles final, Björn Borg against John McEnroe.'

It is time! A Wimbledon official calls Borg and McEnroe. He takes them to a waiting-room, but before entering they pass, perhaps not noticing, but aware of an archway inscribed with Rudyard Kipling's stirring challenge, 'If you can meet with Triumph and Disaster and treat those two Impostors just the same'.

'That final wait in this empty room is akin to awaiting your execution call to the gas chamber, so they say,' whispers the Spirit. 'It is quiet and eerie for some. The regal surroundings, the hushed galleries, the legendary figures that step out of the record books to watch the current generation, and the ever present sense of history, haunts them, reminding how much is at stake. For others like Björn and Boris, and Martina and Billie Jean, it's coming back home. Aah! Here's Newk. What have you to say about this Centre Court?'

'When you walk onto that Centre Court,' replies John Newcombe, three time champion, 'it's like jumping into a bottomless pit. You can find out anything you want to know about a person by putting him on that court. It's an ultimate test of the self, an examination of your desires and abilities. What happens on the Centre Court is that a player's character unravels, strand by strand.'

Finally the moment the world over has been waiting for, arrives. Borg and McEnroe, the two gladiators, make their way through the frosted glass doors, and led by Leo the locker-room attendant, a porcupine under an assortment of rackets, they enter the hallowed shrine.

'The gentlemen's singles final, the blue riband of tennis! The one they all want to win,' says the Spirit. 'Oh, here's Nasty. You care about winning Wimbledon?'

'I care?' asks the supremely gifted, enigmatic Ilie Nastase. 'I tell you how I care. I have a dream that comes to me all the time during Wimbledon. Finally I win. I win this son-of-a-bitch tournament. Then I take my trophy and I go all around that crazy stadium, bowing to the people and giving the finger to everybody. Then I take my rackets, and break them up with my hands. Then I throw them in the river and I stop playing tennis.'

'Nastase has never won Wimbledon,' the Spirit whispers to Justin, 'but he cares! Win Wimbledon and you win the world!'

As the Centre Court erupts in applause, Justin concurs, 'Yep! One thing's for sure, Borg and McEnroe care. They'll battle to the death this afternoon to win this most coveted of championships.'

Peter Jones of the BBC, '*And here, two men so very different in temperament, so different in style. And John McEnroe with that scarlet headband, keeping that brown hair tidy, and that red and blue track suit top.*

'*And Björn Borg, again looking as if he's strolling around the island that he owns off the Swedish coast. He looks so relaxed, again with the headband and the long blond hair. I suppose you could call him the classic Swede. Tall and blond and quiet and cool. I remember last week when he came off Court number one, surrounded by teenagers, hundreds of them, literally, and about six or seven policemen guarding Borg, it looked really quite frightening to me, and Borg looked neither to left nor right, those ice-cool eyes looking straight ahead. Doesn't seem to be affected by anything at all. Somebody was saying the other day he looks as if he's made of enamel. He can't be scratched, he can't be bruised. But certainly, I think there'll be a fair amount of seething going on inside him, because we know how ambitious he is.*

'So, Björn Borg, the classic Swede going for five consecutive titles, a record in fact that might never be equalled in tennis history. He's already had a record 34 successive wins here, and when it's all over, so I'm told, he's going to have a couple of days on that Swedish island, because what he likes is peace and quiet, and John McEnroe.'

The players come out to play, Borg at the Royal Box-end, McEnroe tying his shoelaces. The crowd is absolutely agog.

'Quiet please, ladies and gentlemen,' calls the umpire. 'McEnroe to serve.'

The charged crowd screams.

'Ladies and gentlemen will you please not call out as a player is about to serve,' instructs the umpire sternly. 'Thank you.'

Silence finally descends.

'Play!'

McEnroe serves from the Roller-end and wins on the volley. First blood to the American.

'Hubba hubba! Mac's start is sensational,' expresses a surprised Justin, 'like a greyhound out of its block!'

'Game and first set to McEnroe, by six games to one,' announces the umpire, a set that is brief and to the point, offering little of the drama to come.

The iceman comes back to snatch the second set out of the clutches of the magician, 7-5, and then the keeper of the Wimbledon castle surges ahead to take the third, 6-3.

'The contrasts are a beaut!' marvels Justin.

'Splendid indeed!'

The left-handed McEnroe, wizard with the volcanic temper, gifted to the hilt to win on grass, slices wide to the two-hander, determined to unseat the champion. The counter, the right-handed Borg, cool as an iceberg, not meant to win on grass with his patient baseline game, races in from yards back with astonishing speed of foot to cut off the angle, executing a rapier backhand pass. But McEnroe dives and intercepts on the volley, sending Borg scuttling across the lawn ...

The elliptical shape as perceived from inside the Elizabethan theatre, serves to heighten spectator concentration on the centre, stage of the unfolding drama. So, during points, the crowd hushes and the sweet sound of the ball against the taut gut of Borg's racket is mellifluous against the dull echo of McEnroe's wand, and has the effect of throwback to yesteryear.

'Wimbledon may be an enclave of old England, you know,' rambles the Spirit, 'a heritage that is stately, traditional and very, very British, where they still quaintly call people ladies and gentlemen, but it is an anachronism yearned for, because the paradox that Wimbledon changes without changing exists too. That's her timeless charm, dare I say.'

'What do you mean?' questions Justin, puzzled.

'Aah! Polished wooden netposts crafted with brass fittings working alongside the magical eye of Cyclops and a Rolex digital scoreboard! ... Players swinging high tech Kevlar-Boron-Ceramic widebodies to hit Slazenger balls used since 1902, in a game no longer played elsewhere on grass! ... Discreet white coolers attached to the same umpire's chair that has displayed an assortment of Robinson's Barley Water since time immemorial, contain Coca-Cola! And—'

'Oh, I see!' interrupts Justin, the penny dropping. 'Hordes of schoolgirls screaming at the sight of their idols, while just over there, those royalty buggers sit erect in their box and gently clap hands after that extraordinary Borg passing shot!'

'Indeed! Somehow, Wimbledon has straddled two worlds with remarkable success, inextricably binding the present and future in the past. She is a cradle of history, a treasure trove of memories.'

'Yep! You can feel it in the air, it's almost tangible,' marvels Justin.

'Tell me what you see.'

'Hmm! Dainty ladies frocked in long hooped dresses, patting balls on sprawling lawns with gentleman in long white flannels, who echo, 'Jolly good shot, old chap!'' mimics Justin in a snooty voice. "Time for elevenses!' so the buggers stop for freshly squeezed lemon juice or hot tea served in fine china from a silver teapot. 'Anyone for tennis?"

Both chuckle.

'Come with me,' beckons the Spirit.

'But we'll miss this great match!' protests Justin.

'Just for a moment!'

They make their way to the sun-decked roof of the Player's Tearoom and lean against the guardrail. From this high vantage point of the ivy-covered stadium, they absorb the splendour that is Wimbledon. Spread out before them against an idyllic landscape of plane trees and poplars swaying and soughing in a gentle breeze on Wimbledon hill with its distinctive silhouette of the St Mary's Church spire, is a panoramic festival of tennis on the outside courts.

'Those courts, each framed by neatly clipped hedges and paved walkways, they're like stamps, rare ones, penny greens!' reveres Justin. 'And on each a story unfolds.'

The Spirit merely smiles.

Spectators roam the picturesque grounds, sampling a feast of tennis. The colour is green, a special Wimbledon green designed for a calming effect, laced with pastel pinks and blues of hydrangeas.

Breathing in the scent from beds of climbing roses and fresh grass cuttings which permeate the air, and hearing the sound of tennis balls popping like champagne corks, Justin sighs, 'The ambience is so beautiful here, one of a lavish but genteel garden party, a unique atmosphere that is forever Wimbledon!'

'Shut your eyes and you'll commune with the spirits of Wimbledon.'

Justin closes his eyes and strolls down the memory lanes between the grass courts, and the ghosts of Wimbledon come out to play.

'This Wimbledon thing,' says the Spirit, 'it all happened, well, quite by accident, you know, when these All England Croquet Club fellows decided to hold a tournament to raise funds to mend their broken pony roller!'

'A croquet tournament?' asks Justin, surprised.

'Oh no! A tennis tournament. A game rooted in inauspicious historical occasions, dare I say!'

'Inauspicious?'

'Oh, yes! They say that Henry VIII preferred playing real tennis at Hampton Court whilst Anne's head rolled! And those fellows across the channel, the, uh, the French, they signed that 'tennis court oath' before starting their messy revolution thing!' the Spirit says distastefully.

'Were you there?'

'Really! How old do you think I am?'

'Um—'

'Ahem! Of course, that was 'real tennis'. The trouble with real tennis was that you had to play it indoors. Legend has it, that some players got bored waiting for a court and started to hit a ball on the grass outside—'

'Giving birth to lawn tennis?'

'No, not quite. You see, the lawn mower had not yet been invented. So it was not until much later when a Major Walter Clopton Wingfield patented his game 'Sphairistiké' on the 23rd February 1874 that we got any resemblance to lawn tennis.'

'This 'hairy sticky' stuff, did it catch on?' asks Justin, intrigued.

'Indeed! Caught the fancy of royals. But it wasn't until 1877, that The All England Croquet Club decided to hold an All-Comers' tournament, announcing their intentions in the FIELD magazine.'

'The All England Lawn Tennis and Croquet Club, Wimbledon, propose to hold a lawn tennis meeting open to all amateurs, on Monday, July 9, and following days; entrance £1. 1s. … Two prizes will be given – one gold champion prize to the winner, one silver to the second player.'

'Who's that bugger under an umbrella?' asks Justin curiously.

'The fellow in white flannel and helmet?'

'Uh huh!'

'Oh, that's the raging eccentric, Henry Jones, the tournament referee. A doctor fellow and very shrewd, I might add. Instrumental in forming all these fancy new rules of tennis!'

'Dispense with 'rackets' scoring!' ordered Dr Jones.

'Why?' wonders Justin.

'Doesn't want to follow those fellows across the way at Marylebone Cricket Club. Never does!'

'The All England Lawn Tennis & Croquet Club will follow real tennis scoring,' declared Dr Jones.

'Real tennis scoring?'

'Well, a bit before my time, of course,' says the Spirit hastily, 'but they say an onlooker scored a match using a clock overlooking the court. With each point scored, he moved one hand a quarter, to 15, then to 30 and 45, and finally to twelve o'clock, for a game won. In later years, 40 replaced 45, for convenience, so they tell me!'

'And what of this weird shape for a court? Nice for a lady, but tennis?'

'Dispense with the hourglass shape and adopt a rectangular court,' ordered the doctor.

'There's the first champion,' points the Spirit. 'Crafty fellow that Spencer Gore. Look at him rushing to the net and hitting the ball on the fly.'

'I can't blame the bugger. Look at the net, it's chest high! How can anyone pass him?' says Justin, admiring the champion's decision to volley.

'Mr Gore, sir! What do you think of this newfangled sport of lawn tennis?'

'Boring! It will never last. Too tepid and monotonous!'

'Did the buggers at the club make a profit?' asks Justin.

'Oh, yes!' replied the Spirit. 'Ten pounds, if my memory serves me correctly. A bit before my time, mind you! But a splendid showing. Prompted them to do it again.'

'Why isn't this Gore bugger defending his title?'

'Oh, he most certainly is. They did rather strange things in those early years. Gore's waiting in the Challenge Round for the All-Comers' champion.'

'So he goes straight to the *final?*'

'Indeed! Here he's playing that fellow, uh, the one who suffered from sunstroke, uh, Frank Haddow. He's also despairing of Gore's aggressive netplay. Can't pass him!'

'Why doesn't the bugger lob?' Justin asks.

After many failed attempts at passing, Haddow risks hoisting a shot high in the air, flummoxing Gore and the champion never recovers.

'So we can thank or curse Mr Haddow for giving birth to the lob!' jokes the Spirit.

'And what of the ladies?'

'Aah, they got their turn eight years later when Maud Watson won the first championship. But it was Lottie Dod who set the ladies' game alight.'

'The 'Little Wonder'?'

'Yes, and no wonder. You see, she could move! Being so young at 15, she could get away with playing in a scandalously short dress. Above her ankles, it was!'

'Who's the 'Washerwoman'?'

'May Sutton. Hmm! ... I wonder if they all roll up their sleeves in, uh, what's that place called, uh, America. She was the first foreigner to win a title at The Championships!'

'You mean all the rest were *Brits?*'

'Don't be too surprised! You must remember that, in those days, most who played were Brits, so not many winners weren't Brits!'

'That Gore bugger was right. This is pretty tepid stuff.'

'But not for long! ... Suzanne Lenglen! Ballerina of the courts!' beams the Spirit. 'Look at those half-length dresses of silk with no petticoat, revealing her silhouette! The first time on court anyone has seen a woman's shape! ... Suzanne would become the idol of women the world over, but she later snubs the Queen and is never seen at Wimbledon again.'

'And the 'Poker-Face'?'

'Helen Wills. She wears that peak so no one can see her eyes in that sculptured face. Marvellous concentration.'

'Hmm! So the ladies' secret, it seems, lies in their attire,' discovers Justin.

'Indeed! But I never could quite find out! Legend has it that only two men have ever entered the Ladies' Dressing-Room. A Frenchman and a blind masseur! The Frenchman was none other than the 'Bounding

Basque', Jean Borotra. They saw to it that he lost his crown that year!'

'You obviously love it here?'

'Oh, indeed! From the Renshaw twins to the Doherty duo, the Four Musketeers to Hopman's dynasty, 'Big Bill' to 'Little Mo'. … Long white flannels and hoop skirts to shorts and wrap-arounds, Worple Road to Church Road, Royal Box to standing room. … The magic that is The Championships. I've seen it all.'

'Really! How old are you, then?' asks Justin slyly.

'Ahem!' the Spirit cleared his throat before changing the subject. 'Of course, rain stops play many times! But marvellous groundsmen, these. Covering the court in 38 seconds!'

'Why's the champion doing high jump?'

'Shamateurism! You see, in the amateur days players were not allowed to receive money prizes, so the referee would make a money bet with the winner by challenging him, say, to jump over a small table and—'

'Oh, I see! So they secretly paid the champion under the table for jumping over it!'

'Yes! But not for long. The public have this misconception, you know, that The All England Club is tradition bound! Predominantly white clothing, and all that stuff. But in 1968 the club opened its doors to the professionals! One small step for Wimbledon, one giant leap for tennis! Now we could see Pancho Gonzales and Ken Rosewall and Lew Hoad play in the same tournament as John Newcombe and Roy Emerson and Tony Roche.'

'And Rod Laver?'

'Oh yes! The amateurs caused havoc with the seasoned pros that year, but there was no stopping Rod.'

'He was always my coach's favourite,' enthuses Justin.

'There he is again, the next year. The small redhead with freckles. You wouldn't believe he could hit a ball so hard! Oh, it's one set all and he's 2-4 down in the third. You are in for a treat!'

Just days before man lands on the moon, the 'Rocket' karate-chops a passing shot, unexplained with calliper measurement, past a flabbergasted John Newcombe to win the last of his four titles and goes on to achieve the Grand Slam.'

'Oh I say! What a peach!' interjects that doyen of commentators, Dan Maskell.

'A year later, here's Margaret Court beating the irrepressible Billie Jean King. They're both injured, would you believe! This match stretches interminably, the longest ever ladies' final, 14-12 11-9, if I remember correctly. Maggie goes on to match her countryman with a Grand Slam and Australian tennis stands proud, but not for long.'

'Why not?'

'Well, Billie Jean won that Battle of the Sexes thing that they had in, uh, what's that place called again, uh, America. Beat Bobby Riggs, you know, the 1939 Wimbledon champion. That conceived the tennis boom and the game has never been the same since!'

'What do you mean?'

'Oh, it's hard to explain. Tennis was once a genteel sport played in white, now colour television brings new pop stars into our lives, players with long hair grunting their way to ever increasing prize money.'

'But the tennis seems pretty darn good!'

'Indeed! Look at Ilie Nastase there, supremely gifted clown entertaining with double features of breathtaking tennis and the finger. He's a corporal in the Romanian army, you know, and here he's waging war in a 1972 classic with an American lieutenant, Stan Smith. He gets unnerved and loses, but he'll be back to try again.'

'Where is everybody?' asks Justin, looking round in bewilderment.

'Oh, it must be 1973. Horror of horrors, the men players boycotted Wimbledon this year! But I don't really want to talk about that. Besides, it's just the quiet before the storm.'

'Storm?'

'Borgomania, they call it! Look at those schoolgirl groupies chasing after their Swedish idol, running onto the Centre Court. Whatever will the committee make of it?'

As they stroll through an unfolding Wimbledon history, Justin remarks, 'I see that the two-hander has come into fashion!'

'Yes, quite a revolution, that, Jimmy Connors and Chris Evert swapping their tennis text books for double-handed backhands and dancing the night away at the Wimbledon Ball as champions and sweethearts.'

'But now it's Borg time!'

'Indeed! Here's your Viking fellow now. Not expected to win Wimbledon with that flick of the wrist ping pong style. But the year 1976 launches a new chapter of tennis history with the seemingly never ending story of Björn Borg as he captures the first of a handful of summers.'

Borg: 'For sure, I wanted to win it. It's my first Wimbledon title.'

'And he never lost a set!' praises the Spirit. 'Marvellous athlete that!'

'Who are those buggers in the Royal Box?'

'Aah, Her Royal Majesty is here. It must be 1977. A hundred years have passed, so a time for nostalgia, pomp and pageantry for the Wimbledon Centenary! Here they come, 80 years old and more, all the living singles champions parading on court in time to 'March Of The

Kings' by the Band of the Welsh Guards, each receiving silver commemorative medals from the president of the club, HRH Duke of Kent. There's that American fellow, uh, Jack Kramer … and Maria Bueno. She played like a swan, so graceful. Oh, and Budge. I still remember him in long white flannels. And Kitty Godfree, the oldest, bless her heart. She still plays, I believe.'

As the great gladiators of the past join arms and sing Auld Lang Syne in a toast to the champions, young and old, there is not a dry eye in the house.

'A splendid time for a British victory,' Justin poses.

'Dare we hope, especially after all these years of titillating disappointment? But you're right!'

Amid emotional scenes never witnessed before at Wimbledon, Virgina Wade, in front of Her Majesty Queen Elizabeth II celebrating her Jubilee Year, flies the Union Jack.

'Couldn't have scripted that better myself!' beams the Spirit.

The men's programme has nothing to do with homeland patriotism, but for quality tennis, it is sensational. Borg emerges slightly more feline than rodent in his semifinal cat and mouse affair with the Lithuanian Lion, Vitas Gerulaitus, then holds a 4-0 lead in the final set against Jimmy Connors. The crowd boos Connors when he comes on court, the villain for snubbing the Parade of Past Champions, but cheers him as a hero as he valiantly expunges his deficit.

'A great fighter, this Jimmy, but here it comes, the double fault,' announces the Spirit. 'Can you believe after that amazing comeback he doesn't win another point!'

Borg: 'For sure, I wanted to defend my title. It's Centenary Wimbledon.'

Borg: 'For sure, I wanted a hat trick.'

'Who holds the record for most Wimbledon titles?' asks Justin.

'Funny you should ask that. Until today it was Elizabeth Ryan. She won 19 Wimbledon titles, all doubles in the early part of the century, and she stated earlier this year that she would never like to see her record broken. Sadly, in a way, she got her wish because only yesterday she collapsed and died in the Wimbledon grounds, aged 87, and her record defied all challengers until this day in 1979 when, as you can see, Billie Jean King is about to win her 20th title!'

'Truth stranger than fiction!'

'Talking of records, your Borg fellow is building up quite a tally. There he is at match point against Roscoe Tanner from Lookout Mountain, Tennessee in their titanic five set shootout. He will say his hand shook so much at match point he feared he would drop his racket.

Nobody will believe him.'

Borg: 'For sure, I wanted to win and break Fred Perry's record.'

'I see they have introduced Cyclops. What did Nastase think of the one-eyed monster?' asks Justin.

'There he is tapping it with his racket!'

Suspiciously, Nastase bends down and puts an ear to the service line calling machine, stands up and claims, 'Made in Russia!'

'Always the clown!' laughs the Spirit.

'You said earlier that the Brits won most of the titles when Wimbledon first started. Has that changed?'

'Oh, yes! Mind you, Chris Lloyd and Evonne Cawley are contesting the ladies' final here today in 1980.'

'But they're not British!'

'Aah, but you see, they are both married to Brits!'

Justin laughed, 'You buggers will take anything!'

'Well, it's going to be a long time before a Brit ever wins Wimbledon again.'

'Then why do you look so excited. You're not anti-British, are you?' asks Justin.

'No, no, no! It's just that we are about to witness something very special. As happy as we Brits were with the enchantment of that ladies' final yesterday, it pales to insignificance compared with this match today where McEnroe wins the battle of the tiebreaker, but Borg wins the war.'

Borg: 'For sure, I'm very, very satisfied now!'

'King Borg V lost his crown, so did the new king, but there was no stopping Queen Martina.'

'What's the buzz?' asks Justin, bewildered

'Oh an upset must be on the cards,' informs the Spirit, as urgent whispers swirl like gusty winds through the stands, echoing the shifting tides of a match. A horde of vultures congregates on the balcony overlooking Court 2.

'The 'graveyard' court?'

'Indeed! Top players say this court is jinxed and play on it in trepidation. Tales of the curse prey on their minds.'

'Jinxed by the jinx!'

'Mmm! Rumour has it that the curse has roots in royalty. In 1926, year of the Jubilee Championship, the Duke of York, later King George VI, became the first member of royalty to contest the Wimbledon championships. Last, too, I might add! A dilemma arose. His tennis would embarrass on the stadium courts, but his status would be disgraced on an outside court so they compromised. He played on Court 2, and lost! Legend decrees he put a hex on this court. So say those old

Wimbledon hands McEnroe, Nastase, Ashe and Wade. They've buried title aspirations there.'

'Now it seems Connors, too!'

'Perhaps Jimbo feels the same way about the Centre Court. He can't hold this McEnroe down today in this 1984 final!'

'Sublime tennis, if I may say!' Justin said in awe of McEnroe's talent.

'Indeed! But another storm is brewing. The power game. Lightning strikes in 1985 with Curren blasting McEnroe and Connors for a grand total loss of 13 games, only to lose to Boom Boom Becker.

'Live by the serve, die by the serve!' says Justin sagely.

'If only they knew then what they know now! In the old days, before my time, of course, it was beneath a nobleman to start a point, so he had a servant come on the court and do it for him. Hence the term 'serve'!'

Finally, Queen Martina abdicates her throne.

'Aah! Here's Steffi Graf! A marvellous athlete! What a joy to watch!'

'Change your racket, Steffi!' whispers Justin.

She does! Down a set and 0-2 in the 1988 final, the princess in waiting launches the most awesome display of scintillating winners ever seen on the Centre Court of Wimbledon, winning in style. Steffi tosses that same racket into the crowd with such *joie de vivre*, and goes on to achieve the Grand Slam.

'Do you always come to Wimbledon?' Justin asks the Spirit.

'Oh, I wouldn't miss it for the world!'

An urgent call taps Justin on the shoulder.

'Come, McEnroe is down 4-5 and two match points in the fourth set against the champion.'

Magically, he plays four majestic points out of his endless well of genius. The set heads to a tiebreaker, and the tennis transcends into the realm of high theatre.

'This is Wimbledon's finest hour!' beams the Spirit. 'Every second point becomes either a set point for McEnroe or a championship point for Borg. What sudden switches of fortune!'

The ice-Borg and the volcanic-Mac lock in a deadly test of skill and will for the sport's most prestigious prize. There are winners off seeming winners, passing shots of pinpoint accuracy, volleys feathered on the stretch, a dead netcord winner defuses a match point, and each player is knocked down to the turf in their death defying attempts to win these vital points.

The spectators are absolutely agog, screaming crescendos of support between points, and biting their nails with nerves during play, hanging onto every point of this spine-chilling, excruciatingly tense, heart attack stuff. In the Viking homeland, the streets and beaches lie empty, and 52 Swedes give up their ghosts watching this crucible of nerve-jangling fare. And after 21 minutes, at which stage fate has thwarted Borg of seven championship points, and McEnroe six set points, the American wins the tiebreaker by 18-16. The fans are exhausted, but there is more to come.

'A marvellous match player, this fellow Borg, consummately imperturbable,' states the Spirit of Wimbledon. 'He loses the first two points here at the start of the fifth set, but then serves out of a mountain, losing just a single point in the last 27, if my memory serves me correctly. It's only a matter of time before this obstinate McEnroe will succumb.'

Just short of four hours, Borg leads 7-6 in the fifth set. At 15-40, McEnroe, without a flicker of temper in this marathon match, his villain tag removed, settles to serve from the 'Roller-end', containing the same pony roller that inspired the first tournament, now too large to remove, and instead, serves as a nostalgic beacon in providing a name opposite the 'Royal Box-end'.

Headband pulled low above the eyes, body crouched and feet lithely pattering on the brown turf in anticipation, Borg once more faces the volcanic fury that has pushed him so close to the edge of the cliff. The arena hushes to a loud silence, agonizingly enduring the slow scissor-like wind up, awaiting the impending attack.

Finally, a grunt propels the white ball towards the impenetrable castle. First, a topspin backhand return sets up the swansong, then Borg's strong, sinewy wrists dig deep and explode upwards into the face of the ball, raking through a crosscourt backhand pass to diffuse the opponent's assault and quench the volatile fire to a whimper. Amid tumultuous applause, he sinks to his knees in relief, as all rise to hail King Borg V.

As the crescendo of applause dies down on the match historians will regard as the greatest ever played, there is a tinge of sadness that it is all over.

'Never mind,' consoles the Spirit of Wimbledon, 'only 50 more weeks until Wimbledon!'

… thanks for the memories!

Justin woke from these memories bathed in the romantic glow of the past. The evening hushed quiet in the extended twilight of late spring, and the famous old Centre Court lay silent, sleeping like an empty cathedral. Even the swish of mower blades was absent, the impeccable grooming almost complete.

He sat in the Royal Box, alone, and gazed at the Centre Court the way some people stare into a log fire, and reminisced, *Borg versus McEnroe*

... Wimbledon 1980 ... the dream, my passion to become the greatest tennis player in the world!

In a week's time, four elderly ladies from the club, frocked in pure white, of course, would play a set and a half of doubles to break in the court, and allow the groundsman to assess the vintage of the lawn and address the final touches, if necessary. Otherwise, there had been no play since the Chairman's Game on the Tuesday following last year's championships, when a group of club officials played a ceremonial match signalling the closure of that tournament. In the interim, 350 days of work, of scary scarifying, replanting, watering, rolling and mowing, with groundsmen on hands and knees furnishing loads of tender loving care.

As The Fortnight approached, the court would be mowed to a height difference of the width of a tennis string, with cuttings so fine they resemble dust, and would fit in the palms of two hands, rolled to look velvet green and lined with whiting, given a drink and put to bed under a cover, all in readiness for The Great English Garden Party.

In the next few days, jets from all corners of the globe converged on London. Aboard, travelled a cosmopolitan army of modern day Vikings, professional tennis players, each burning to plunder a little corner of South-West London to conquer the biggest prize of all.

Six weeks before the first Monday in August, Justin's debut Wimbledon arrived.

'Wow!' exclaimed Justin, on learning that the committee had scheduled him, the 7th seed, to play second match on, where else, Centre Court. *That's such a thrill. Many players have combatted at the Big W for a lifetime without ever setting foot on that cherished Centre Court.*

Justin's first venture on opening day was a surprise visit to the BBC world service radio commentary booth, seed of his dream.

So this is where the dream began!

His curiosity satisfied, he joined his International Management Group representative, Marco Ponti.

Justin sat in a blue wicker chair in the Player's Lounge, the meat market of tennis, where big businesses conclude high-priced deals with the pedlars of their products, the players. So many thousands or millions for wearing a company logo on their sleeves. And not lire or yen, but dollars or pounds! For top players, this avenue of income can outweigh prize money many fold. It all depends on star quality, the right mix of popularity, likeability and believability.

'It might be presumptuous to speculate on your chances of winning Wimbledon,' commented Marco, 'but the outcome here will be crucial to your endorsement potential. You are already hot property, especially with British companies who are champing at the bit to contract you. Still, if you win Wimbledon, you'll be dynamite. But should you—'

'If I cock it up, my value will be sullied!' interjected Justin.

'Right!'

'So you want to know if I should sign now or risk the outcome of Wimbledon.'

'Right!'

Flushed with success at Roland Garros, his expectations high, Justin pondered his chances of winning Wimbledon. *Only Rod Laver and Björn Borg have won the French and Wimbledon duple in the professional era ... Hmm! To cross the great divide from the gruelling marathons on the slow clay courts of Roland Garros, to the explosive cut and thrust one twos on the fast grass of Wimbledon, in a matter of two weeks, is a severe test in tennis. And all the money in the game has brought about specialisation of style to suit court surfaces, making it bloody difficult to win on both fast and slow courts. It's true, I don't possess the one-dimensional brick wall defence Sern Stenmark has on clay, nor do I own the brutal serve that brought Roland Drechsler his Wimbledon title on grass, but I complement my all-court game with my legs. I was born to run, I'm fast, and my legs carry my greatest weapon, my mind. I learned my game on clay, that nurtured mental toughness, but I'm also a natural player, a gift on grass, where every point played is a crisis.*

'Delay any decision until after Wimbledon,' Justin confidently told Marco Ponti.

He glanced up at a TV monitor that beamed the end of the opening match featuring Roland Drechsler. As defending champion, it was the German's privilege to open proceedings.

I wish that were me! One day, I'll have that privilege.

At last his time came to take centre stage in the world of tennis. Stepping onto the hallowed Centre Court, adrenalin pumped through his body. Around him, the stadium reverberated as if he had already won the match.

Mmm! That sounds good!

For Justin, nothing came close to the sound of applause to arouse his senses and prime his game to offer more to receive.

I love this place Wimbledon, especially this Centre Court, coveted Justin. *This is home!*

His opponent was the Russian qualifier, Vladimir Vsevolozhsky, a name to put 'she sells seas shells on the sea shore' in the kindergarten bracket. Umpires warned their peers to be tee-total when taking the court with Vladimir Vsevolozhsky.

But on grass they need not have worried. They could have joined the

Russian under the weather, because he played on grass as if he smoked it!

He had battled his way through three qualifying rounds at Roehampton the week before, and now wished for a giant rock to hide behind. The infamous Wimbledon nerves struck his body rigid. But this court offered not the slightest hint of even the tiniest pebble! On this first day of the championships, it was like velvet.

Justin did not disappoint his fans. He was quicker and more scythingly penetrating than Vladimir Vsevolozhsky could ever have imagined. His skills proved too much for the hapless qualifier and he raced to a 6-2 6-2 2-0 lead. That there was no contest did not bother his fans, some who had travelled many miles to watch the saviour of British tennis. The exhibition of Justin's superb grass court skills amply compensated.

Then the rain came. It would just not be Wimbledon without a dose of fine drizzle! The ball began to resemble a mango pip and the court became slippery.

Call off the bloody match! Justin mentally urged the umpire.

He tapped his shoes to aid traction — European clay habits die hard —and played another point.

Shit! Does the umpire think I'm going to beat the rain? Does he think calling off the match will stir a riot? Come on! Damn!

'Hey, Rusky! Agree to stop?' asked Justin, rain pelting down in his face.

They jointly abandoned play.

They waited and waited in the locker-room. The erroneously perceived glamorous world of tennis is actually a succession of bitter confrontations, punctuated with oodles of boring waiting, and waiting, and waiting. Waiting in airports through flight delays, waiting for matches to end for yours to start, and waiting for rain to let up to continue a match. This is the lifestyle of a professional tennis player. The difficulty is having to switch one's concentration off and on in an instant. To bide their time, players strap on Walkmans or play backgammon. Justin slept.

On the second point upon resumption of play, Justin served, and made a beeline towards the net to volley. On checking his flight to pick the direction of the return, his foot caved in on the slippery T-junction, and he fell on his butt. But instinct driving him on, Justin rose without the use of his hands, hit a winner, then came crashing down and lay supine on the turf nursing a twisted right ankle.

'Aagh!' Justin cried out, grimacing, but quickly masked his face. *Never show a weakness.*

The crowd emitted a deep bellow and went silent, like a dying animal sighing its last breath. They waited in trepidation.

Damn that bastard umpire for not calling off the match sooner, cursed Justin.

The umpire's delay caused the already slick grass to become soaked, and whilst the grass was now playable, the lines were still slippery.

Shit! What now? wondered Justin. Hmm! *A few years back, another bugger also slipped and twisted his ankle in an early round. He called off his match, but his quick-thinking manager urged him to change his mind and take an injury time out. He resumed play, won the match and went on to win Wimbledon for the first time. Boris Becker!*

Justin slowly rose from the grass and limped to the umpire's chair, deliberately testing his ankle.

'An injury time out, please. May I have the trainer.'

The ATP trainer, Norrie Bowden, sprayed an anaesthetizing solution out of his magic can onto Justin's ankle, and then bound it tight with tape.

What the hell do I do? wondered Justin, gingerly testing his ankle and debating a heart-wrenching dilemma. *If I carry on playing I could permanently damage my ankle and bugger up my tennis career. But this is my first match at Wimbledon. I shouldn't risk it, but …*

To the relief of the spectators, he signalled his intention to continue.

He reached 5-2 and match point in the third set, but a nagging doubt unnerved him.

It's hopeless, he cried, agonizing over the worst dilemma a tennis player can confront. *I'll never be able to continue in the tournament.*

Biting his lip, tears moistening his eyes, he limped to the net and shook the hand of a sympathetic but delighted Russian. Rather than beat Vladimir Vsevolozhsky and then withdraw from the tournament and leave an empty pocket in the draw, Justin defaulted to let through his opponent. The perplexed crowd seemed on the verge of booing, they felt so cheated. Only later that day would they understand. Then they would say, 'A chivalrous decision that. We may not have a Wimbledon winner this year, but we have a good loser!'

What rot! That's a major problem with British tennis, thought Justin. Winning is all that matters. It's not enough to play well! Nope! Not ever! It's most important to win. Only important to win! It's not good enough for a big cat to make a kill and lose his prey to a cheating pack of die-mad hyenas. That'll weaken him, leaving him without the strength to make another kill. Then he dies! Tennis is designed to produce a winner.

A forlorn and dejected figure of a broken man hobbled off court. His love affair with Wimbledon was short and sweet, but the divorce bitter. Having tasted the sweet nectar of Grand Slam fare at Roland Garros,

Wimbledon served Justin, not strawberries and cream, but a lemon.

One day I'll have a happy reconciliation, vowed Justin.

In the locker-room, Justin peeled off the bandages and winced as his bruised ankle swelled visibly before his eyes to the size of a large grapefruit.

I was bloody right! he exclaimed, his decision vindicated. 'What's the prognosis?'

'Firstly, you're out of tennis for six weeks!'

'Wha—?' responded Justin, his heart sinking low.

'Yes! And that's if treatment works.'

'What treatment?'

'We'll pin our hopes on aspiration-and-steroid treatment to reduce this grim swelling,' outlined the trainer. 'If the tissue has hardened, we'll try laser and ultra-sound treatment coupled with – ha, ha – cross-ply massage.'

'What's so funny?'

'This pain is a tickle compared with cross-ply!'

'And that's funny?'

'And then we'll try to recapture your lost mobility.'

Suddenly, an incensed man with a silver mane erupted into the locker-room.

'Quit mooning the famous centre courts of the world,' bellowed the deep voice of leonine Larry King.

'Hoss!'

'Every time I see you on court, you're on your backside! Ever heard of these?'

Larry handed Justin a pair of grass court shoes proudly featuring numerous rubber pimples on their soles to aid traction.

Damn! cursed Justin, feeling sheepish and dejected. *There's no excuse for this. Bad luck played no part in this swollen ankle. A professional tennis player must always be prepared for unforeseen circumstances. Injuries must be prevented through hard training and judicious planning.*

Justin slumped forward in his seat.

'Damn! Damn! Damn! I'm a bloody idiot!' he screamed. 'How could I jeopardise my career?'

Unfortunately, Larry's advice came too late this time. A double blow, this, for Justin.

Shit! Even though the chances were small, I really wanted to become the first official World Champion of the newly modified ATP Tour, my brainchild. Six weeks off without the chance to pick up valuable computer points will surely squeeze that scant chance lifeless.

While Tyrone spoiled Roland Drechsler's chance to go Double Deutsch again with Heidi Schültz, Justin felt bored and miserable with his enforced exile from tennis.

§

'I'm going home,' cried a dejected Justin. 'Home to Africa.'

Justin toured Central Africa.

This is appalling! grieved Justin.

Bloated elephant carcasses littered the killing fields, filling the air with an unbearable stench. A poaching trail of shame headed to the Far East.

'All for 'white gold', ivory!' spat a bitter Walter Steele. 'A poisoned arrow did not kill these once majestic creatures. Whole herds were mown down with AK-47 assault rifles, their tusks frantically hacked from their skulls while some were still alive.'

'The young ones?' asked Justin, repulsed.

'This orphan died of loneliness,' cried out the distressed conservationist, pointing to a calf nestled against its slaughtered mother. 'An orphan elephant will linger by its dead mother until it dies of starvation. ... Can you believe that tusk sizes have halved in the last 10 years! Poachers have wiped out the older elephants.'

When they got back to camp, a cluster of tents in the middle of darkest Africa, a little boy shouted, 'Hey, it's Justin Forrester. Can I have your autograph?'

Justin dutifully obliged.

Sickened to the core by the stench of death, Justin returned home to Swaziland. North of where his parents lived, he marked out an expanse of land and declared, 'One day I'll dedicate it to wildlife. I'll call it Tamboti.'

§

If I can make it there,
I'll make it anywhere ...
It's up to you, New York, New York!

Sitting in his suite of the Grand Hyatt Hotel on 42nd Street, Justin twirled his thumbs, impatiently waiting to see the new American tennis sensation, Dayack Sassoon.

Is this bugger going to be my next opponent in this US Open? wondered Justin. *And what's all the ballyhoo?*

Instead, his television set mirrored himself, beaming his latest press interview, a particularly irksome verbal diatribe.

'Ted Parsen of the *London Daily News.*'

'Uh huh,' sighed Justin, heart sinking, dreading the expected assault.

'How can you justify the disproportionate prize-money?' challenged Ted Parsen, tossing a stone into the calm pond that was Justin's tennis world.

For the first time in tennis history, a Grand Slam tournament offered a $1 million first prize, bringing the cynics crawling out of their holes with vengeance.

'I can only assume the sponsors believe the value of winning the US Open warrants a $1 million prize, or they wouldn't offer it!'

'Making you a money whore!' accused Ted Parsen maliciously.

Be patient, Justin! Be patient! 'Quite the contrary. Money in tennis is a by-product. Without it, the same players would play and win the same tournaments. We play for the love of—'

'But instead, you demand a king's ransom!'

'Not demand. Our value *commands* such amounts or more. If a billion viewers tune into a final, the million dollar cost to them is one tenth of a cent. That's good value!'

'Pah! Shouldn't a nurse, whose job saves lives and is indispensable, get paid more than a tennis player?' asked Ted Parsen.

'Or more than a reporter?' Justin retorted.

'The public has a right to be informed,' defended Ted Parsen. 'Especially on an injustice such as this!'

'And they *want* to be entertained, and are *willing* to pay for it!' responded Justin.

Attacked, but given a way out, he seized his chance and turned to address the rest of the press crew. 'Tennis players are hostage to a spoiled, overpaid, prima donna image. The fact is, most nurses *do* get paid more than tennis players. The few wealthy players you see are the tip of an iceberg. The balance receives a pittance in a profession that is prohibitively expensive and over in 10 years. These buggers sleep under the stars and beg or borrow just to pursue a passionate dream. Sadly, such plight has even led to suicide. Without the rabble, professional tennis would cease, and you buggers would be without a job. *We* are the lucky ones!'

Justin turned to address Ted Parsen, his chilling blue eyes moving the reporter uneasily in his seat. 'Mr Parsen, you'll find your pecuniary reward is proportionate to your skill. *If* you get to the top of your field, and *if* you command a readership of a billion people or more, then you, too, might find a champion's prize in your pay-packet!'

Stung by this barb, Ted Parsen attacked below the belt, putting Justin on the spot with a controversial topic. 'It must bother you, then, that the woman champion will also receive the ridiculous sum of a million dollars?'

'Not at all. She—'

'Pah!' spat Parsen. 'Tyrone Summers finds women's play so boring he's thankful their matches are over so quickly. You mean to tell me you regard their tennis as equal value?'

'Nope! Not in a tennis sense. But they have something else to offer. Something—'

'Sexy legs!' interjected Dan Welding of the Boston Globe.

'Right!' smiled Justin. 'There's an intangible compelling quality about the women's game. Otherwise, they simply wouldn't get paid. … I see our sports differently and I do not think they should link our prize money just for the sake of equality. But I am a great believer in free market forces, so if they can organise all that lolly – in fact, if they got paid twice as much as us, then good luck to them. Let the market-place decide.'

To ease Justin out of the heat of a controversial topic, Dan Welding altered the angle of conversation. 'Do you watch ladies' tennis?'

'Not really …,' replied Justin, but after a moment's thought, 'except Heidi. But then her legs are sexy!'

Irritated by this interview, but impatient for the Dayack Sassoon match to start, Justin temporarily switched channels, finding another Justin Forrester interview. The television showed him sitting in the interview room wearing a T-shirt emblazoned, 'AIN'T GOT WHAT IT TAKES? GET HORNY ON PORN, NOT RHINO HORN!'

This blond wonder from the bush of Africa who had taken the tennis world by storm, captured the imagination of the American public. The media waxed lyrical about Justin and played the wildlife angle to the hilt, eager to scratch away the aura of mystique that cloaked this quiet but fiercely determined man.

'When you're hunting back in Africa and aiming your rifle at a big cat, do you ever see Tyrone Summers in your sights?'

Justin glared at the man with his piercing blue eyes, cutting right through to the reporter's core. The paunchy man turned this way and that, desperate to get out of Justin's sight, sweating in trepidation. Very deliberately, Justin spat with venom, 'I hunt the hunter!'

Justin flipped channels once more. A karate expert demonstrated the art of extracting hidden powers from the body.

'Brace yourself at the hip before you strike. Better still, thrust your hip forward and you'll crack nuts!'

Interesting, thought Justin, flipping channels back to the tennis. 'Aah, at last! Dayack Sassoon versus Larry King!'

Dayack Sassoon had become the storyline of the US Open Championships. Tall! Black! Luminous in a reggae Day-Glo suit! Sporting flying Rastafarian dreadlocks! In combination with the loudest decibel grunt measured on the gruntometer, these were good enough to scare his way into the quarter-finals.

But how good is his tennis? wondered Justin, knowing he had to play the winner of this match for a place in the US Open final.

The public did not care. To grunt or not to grunt, that was the question! In his previous match on Court 3, they had packed like sardines on the outside ramps of the main stadium, just to catch a glimpse of the unheralded but audacious upstart frying the Frenchman, Jean-Pierre Perrot.

Now as the sun set on this final day of August, Lady Liberty basked in the reflected glory of American tennis from Flushing Meadows. With Tyrone Summers carving his way through the top half of the draw, young challenged old for a possible all-American final.

Dayack stunned all with his spectacular launch, obliterating the old warhorse 6-2 in the opening set. Larry had grown his white hair long for this tournament, claiming that, as with Samson, it would give him strength, but something was wrong.

Something's amiss with Hoss, deduced Justin.

No sooner had he entertained that thought when a florid-faced Larry, clutching his stomach, went over to his wife, Jeanie, sitting in the front row.

'I ain't goin' to finish this match! My plumbing works are leaking!'

Hoping for a dogfight, this sight dispirited the spectators. But a surprise awaited them.

The scent of a quick and easy victory allured Dayack, but astonishingly, his visible effort to nail down the ailing Larry King, backfired.

That's so typical, chuckled Justin. *Forcing the pace has thrown his rhythm, causing a glut of unforced errors. The bugger's grown frustrated, and now distractions loom larger than life!*

The crowd came alive at the prospect of a fight. New Yorkers love a scrap. So, in competition with the rolling thunder of jet aircraft overhead and the Long Island Railroad just a lob away, they yelled and screamed vociferous support. The noise was irregular, irritatingly irregular.

At one point it reduced Dayack to despair. He pointed his racket to the sky and mimicked shooting the jet aircraft with his bazooka. When that did not help he hammered his racket against the netpost.

'Noise, noise, noise!' he of all people screamed.

No one heard him, there was too much noise! A bagel set to King, 6-0.

Strangely, the feeling of urgency now dissipated, Dayack regrouped to take the third set and served for the match at 5-4.

Aah! The moment of truth for any tennis player, declared Justin. *To finish a match is the ultimate test of one's self.*

At 30-all, Dayack became as stiff as a poker and elected to drive-volley a shoulder high ball. It sailed long.

A dose of major gaggage! Choking on the Big Apple! chuckled Justin. *I've seen enough! Now where's some OK Corral?* he wondered, fondling the remote control.

With the day off, Justin woke early, togged out in tennis gear, left the Grand Hyatt and headed straight into the adjacent Grand Central Station of mid-town Manhattan. He boarded the No. 7 Flushing Line subway, taking him eight miles east across the East River into the heart of the borough of Queens to Flushing Meadows, home of the United States Tennis Association's National Tennis Centre, where each year as August rolls into September the tennis pros contest the US Open.

The subway dumped him at Shea Stadium, home of the New York Mets. Walking across the scalper infested boardwalk to the National Tennis Centre, a wonderful fever of anticipation gripped Justin, washing an air of excitement over him like a fresh summer breeze.

Sixteen years before, USTA president Slew Hester, an oil man, flew into New York to discuss a new site for the Open. As his plane jetted into La Guardia airport on that wintry January day, he gazed below to the old abandoned Louis Armstrong Stadium, framed in a blanket of snow, and a vision was born. Although accorded questionable immortality in *The Great Gatsby* as 'a valley of ashes', the cigar-chomping Louisiana wildcatter jazzed up the derelict stadium in record time, and like the mighty birds that take off from La Guardia, the phoenix rose out of the ashes and gave birth to the glitzy showcase of American tennis that is Flushing Meadows.

An international array of tennis fans converged on Flushing Meadows for the grand premier. Bob Hewitt blew it, opening proceedings against Björn Borg with a double fault! An omen of things to come?

Perhaps! On the day of discovery, a blanket of snow gave a sterile appearance and a north wind blew so there was no plane noise. But

Flushing Meadows is slap-bang in the middle of commuter and airport traffic, ear-splittingly close to La Guardia airport. Getting there is a nightmare, especially on double feature days when the Mets are at home, and once there, it is hot, humid and noisy. And just to remind us of the notorious past, each year the Stadium Court sinks further back into the swamps from which it flourished, and relics from the past rise out of the green surface, coming back to haunt like some swamp monster lurking in murky waters.

Like a teeming microcosm of New York, Flushing Meadows is a stifling asphalt jungle with a pace that is kinetic and frenetic, a literal definition of extraneous distraction, where life is four parts in five, an argument. While Wimbledon is synonymous with genteel croquet, the Open gauchely exudes Wrestlemania. As the pugilistic five times champion, Jimmy Connors, once said of the New York fans, 'They like you to spill your blood and guts. At Wimbledon they'd ask you to clean it up!'

Yep! If you like your tennis raw, then the US Open is the place to taste! chuckled Justin. With the excitement of a child going to a circus, he bubbled with enthusiasm, *And I'm in the semis, a tournament I have to win to keep alive my puny hopes of becoming World Champion.*

Carrying a bucket of balls, Justin walked past a medley of grunts to Court 12, opposite the Grove, and practised his serve. Only this time he consciously swivelled his hip forward to, 'Crack nuts!'

I'll be a son of a gun! It works! expressed a surprised Justin. *At least another five percent more power in there.*

After an hour of service practice and a workout with his latest victim, Byron Belvedere, on leaving the National Tennis Centre, Justin suddenly saw a billboard screaming the shocking news, 'LARRY KING TO RETIRE'. His heart thumped with mixed emotions.

What? Did he lose to Dayack? I'd have laid my cock on a chopping block that Hoss would win that bloody match! ... Damn! I can't imagine the tour without Hoss! grieved Justin, but immediately refocused his mind. *Hmm! Dayack Sassoon.*

§

On returning to her den the leopard calls softly to warn her cubs of her approach. Since she is a solitary hunter, and her cubs are vulnerable, she will frequently move them to diminish the risk of being found by other predators. Now she must take them to her kill.

Suddenly the wind changes. Danger! Lions! What follows is gruesome to all but those who know the ways of the wild. The lions move in on the leopards.

136

Sadly, only one cub has the instinct to follow the white tipped tail of its mother. The others try to hide. But the lions find them and swiftly kill the cubs, significantly, not eating them. A territorial imperative drives them to eliminate all competition. It is grim, but is the process of natural selection.

On return, the surviving male cub mock kills the already dead duiker, honing his skills for later life.

§

The US Open bows to one god, television. And so there is Super Saturday, an intoxicating day night extravaganza that draws excellent ratings, but to do so, absurdly sandwiches the ladies' singles final between the two men's semifinals. If all matches go the distance, the winner of the second men's semifinal could be, well, less than fresh for the final the next day.

Tyrone Summers found himself in a marathon argument with Roland Drechsler, lasting four and a half hours. More surprisingly, Heidi Schültz lost the first set in her final.

Damn you, Heidi! Pull your thumb out and get on with it! urged Justin. *Bloody television! Stupid Super Saturday!*

Justin's opponent would not be Dayack Sassoon, but his old nemesis, Larry King. The old-timer announced after his win over the kid from Atlanta that this tournament would be his final curtain call.

Great! exclaimed Justin. *I've still to settle a score with Hoss, avenge my defeat here last year.*

Larry sat in the locker-room, not 10 paces away and the only communication between these two good friends was a gentle nod of the head in greeting.

Maybe I should go over and wish him well in retirement, perhaps even change his mind, Justin's heart fleetingly reached out to his friend, but suddenly his tennis instinct absolutely forbade expression of feeling. *Shut up! Shut out all human emotions, all weaknesses. He's my friend, but he beat me here last year. He can do it again, so watch out! We're locked in a territorial battle in a rarefied atmosphere that only tolerates space for one, so until the final point of our match is history, keep an invisible space and remain aloof.*

Heidi struggled not with her opponent but herself, so elected to run a marathon, stopping just this side of doom. It was 8.05 p.m. before Justin and Larry walked out onto the Stadium Court to a crescendo of welcome. The two matches before were an endless bowl of peanuts, the hand just went out for more. But now the entrée was ready. The cordon bleu chefs, Justin and Larry, served up sumptuous fare.

New Yorkers like a winner, but above all they love a fighter. They knew Larry King was a fighter. Where speed and reflex diminished with the ravages of time, the veteran compensated with wile and guile. To beat him, the grand old man of tennis would have to die in the saddle. They had read and heard of Justin's marvellous episodes of escapology at Roland Garros. In Larry and Justin they had two of the game's best fighters. They loved them both.

But this was Larry King's last tournament, and he was American. This explained the euphoric adulation as the man with the silver mane took the first set.

'First set to King, 6-4,' called the umpire.

Damn! swore Justin, biting his lips. He quickly consoled himself, *Okay, relax. Just have to be a bloody four setter!*

Old Man River kept rolling on. Riding the crest of a wave of euphoria, Larry got feed-off from the crowd and played stupendous tennis.

Is my friendship undermining my killer instinct? Justin wondered fleetingly. *No! No! Absolute nonsense!*

'Second set to King, 6-4.'

Okay, relax. Just have to be a bloody five setter! Justin admonished. *Damn! That means the match is going to last long into the night and jeopardise my chances in the final!*

Two hours of sensational tennis had passed and the crowd witnessed the unbelievable. Father Time turned back the clock and seemed set on retooling reality into a fairy tale. The US Open, the apple pie of international tennis, was the only tennis title to elude the old maestro. Now the world braced itself for a sensation.

No way! rejected Justin. *Fairy tales formed no part of my educational diet. I live by the tales of the wild, where all adhere to the age-old adage, 'survival of the fittest'. Dig deep!*

On the very brink of extinction, Justin gritted his teeth, pursed his lips, steeled his eyes, searched deep into his bottomless pit of fight and clawed his way back in, scratching inroads into Larry's game. Like a cyclist strenuously peddling a steep incline to its crest, Justin pushed the match to a nub, and with his endless physical resources, burst through, wrenching Larry's grip from the match. He could now free-wheel to the finish.

'Third set to Forrester, 7-6.'

The energetic Justin continued to press forward, stamping his authority on the match, while Larry, looking a misfit living on borrowed time, shuffled slowly around the court between points.

Gotcha! His legs look rubbery, remarked Justin with glee. He looked up to the sky that drizzled ever so slightly. *Yep! You do that. Weep the mournful song of a passing legend, because this bugger's history!*

Still Justin exerted more pressure, and was all over the old-timer like a rash, the pupil giving the teacher a lesson.

'Fourth set to Forrester, 6-2.'

As Super Saturday edged into Sunday and the match entered a fifth set, Larry rejected Justin's obituary, rolled back the years and fought fiercely to show that his last US Open would be remembered.

Hmm! This bugger's a fighter, cut from the same cloth as me! Seems as if he let the fourth set go to replenish for a final set onslaught. Suddenly there's life in him and he's showing perfect recall of his genius.

Suddenly a perturbed Justin cautioned himself, *Watch it! This is treacherous. Revved up emotions fuelled on adrenalin, can be dangerous in the lottery of a fifth set. Come on, Hoss! Break your leg!* implored Justin, then sharply rebuked himself for hoping his opponent would crumble. *No negatives!*

Matches between Justin and Larry were memorable encounters. The two men were friends and practice partners, and had inside knowledge of each other's play, a telepathy that enabled them to start running before the other executed his shot, homing in on the expected ball like a heat seeking missile. Tapping into an opponent's psyche to discover before time the next play, is of paramount importance to winning in tennis. They call it anticipation. With Justin and Larry, anticipation shook hands at the net.

Incredibly, the tempo quickened and the match became charged with emotional electricity. There occurred the most artful exhibition of the highest class of tennis, each warrior elevating his game into a purple patch, fighting for domination.

The mystical seventh game, as pundits have tagged it because of its apparent proclivity to furnish more service breaks than any other game, proved a flashpoint. It was an astonishing game of mammoth proportions as deuce followed deuce followed deuce. A splendid slugfest destined to last 18 minutes!

'Game, King. He leads 4-3.'

Phew! exclaimed Justin, wiping sweat from his body. *Okay, I lost it, but maybe it softened him. So often after a long point or game, when the guard is down, an opportunity presents. Gaining the edge now will be crucial. Intensify!*

He did. But so did Larry. With a touch of gamble, the American broke through and held serve to lead 5-3.

'Way to go, Larry!' screamed his vociferous supporters.

Damn! Damn! Damn! What the hell happened? Suddenly we're at the business end of this set, this match, where one stroke of the racket can conclude the deal!

Far more fans watched the dramatic encounter than there were seats. Down in the bowels of the stadium, people fought desperately to get in, just to catch a fleeting glimpse of the extraordinary drama. They sat in the aisles, and on the steps, and on the walkways. Flushing Meadows had a way of getting more than a capacity crowd into the stadium. It overflowed.

Gambling like a high roller, Larry launched suicidal attacking returns. Alternatively they worked.

'Thirty-forty.'

Damn! Match point down! He's playing like a bloody maniac, lamented Justin, biting his lip, his eyes burning.

The New York spectators stood to their feet, baying for blood. There was no keeping them quiet!

Shit they're drowning me. Can't hear myself think! Justin fretted. But don't give up. I've still one gasp of air. Surface to fight on. Keep looking for the edge!

Then above all the din, he heard the faint noise of a jet labouring down La Guardia's runway 13 and up into the balmy New York sky.

Oh, great! Just to add to my … Aah! A chance! exclaimed Justin, ever aware and quick to spot and seize an opportunity afforded by his domain.

Uncharacteristically, he stalled for the briefest moment. He bent over to tie his shoelaces, then blew into his racket hand like a cowboy blows smoke from his gun.

By this time the jet was passing low overhead, seemingly closer to the spectators sitting in the nosebleed seats up on the lip of Louis Armstrong Stadium, than they were to the tennis. The noise drowned the noisy crowd and the stadium shuddered.

On cue, Justin threw the ball into the air and served, imparting manic slice spin, directed to Larry's backhand. The ball bit into the Deco Turf II surface and violently swerved back into the King body, the snorter climbing viciously, nearly taking off poor Larry's nose!

Gotcha! exclaimed Justin.

Amid the mayhem of supercharged emotions and noise, Justin nullified a principal but underrated sense of a tennis player, hearing. Unable to discern the duller swish sound of Justin's racket brushing the ball, and unsuspecting of ferocious slice, not having received it so far in this marathon match, Larry found his feet all tangled up, and missed the ball. Did he know why? Perhaps not!

The match point expunged, Justin won his serve, but was still down a break.

It's the 11th hour, a do or die game. This bugger's feeding off crowd vibes. Take a gamble, immerse yourself in pure inspiration and neutralise it.

He risked all on the first point, chipping and charging, then hoisting the sweetest lob-volley over the maverick's head.

'Yow-ee!' screamed the sharply banked Stadium Court, throbbing with life in a cauldron of noise and swirling motion, the rapturous ovations raucous.

In one fell swoop, Justin switched off the drip from which Father Time sapped life. There was no supporting of a particular player now. The incredible quality of tennis, as each protagonist wore his heart on his sleeve in a toe to toe battle, so captured the dizzying wall of faces that funnelled up to the nocturnal sky, they lavished waves of emotion on the match.

'Love-fifteen.'

Justin fought back with the fury of a wounded but indomitable lion who knows he has to kill or be killed, rifling three passing shots for clean winners. Perhaps Larry was a little down at missing on his match point. The crowd would never know, but Justin's riposte was a joy to behold.

'Games are 5-all,' announced the umpire.

Dare this match go to a fifth set tiebreaker! How else to separate the hornlock?

Yes, in keeping with the Open's glitzy razzmatazz and its blood and guts drama, they do not permit a fifth set to protract, but end it in a nerve-jangling 'now or never' final set tiebreaker.

'Games are 6-all.'

As the titans clashed in the final showdown, the noose tightening, both explored their technical, tactical and emotional resources to the limit, defying each other's fountain of inspiration to run dry. Relentlessly the pressure surged to the bitter end, but each refused to budge.

As the five hour mark passed, the match quivered at two sets all, six games all, and five points all. Playing a tiebreaker is akin to each being given a bag of marbles. You have to protect them from being stolen. Who would steal the match, Larry or Justin? The player who gained a two marble advantage would win the lot.

A crumb! A scrap! That's all it's going to take. Keep looking! Tap into his psyche, urged Justin. This for match point.

At 5-all Justin served wide to the deuce court and fenced the return deep with a piercing volley into Larry's backhand court.

No way the bugger can pass crosscourt! flashed through Justin's mind. *Blanket the down-the-line pass.*

Larry charged across the baseline, and as Justin expected, he lunged, almost played the shot behind him, sending it down the line as he lay sprawled and grazed on the cement. The ball struck the very tight netcord of Flushing Meadows and popped straight over the stranded Justin. It was the only possible way Larry could have won the point.

Nooooo! cried a devastated Justin, suffering Larry's strong sinewy arms plunging into his chest, and with his bare hands, ripping his heart out. But it never showed.

'Six-five, King.'

The overflowing crowd went berserk. Match point with two serves at Larry's disposal, the Sword of Damocles hanging precariously over Justin's neck.

Damn! His eyes are brimming with fire, observed Justin, the American's eyes nearly popping out with a rage of determination. *Dig deep. Go with the gut.*

With a trick of his own up his sleeve, Larry served a three-quarter pace kick serve wide to the backhand, and raced in pursuit of the net to surprise Justin. He did.

Shit a brick! A super rubber ball with a raging Samson charging into the net behind it! What the hell do I do?

Like a drowning man viewing his lifetime flashing before him, Justin, himself dying, assessed his options with lightning pace.

Lights! Lob! cried Justin, thinking in motion.

With an intangible sixth sense about what the moment calls for, he did no more than push back a defensive lob, his first in the match, deep into Larry's backhand corner. No pace in the lob, no spin, no time for such condiments. No possibility for an outright winner. But he was hoping …

After a long and gruelling five hour match, Larry skipped back, had the lob covered, his left hand desperately tracking the flight of the ball like a radar station. Then suddenly, he mysteriously let the ball bounce, almost shaving his mane. He raced back, and arms flailing bravely but futilely in all directions, searched for the lost ball, desperately poked at it and made feeble contact.

Go for it! urged Justin, tearing in pursuit and punching the volley for a winner.

'Six-all,' called the umpire, each player just two points away from the last rites.

Sneak a glimpse at his eyes, Justin said to himself, as they changed ends. *Gotcha! They're stunned, dazed! It worked, and he knows it!*

When Justin hoisted that simple lob, it contained the venom of primeval instinct, perfectly backdropped by a bank of floodlights that bleached Larry's retina and caused a millisecond of blindness.

Justin crouched to receive serve, his body rippling in anticipation. In contrast his head remained perfectly still for utmost concentration.

Larry served down the centre and came in. Justin stalked forward, softened the wrist and met the ball on the rise with a lifeless, off-backhand, sliced dink. Larry groped to his right, scooped the ball up into play but fell on his knees. Like a man treading water to save his life, he battled furiously to recover, desperately grappling forwards to close the angles of pass.

The perfect time to lob! judged Justin, sensitively attuned to opportunity.

He sailed a majestic, topspin, backhand lob over the King head, accurate to a dime, the ball scuttling away like a jackrabbit.

Gotcha! I will *not,* will *not lose!* cried Justin, even though logic most firmly insisted on it.

All marvelled at such exquisite skill afforded by instinctive thought.

'Seven-six, Forrester,' called the umpire.

My first match point. Dinosaur, get ready for extinction! Thrust the hip forward, Justin reminded himself.

An ace! The King was dead. The old gunslinger died in his saddle while the miracle man continued. In tennis, one wins, the other loses. Something else does not exist.

'Game, set and match, Forrester. He wins 4-6 4-6 7-6 6-2 7-6.'

Around Justin the stadium went berserk. But he walked very quietly to the net, his eyes trained on the ground, not wanting to be showy in front of his friend who might be hurting. There they embraced like two long lost friends who had found each other.

After their torturous match, a television interviewer spoke to the two drained warriors, courtside.

'After Paris I wanted to play him again, just to see what he is really like. I busted my ass for, what's it ...?' Larry queried, looking up at the clock, 'Five hours! Wow! But so did he. We killed each other out there. With him, as they say, 'It ain't over 'til it's over!' If I had to lose to anyone, I'm glad it was Justin. He's the champion of the future.'

'It's a thrill for me to play Hoss! The bugger played here before I was born!' said Justin, choking back tears. He turned to the weathered Larry, 'It's an honour for me to be on the same court as you, Hoss! You've been a great champion for the game. I just hope after tonight you change your mind about retirement!'

After the battle smoke cleared, the cordite still fresh in the nostrils, the battle-weary trudged off court. Exiting the Stadium Court, the swashbuckling old-timer turned around and waved goodbye to his adoring well-wishers for the last time, to an emotional standing ovation. The night Larry King bowed out in a blaze of glory, if not a winner, he left behind him some truly great tennis of his era. It was time for him to climb onto the shelf to rest and reflect on the glory and memories of surrounding trophies. Vale Larry King! Thanks for the memories.

Super Saturday had lived up to its billing, but at what cost? When Justin left the Meadow that night, he left behind his flesh and blood.

Not 12 hours later in the locker-room, minutes before the title match, the two protagonists made their preparations. Tyrone swatted his racket at imaginary flies, expending nervous energy. Justin stretched, before donning his new line of STEALTH clothing depicting a leopard, manna from heaven for the greening of the human consciousness. The gladiators waited to go into the great big bowl to do battle, fight to the death in front of a chanting crowd.

Shit! I should have butterflies, complained Justin. *But I feel so stale. This before a US Open final!*

As the clock struck 4.00 p.m. on a very hot, cloudless day, the adversaries made their way to the Stadium Court. Justin entered the long, dark tunnel in the direction of light. The blond hair fell away from a face gazing at the floor as he walked. Always the piercing blue eyes looked to the ground. The gait was firm but light, with just the slightest hint of a swagger, his body lean and wiry and tanned golden brown. An eerie serenity shrouded him, a mystical aura, a touch of aloofness of a man who alone knows what he wants.

But who was this kid, the American public had asked for two weeks? He came from a foreign land, from the wilds of Africa, to play tennis in New York. He did not smile. If he were losing or if he won, still no smile. A man on a mission, who came to conquer. But who was he? Suddenly the tunnel gave way to a pea green tennis court, the battleground of this warrior.

The court is not the only battleground at the US Open. So is the stadium, which bustles with activity like an anthill. No sooner do the spectators arrive, when they whisk off in search of junk food to feed their faces. Having sunk their teeth into an array of goodies from French ice-cream, to Mexican tacos, to plump, Texas-size, charcoal-grilled hamburgers at the International Food Village, they return to the tennis laden with consumables, only to collide with rivers of others marching off in the direction of the smell of food. Congestion builds at the entrances and fisticuffs break out. When a spectator does finally return he will most probably find his seat taken, sold by a crooked usher. Only Flushing Meadows can allow 22,000 fans in a 20,000 seat stadium, resulting in a wild game of musical chairs for those coming back from the food stalls.

Justin had walked the tightrope of what might have been a villain in his match against Larry King, to sentimental hero in his confrontation with the brash, exuberant, obscenely combative man New York loved, Tyrone Summers. They loved to hate him! The pairing made the classic match-up, perfect foils for each other. Fire versus ice. Volcano against glacier. Irresistible force opposing immovable object. The force of light against the force of darkness.

After the contestants took their respective ends for the warm-up and the umpire announced the tale of the tape, Tyrone walked up to a lineslady, and in a parody honouring Romeo and Juliet, bowed, took her hand and kissed it, then presented her with a red rose and the sweetest of smiles.

The crowd giggled and wondered at this man whose cheeks bunched into rosy apples, squinting his eyes into impish twinkles. Tennis would just not be the same without the world number one, Tyrone Summers!

He played tennis as sweet as his gesture, entertaining with a wild hitting spree, unleashing the blinding speed that was his speciality, whipping fans into a frenzy with his 'spill your guts' type of play. A miler running each lap as though it was his last.

Justin was still in the starting block, startled that the gun had gone off and he had not heard it. He looked up to the sky and saw the Fuji blimp floating lazily across the New York skyline like a bloated fish in an aquarium.

'That's how I feel!' he mumbled wryly.

Tyrone blasted another humdinger past Justin.

Shit! My legs feel stiff and sore, complained Justin, suffering a profusion of microscopic muscle fibre tears caused from last night's marathon duel on the cement-like Deco Turf II surface of Flushing Meadows. A surface as forgiving as playing on the tarmac of La Guardia, prompting players to always apply ice or wrap themselves up like a parcel in bandages, looking like Napoleon's battle-scarred geriatric tour trudging back from Russia.

Tyrone surged to a 4-0 lead with sublime tennis, against a humdrum opponent again fighting a rearguard action.

Not another bloody long drawn out match, lamented Justin, tormented by an unenthusiastic body.

He jumped up and down, swayed from one leg to the other before returning serve, trying to shake the cobwebs out of his game. It was no use. He continued playing lethargic tennis as if he had not wound up his clock that morning.

Justin lost another game and the crowd booed. Out of the corner of his eye he detected a missile whizzing in his direction.

Look out! he cried, but his reaction was too slow to dodge, and an apple core stung him squarely on the thigh. *Ouch!*

Serving at 30-all, Justin's first volley hit the tape and popped up nicely for Tyrone to pass down the line or crosscourt, or lob, but he elected a fourth alternative. He pummelled the ball straight at Justin, hitting his right shoulder. Justin fought a natural instinct to rub the pain away. He forbade his pride to hurt. Unflinching, he turned, walked to the baseline to serve at set point down, and then on impulse, massaged his left shoulder. The crowd applauded.

Why the hell did I do that? asked Justin. *Hitting an opponent is fair game in tennis. If I go to net, I accept the risk of being used as target practice. Is Terror testing my reactions, or the lack of them?*

Set point down, Justin unleashed a corker, smacking the ball into the tape. To everyone's amazement, the netcord broke, sending the net limp at its station. Both players momentarily stood dumbstruck, like spare parts, not knowing what to do.

That's a first for me!

A comedy of errors ensued as officials tried all and sundry to remedy the sagging net. Tyrone paced up and down like an impatient man waiting outside a maternity ward.

Justin calmly walked to and slumped in his chair. With vacant eyes, he stared at the ground. *The US Open final, and I feel like it's a bloody Sunday afternoon social. Damn the bizarre scheduling! Damn television!*

My body's aching, but I can deal with that. The problem's in my mind. That immense concentration against Hoss last night has sapped my mind dry. I've nothing left to give, realised Justin, his throat tightening with frustration, but feeling helpless like an inebriated partygoer finding someone trashing his car, and all he can muster is a dazed laugh, 'Ha ha! He's trashing my car!'

Snap out of it, Justin, he reproached himself. *I'm a ball hair away from the US Open title. What's wrong with me?*

Leaning forward, he poured a jug of cold water over his blond hair, shook his head violently as a wet dog would, then pulled a towel over his head and shoulders, closing himself off from the world to meditate on his plight.

For a brief moment, Justin stilled his mind, purged it clean of doubt. Then he embarked on a process of steeling his will. First the motivation.

This is my dream! The US Open final. I've beaten this bugger before, I can do it again. I want to be the best tennis player in the world. I want to be World Champion.

Then almost entering a trance, Justin chanted to himself over and over again, *I am the best! I can and* will *win! I am the best! I can and* will *win! I am …*

In the cauldron of the towel swathed over his head, he conceived the will to win, and with each chant, fertilized it, so it grew and grew until the pressure pot burst. He threw back the towel.

I'm ready! he declared, flames dancing in his eyes.

Twenty one minutes elapsed before a new net eventually replaced the old.

'Thirty-forty. Two serves to come, Mr Forrester,' reminded the umpire.

During the break, Tyrone had grown progressively tighter. He left on his tap of the nervous energy he needed to play his tennis, and with no relief, his vessel filled to bursting point.

'You've gotta be gaga!' exploded Tyrone. 'Why does he get two serves?'

'Mr Summers, interference with a point warrants the whole point to be replayed.'

'Yeah, but *he* caused the interfer—— Hey what's this?'

A pretty streaker pranced across the court.

'You've got a cheek! Get the hell out …,' Tyrone shouted, but changed his mind.

He thrust his racket suggestively between his legs and beckoned the girl to approach him. She did, but just as she got near, she turned to run away and Tyrone quickly chased and smacked her on the bottom.

'Now, get outta here!' he ordered. Tyrone turned to the umpire to continue his complaint.

'Aw, what's the point of talking to you. You never listen. Always conspiring against me,' Tyrone muttered, walking away scratching his head.

With the highly strung American in such brittle frame of mind, Justin uncurled from his mental catnap and stirred into action. His spark ignited, he mounted a blistering comeback to square at 5-all, much to the appreciation of the crowd.

Maybe Tyrone froze, knowing Justin's reputation for coming back from the dead. Then almost as if he needed the spur of Justin's rejuvenation, Tyrone loosened, and the tennis sparkled into a tiebreaker, which he annexed 7-5.

Just as the match seemed to grow in stature and promise a memorable contest, a rasping Forrester return caused the incoming Tyrone's half-volley to pop up in the air. Justin raced in to kill. Tyrone baulked, causing Justin to smash blindly, and the ball struck his opponent plumb on the nose. Tyrone sank to the ground, blood streaming down his face. The New York crowd loved it.

Jimbo's right! chuckled Justin, his own nose aching in sympathy.

He stepped over the net to administer aid, fetched an ice-pack and held it over Tyrone's face.

'That's twice you've body-lined me,' Tyrone accused out of the muzzling ice-pack, alluding also to the French Open final. 'I owe you one!'

'You should've ducked. The ball was going out!'

'Better the ball hit me where it's going out, than where it'd go in!' joked the stricken Tyrone.

Norrie Bowden, the ATP trainer, arrived on court to nurse the injured Tyrone.

Justin walked over to the umpire and advised, 'Give him all the time he wants to recover.'

'I can't! He has three minutes. More than that and I will have no option but to disqualify him.'

'That's bloody ridiculous. Surely if I'm willing—'

'I'm afraid not.'

Well, stick it up your clay pipe! Sure, all tennis players accept the risks of netplay, and it's true that Terror deliberately hindered me instead of accepting the loss of that point, but an unwritten code prohibits directing a sitter smash at a helpless opponent, Justin mulled over in his head, then declared with horror, I don't want to win the US Open by default!

As the three minutes ended, Justin approached the umpire again.

'I wish to go and pee!' informed Justin, buying a second time out.

The umpire wore a hundred looks that said no, but he had to agree.

Gotcha! exclaimed Justin gleefully.

As he passed his afflicted opponent, purportedly on the way to commune with nature, Tyrone nodded his head in appreciation.

On returning, Justin met the ATP trainer in the tunnel. 'Is the bugger okay?'

'He'll be alright. You broke his nose, although he doesn't know it.'

Amazingly, the tennis resumed at a superb level, but Tyrone was in tetchy mood, his nose sniffing the blood of confrontation.

'There was chalkdust. Didn't you see the chalkdust? Everybody saw the chalkdust. I mean, I did!' rambled Tyrone.

Of course, the lines are painted on the hardcourts of Flushing Meadows!

'Oops!' he uttered, his grimace suddenly dissolving into a sheepish smile. He slunk back to the baseline like a thief caught red-handed.

At 3-all and 30-all, the mystical seventh game, a big point. Justin served down the middle. Tyrone returned into the net.

'Fault!' called the centre lineslady, the recipient of Tyrone's red rose.

Hmm! I accept, decided Justin. *It could've hit the ghost-line on a poor television reception, but definitely questionable.*

Both players stood their ground ready for the second serve.

'The ball was good, 40-30,' overruled the umpire.

Uh oh! Justin sounded the alarm.

A black cloud seemed visibly to shroud Tyrone, whose blood-stained nostrils appeared to snort fire.

'What do you mean? The ball was out! Haven't you got ears?' Tyrone attacked the umpire. 'You heard her. She called the fucking ball out.'

'I saw the ball good,' countered the umpire.

'You saw the ball good. Hah! Well the least I get is a let,' commanded Tyrone, walking back to the deuce court.

'The call came after you struck the ball,' announced the umpire defiantly.

Tyrone turned round with rage.

'Now you're a bloody mind reader, too!' accused Tyrone, implying the umpire had judged the call to have no effect on his return.

The umpire did not respond.

'Are you so sure the call didn't put me off?' demanded Tyrone, marching back to the umpire's throne. 'Tell me, loony tune. Damn you!'

No response.

'Are you deaf?' shouted an infuriated Tyrone. 'Then how the hell did you hear her call *after* I hit the ball?'

'Time delay. Warning, Mr Summers.'

'What did you say?' a red-faced Tyrone yelled.

'I've just given you a Code Violation.'

'Oh! Thank you very much!' retorted Tyrone, bringing a round of laughter, but suddenly turning vitriolic, 'And what do I give you for not doing your job properly?' Tyrone stood staring at the umpire. 'I can't believe this!' he screamed, frothing at the mouth, and reacted in temper by swiping his racket at the netpost. It cracked.

'Racket abuse. Penalty point Mr Summers. Game Forrester. Four-three.'

'Now you go by the rules,' said Tyrone drily. 'Is that fair, suddenly to go by the rules?'

No response.

'Is a cracked racket broken?' asked Tyrone meekly, the ancestral Paddy eking out of him.

Justin slowly walked to his seat for the change-over, and sat, his mind shaking its head.

All this and Terror could be right. The ball did seem a tad wide, conceded Justin, who refused to enter a line decision fray, not since that day back at school when his headmaster banned him from playing tennis for six months.

The penalty point decision might just as well have sailed over Tyrone's head. He had passed the point of reason and his blind temper switched to autopilot. He stubbornly refused to accept the umpire's stance. Instead, he marched back to the deuce court and stood firmly, lips pouting, still awaiting the service let. The change-over ticked by.

Justin stood up, but waited at the umpire's chair, biding the dilemma's outcome before crossing sides, while the crowd slow-clapped the stalemate.

After a seeming eternity, Tyrone started to cross sides, but then suddenly returned to the lineslady at the back of the court.

'Why the fuck did you call it out if it was in?' asked Tyrone petulantly, unwittingly accepting the umpire's decision and steering the blame. 'Why? Just tell me why, because I don't understand!' his mouth flailed away in the clutches of his private demon. He was hardly aware of what he was saying. But he just had to say something. 'It's hard enough for me to win without you screwing it up for me. Take off your shades! Maybe you'll see a little better!'

The lineslady said nothing.

The umpire leant forward to his microphone, about to award a penalty for badgering the lineslady. That would mean automatic disqualification.

Justin quickly reached up and clutched his arm.

'Hang tight,' he whispered urgently to the man sitting above him.

'What do you know about tennis, anyway?' Tyrone asked the lineslady. 'Have you ever played this fucking game?'

'No! Not men's singles!' replied the lineslady, unable to resist.

'Aw, shuddup,' spat Tyrone. Dawdling away from the lineslady to the other side like a schoolboy returning home with a bad report card, even kicking an imaginary stone, he mumbled under his breath, 'Hope you prick yourself on a rose thorn!'

Mostly Tyrone's antics resembled a game of chicken. His outbursts invited his opponent on a joyride, racing in opposite directions towards a head-on collision. Then for Tyrone the thrill was over. He simply popped the valve on his pressure cooker and left his opponent trembling with nerves. But in Justin he found a man better at the game. Mentally he simply refused to be drawn into the fracas.

His morale's low, judged Justin. *Press for an advantage.*

He stung with a break of serve.

Great! Now keep it up! urged Justin, keeping a high tempo. *Hmm! We've entered the twilight zone of dusk. Let me try serving straight arrow serves into Terror's body. The bugger'll have difficulty picking the flight of the ball in this light.*

In a flash the second set was Justin's, 6-3.

He broke serve immediately and cracked the Summers back. The American's game deflated with the suddenness of a nail puncturing a car tyre, the tide irrevocably turned.

As the sun took its nightly bow on this stage, mesmerising the silhouetted Manhattan skyline with magical glows of salmon, rose and orange, the mood of Justin's tennis smouldered seductively. With a mental lock on his opponent, buoyed in spirit, Justin rolled on, an irresistible tide of skill and genius, metering out severe punishment, picking Tyrone's game apart, guilefully and dispassionately, with his oblique strategies. There was no stopping him now. With the bit between his teeth, he headed for home in style.

Three match points to Justin. A string of pearls to a tennis player. Suddenly the racket hand got a little more sweaty, the heart beat like a war drum and his legs felt like jelly.

Tyrone laboured through his usual Fabian ritual of bouncing the ball and wiping sawdust on his racket handle. Shavings fell to the floor. It seemed that Justin, like a dressmaker undoing a garment, had picked the seams of Tyrone's game apart leaving them threadbare, and his stuffing spilled out.

Tyrone served and charged to the net. Conquering his nerves, Justin skipped forward, sought the ball like a tracer, and with a truncated backswing repelled it, dipping the ball to the incoming server's feet. A split second to assess the quality of shot, then Justin pounced, punishing the weak reply with a pulsating volley.

Gotcha! exclaimed Justin.

Amidst the roar of the crowd the umpire announced the score, 6-7 6-3 6-2 6-1. Justin had gracefully sutured Tyrone in a resounding victory.

Justin bowed his head slightly, shook hands with his despondent rival and nodded, then retired to his seat. A hive of activity surrounded him, with a posse of cameramen and newshounds jostling for position courtside to catch a glimpse of the new champion.

But for a moment Justin sat still, staring at the ground, shaking his head.

What an amazing two weeks! That sensational tennis with Hoss! This bizarre match today! What a pathetic start, but I turned it into sublime tennis! Once again, a weird bout with Terror. … Hmm! That Terror! thought Justin before the floodgates opened and a rush of joy and happiness consumed him. *Wow! I can't believe it, I'm the US Open champ! It feels so good, so tingly inside, so warm!*

151

A dissonance of boos disturbed Justin's bliss. He looked round and saw Tyrone and his brown paper packet storming from the court in a tide of anger and humiliation.

I feel for you, sympathised Justin. *Losing in a Grand Slam final must be the pits, yet the knockers stone you until stripped naked. Why stick around for the prize-giving for the rabble to scorn?*

'Ladies and gentlemen, a great hand for our new Open champ, Justin Forrester,' broadcasted the CBS microphone man.

Around the shining light of tennis hovered a mob of hangers-on like moths to a flame, all trying to get in on the act. Then it was the turn of the sponsor.

'Ladies and gentlemen, we are proud to be associated with United States tennis, and have the greatest pleasure in awarding Justin with this milestone prize, the first million dollars for a Grand Slam tournament.'

Justin loved to win, but trudging forward with his head bowed between his shoulders, he felt almost embarrassed amid the crescendo of applause.

The sponsor presented Justin with the cheque. 'You're a fine champion. You deserve this.'

The Flushing Meadows crowd lavished adulation upon him, adoring this man who simply and utterly refused to lose.

'Justin, a few words?' asked the CBS man. 'A million smackaroos. How does that feel?'

He thrust a microphone into the champion's face.

'Yesterday was—'

A jet flew low overhead and drowned out Justin, the first since the match began. La Guardia had kindly steered their noise away from the Louis Armstrong stadium during the final, but wasted no time in resuming their normal flight path.

The US Open champion looked skywards and spontaneously blew a kiss. The crowd laughed at his gesture, but no one could have known why.

'Yesterday was the greatest day in the history of Flushing Meadows. Today was the greatest day for me. I'm very pleased! Very happy!' exclaimed Justin, purring his burp of contentment, warm blood smudging the leopard's whiskers.

'What do you think of Tyrone Summers slinking off court in humiliation like some wounded animal?'

Justin ignored the question. Instead, he thanked the ballboys and ballgirls.

'Thanks a lot. Without you, tennis wouldn't be half as much fun!'

The USTA president presented Justin with the US Open trophy, and as he lifted it high in the night that winked and blinked with the city lights, there could not have been a happier man in the world.

I'll rise to number two in the world now, the highest camp pitched in my climb to the summit of the game, ranked only behind Terror, and I've now beaten the bugger twice!

As Justin left the stadium that night, he momentarily gazed at a giant globe of the world in Flushing Meadows, a relic from an old World Fair.

Hmm! The race for World Champion! If I can make it there, I'll make it anywhere. … It's up to you, New York, New York! It will be very exciting indeed!

Sitting in Vasata eatery on East 75th Street, Justin and Heidi, and Larry King and his wife Jeanie, dined on roast pork sprinkled with caraway seeds and potato dumplings.

Justin took one last bite and left his meal unfinished. He had an inbuilt scale, meticulously keeping his weight dead on 75 kilograms to maintain the dynamics of his stroke play in perfect harmony. As the others rounded off a scrumptious meal with Balacinky, an apricot pancake dessert smothered with chocolate sauce, Larry looked to the conqueror of his memorable epilogue.

'Let's peek at that cheque you stole from me?' asked an impish Larry.

Justin put his hand in his pocket. After fumbling without success, he searched another pocket, and another.

'You're not going to believe this, buddy, but I haven't the foggiest idea where it is.' *And I don't care! I'm in dreamland, and the trivial issue of a lost $1 million cheque is not going to dampen my joy!*

Larry looked a trifle surprised at Justin's lack of concern. 'When last did you—'

'In the change-room. Some bugger asked to see it. I can't remember.'

'You must be tired. I'll recover it for you,' volunteered Larry.

'Thanks, Hoss! You're a star,' acknowledged Justin, then shot with an impish grin, 'But don't forget the cheque is mine!'

Whilst the two million dollar couple repaired to Justin's hotel suite, Larry motored to Flushing Meadows. The deserted stadia eerily reeked of the stale pall in the aftermath of a festive party. Larry waded through the litter to the locker-room and there on the floor, completely forgotten, lay $1 million.

Justin temporarily excused himself from Heidi to the seclusion of a private telephone. He dialled the number of his IMG agent, Marco Ponti.

'Sorry to call you at this hour, but there may be a delay with the cheque. When you receive it, please credit half to the following bank account.'

Justin recited a bank account number from a slip of paper. Above the number, read, 'SAVE THE ELEPHANT FUND'.

As Heidi lay naked on the bed in Justin's arms, thinking of their progeny he titillated, 'Are you aware of the kind of babies we can make?'

'Yes! They'll have graphite teeth and furry yellow eyes set in a round head strung to a frame that wears leather gloves,' laughed Heidi. 'And they'll cry thwack, thwack, thwack!'

'Yech!' scowled Justin, then stroking her clitoris, he asked, 'Are you protected then?'

'Of course!'

In the serenity that stills the excitement of victory, two Olympian athletes bonded warmly in the heart of their conquered land and made love.

A knock on the door rudely woke them from their precious sleep.

'It's room service,' Heidi enlightened a groggy Justin. 'I'll get it.'

She quickly donned a pair of panties and a tennis shirt of Justin's and scampered to the entrance door, opening it to allow the waiter to wheel in the breakfast trolley.

'What's going on?' drawled Justin sleepily, staggering naked into the living room like a dazed boxer.

As quick as the flash of his camera, a photographer stealthily entered the suite, snapped a picture and disappeared.

The following day, Justin jetted into Heathrow aboard a Concorde.

Shit! cursed Justin, his heart plunging in despair.

Suddenly his fairy tale developed a sinister twist. On the front page of the *London Daily News* splashed the photograph of Justin and Heidi with the headline, 'CHAMPIONS CELEBRATE WITH ORGY'.

CHAPTER 8

Borg thumped, 6-1 6-1 6-1! McEnroe, too! Becker overpowered, 6-2 6-1 6-0!

'G'day, mates,' Bob Wallace addressed Team BB, then focused on Amos Creighton. Beaming, he announced, 'The Big Bastard's ready, chief. 'E's unbeatable!'

'What of this Forrester character?' queried a cautious Amos Creighton.

'For obvious reasons, ve don't have a vast data bank on Forrester,' answered Otto Weiner. 'He's a vild card, but ve're confident ve'll ace him!'

Over the past five years Boris Bauer had played the game's all-time greats in the big finals of the Grand Slam events, all simulated on court with Otto Weiner's computerised ball machine. He beat them all, convincingly!

First, he would take the part of Connors in his 1982 US Open final against Lendl, and play the Czech until he demolished him. Then he would reverse the order, and annihilate Connors. Indeed, Team BB extended Boris Bauer's abilities by increasing the difficulties of each match he played far beyond reality.

For nine years, Boris Bauer's game plugged into a multi-point adaptor of expertise. Out of a man born of Czechoslovakia, a country that gave origin to the word 'robot' from Karel Capek's *Rossum's Universal Robots*, Creighton built a cyborg, a machine man, expertly primed in the sport of tennis. Now he was ready to be set loose in the tennis world.

'The Big Bastard's ready for the litmus test,' voiced Bob Wallace. 'Satellite tournaments.'

Team BB concurred.

'Thank you, gentlemen. You will be taken care of,' announced Amos Creighton. Then he spoke privately with Vich. 'I want that masseur without delay!'

§

Robin Wallenborg returned from Göteborg's traffic department with great excitement and burst through the door to her father's apartment.

'I got it, Daddy!' the auburn-haired 18 year old cried with delight, proudly holding up her brand new driving-licence.

'Congratulations, pussycat!' offered her father, hugging her.

A year ago, Carina Wallenborg died of cancer, leaving behind a young daughter and a distraught and desperate husband. Desperate because in 45 years, Sven refused to learn to drive a car. Robin's driving-licence would cut the umbilical cord to the void her mother left behind.

'Come, Daddy. Let me take you for a drive. Please?'

'Sure.'

The two climbed into an old grey Saab, Robin at the wheel, and rode off into their newfound freedom. Perhaps this excitement accounted for Robin not noticing the danger sign. She was red and green colour-blind and failed to see the position of the shining light.

A loud crunching of metal and crashing of glass abruptly woke Robin from her joy, a joy which turned to horror.

'Daddy!' she cried, turning to her right.

There was no response.

A battered and bruised Robin reached over to her father whose legs were buried under mangled metal.

'Daddy! Daddy!' she screamed, tears streaming down her face. 'Talk to me!'

An eternity passed in Göteborg's Sahlgren Hospital. Finally Dr Karl Stranlund approached an agitated Robin.

'I'm afraid the news is not good,' he told her sombrely.

'Oh, no!' cried Robin, burying her head in her hands, her shoulders shaking with sobs. Then she raised a white, strained face to the doctor and braced herself for the grim tidings.

'Your father is paralysed in the legs and—'

'Is it permanent?'

'We're not sure. There is some damage to the spinal cord, but not severe enough to cause this paralysis. It appears that his concussion stunned his brain, so to speak, and it is not communicating with his legs. Only time will tell. The best we can do is to treat him with intensive physical therapy in the hope that we can reawaken his brain to the legs.'

'Where do I learn this therapy?' Robin asked determinedly.

'…, thank you ladies and gentlemen,' the 27 year old Robin Wallenborg said after receiving a standing ovation at the Alternative Medicine Symposium. The occupational therapist had delivered a paper on shock treatment massage, a technique she had discovered to bring life back to her father's legs.

'You've sparked their interest, Robin. You must be a very proud lady,' praised Dr Karl Stranlund.

Robin looked despondent.

'Is there something wrong?' asked the doctor, concerned.

Robin choked back disappointment. 'There has been a relapse, Karl. Daddy's losing it. The paralysis is returning. His life is ebbing away. And it's all my fault!' She looked away. 'I'm desperate!'

A moment's silence.

'Robin, I don't wish to falsely raise your hopes, but a friend of mine, Professor Carlsson of Karolinska Hospital here in Stockholm, has been working on a technique to help paralysed victims. He and his colleagues have isolated nerve growth factors which they hope to apply as a stimulus for spinal cord regeneration. But there are problems of reconnection. Professor Carlsson hopes to short-circuit the damaged spinal cord by simulating the normal electrical impulses running through the nervous system with a computer. I'll introduce you to him. But I warn you his research is at the embryonic stage, and if he makes a breakthrough it'll be very expensive.'

'You'll be rich,' growled Vich, thrusting a contract under Robin Wallenborg's nose. 'Sign!'

§

Boris Bauer played in three satellite tournaments, each in a different continent to detract attention, and in each, he easily reached the semifinals, playing like a cat toying with a mouse, well within his capabilities. At this juncture he defaulted each time, to prevent winning and bringing notice.

Also, Team BB forbade him to lose purposely and risk developing the bad habit. They conditioned Boris Bauer only for success. Partial failure was incomprehensible. Playing these tournaments dualled to accumulate sufficient ranking points to gain entry into the qualifying tournament for the upcoming Australian Open.

Now to wrap up preparations for the Grand Plan, Amos Creighton said to himself, rubbing his hands with glee. *QE2, meet your iceberg!*

Like a high roller, Amos Creighton travelled a whirlwind globe-trotting tour, salting away $10 million in bets with anyone from Ladbrokes and William Hill in the UK, to syndicates in the United States, to the betting penchant of the East. He kept each stake small to prevent suspicion, but also because the staggering odds thrust potential pay outs up to ceiling limits.

'What? You're crazy! No one can ever achieve three Grand Slams in a row!'

'The odds, please?' Amos Creighton asked defiantly.

When Donald Budge won the four major titles of Australia, France, Great Britain and the United States in 1938, Allison Danzig of *The New York Times* coined his feat a Grand Slam, and these tournaments subsequently became known as Grand Slam tournaments. Ever since, this magical mystery tour has become the mythical pinnacle of the sport. Every tennis player in the world dreams of achieving a Grand Slam, but few ever believe it possible.

More astronauts have walked on the moon, or mountain climbers ascended Mount Everest, than tennis players have conquered this elusive, almost sacred species. Since Donald Budge, only Rod Laver of the men players has surmounted this celestial height of winning the four Grand Slam titles all in the same season. Amazingly, the 'Rocket', wizard of the grand dynasty from the Golden Age of tennis in the Land of Oz, did it twice, once as an amateur and again as a professional. Three ladies have tasted the *crème de la crème* of tennis. 'Little Mo' Maureen Connolly was first, followed by Margaret Court, and lastly, the astonishing Steffi Graf who gilded hers with gold at the Seoul Olympic Games for the only 'Golden Grand Slam'.

To accomplish three consecutive Grand Slams necessitates winning 84 consecutive matches of the highest calibre. Allowing for a range of a 99 percent success rate in the first round of a Grand Slam championship to 70 percent in the final, the odds of annexing three consecutive Grand Slams, amounts to one chance in a million! And that is discounting the possibilities of extraneous intervention. What if a war erupted or if tennis politics interfered? A bad cold or flood rains or food poisoning? Even grappling with the affliction of menstrual cramps has dashed Grand Slam hopes. Not that this should worry Boris Bauer!

'You're mad. You own some mutant superman, or something?' laughed the broker. 'But I'll give 1500-1.'

Ten million dollars at such odds will pay out $15 billion, calculated Creighton.

Back in his inner sanctum at his home in Greenwich, Connecticut, Amos Creighton paged through the latest edition of FORTUNE magazine. It listed the Queen of England as the richest woman in the world, behind only three men.

That should take care of QE2 and give me dominion over women. Thereafter, I'll conquer the world, boasted Amos Creighton excitedly.

A knock rapped on his door. Amos Creighton waited awhile, as was his custom, before attending.

'Your masseur,' announced Vich to a raised eyebrow query from Creighton. 'She's outside.'

'*She! She!* Robin Wallenborg is a *she?*' foamed Creighton, nearly hitting the roof.

'Hmmph!'

'I expressly forbade you to contract any dirtbags to Team BB!'

'You want the best? It's a woman!'

'Impossible!' spat Creighton, pacing up and down the room like a caged animal.

'You want Team BB down the toilet, I get rid of her. You want to stink with money, you stick with the girl,' Vich spelled out the options.

Creighton agonized in deliberation. 'The girl stays. When the operation is complete, eliminate her!'

CHAPTER 9

The new US Open champion returned to his home in Hampstead, London, to map out a plan of action that might, just might, allow a whiff of the World Champion title. That evening, a knock on the door disturbed Justin.

'Mr Forrester, the name's Jerry Bead, your new neighbour,' introduced the grey-suited man, offering his hand.

Justin shook hands almost reluctantly through shyness. 'Please come in. Call me Justin. Have you been here long?'

'Since the end of July.'

'Really!' expressed a surprised Justin. 'A week after I moved in.'

After a few more exchanged pleasantries, Jerry Bead reached into his briefcase and withdrew a portfolio.

'As I was saying, I work for Pegasus Sports, and we've come up with this wonderful proposal for you to wear our sports apparel. The image we project is a good, wholesome, quality product, all Justin Forrester. We have taken the liberty of drawing up a contract. We're confident you'll find it favourable.'

Jerry Bead handed Justin a cheque for $2 million.

'Consider that a gift from the company. Each year another of those will be yours in return for wearing our sports clothes.'

'Jerry, I hate to disappoint you, but I've just started my own clothing line.'

'Mmm. The animal ones. Justin, that's not you. You have class. Panache. You belong—'

'I'm afraid not, Mr Bead,' interjected Justin, peeved at Bead's disparaging assessment of his association with wildlife. 'You'll never understand!'

Jerry Bead wrote out another cheque, for $3 million.

'I'll increase the figure all round,' Jerry Bead said, smiling with confidence.

Justin tore up the cheque without looking at the sum endorsed.

'Five million dollars a year. That's my final offer.'

'Then leave it as a bloody offer!' responded Justin firmly. 'Now will you please excuse me. I have work to do.'

Justin ushered his neighbour out with the same feeling as sweeping dust out of the house.

That night, Justin mapped out a plan to maximize his chances of gaining as many ATP Tour points as possible.

At ten o'clock, a ringing telephone woke Justin.

'You're awfully difficult to get hold of. I've started writing a biography of Justin Forrester. Could we meet and—'

'A bit early in my career, isn't it?'

'No problem. The interest is overwhelming. That's—'

'The public has seen my tennis on television,' said Justin, his ire stirred. '*You* want to write a kiss-and-tell-all story. An account of my first sexual experience—'

'Your tennis records will be included in an appendix.'

Justin slammed down the phone and pulled out its plug.

The following morning, as Justin prepared to depart on an airplane booking errand, another knock rapped on the door.

'Mike Bernstein, your new neighbour,' introduced the short bespectacled man with an outstretched hand.

Justin looked at him suspiciously, and tentatively reciprocated. 'You bought from the Eldens?'

'Yes! Around the end of July!'

Justin put two and two together. He had heard stories of companies that would purchase the house next door to a champion in a maniacal drive to extort star endorsement for their products, in the hope that saturation pressure would wane resistance, sway the mind and reap the desired response.

'You have a bloody contract for me to sign?' shot Justin.

The man's eyes nearly popped out with surprise.

'Uh, um, if I could have a minute of your time,' not knowing if he should feel happy that he had hurdled the sensitive matter of introducing business or if Justin was pulling the welcome mat from under his feet.

'I'm afraid, Mr Bernstein, the answer is no!'

'But you haven't any idea the enormous figure we're offering for your services,' protested the neighbour.

'Mr Bernstein, money will not buy an attitude. That's what *I* have to sell!'

Justin immediately changed his telephone number for an unlisted one, and hired a PRO worker to deal with the more than 400 telephone calls and mailbags of letters he received every day.

§

In a frantic attempt to close the gap on Tyrone Summers, Justin criss-crossed the globe like a human yo-yo, searching for elusive ATP Tour ranking points in his single-minded quest to become World Champion. In the tennis world, the computer ranking is the central nervous system of the tour, the yardstick by which players measure themselves, and the points are worth their number in bars of gold. They determine acceptance into tournaments, seedings and commercial opportunities. Players live and die by their rankings. But more importantly for Justin, they evaluated the best player in the world.

The ATP Tour is like a reservoir of water, too deep to stand in, with the title of World Champion suspended overhead. The prize lures players into the treacherous water, but there is no way to get to it alone. So they tread water, and soon a pyramid of people forms, players clambering in mass hysteria, tearing and pulling, climbing up in a desperate attempt to reach for the sky, for the mythical honour of being number one. The sides are wet and slippery. One wrong move and a player tumbles down, like wax melting off a candle. The others kick him in the face, shove him down below, perhaps under water, never to surface again. Maybe a lucky turn, a loophole, or a clever move and the upward struggle reaps better fortune.

The one who makes it to the top is the strongest, the shrewdest and a touch lucky. But a moment's relaxation, and the tour flushes him down the ranks with a hungrier opponent filling the void. Yes, the plentiful weak support the predatorial few. It is 'survival of the fittest' in the dog-eat-dog world of tennis. That is the law of the jungle. That, too, is the law of tennis.

Waltzing to the Sound of Music in Kitzbühel, boogieing to the beat of the Beach Boys in Los Angeles, doing the Fandango in Madrid, hup hupping the Hopak in Moscow and clogging a Dutch treat in Amsterdam, Justin greased the rungs of the tennis ladder in a stellar campaign to crest the rankings, and his opponents all came tumbling down. In a final whistle-stop tour, he fleeced titles in the Yoyogi Stadium in Tokyo and the Omnipalais in Paris. By the last tournament of the season, he strode the tennis world like a colossus and stood within striking distance of the title he cherished, World Champion.

The tour headed for Frankfurt, Germany, for the wind-up tournament of the season, the ATP Tour World Championships, a glittering showcase for the world's eight best players to put their final case forward for the debate of World Champion. Two players artfully slit throats in each round robin group. They decided the match everybody expected and wanted. A final showdown between Tyrone Summers and his pretender to the crown, Justin Forrester.

In my wildest dreams I would not have imagined my idea of the ATP Tour as a world championships going down to the wire in its inaugural year! thought Justin, amazed. *And the icing on the cake, I'm a contestant for World Champion!*

After a long and gruelling season, only 70 ranking points separated the two masters of the game, Justin Forrester and Tyrone Summers. With exactly 100 points on offer to the winner of the final, all the marbles were up for grabs in this, a black ball game for the title of World Champion.

At 8.00 p.m., Frankfurt's famed Festhalle lay in darkness, awaiting the protagonists. Suddenly, a spotlight escorted onto court, first the challenger, Justin Forrester, French and US Open champion. Then came world number one and Wimbledon champion, Tyrone Summers.

Together this unlikely couple, the yin and yang of professional tennis, had captivated the sport in a fascinating race for World Champion. Justin, quiet and serious, magnetic but aloof, cloaked in mystique, but burning with ambition to be the best. Tyrone Summers, extrovert and brash, loquacious and jovial, already the best. A morality play in the truest sense.

The German crowd bristled with anticipation. Who would become World Champion?

Two months earlier at the US Open championships, Justin came back from a set down to steamroll Tyrone Summers into submission, 6-3 6-2 6-1. Many who watched the match felt that had they played another set, Justin would have continued the blitz pattern to 6-0. Now he did!

The match began in a flurry of Forrester brilliance, casting the die. With total concentration manifesting in an aura of supreme calmness, Justin scaled the zenith of his all-court tennis skills to embrace tennis nirvana.

Playing to a maxim of 'divide and conquer', and moving with a lightness and stealth evoking images of Björn Borg and Steffi Graf, Justin lithely carried his consummate mastery in full flight to all corners of the court, where he teased and toyed with Tyrone as one might fox a tethered dog into winding itself round and round its kennel. Inexorably the chain shortened, as sublime strokes – gossamer drop-volleys of a John McEnroe, melting like a hot knife through butter, lob-volleys reminiscent of Henri Cochet, hobbling the opponent at the net in despair, skewered backhands of poetic Rosewallian precision, and volleys of Frank Sedgeman, attacking weak half-volley replies with impunity – flowed from his racket until no response issued from the impotent Summers. With Tyrone snared in his kennel, Justin stole the bone.

Then with the deft skills of a detached surgeon, he performed a surgical strike on the sacrificial lamb, rearranging the organs and ablating the oomph from his game, leaving him naked of weapons and bereft of ideas to tame the rampant tide. But he forgot to stitch up his patient, and the American's lifeblood bled dry.

To Tyrone, it seemed that Justin had concocted a diabolical plan to drive him mad. This was minimalist tennis played at the razor's edge, classical, economical and brutal, kindled by an inner rage for perfection an ordinary man could not comprehend.

On the bagel end of a shutout first set, drawn and quartered by the incisive play of Justin, Tyrone looked at his opponent warily, rather like a man might look at a dog that has previously bitten him. Having the best view in the Festhalle to witness the avalanche of winners from the awesome Forrester roll, was his only consolation!

The drama was whether Tyrone could get a game. He did! At 1-4 down in the second set, stripped of tennis skills and looking utterly resigned, Tyrone was in dire need of a new lease of life.

'Gimme a warning?' a tame Tyrone asked the umpire, hoping such an incident would spark zest in his subdued game.

The crowd giggled.

'I cannot do that,' disappointed the umpire.

'Aw, go fuck yourself!' responded Tyrone, always at odds with authority.

'Warning, Summers! Verbal obscenity,' announced the umpire.

'Mr Flodrops,' Tyrone reacted pettily, '*you* call me *Mr* Summers!'

'Warning, Mr Summers! Verbal obscenity.'

To the amazement of the German spectators, Tyrone grew mad with the umpire.

'*Now* you give me a warning. What obscenity? You don't hear so good. I told you to go *phuck* yourself, with a p-h, as in phone! Is that obscene? I ask you a favour, but no! Nothing doing. Now you make me look bad. Are you satisfied?' screamed Tyrone.

'Please play on, Mr Summers!' ordered the umpire, checking his watch for a possible time warning.

Tyrone sighed with a deep exhalation of breath, but grudgingly complied, now crackling with the sparks he so desired. But to no avail. The problem lay not in his game, but in the majestic impact of his opponent's. With the exquisite shotmaking flair of a John McEnroe, the animalistic street-fighting spirit of a Jimmy Connors and the resilient athleticism and indomitable iron-will of a Björn Borg, Justin effectively imposed the ultimate military strategy on Tyrone. By containing his opponent's game, he prevented the match developing into a scrap.

No longer did he play against Tyrone Summers. Instead he flirted with perfection. In tennis parlance, Justin played 'in the zone', a seemingly unreal flow state where everything is like a dream, and the match seems to unfold in slow motion. In this surreal trance, unfettered instinctive winners flow from the racket as if by magic, and the possessed player knows exactly where the opponent's shots are going, as if watching the match as a whole on television.

'Set Mr Forrester, 6-1.'

Justin walked to the umpire's chair in a trance, Tyrone in a coma. As the players passed each other, Tyrone interposed Justin's mind.

'Slow down Pale Wog! Two sets gone in only 39 minutes. Give the spectators some value for their Deutschmarks!'

Why is Terror of all people worrying about the spectators, especially during a match? Justin fleetingly wondered.

He quickly dismissed the thought, sat in his chair and towelled himself down. As he swigged back some cool water, Justin noticed the elapsed time on the courtside clock read 39 minutes.

Hubba hubba! Terror's right! exclaimed Justin. Two sets in 39 minutes! That's pretty good going! I must be playing well!

Unknown to Justin, the shrewd Tyrone Summers had brilliantly orchestrated the craftiest gamesmanship trick in the book, and it worked. He subliminally brought to Justin's attention that he was playing superbly. Such thoughts broke his trance of total concentration, led to a logical analysis, and with it, a disintegration of his game.

Suddenly, the die recast and the match became a dogfight. Justin's timing relentlessly slipped from his grasp, and he went down 0-3. Crisis time.

Run. Guts it out and run! Justin exhorted himself.

To compensate for the sudden loss of form, Justin's primordial instinct resorted to innate athleticism. He fought like a junkyard dog to restore the balance. Tyrone held serve for 4-3.

At 30-all, Justin prepared to deliver a second serve when Tyrone turned his back on him. A double fault!

Damn that Terror! Justin seethed below his glacial mask, peeved more with himself for succumbing to the gamesmanship, than with the propagator. *Now he's got break point!*

Again Tyrone stalled. But this time Justin ignored him and served an uncontested ace.

Take that, Terror! hissed Justin.

'Deuce,' announced the umpire.

Tyrone stood his ground, hands on his hips and spelled out in a deliberate tone, 'I was not ready!'

'Deuce!' repeated the umpire.

'Listen, loony tune, read my lips. I have 25 seconds to get ready. The point gets replayed!' Tyrone confidently ordered.

The umpire struck back. '*Mr* Summers, the rule is quite clear. The receiver must play to the pace of the server. The score stands at deuce!'

Tyrone screamed, shook his head violently to shake the curse of authority out of his mind, and grudgingly returned to his domain, scratching his head in puzzlement. 'You're all out to get me!' he mumbled dejectedly, readying to receive serve. More a cry of despair.

Justin turned another notch in the ratchet, caught Tyrone by the tail, took control of his rudder and steered him off track to snuff out his revival. He surged to 5-4 and 40-love, poised on the threshold with triple match point.

He served wide to the left-hander's forehand, and followed in with his *coup de grâce*, a feathered drop-volley. Brave or foolish? This time brave, the execution couched in panache. The torch passed to the crown prince of tennis, hailing Justin king of the Festhalle. He raised his arms high in the air and allowed just a little smile. He was World Champion.

'A prodigious performance by Justin, one that will long linger in the memory. What have you to say?' a television interviewer asked Tyrone Summers at the presentation ceremony.

'I'm not sure!' answered Tyrone, surprised at being the sudden spare player in a game of musical chairs, dislodged from the summit of world tennis. 'I was too busy trying to rattle him, but he was kicking my ass!'

'Do you have any chance of beating him?'

'You feel you have a chance,' replied Tyrone, shrugging his shoulders. 'I mean, you *have* to feel you feel you have a chance!'

'But can you beat him?'

'Sure!' replied Tyrone, rubbing the kink in his broken nose. 'I just have to improve some on my groundies and my volleys. Add some pep to my serve and get a bit faster. Sure I can beat him!' Tyrone answered with weary humour. 'He has this weakness, you know, he's not so hot at killing a sitter at the net!'

The rest of the field needed some illusion to cling to, some real or imagined weakness that cast a ray of hope into their gloom generated by Justin's utter domination of the sport. In effect, Tyrone implied that Justin lacked weakness.

He then paid the ultimate compliment, admiring the sheer genius of the man. 'I played well enough today to beat most players, but whatever I did, he came up with something better. I just couldn't hold Pale Wog down, tonight. I don't know what else to say. What can you say about him? He says it all with his tennis.'

The president of the Association of Tennis Professionals addressed

Justin. 'A little something for you,' he said, presenting a trophy and a $1 million cheque to the winner.

'Ladies and gentlemen,' continued the president, 'the ATP Tour has ended, but there remains one item. A big hand, then, to salute the champion of champions, the World Champion, Justin Forrester!'

Justin rose onto a pedestal, untouchable monarch of the courts and accepted the trophy to the thunderous sound of applause. And with it a cheque for $5 million, the biggest prize in tennis history. A myriad of flashbulbs sparkled like newborn stars, seeking to capture one man. Just one name reverberated around the world, Justin Forrester. With the grace and dignity of a knight in shining armour, he had conquered the kingdom of tennis, and entered the realm of tennis mythology. He stood a proud man, haloed with the serene aura of an invincible champion, the tennis world at his feet.

World Champion! exclaimed Justin, shivering, goose bumps flecking his skin.

His mind still reeling from the euphoria, Justin entered a press conference.

'Justin, I think the rest of the press corps agree with me when I say that tonight you played the supreme exhibition of tennis. What do you say?'

'I'm still in a state of shock,' replied Justin, feeling giddy. 'From the moment I took the court and hit the first ball, I felt I was gliding. I could walk on water out there. I couldn't miss. I really psyched myself up for this match. You know, World Champion on the line. It was my best tennis ever,' Justin described his sublime ballet of precision power. 'It's a wonderful sensation knowing that you're on. I felt moved to try any shot from any place on the court. I felt all tingly inside. It was eerie, but fun!'

'Was your performance motivated by the chance to become World Champion?'

'I *always* try my hardest. Tonight I was lucky I had one of those few times when a tennis player becomes zoned.'

'You lost that in the third set?'

'Yes. I fell into the trap of thinking how well I was playing. Then it was a bloody struggle. Tyrone's a good player.'

'What do you want now?'

'My opponents to feel they never want to play me again!' responded Justin with a wry smile. 'Seriously, to win the Grand Slam tournaments, especially Wimbledon, of course, and remain World Champion.'

'Is becoming World Champion more satisfying than winning the French or US Open championships?'

'It's difficult to say. Everything stands for itself. But winning the French and the Open enabled me to become World Champion.'

'Will you ever tire of winning?'

'Impossible!' answered Justin, feeling a never ending joy. 'Winning is the most beautiful thing for a tennis player. It doesn't matter how much you win, you are so happy. The way you dream of success and the way it all turns out. It's a wonderful feeling, like you're on top of the world. It's a dream!'

'Ted Parsen of the *London Daily News* …'

Justin tightened like a cat dangled over water, his defence immediately commissioned.

'What did you take to give yourself such a lift?' Ted Parsen asked, a question loaded with accusation of drug imbibement. 'I mean, what did you eat?'

'Eggs. Snake's eggs. They give my reflexes extra venom!'

Ted Parsen shuffled uncomfortably in his seat.

'What is your relationship with Heidi Schültz?'

'You'll find out soon,' came Justin's deadpan answer without a second's thought.

A buzz permeated the press conference room like a plague of locusts.

'That's enough questions. Thank you.'

Justin stood up, walked out and headed straight for his hotel where he rang Heidi.

'The sphincter stinker's nibbling the bait! You can wear that engagement ring now!'

Justin phoned his agent. Reaching blue chip status, he anticipated a stampede of commercial opportunities.

'Marco, the time is ripe to cash in long term. Oh, and I need that prize-money liquid.' *I will buy Tamboti, my own tract of African bushveld.*

Justin sat down on his bed and thought about his performance. *Today I probed the limits of my skills, touched celestial heights. I saw the zenith!* he thought, shaking his head in amazement. Suddenly he felt apprehensive and a chill ran through his body. *Shit! All else will seem stale after today!*

Damn it! Stop it, Justin! he reproached himself, panting.

To escape this false panic, armed with a racket and a ball, Justin disappeared into the dark of night to bash about a ball.

§

The tour ended, but one more event on the calendar captured the attention of the tennis world, the inaugural World Cup Tennis, brainchild of Justin Forrester, conceived in the spirit of team support at the Barcelona Olympic Games.

In the middle of December, 16 national mixed men and women's teams paraded onto court underneath their national flags in Munich's Olympiahalle, for the opening ceremony of World Cup Tennis. While the president of the WCT committee declared the meeting open, goose bumps flecked Justin's skin.

Wow! Multiple wow! World Cup Tennis to determine the best tennis playing country of the year. Justin you've surpassed yourself, even if I say so myself! And to think that it's revived flagging doubles and mixed doubles at the Grand Slam tournaments! he thought proudly, since performances in all the events of the Grand Slam championships during the year determined the selection of teams, and all the top players had contested these events to help their countries qualify and possibly get seeded for World Cup Tennis.

Britain was seeded fourth in the knockout competition. Buoyed by Justin's recent conquests, huge doses of team spirit helped the British team scrape through to the final against the top seeds, Germany, spearheaded by the Deutschland Duo, Roland Drechsler and Heidi Schültz.

Heidi opened with a straight sets shellacking of Lucinda Parkinson.

Thanks, Heidi! Justin thought sarcastically. *You're a great bloody help!*

He and the much improved Byron Belvedere, with his overhauled body and confidence to boot, squared the tie with a three setter, only to see the ladies bravely but futilely succumb to the blonde bomb and her ally. Justin made amends with a fine victory over Roland Drechsler.

The tie boiled down to a fifth and final rubber, the mixed doubles. This for World Cup Tennis!

The odds weighed heavily against the Brits and the German public knew it.

'We can do it, Mimsy,' Justin urged, using his pet name for the refined Lucinda, his partner, on paper the weak link of the foursome. 'This is it! Britain's chance to redeem herself in the world of tennis. We can do it!'

The setting was marvellous. The tournament had captured the imagination of the world. Where else did a contest bring together the top man and woman against each other in a territorial battle for sports supremacy? The Brits turned out in droves to wave the Union Jack, and swells of national fervour spilled over in the Olympiahalle.

But when Roland Drechsler and Heidi Schültz went up a set and 5-2, one game away from World Cup Tennis, the smell of steins lifted high to the sky and the loud ringing oompah-pahs in the ears, cornered Justin.

The World Cup Tennis final had long developed into a tit for tat between two good friends, Justin and Heidi.

Get out of my mind, Heidi! Justin castigated himself at the change-over, and steeled his weapon against her heart and armour.

'Care for me to step aside?' asked Lucinda in a high-faluting voice. 'Can you? Can you do it?'

'No, Mimsy! Not ever!' Justin replied in kind. 'It just doesn't work like that. But listen, we're only down one service break. It's critical, but not impossible. Here's my plan. Make love to the net. Get in real close. They haven't lobbed much. Both are power players. Then cover the alley like a terrier. Leave the rest to me. Got it, Mimsy?'

'My pleasure, sir!'

'Stay in your island, but defend it with your life,' advised Justin. 'Oh, and one more thing, Mimsy. Hit everything to Roland!'

Lucinda wore an incredulous look at this last suggestion, but dutifully resigned herself to this new tactic.

It worked with aplomb. Heidi had relished her duel with Justin, especially with knowledge of support from Roland Drechsler. She thrived on this exploit and it rattled Justin. Now he excluded her from the duel. With Lucinda banished to a small but critical corner of the court, Justin took the match to Roland where he felt more comfortable. And he ran and ran, and stretched and dived, and ran and ran some more. They expunged the deficit to the raucous roar of the British fans and a more muted, *'Wunderbar!'*

The final set developed into a climactic gem. The pressure mounted, the tension grew taut and the opposing fans deliriously cheered their countries. The match headed to a final set tiebreaker. And still it grew in stature as point after point raised the hackles on the back to a nerve-jangling pinnacle.

Britain reached match point at 6-5, but service switched to the Germans, Heidi to serve to Justin in the backhand court. She tossed up the ball to serve, but it hardly left her hand. A fault.

Oh, my gosh! She's nervous! Justin discovered with delight and amazement. He had never known Heidi to exhibit the slightest trace of nerves on court. *Could it be, in this moment of truth, that playing me is unnerving her?*

The air grew taut with tension from the crowd. Everyone held their breath. Justin quickly moved forward a couple of paces, pressuring the server, announcing intentions to chip and charge to the net for the kill. Radiating aggression, he glared at Heidi. Her eyes looked like a frightened fawn's. She quickly dropped her gaze. The ball barely reached the net. Double fault. Match to Great Britain! World Cup Tennis!

The Olympiahalle exploded in a tumultuous storm as emotions rained down onto the court. Justin hugged his partner, and then quickly ran round the netpost and embraced Heidi, his great friend in need.

Shit a brick! Britain has won World Cup Tennis! it suddenly dawned on him.

He waved to the large contingent of supporters in the stands who echoed their appreciation.

Before the presentation, the president of the WCT committee rushed over to Justin.

'Splendid news! Preliminary reports suggest the highest television viewership in sporting history! Well done!'

On their return to Britain, Justin and his team mates received a welcome they could never have imagined in their wildest dreams. A ticker-tape parade through the streets of London. The newspapers were awash with headlines of the resurrection of British tennis. Justin was suddenly in great demand for talk shows and interviews, and besieged for autographs.

I can't go to a restaurant without hordes badgering me. I know they mean well, but ... And my neighbours have hemmed me in, pressuring me to sign contracts, and others stampede to my front door asking me to sign, complained Justin, trapped in the wake of his fame. *And then there's the pesky yobloid press!*

'Ted Parsen, of the *London Daily News*. Mr Forrester, have you seen the article about yourself in yesterday's edition? Front page.'

The *London Daily News* triumphantly announced the engagement of Heidi Schültz to Justin Forrester, and included a close-up picture of the lady wearing an engagement ring.

'Since the US Open I don't read any articles on tennis, or myself,' replied Justin, aloof.

'I'm a tennis reporter, so you know I'm not responsible for that article. But can you tell us if it's true? Are you engaged to Miss Schültz?'

Ted Parsen itched, but Justin declined to scratch. 'If you only write about tennis, then I will only speak of tennis,' Justin emphatically replied, and then turned to face the other reporters. 'Any tennis questions?'

'World Champion, now you win World Cup Tennis for Britain—'

'Oh no!' interrupted Justin. 'This was a team effort. Clearly my team mates played solid tennis. Without them we could never have won. Don't forget them.'

'Perhaps, but it seems to us you've instilled a spirit in your team members that urges them to win. Still, they're not you! A most curious irony is that Britain, home of lawn tennis, host of the greatest championships in the world, is comatose, unable to produce a champion. Yet Swaziland, an ex-colony can! What the bloody hell is wrong with British tennis?'

'I'm not sure. Champions exist in people. Um …'

'But no champions in British tennis?'

'Not at the moment!' replied Justin, getting a round of nervous laughter.

'Where does your fanaticism, this almost unbridled, naked fanaticism to win, come from?' asked another reporter, intrigued.

'I hate to lose at anything. I would rather die out there than lose. When it comes to the big tournaments, I love to win, an unquenchable passion to win. It's food for my inner being. But more than that I don't know. If you analyse it, you might lose it. I just look forward to my next tournament. I want to win it!' said Justin, his eyes burning with ambition. And then after a brief moment of reminiscing, 'It's weird, but if my father had not won a regatta, I'd never have played this crazy game. But I'm absolutely convinced I would've been a champion in some other sport. I burn inside to win.'

'And British tennis players? Is there not the raw material?' questioned a reporter, mystified.

'It's wrong to blame the current players. That's a big problem with British tennis. You knock the buggers too much. It makes tennis unattractive to people looking for a sport to play. The players you see are doing the best they can. I can only assume tennis loses its champions to other sports. The talent is there, it has to be with 60 million people. Britain's had great champions in other sports. The great middle distance runners, Coe, Ovett and Cram … Torvill and Dean were pretty good … Nick Faldo … Daley Thompson. And what about Steve Davis? There's a champ with the killer instinct if ever I saw one. Yep, the talent is there.'

'But?'

'British tennis simply does not attract them.'

'Why not?'

'The game's too stuffy! It has that stiff upper lip of an old boy's club,' replied Justin, pulling no punches. 'They chased me off court because I wasn't wearing white, and 'white apparel is *de rigueur*',' mimicked Justin in a supercilious tone of voice. 'And then they wanted to change my game—'

'Who are they?'

'Just they. The stiffs who run the show. They chased me away to an American college. It was easy for me to go, I wasn't leaving home. I knew what I wanted and I would go to any lengths to realise my ambition, globe-trotting to find a place to nurture my talent. But if I was a kid starting here in Britain, I'd give up tennis for another sport.'

'What's your solution?'

'Lighten up a little. Then there're three things you can do. Make tennis freely available. You get enough money from Wimbledon profits, so give the kids a racket and a ball. Secondly, hold masses of competitions for players at all levels and for all ages, 6 to 60. Do that and you'll extend the net to attract many more people to tennis. Thirdly, play more on clay. It'll give you Brits a spine.'

'Will that produce champions?'

'Sure to give you a better chance. But you can't order champs on a plate. Anyone who believes you can manufacture a Wimbledon champion is suffering from delusions of grandeur. Like I said, champs exist in people. They're the crazy buggers who have that absolute fire, an intangible passion to win. Do what I said and someday, somewhere in the net, there'll be a champion. Look for him. He'll be the one who concentrates and runs well, not the classical grooved stroker. Then leave him alone, don't mould him, he'll take care of himself. And don't knock him or you'll lose him.'

'Björn Borg coming from a snow-bound country not known for its tennis and conquering the tennis world like a Viking must be one of the most incredible success stories in sport, and spawned a generation of Swedish players,' commented a reporter. 'Will—'

'Exactly!' interrupted Justin. 'Had Borg not existed, many of those players might have become champions in other sports.'

'Will Britain follow the same course in the wake of your success?'

'I warn you, maybe not! The demand will increase, I'm sure. But if the stiffs don't take care of the sport and satisfy the need, they may well turn away. The Swedes converted Borg's success into further success.'

'Where do you go from here?' asked another reporter.

'I want to be the best. I—'

'You *are* the best!'

'Perhaps, but I want to win Wimbledon!' commented Justin, embracing the greatest tournament in the world as his inalienable right. 'I will always have this stirring restlessness until I win Wimbledon.'

'You're not alone, Justin. I don't think Britain can wait the six months until Wimbledon. There are many aficionados of long standing talking of you achieving the Grand Slam next year.'

Justin went cold for a moment. Caution pervaded his being. 'It's not right to talk about the Grand Slam. No one has any business to talk like that. It's too much.'

CHAPTER 10

Sitting in his hotel room on the 42nd floor of the Regent Hotel in Melbourne, Australia, Justin perused the ranking list in the latest copy of International Tennis Weekly.

Number one in the world! exclaimed Justin proudly.

He walked to the window and peered out into the night air. Like a fairy ship glittering on the horizon, glowed the futuristic National Tennis Centre in the tree-lined Flinders Park, astride the banks of the Yarra river in the heart of old Melbourne. Long considered a second class citizen of Grand Slam events, but with a yearning to belong, the Australian Open, in one fell swoop, had burst out of the cocoon of Kooyong and into the next century with a grand state-of-the-art showcase for tennis, boasting a centre court stadium with its crowning feature, a retractable roof. They could play when it rained!

The first Grand Slam tournament of the year would commence the next day, and as the curtain went up all eyes would be on the best player in the world, the top seed, Justin Forrester.

A Grand Slam? The Australian, French, Wimbledon and US Open, all in the same year. I can do it, fantasized Justin, but very quickly castigated himself. *Stop it, Justin! Take it one tournament at a time, one match at a time.*

The court surface at Flinders Park is Rebound Ace, the base, shredded car tyres. The oppressive Australian summer sun bakes the rubber, sometimes nudging the mercury on the court surface to over 65°C, creating an oven effect. It saps the player's energy, and with it the fruit of their game, to leave behind a raisin. Between points some stand on the white lines or quickly enter the sanctuary of shade at the back of the court for a brief respite from the crucible of heat, only to have to enter hell again.

They come armed with a panoply of imagination to deceive the scalding Melbourne sun, painting their noses with a variety of shades of zinc ointment, cutting strips of towels to dip in iced water and tie round their necks, or even placing moist cabbage leaves under French legionnaire's hats! Others pray for a stealthy night-time route to the final, to escape the heat exhaustion.

But whilst his opponents wilted under the merciless broiling sun, Justin, the top seed, blossomed at Flinders Park, rubbing salt into their sunburn by barbecuing them with his white hot game. He was all perpetual motion, the perfect antidote to his opponents, the baking court and the pesky Australian fly.

And he was perpetually in demand. To escape the swarm of activity that surrounded him, Justin and Heidi motored miles away from Melbourne centre to Brighton Beach.

To his utter dismay, hordes flocked around him like moths to a flame, ceaselessly hunting for his autograph.

'They're staring,' Justin whispered, jailed in the public's attention. 'I can feel it in my back!'

'Just ignore them,' advised Heidi, herself having suffered the annoyance of those who pester.

'Damn! Now they're whispering about us!' complained Justin, agitated. 'I can't take this any more. Let's escape!'

'Why don't we have a relaxing meal in that Chinese restaurant over there.'

'Think they'd serve lean beef and potatoes?'

'Oh, Justin! Get a life!'

No sooner had the two sat down to lunch when a middle-aged lady approached their table and asked Justin, 'Oh, um, would you mind signing this serviette?'

He obliged. While he struggled to write legibly on the crinkled paper, the lady droned on in the background.

'You know, I have a son who plays tennis. He's in the fourth grade this year. I've wondered lately if he should stay back a year. Oh, he's a fan of yours, so he's going to be jealous of me, alright. Do you think you'll still be here in half an hour? Maybe I can bring him around.'

Justin stared at the lady, incredulous.

'Bye!' she giggled and left.

'Justin!' bellowed a silver-haired man, patting him on the back. 'I'm shooting this movie, CALL ME JANE. It's kind of a Tarzan story set in a hammock. When I saw you on Channel 7 yesterday, I just knew I had to have you star in it. Here's the script. Read it through and let me know before you leave—'

The man suddenly went silent, staring contemplatively at Heidi.

'Jane!' he exclaimed, snapping his fingers.

'Excuse me!' Justin curtly interrupted. 'Thanks, but no thanks. We're tennis players.'

The man looked enquiringly at Heidi.

'I'd love to do it,' she said with a smile. 'Call me next century!'

'Pah!' spat the man, snatching the script from the table. 'You'll be sorry. You could've been famous with me!'

Justin turned to Heidi and said, 'Fame. Now *that* I can do without!'

'You're going to have to learn to deal with it,' advised Heidi. 'Muffle it, or it'll get to you.'

'I swear, a year ago if I had discovered a water substitution for fuel I would have experienced the rejection of a door-to-door salesman. Now they hunt me down. And it's so crazy because I'm the same person. … Have you been asked to pose nude?'

'Yes! And be paid $1 million.'

'Oh!' said Justin, indignantly. 'I was only offered half that!'

Precariously juggling a grain of rice on chopsticks, anxious to taste his first morsel of chopsuey, Justin noticed the waiter approaching their table. Expecting him to ask if they were enjoying their meals, Justin looked up at him.

'Mr Justin. Is communism dead?' asked the waiter.

'Huh?'

'If communism is dead, maybe I go back to mainland China!'

'You do that!'

Justin looked disbelievingly at Heidi, who merely smiled.

'Look at them, Heidi! Look at that window. There're dozens of them peering in. I feel like a monkey in a gold cage. Next they'll throw sweets at me!'

Just then someone tugged him on his shoulder and peered round from behind him.

'Yes, Marge, you're dead right. His eyes *are* blue!'

'That's it!' screamed Justin. 'I'm out of here. Came here for some bloody peace, but no, they have to bug, bug, bug! Damn, it's so draining! And detracting! You tell me it's more difficult sustaining number one than earning it. Well, I want nothing more but to stay at the top of the tree. But this fame stuff is going to exhaust my energy and destroy me first!' griped an exasperated Justin. He stood up and said, 'Come, let's go and lock ourselves up in our hotel.'

'You and me in a cocoon?' teased Heidi.

'Mmm! Yep! Let's play find the worm!'

'More like a snake!'

Suddenly Justin found life at the crest of tennis a lonely and curious one. Lonely because his domination produced distance. He became an island. It was silent there. When he walked into the locker-room, fellow players felt in unutterable awe of him. They stared from a distance, intimidated by his glacial aloofness. He was different.

Curious because his star status reaped dividends, too. Justin began to win matches because his growing legend unnerved opponents. There were 128 players in the draw, with 127 huddled in the shadow of one man, Justin Forrester.

As Justin got up to leave the interview room, a man burst in, bubbling with enthusiasm.

'Steve, have you seen this qualifier, Boris Bauer?' he asked, unable to contain his excitement of discovery.

'No! Not heard of him.'

'He just beat Manolo Gonzales. Four, four and four!'

'So what! Waltzing Matilda can beat Manolo on his off-days!'

Leaving the interview room, Justin pondered the conversation he had overheard. *True, Manolo can beat or lose to anyone. But a bloody qualifier in the quarters! Who is this bugger, Boris Bauer?* He quickly dismissed the thought from his mind and focused on his next match. *Naresh Singh.*

Flinders Park unfolded into a canvas on which Naresh used his silky skills to paint beautiful pictures with his tennis artistry, prompting members in the crowd to hold up banners, 'SINGHULAR SENSATION' or 'SINGH'S SHOT SINGS'. An artist stands in his own niche. Da Vinci. Picasso. Neither of these two artists competed against each other. Neither lived with head to head records. But Naresh Singh's chosen *métier* measured him against his fellow man in a profession that honours one man, the king of the hill.

Judged solely on his artistic impression, Naresh would be king. But tennis is more than art. Justin plied his rich and varied talents to smudge the Indian's pictures for two sets. Then in the heat of the battle, Naresh Singh's shoe stuck to the tacky rubber and he went over on his ankle like a withered flower, sitting dead still where it happened.

Justin raced to the other side of the net and applied ice to the agonized Indian. The match over, a wheelchair carted Naresh Singh off the court.

In Justin's mandatory press conference, only one question pertained to his match.

'Naresh is the third player to twist an ankle. The buzz is that the courts are treacherous in this hot weather, like running in chewing gum, and the players are taping their ankles in precaution. Have you taped your ankles?' asked a reporter.

'I have, ever since Wimbledon last year,' answered Justin, remembering his heart-rending injury. 'Grass at Wimbledon. Rebound here. I'm not sure it's the court surface.'

'Have you seen this Boris Bauer?' questioned another reporter.

'Nope!'

'He just beat Roland Drechsler!' the reporter spilled the dramatic news.

Immediately Justin's mental ears pricked up.

The newsman continued, 'Wait for it, 6-2 6-0 6-1. His initials are perfect for …'

Justin remained quiet, but sifted an assortment of mind flashes. *Seldom does a dark horse creep up on the tour and sneak a surprise victory. Nope, the grapevine runs deep and long. Was Roland injured? Maybe! But then he also beat Manolo! Shit! Who is this bloody qualifier, Boris Bauer? a concerned Justin asked himself. New blood on the tour. I can handle that. But what a hiding! Roland's number three in the world and defending champion!*

'Do you realise that Boris Bauer is only the second qualifier to get as far as a Grand Slam semifinal?' another journalist asked.

'I'm well aware,' answered Justin, remembering the other to be John McEnroe at Centenary Wimbledon.

'Do you think he can beat Tyrone Summers in the semis?'

'I can't say. I've never seen the bugger play.'

'Is it possible for a qualifier to win a Grand Slam tournament?'

'It's possible,' answered Justin, not giving anything away.

The questions about Boris Bauer continued until the end of the interview.

The sudden and interesting turn of events did not displease Justin. *At last the pressure is off me a little,* he sighed. *Phew! Thank goodness for this bugger, Boris Bauer.*

Justin rushed straight back to the Regent Hotel, ran up all 42 flights of stairs to avoid the risk of catching a cold from a sneezer in a lift, besides, it was good training, entered his room and rewound the tape in his VCR. He had set the machine to tape the Boris Bauer match off Channel 7 Sport, wanting to know about this player who had grown in menace, round by round.

'Hubba hubba! What bloody power!' exclaimed Justin, watching intently, absorbing every detail of the big man's game. 'But how good is he?'

Boris Bauer simply devoured the power of Roland Drechsler, stoking it up and exhaling it like some fire-breathing dragon, scorching the German. Being Australia Day, cannons on the far banks of the Yarra river sounded a 21 gun salute. One could believe they recognised their kind and stirred to life like some long lost friends finding each other. Their echoes sounded the death knell for Roland Drechsler.

What a whitewash! thought Justin. *But not being under any pressure, it's difficult to assess his true ability.*

After the match, the press interviewed Roland Drechsler.

'Do you think Boris Bauer can actually win the title?'

'No! Not this year,' answered Roland, settling back into his chair. 'Sure he can win it,' he continued, shaking his head, 'but not this year!' He shrugged his shoulders, pondering the unthinkable. 'A qualifier? A novice to Grand Slam tennis?'

The first semifinal featured Justin against Sern Stenmark, the doomsday stroking machine of the clay courts. The Rebound Ace at Flinders Park favoured neither the serve and volleyer nor the baseliner. But out of the domain of his beloved red clay, Sern Stenmark found himself a Swedish mackerel in the Australian coastal waters, home of the Great White. Justin's marauding game devoured him in a feeding frenzy, silencing the cry of a large perennial contingent of Swedish supporters, warpainted in their national colours of blue and yellow.

As Justin left the court, autograph hunters bogged him down. He dutifully signed, but he was anxious.

Come on! Come on! Come on! I want to go back to my hotel and see Terror play this Boris Bauer. To see this bugger you have to be punctual. He doesn't stick around for very long!

Lastly, an old man thrust a programme in his face. 'For my niece!'

'What's her name?'

'Oh, just make it Jack!'

In his press conference a reporter asked Justin, '*Now* have you seen Boris Bauer playing?'

'Uh huh!' replied Justin.

'And?'

'Powerful!'

'Can he beat Tyrone Summers?'

'Anything's possible.'

'Can he beat Justin Forrester?'

'You'll just have to wait and see!'

Only on completion of the first semifinal did a buzz permeate the stadium. Heralded by the thunder, triggered by the lightning, the supersonic Boris Bauer became the talk of the tournament. Hundreds of reporters from around the globe heard the news and flew into Melbourne to witness this sensation who hit the tennis world like a howitzer striking a zeppelin, blowing to bits the cosy world of its inhabitants.

Back at the Regent, Justin switched on the television.

Terror's a different species from Roland Drechsler. He's got that absolute fire. Many jokers up the tyrant's sleeve, too, assessed Justin. He'll provide a real test for Boris Bauer's ability. Show the bugger up for what he is.

Boris Bauer made a mockery of expectations and mercilessly destroyed Tyrone Summers, 6-1 6-2 6-1, just as he had done so often in Greenwich, Connecticut.

As shell-shocked as Tyrone, a puzzled and concerned Justin hurriedly retrieved his copy of International Tennis Weekly, and surveyed the columns of rankings. Who was this runaway juggernaut with the bludgeoning serve and volley blitzkrieg of a Boris Becker, and the relentless awesome ground stroking power of an Ivan Lendl?

'He's only ranked 237!' exclaimed Justin in utter disbelief. *In a blink of an eye he's transformed in a quantum leap from obscurity to greatness. A giant among midgets!*

Almost unnoticed, Tyrone Summers passed the $7,500 fine barrier when he cracked a racket. Banned from playing the next Grand Slam tournament! The press seemed unconcerned. They wanted to know about Boris Bauer.

'What is it like to face Boris Bauer?' a reporter asked Tyrone.

'Teach a gorilla to serve and you've got that Scudface!'

'What do you mean this guy doesn't talk? Is he dumb or something?' asked a disbelieving reporter who had just flown in to Melbourne.

'Hmmph!' answered Vich, Boris Bauer's mentor.

'Where does he come from?'

'Hmmph!'

'Where has he been?'

'Hmmph!'

'Who taught him how to play?'

'Hmmph!'

The international media went at Vich like a pack of hungry wolves, but he gave very little away. The fortuitous ailment enabled Amos Creighton to shield his protégé from the fangs of the media. They soon grew tired of the mumbling Vich, but the Boris Bauer bubble of intrigue, swelled.

§

The strength of the lion is the pride, and the strength of the pride is the lion.

§

The Team BB entourage drove to their hide-out on the outskirts of Melbourne where Creighton had built a replica of Flinders Park. Boris Bauer had used it for two months to hone his game for the Australian Open championships.

The following day he walked out onto the replica of the centre court stadium. Instead of people in the seats, thousands of suspended squares of aluminium took their place. They reflected light and shivered, making a restless noise, all to simulate the real thing. Even the blue Ford billboards separated the playing area from the aluminium spectators with a buffer zone, creating the unnerving spatial dimension warp that exists at Flinders Park. They emulated the identical routine used at the Australian Open, right down to the toss for service and the use of an umpire.

Boris Bauer walked out to one side of the court and turned round to face Justin Forrester, the OTTO ball machine.

Early Sunday, morning of the final, Boris Bauer went through his pre-match massage ritual.

'First your aperitif,' instructed the pretty auburn-haired Robin Wallenborg, offering Boris a tray of five glasses of water. They were alone. 'Take two hours.'

She proceeded to massage the waterlogged body, first with long strokes, then kneaded the muscles, unlocking lactic acid particles to flow into the bloodstream and eventually flush out in the urine. As the outer layers softened, she delved deeper and deeper to the bone, priming him into peak condition.

'Your after dinner mint!' said the masseur, offering him another two glasses of water. 'Bottoms up. Then go and wee.'

Boris Bauer drank the water then started to leave.

'Boris?'

The tall man turned around.

'Good luck, today!' said Robin with a smile.

Boris Bauer stood still for a moment, his eyes searching into hers. He longed to say something. Then he turned and left.

Justin finalised his preparations in the locker-room, stretching and gathering his gear. He sat alone, in contrast to all other players who surrounded themselves with a coterie of advisers. The shy man looked almost vulnerable. But every eye watched him. Nobody failed to see him. They knew who he was. All that changed on a tennis court, where he implacably dominated his sport. When called to go on court, he nodded his head to his 20 year old opponent as a mark of respect, but Boris Bauer merely gazed with a vacuous stare.

Shit! He's oblivious of anyone and anything around him, thought Justin.

Boris Bauer won the toss and mimed his choice to serve first.

He's weird! thought Justin.

Turning round to commence the warm-up, the appearance of his towering, short-cropped, black-haired opponent, completely dressed in black, struck him. *Hubba hubba!* exclaimed Justin. *The bugger's chiselled out of granite!*

Damn! I've no idea how to play this bugger, lamented Justin, perturbed. *Okay, so I know he hits with power. But what else? This warm-up is giving me no clue! If need be, I'll just have to use my legs to run down his shots,* he consoled himself.

'Ready gentlemen. Mr Bauer to serve,' called the umpire.

Boris launched his delivery with devastating force. Justin barely got a racket to it.

'Fifteen-love.'

Second point. The ball hissed, skidding off the pea green Rebound Ace, uninterrupted by a Dunlop Max 800i. A sparkling ace.

'Thirty-love.'

First serve fault.

Aah! Here's a chance, thought Justin, moving forward to take the second serve.

Boris Bauer crashed down the second serve with equal power to his first delivery. Again, Justin barely got a racket to the ball.

'Forty-love.'

'Servin' two first serves makes the game simple, like a bloody square wheel, chief,' outlined Bob Wallace. 'The Big Bastard'll 'ave only one action to learn. Ya see, chief, a bugger normally wins only about 'alf the points on his second serve. By 'avin' one action, the Big Bastard'll increase both his first serve percentage and the number of points won on his second serve.'

'But double faults will increase,' countered Creighton, concerned.

'Righto, but there's a bonus. 'Is opponent either faces a mule kick or a double fault. The bugger can't get into a rhythm. Won't feel like 'e's won the bloody point on a double fault, rather, the Big Bastard *lost* ut!'

Boris Bauer closed out the game with another cracking ace down the centre.

'Game, Bauer. He leads 1-0,' announced the umpire.

The crowd buzzed with anticipation after Boris Bauer's sensational start in his first Grand Slam final.

It's one thing to serve like that. Let the bugger try receiving serve, countered Justin, walking to his seat at the change-over.

On passing each other, those eyes again struck Justin. *They're blank, like a robot!* He set great store by reading innuendos – arguments, a shrug of the shoulders and especially the eyes – striving to find soft spots to help devise a strategy to swing the match in his favour. *He's like me! He doesn't show anything. Emotionless players are the hardest to deal with. I'll have to keep grinding away to reveal the inside!*

Sitting in his chair, shaded by a beach umbrella, Justin noticed Boris Bauer walk straight to the other side. *Talk about rushing an opponent!* criticised Justin. *And I thought my tempo was fast!*

Team BB had instructed Boris Bauer to skip the first changeover, to use the extra time to acclimatise to the different perspective offered by the other side of the court.

Justin served straight as an arrow down the centre. Before he had finished the follow through, Boris Bauer's full-blooded return sizzled by, leaving the nimble Justin tottering off balance in no man's land. The ball had mild topspin for safety, the rest, bludgeoning power! Same for point number two, Boris Bauer uncorking a powerhouse down the line for a clean winner.

Shit! I feel like I'm playing that game 'stuck in the mud', felt Justin sheepishly, his tennis shoes seemingly melted and welded to the tacky rubber court.

'Love-thirty.'

He's a big bugger. How quick is he? Justin questioned first himself, and then Boris Bauer by spinning a wicked serve wide to the forehand side. He followed the serve up to the net. Boris Bauer leapt to his right side with lightning speed for his size and crushed the ball, deforming it with force. Justin reached out for the volley, but the sheer power in the ball caused a miscue and the ball sailed over the baseline.

Shit! Triple break point in my first service game! cursed Justin. *I'll test a point staying back.*

The rally quickly suckered Justin deeper and deeper into trouble, Boris Bauer jerking him around the court, finally catapulting a winner down the line.

'Game, Bauer. He leads 2-0,' announced the umpire.

The break of serve stunned the crowd. The only communication came from a lone poster, 'BRAVO BORIS'.

Shit! This is a nightmare. Nothing seems real, whined Justin. He shook his head to clear it.

Preparing to receive serve, he looked up at Boris Bauer and thought,

He makes the court look small. He's a bloody monster! Those legs look like tree trunks and that burly frame belongs more to a Canadian lumberjack! And shit, look at those large hands dwarfing that odd-looking racket, manoeuvring it with the ease and insignificance of swatting flies with a fly-swatter. I feel like a middleweight boxer in a division of heavyweight sluggers!

Boris Bauer served out the third game to love. The pace was hot. Rubber burned. He began like a bat out of hell, and observers quickly dispelled any doubts about the efficacy of Boris Bauer at top flight tennis.

Crisis time! worried Justin, towelling down. *That bloody serve is killing me! It's the bedrock of his game, the launching pad from which the bugger strikes. He just winds up and booms, and my returns sit up like big juicy plums inviting to be picked off on the volley!*

Hearing a murmur reverberate around the stadium like a stream tumbling down a waterfall, the blood drained from Justin's face.

World Champion and I've lost the opening 12 points to a qualifier! My legs and my mind, my great weapons, have screwed me, griped Justin. *But a quitter, I am not! I will run the full gamut of my abilities to stem his glut of winners, and beat that Boris Bauer!*

In the next game, at 40-30, Justin served and attacked. His racket popped up the ball with pirouetting underspin, so wild, it bounced on Boris Bauer's side and spun back to Justin. Boris Bauer was there to hit it, but did not. Team BB had failed to prime him on the rule that allowed you to reach over to the opponent's side without touching the net, and hit such a ball.

On the scoreboard at last! thought a relieved Justin.

But such luck was not enough.

'Game Boris Bauer. He leads 5-2. New balls please,' called the umpire.

During the change-over, Boris retrieved a brand new racket from a cellophane bag. Team BB trained him to do so each ball-change, to parallel the dynamics of his game to the wear of the ball, thereby minimising adjustment.

Before serving, Justin showed Boris Bauer the new balls, an unwritten code between players. It went unnoticed. With his new racket, Boris Bauer broke serve and took the first set 6-2. He pillaged the second, also 6-2.

Down 0-1 in the third set, Justin sat at the change-over and poured ice-water over his legs.

Shit! This stadium's on heat! he complained.

But it was no hotter than any other day, and it never worried him before. His mind started to deceive him, looking for problems, subconsciously seeking an alibi for failure. Heat became unbearable, noises magnified.

Snap out of it, Justin. Work your butt off. I've turned many matches around before. I'll do it again!

Still the supersonic serves relentlessly rained down in a blitz of smart laser-guided missiles.

Damn! I just can't seem to break through. I can't get to the bloody ball to do anything with it! lamented Justin, feeling himself sucked into the black hole of defeat, helpless to resist.

Sheer guts held the third set to 3-all.

At last! The hardest thing in tennis, the severest test of the mind, is to close out a title match. Let's see what this bugger's made of!

Such talk was to be Justin's last hurrah. He tried gallantly until the last point, but never won another game. There *was* no mental test for Boris Bauer. Team BB stilled his mind of all thought, except power. In an hour and 10 minutes, the white hot game of the puissant Boris Bauer, neither weakening nor gaining strength, melted the ice-man's game to a puddle.

'Game, set and match to Bauer, 6-2 6-2 6-3,' called the umpire.

Boris Bauer raised his arms in triumph before the two opponents shook hands. His eyes never met Justin's.

The same expressionless eyes, observed Justin, still shell-shocked by the blitz.

'An incredible day for tennis, but not for you, Justin!' remarked a reporter at a press conference.

'Nope! Most certainly not,' replied a dejected Justin, suffering his first loss since his default at Wimbledon last year.

'When Boris Becker lost early one year at Wimbledon, he said he had just lost a tennis match, not a war, that nobody died out there, and these things just happen. What—?'

Justin wore a dazed look on his face, but slowly shook his head in disagreement. 'For me, tennis is a war. For you it's no big deal. Today I died. Each time I lose, I die a little. When I win, I am reborn. That's war!'

'We all surmised that in the final, playing the World Champion, and with the world eye on him, Boris Bauer would crack. It did not appear so.'

'Nope!' replied Justin emphatically.

'How did you feel out there?'

'Overwhelmed!' exclaimed a stunned Justin. 'Everything felt so fast. Even the change-overs and between points. I felt rushed. Normally my opponents feel that way, I think. The match just finished without me. I guess he plain kicked me in the clay pipe cushion!'

'How hard was his serve?'

'Pretty hard!' answered Justin with a wry smile. 'He has no second serve. He just hits another first. I needed a bullet proof vest!'

'Did you run out of tactical ideas?'

'Pretty much! He plays one way, with power. He serves hard, bloody hard! He pulverises his groundies and crushes his volleys. I just had no time. No time to think. It's weird, because you know what he's going to do, but there's not much you can do about it. His power causes strategic paralysis. Eventually I just tried to hang in there, but he was simply the best player on the day.'

'Was this a freak tournament for him?'

'Nope!'

'Then it looks like the sky's the limit for him. Where does he go from here?'

'I have no idea,' said Justin, shrugging his shoulders. 'Tennis has never had such a weird species. He played tennis I would never have believed possible!'

'Can he win the French Open?' asked a reporter, thinking ahead to the next Grand Slam tournament.

'Normally it takes more than power to win at Roland Garros. But here he played tennis from another planet, so I'll withhold opinion. I look forward to playing him at Wimbledon!'

Amos Creighton called a meeting of Team BB.

'Instruct the boy never to show emotion at winning again!' ordered Creighton, fuming that his protégé had. 'Only when I laugh all the way to the bank!'

That done he assumed a quieter tone. 'Gentlemen,' started Creighton before adding the faintest nod to Robin Wallenborg, 'one down, eleven to go!'

The first wave of trepidation rippled through the betting houses.

While Ford bound for Tullamarine airport, Justin saw *The Age's* billboard screaming, 'BIONIC BRUTE BULLIES BRIT'.

I can't believe it! he thought, still shaking his head. *Damn! I feel so cheated,* moped Justin, thinking back to the evening before the tournament. *Only a moment ago I towered as the undisputed best player in the world. I felt so sure I would win the Aussie Open. Now Boris Bauer, a qualifier, gatecrashes a party reserved for the tennis élite, never to be denied a future invitation.*

Justin gazed out the window at a great expanse of the world and decided, *I look forward to a rivalry with this Boris Bauer bugger. I'm not dead. I'm wounded. I'll heal. The beauty of this game is that I may have lost to him today, but I can play him again tomorrow. I'll follow him to the ends of the earth to play him again, and beat him!*

§

'Damn Boris Bauer!' Justin cried to Heidi in a cross-Atlantic call. 'The bugger's disappeared!'

'You're joking!' she replied.

Long after the Australian Open, the talking point of the tennis world still centred on Boris Bauer. Yet, no longer did the topic concern his staggering triumph at Flinders Park, but his sudden disappearance. As quickly as he surfaced, he vanished!

'Nope! He's nowhere—'

'But how can he maintain his competitiveness?' wondered Heidi, bewildered that Boris Bauer contested no ATP Tour events.

Where Justin shone in full glory on the tour, winning titles at Key Biscayne, Monte Carlo and Hamburg, Boris Bauer was non-participant. Month after month passed without a word about him. Would he play the French Open?

'Damn! Damn that bugger!' cursed Justin, irked. Defeat never rested easily on his shoulders. He itched to pursue a rivalry to settle a score, peeved at his deprivation to exact revenge. 'And damn your tour! You've *gone* a long way, baby, rationing our rendezvous to Grand Slams. I need you, Heidi!'

'Paris! I can't wait!'

By rationing Boris Bauer's trenchant, bullying skills to Grand Slam fare, Team BB kept him fresh, unfamiliar and invincible. They hibernated in a simulated environment of Roland Garros at Creighton's tennis complex in Greenwich, Connecticut, oiling the machinery for Act 2.

Justin was right. Winning the French Open loomed as Boris Bauer's most difficult hurdle of the famed foursome. Fortunately for him, he had four months to prepare, and prepare he did! For six hours every day, he lived on red clay! His morning session consisted of drills extracting consistency from a man who continued to hit with potent power. And to keep match tight, Boris Bauer spent the afternoon playing several opponents in the form of Otto Weiner's ball machine, the data captured from last year's French Open.

Three weeks before the French Open, Team BB acquired another member, a sports nutritionist. A disciple of pasta, Romany Fatignon shed light on performance enhancing through diet, at his first meeting with

Team BB, in Creighton's replica of Roland Garros.

'Martina Navratilova's pasta diet is legendary. Many tennis players have followed her example. That, we know. *I* have been experimenting with a variation,' declared the slick, dark-haired Frenchman. 'For some time, now, long distance runners have used carbohydrate-loading to gain that extra mile before hitting the wall. Since winning the French Open is equivalent to seven marathons, it is prudent that we follow suit.'

A week before the marathon on red clay, Boris Bauer commenced a carbo-loading diet more scientific than palatable.

'The most efficient energy source in the body is glycogen in the muscles,' explained Romany Fatignon. 'But the limited stores burn up quickly. After that, the body fires on fat, inefficiently.'

'Is this when those bloody runners 'it the wall?' asked Bob Wallace.

'Exactly! When their glycogen depletes, they experience a marked deterioration in performance due to the decreased efficiency of energy supply.'

'And pasta fixes this, mate?' asked Bob Wallace. 'A can o' piss does ut for me!'

'Partly,' responded Romany Fatignon, ignoring the Australian's penchant for beer. 'Eating carbohydrates elevates the glycogen supply, but using my carbo-loading technique, you can artificially expand this reserve.'

'Makin' a bloody camel with a long distance storage tank!' offered Bob Wallace.

'Precisely! And the first step towards our dromedary, is to deplete the current supply of glycogen,' announced Romany Fatignon.

The nutritionist instructed Boris Bauer, 'Train for five hours against a ball machine and run a distance of 20 kilometres. And drink only water, nothing sweet.'

'The next three days, instead of pasta, eat fats and proteins,' ordered Romany Fatignon.

''As your block conked?' asked a disturbed Bob Wallace.

'No!' responded the nutritionist. 'He must eat eggs and cheese, and fish and green salads. To drink, only artificially sweetened beverages.'

'Back to front, ain't ut, mate?'

'For the moment, yes!' replied Romany Fatignon. 'Oh, and no tennis, just physical training.'

'Bloody 'ell 'e won't!' bellowed Bob Wallace. 'The flippin' French Open's next week. You can be damn sure 'e'll play tennis!'

'It'll be useless,' defended the nutritionist. 'His fine-motor skills will regress.'

Vich looked menacingly at Bob Wallace, fondling his Donnay Allwood.

For the next three days Boris Bauer continued only his physical training. Disturbingly, his performance nose-dived. The robot grew human. Listless. Irritable. Depressed. He looked gaunt and pimply, and his times grew slower and slower.

'What've ya done, mate?' a disturbed Bob Wallace asked Romany Fatignon. 'The Big Bastard looks bloody pathetic.'

'Then it's working!' smiled Romany Fatignon. 'The worse he gets, the greater the benefits! That hard workout Monday, plus this training, will totally deplete his glycogen level. Be careful he does not come into contact with people. In this state he's very susceptible to picking up a cold.'

'Not bloody likely 'e'll meet any bastards, mate!'

Boris Bauer collapsed in a pitiful heap.

'Tomorrow he'll rise from the dead!' pronounced Romany Fatignon.

On the fifth day, Romany Fatignon arrived at the Roland Garros replica with a basketful of cereals, bread, rice and goodies such as chocolate éclairs, sweets and syrupy drinks.

'Train on this!' ordered Romany Fatignon. 'And relax. No exercise. No tennis.'

A gaunt Boris Bauer wolfed down the masses of carbohydrates. But the supply coming out of the basket was endless. As the day wore on and he fed his face, life flushed back into his body, until by the end of the day, like a dog after a postman, he was hard to restrain from playing tennis.

'You see, with his glycogen supply totally depleted over the last three days, loading takes place to a degree not normally possible. It's as if starvation expands the body's capacity to store glycogen. *Now* he is a camel of energy!' declared Romany Fatignon. He produced a whopping chocolate cake from his magic basket and ordered Boris Bauer, 'Eat!'

On the sixth day, Boris Bauer resumed light tennis work.

'How's he doing?' asked Romany Fatignon.

'I 'ate to admit ut, mate, but the Big Bastard's playin' better than before!'

'That is to be expected. Not only did BB suffer physically during the depletion stage, but it brutalised him psychologically,' expounded Romany Fatignon. 'Now he is reborn, mentally refreshed and playing with new vigour. On top of the world!'

'Is the carbo-loading process complete?' asked the business-like Amos

Creighton.

'Mostly. But this is where tennis is different from running. Since the arduous matches are likely to come later in the tournament, he has to maintain these glycogen levels for two weeks. From now on, he must ingest large supplies of carbohydrates to replenish lost reserves and maintain his boosted capacity. In essence, we have added a reserve tank as an emergency for a tight match.'

Syphoning corn syrup, Boris Bauer ploughed a furrow *en route* to the semifinal where he met a potentially dangerous opponent in Sern Stenmark. But firing on all cylinders with a storm of energy, he demolished the Swede 6-0 6-0 6-1.

The Australian Open had come and gone and so had Boris Bauer. The tennis world had to pinch itself to wonder if it had temporarily lapsed into a dream, but it was true. If one checked the name engraved on the Norman Brookes Challenge Cup, it was indeed Boris Bauer. Nobody had expected him to do it again, least on the slow red clay courts of Roland Garros. But he did. He blazed through to the final in sensational style, not losing a set, stunning the international tennis community.

For Justin, it was back to his happy hunting ground, Roland Garros. In the quarter-finals he dispatched Manolo Gonzales with ease.

A reporter at a press conference addressed Justin, 'You once said that a player must be careful not to expend unnecessary drive early, yet have reserves for an unexpected test. Beating Manolo so easily, are you not peaking too soon?'

'It is true that Grand Slam tennis requires perfect pacing, a slow tightening of the nuts and bolts as the tournament progresses to the final,' replied Justin. 'But no, I've got a trick or two left up my sleeve!'

'You are the champion. Would it mean more to defend your title successfully?'

'The first time was special, and will always be. But now, if I lost, I would feel deprived of something that belongs to me. I will fight to the bitter end and more, and if I succeed, that would be very special too!'

'Do you know where Boris Bauer has been hiding out?'

'Nope!'

In the other semifinal, Justin found an old and wily enemy in Tyrone Summers, absurdly unseeded. Her son banned from Roland Garros for exceeding the $7,500 fine limit, Tyrone's mother found a loophole in legality. He could play if he qualified!

Debated under a mournful and leaden Parisian sky, the match attracted controversy like children to the Pied Piper. It was treated to the entire Summers carnival and started in typical Tyrone unpredictability.

'I'm ready!' he declared, refusing to warm up with Justin.

Tennis subscribes to an extraordinary ritual of the antagonists warming up with each other before a match. Amazingly, the players observe the routine in dead silence, each fine-tuning his game with a telepathy of understanding.

The umpire scratched his head. He was baffled. What to do?

'It's okay,' Justin advised the umpire, holding up his hand like a traffic warden to ward off any confrontation. 'I'm ready, too!'

That was the only resistance Tyrone offered for the first 30 minutes as the champion raced through the first set, 6-0. The calm before the storm.

Be careful! Keep the bugger under wraps, warned Justin, aware that winning a bagel first set can sometimes backfire. My score cannot improve, he cannot get worse. *The shift in balance can snowball.*

It did! Serving with advantage at 3-all in the second set, Justin raced to his forehand side and flicked a sizzling topspin pass on the stretch. Tyrone dived and miraculously half-volleyed an uncontested drop-shot. The sideline linesman's hand went out late, casting a shadow of doubt in Tyrone's mind.

'No, no, no!' protested Tyrone, quickly coming across to Justin's side to inspect the mark. He looked up to the umpire, 'The ball was in. There's no mark!'

Hmm! I'm not sure of the call, thought Justin. *Sure, it landed close to the white line, that dividing line between perfection and disaster, but I was too far away from the scene of the crime to judge. But I'll exploit the question mark and let Terror blow up emotionally and lose control.*

The umpire suddenly appeared dismayed, as if he just got word that he would have to umpire a Tyrone Summers match. A 'why did this have to happen to me' type of look. He glanced at the linesman, then back at Tyrone, then again at the linesman. He clearly seemed unsure how to handle this close encounter of the Tyrone Summers kind. Not calling the score before Tyrone got his mouth into the act, now provided a dilemma.

He signalled the linesman to go and look for the mark. The linesman dutifully complied, searched for awhile, then his face radiated a triumphant grin and he held out his hand again.

'Jeu, Forrester!' called the umpire, giving the point and game to Justin.

'No way, loony tune. That's my footprint!' screamed Tyrone. He quickly dragged his foot over it, rubbing out the mark, reaping a mixed bag echo of laughter and jeers from the crowd. 'There's no mark! Come see for yourself.'

The umpire shifted uneasily in his chair.

Tyrone put the palms of his hands together near his heart in prayer mode, pleading with the umpire to dismount his high horse and inspect the dearth of a ball mark. This point to Tyrone would aid his case for a crucial break of serve in the mystical seventh game.

'Please?'

To the amazement of everybody, the umpire raised his eyebrows questioningly to the netcord judge for his opinion. Sitting on the far side of the net from the umpire, the netcord judge sat only a couple of paces away from where the ball landed. He held out his hand, level.

Tyrone walked in the direction of the umpire.

'Are you kidding? *He* calls the lines,' shouted Tyrone pointing to the linesman, and then pointing to the netcord judge, instructed the umpire, 'and *he* calls the net. *You* call the score. Now go and see if you can see a mark.'

Tyrone went to sit in his chair. Photographers fanned the embers by poking their lenses into his face and the crowd around him bayed for blood. Suddenly everything came tumbling down, including, alas, Tyrone's shorts, giving the photographers a bird's eye view of a new moon.

Terror! Terror! Terror! The cheek of it! chuckled Justin. *This from a bugger who refused to play mixed doubles in disgust of some women storing the spare ball inside their panties!*

The umpire leant menacingly forward in his chair.

'I'm just changing my shorts!' protested Tyrone, who did just that.

Still the photographers baited him.

'Do your job and tell the crowd to shut up,' ordered Tyrone.

No response from the umpire.

'If it helps, *please!*'

Still he did not respond.

'Shut up, you!' screamed an enraged Tyrone, rushing the enemy and swiping his racket at the photographers. 'Or the next time you open your mouth I'll shove a ball down your throat and shut you up!'

The photographers dispersed like a swarm of flies swatted away from rotting fruit, only to return. Attempts to capture Tyrone Summers on film were fraught with danger!

Slamming down his racket, Tyrone sat in his chair, turned his head round and shouted in pidgin English, 'Me play tennis. You shut up!'

Meanwhile, the umpire descended from his perch and took a cursory look at the questionable patch of clay. Unable to find a mark made from ball or shoe, he reversed the point.

'*Égalité!*' announced the umpire to a round of derisive whistles.

Tyrone threw up his hands in mock triumph. Over six minutes had elapsed due to this altercation, when the rules permitted only 25 seconds between points.

Bloody hell! I wish linecalls were decisive, without recourse for intervention, yearned Justin, peeved. *That way play would be continuous! … Now focus all on the next ball.*

During the following point, a Forrester lifted backhand landed perilously close to the sideline. As Tyrone scooped it back, he pointed to the line, communicating to the umpire he felt the ball was out. Only then did the umpire concur in judgement and overrule the linesman.

'*Avantage,* Summers!' called the umpire.

This umpire's under his bloody thumb! bemoaned Justin. *And this match is draining away from my tennis control.*

With advantage to Tyrone, the champion faced break point on a second serve. Justin stuttered through the service motion and the ball clipped the net and fell on the centre line. Tyrone immediately walked to the chair in his confident, cocky gait.

'*Jeu,* Summers!' announced the umpire.

Justin took a deep breath and swore, *Shit! Terror's body language and the threat of another altercation swayed the bloody umpire! Now I'll have to break back. Quickly too! And not hit near the lines!*

With that break of serve Tyrone stole the second set against the run of play, 6-4.

At 2-all and 30-love in the third set, sickened by his tame forehand error into the net, Tyrone looked this way and that, sniffing a target for his vitriolic temper.

'Could you check the ball please? The one I hit felt soft. It could be popped.'

'It's mixed up with the others,' said the umpire.

'Then check *all* the balls. If the one I just hit is popped, I get a let,' said Tyrone in raised tone, angling for a replay of the previous point.

'But we don't know which ball you hit!' countered the umpire.

'Shit! Do I have to stick my dick in your mouth and fuck some brains into you?' mumbled Tyrone under his breath.

He turned to a ballboy and ordered him, 'Check the balls!'

Pinching yellow nap between his fingers, the ballboy held up a ball to his nose, sniffed, and replied with a shrug of his shoulders, 'It's okay!'

Biting his tongue, Tyrone glared disbelievingly at the ballboy for a few moments, then tired of him, he returned to the umpire. 'Damn you! All I ask is for you to check the balls.'

The umpire sat in silence. Tyrone eventually plodded back to the baseline to receive serve.

Justin received a second ball from a ballboy.

Terror's right. A ball is soft! said Justin, kneading it in his hands.

He returned it for another and went on to win the game for a 3-2 lead.

'Pass all the balls, please!' Tyrone demanded of a ballboy at the change-over.

The ballboy complied.

'This one's soft,' Tyrone indignantly notified the umpire.

'It may not be the one you hit,' replied the umpire pompously.

'It's unlikely there'd be two soft balls!' Tyrone looked at him pleadingly. Then he mumbled, 'Yours, perhaps!'

A drone of taunts issued from those in earshot. Tyrone took his cup of water and sprayed its contents over them, to the merriment of those who watched and stayed dry. Then he slammed the popped ball into the crowd, proceeded to the other side and prepared to serve, getting two balls from the ballboy on the far side.

'This fucking ball is also popped,' whined Tyrone, haunted by soft balls.

The crowd laughed, whistled and booed. Tyrone whacked the ball out of the stadium, got another from the other ballboy, served and won the point.

About to serve again, the left-hander caught a flicker of activity out the corner of his eye.

'Hey, you moronic jerk,' Tyrone shouted at the ballboy standing in the advantage corner of the court.

He rushed up to him, cuffed him on the head, grabbed a handful of hair and dragged him to a flummoxed umpire.

'*Now* do you believe me?' Tyrone triumphantly challenged the umpire.

From Tyrone's hand, hung a ballboy guiltily holding a tennis ball and a tack. He had mischievously taken to puncturing tennis balls!

'I deserved a let. All I asked was for you to check the balls. Now I get a bad reaction. What have you got against me?' Tyrone screamed.

Again, all hell broke loose in the following game, also the hoodoo seventh game, this time in the third set. Justin had hit a ball deep to the left-handed Tyrone's backhand side, perilously close to the line. There was no call. During play, Tyrone held out his hand as if to say, 'Did you see that?' sowing the seed of doubt in the linesman's mind. The rally protracted, but Tyrone played with little conviction, and eventually netted.

With the memory of an elephant, his eyes wild, Tyrone immediately looked to the umpire, questioning a judgement call long forgotten. The umpire shrugged his shoulders in utter non-comprehension, as only the French can. Tyrone fumed, the demon of rage consuming his sense of reason.

That swarm of bees is buzzing in his head again, thought Justin, bracing for another test of his patience.

'You come and check the mark or I'm outta here!' demanded Tyrone.

After a brief moment of indecision, the umpire descended and walked over to the baseline. He confirmed his call as good. Infuriated, Tyrone demanded the presence of the intimidated linesman. Nervous and on edge, and more likely to rule in Tyrone's favour, the linesman indicated a mark past the baseline.

Quite amazingly, the two officials animated their debate over the questionable mark.

Neither bastard is correct! observed an angry Justin. *The ball landed closer to the sideline.*

With the benefit of television replays, the world over itched to inform officialdom of their misguided judgement, but had to remain mum.

The argument gained momentum. Tyrone looked perplexed, perhaps not understanding his absence in controversy. Justin grew angry that the umpire had let the match deteriorate into a circus.

This calls for action, pronounced Justin. *I'm not going to lose my title because of a bloody incompetent umpire!*

With tensions percolating, Justin walked over to and waited by the hot seat to take umbrage with the umpire. The *arbitre de chaise* eventually pulled rank on his linesman and returned with a self-acquittal verdict.

'I want the referee! *Now,* please, before I play any more!' demanded Justin, to the astonishment of the umpire.

'You must carry on playing!' ordered the umpire.

Justin slumped into his change-over chair and kept silent.

'Mr Forrester, please play!'

Justin refused to budge. He sat with his gaze lowered to the ground.

'Warning, Mr Forrester! Time violation!' announced the umpire, assuming an autocratic stance.

This sudden turn of events stunned the crowd. Still Justin remained mute in his chair. He had made his case known to the umpire. He wanted to speak to the referee and would not budge until he had his say.

'Point penalty, Mr Forrester! Time violation! *Trente-à.*'

A great outcry emanated from a bewildered crowd. It equally flabbergasted Tyrone Summers that Justin Forrester had violated authority.

Still Justin refused to move. The stadium went silent. Each person strained to see what turnabout would transpire. The umpire looked at Justin, then at his watch, then back at Justin. He shuffled nervously in his seat, not knowing what to do next. The law compelled the next violation to be disqualification. How could he back down? How could he disqualify the defending champion?

He squirmed and sweated in his seat. Fifteen thousand pairs of eyes stared at him in silent anticipation. Twenty five seconds from the last warning went by, then a minute. The umpire looked at his watch again, then back at Justin. Another minute went by. A restless stir swept through the crowd. Another minute passed.

The umpire leant forward to his microphone and the crowd hushed to catch the latest news.

'Disqualification, Mr Forrester! Match to Summers by default!'

Out went the champion! Tyrone Summers entered the final! It is the fate of kings to be deposed, but by default?

A stunned silence erupted into a cacophony of boos from the restless crowd. Tyrone looked bewildered, hovering around like a spare part. No one had yet managed to lasso the rope around his neck.

Biting his lip until he tasted blood, Justin sat and stared at the red clay in front, unmoved in outward emotion, inwardly, bitterly stubborn as the news of disqualification swirled inside his head.

With an impassive face and deliberate movements, he rose from his seat, packed his belongings and walked the expanse of red clay to the exit. Behind him all hell broke loose, angry spectators pelting the umpire with an assortment of trash, but Justin looked neither left nor right. Eyes trained to the ground, he walked off the court, out of the lewd and vulgar stench and straight to the locker-room, locking himself in a cubicle.

Sitting on a closed toilet, his eyes moist, throat tight, black gloom clouding his face, he pondered the staggering moments that had transpired.

I've always prided myself in sportsmanship, and for years these tirades have chipped away, chipped away, chipped away at my granite veneer. Don't they know I'm human inside! And with my title dissipating before my eyes through ineffectual umpiring, once, just once, I stand up for my right for continuous play and I'm kicked out of a Grand Slam championship! Stripped of my title! mourned Justin.

Punching his fist in his hand he cried out to himself, *'Why are those blimmin' umpires so spineless? I can handle Terror and his gamesmanship, but not without an impartial umpire. Damn them! Why are they so inconsistent?'*

Over the years, Justin had borne the brunt of the umpire's easy option. Instead of risking a bitter battle with a bad tempered player over a questionable linecall, they overruled against quieter demeanour, leading to the irritating habit of players incessantly whining over linecalls, not in the hope of reversing them, but to bear pressure on the umpire's mind to favour them in a later dispute, or risk war. Clay court tennis is the exception! A comedy of errors occurs over the absurd procedure of checking the mark.

How on earth can they stoop so low? Arguing with a linesman over a mark, when both are wrong! Don't they believe in their judgement? wondered a bewildered Justin.

Why the hell don't they play according to the rules? questioned Justin. Then burying his head in his hands, he sobbed, *Why didn't I? I went back on my word never to enter a dispute, now I've sabotaged my own fate. Why? Why didn't I play by the rules?*

For three hours, Justin sat alone, locked in a toilet cubicle, coming to terms with his predicament. He had filled his mind with the dirty water of his horrendous disqualification and its ramifications, now it was time for a cathartic pulling of the plug.

I expect them to rule by the letter, but I didn't, so I must accept this default. I was wrong to buck the system! admonished Justin. *I swear that if they don't overhaul the issue of challenging linecalls, I'm out of this game. I'll simply have to change the system!*

Justin unlocked himself out of his impasse. An agitated Jean-Pierre Perrot confronted him.

'Justin! Where on earth have you been? The referee has gone crazy trying to find you. He's making noises, you know, uh, like he's giving birth to a cactus!' expressed an equally animated Jean-Pierre.

Justin merely nodded his head in thanks, took off his clothes, showered and re-dressed. Then he proceeded to the referee's office.

'Justin! Justin! Where have you been? You make me go grey!' exclaimed an excited referee, throwing up his arms.

Justin remained silent.

'Take a seat,' offered the referee. 'My apologies for the umpire. I should have intervened. He was out of line defaulting you.'

What? What's the buzz? wondered Justin.

'The committee has reviewed the match and reinstated you! We have defaulted Mr Summers!' the referee beamed his good tidings.

Justin stared at the referee with his icy eyes. 'I cannot accept!' he refused. *Why be so bloody stubborn?* he debated, thinking of the chance to defend his French Open crown.

'*Non.* You don't understand. You are in the final,' expressed a concerned referee, desperate for acceptance.

'Then I shall have to default!'

'You don't understand,' said the agitated referee, his eyes dilating as he recommenced labour pains. Wringing his hands, he continued, 'We have already defaulted Mr Summers. This is public knowledge. We've reinstated you. *You* are in the final!'

Justin relinquished the defence of his title, 'I decline, thank you very much!'

He stood up and left behind an office with a referee running about like a chicken with its head cut off. The French Open championships would be won by Boris Bauer, horror of horrors, by default!

Justin walked straight into a press conference. The hungry reporters hovered like vultures craving their first morsels of a rotting carcass.

'I will not field any questions, but instead, will make a statement. The referee has just informed me of my reinstatement into the tournament, into the final. However, I have thought long and hard about this. It was wrong of me to disobey the umpire. Whatever happened prior to that incident is of no consequence, so I have no option but to decline his offer.'

Pens burned paper and micro-cassettes whirred at full speed.

Justin solemnly continued, 'Whether the referee will now reinstate Tyrone is a matter for him to decide, but he was wrong to make decisions for me publicly, and use me as a pawn. Thank you.'

Leaving the interview room, a flood of cameramen shoved their lenses in Justin's face and masses of reporters asked a pandemonium of questions. Again, he looked neither left nor right as he slowly shouldered his way out of Roland Garros.

Back at his hotel, Justin switched on the television. The afternoon's drama captured the city in animated debate, trying officialdom for sacrificing the climax of a high point on the sporting calendar. Highlights of the afternoon's drama replayed ad nauseam, clearly indicating the umpire and linesman arguing over an incorrect mark!

Just as I thought, the bastards! Justin remarked to himself, but with little consolation.

The press conference concerning Tyrone Summers and his disqualification, followed.

'I hate the stupid game anyway!' Tyrone responded moodily.

'I'm sorry, Justin,' commiserated Heidi.

Lying in her arms, he did not hear. Wallowing in abject misery, Justin desperately needed to come up for air. Alone, he left his hotel and drove off into the Paris night.

A year ago, how wonderful it was! he thought, remembering his first Grand Slam title, won in dramatic style. But on a day cut from the rougher cloth of fate, his cup of misery overflowed. *Now I suffer the stigma of disqualification. They robbed me of my crown, took away my pride. I feel naked.*

It's a funny ol' world, this, mused Justin.

§

Justin stood in a queue in Aérogare 1 of Charles-de-Gaulle airport, determined to leave behind his woe. The scream of a lost child suddenly pierced the airport noise.

Should I go and help? Justin pondered, wrestling with his shyness.

To his astonishment, a man with a page-boy haircut and a pixie face shielded by sun-glasses, came to the infant's rescue, picked her up, walked to a shop and bought her a packet of sweets. Then he waited with her until airport officials contacted her mother. No one else noticed.

Tyrone Summers! Saint or sinner? ruminated Justin.

For a brief moment, away from the court, the schizophrenic Tyrone dropped his game face and assumed his mild-mannered guise, revealing himself in the most innocent of situations. This did not go unnoticed by Justin.

In London, the Brits were indignant that bumbling French officials had dethroned Justin Forrester from their English kingdom in France.

Reporters besieged Justin.

'Are you married?' asked a reporter. 'A source of mine informs me ...'

Justin looked to Ted Parsen, then back at the reporter. 'Is your source reliable?'

'Well, uh, hmm!'

'Do you know where Boris Bauer is?' asked another reporter.

'Nope!'

'What of the news of Tyrone Summers?'

'What news? I don't read tennis!'

'He's banned from the game for a year!'

'For *what?*' asked Justin, staggered.

'Aggravating behaviour.'

Banning is not a solution. This can only hurt the game! thought Justin, stunned at the news. *And it's not entirely his fault.*

'I miss you on tour,' Justin moaned to Heidi after a practice session at

Cumberland Club. Then climbing into his wine red Mercedes-Benz 500 SE AT, he looked into her eyes and said, 'I'd like you to move in with me during Wimbledon. Can you cook?'

'Not really! But I can warm up dishes like you!'

'Tabasco, I'm ravenous. Let's go!'

Turning into Ingram Avenue in Hampstead, Justin braked sharply.

'Justin! What's wrong?' cried out Heidi.

'Sphincter stinkers!'

A posse of newshounds camped on Justin's property verge. For a brief moment he sized up the situation, then suddenly revved up the car, turned round, wound up to and entered Winnington Road and drove to the Hampstead Golf Course, which abutted his property from behind. He burrowed a hole in the fence of his backyard tennis court, the border of his property adjoining the golf course, and the two slipped into his home via the back door. Justin went upstairs and peeped out of a bay window to his front verge.

You bunch of blood-sucking idiots! cursed Justin.

He telephoned Tyrone Summers.

'I've just heard.'

'Yeah, screw them!' whined Tyrone with little bite to his bark, his tail between his legs and with good reason. A year's banning would effectively end his career.

Justin made him an offer. 'I'll kick backsides to try to overturn your banning, but I need your help. As an appeasement, I need you to agree to a new Code of Conduct.'

'How can I refuse!' acceded a tame Tyrone.

'But one thing is clear. You do it *my* way.'

Justin contacted the chairman of the sport's Disciplinary Council and convened an extraordinary meeting at his mansion.

Prior to the meeting, he called his friend Larry King, who had kept his finger in the tennis pie through administration, and coached him on his new Code of Conduct.

'Gentleman, Tyrone has asked to sit in on this meeting. I hope you will accommodate him?'

Surprised looks creased the council members' faces, but they acquiesced.

Justin summoned Tyrone, whispering to him, 'Just do it with a smile!' He then addressed the council. 'My concern with the present code is that its harshness prevents umpires from effectively implementing the rules. A player whacks a ball into the stadium three times and they disqualify him. That's bloody ridiculous! Maybe they ban him from the next tournament, too. Then those buggers get punished!'

'That's unfair!' smiled Tyrone, bringing a round of laughter. 'The players should call their own shots!'

'And inmates should run their own asylum!' rebounded Justin's repartee, defusing the tension by laughing at his partner in crime. 'Seriously, the upshot is that the umpires are inconsistent with their application.'

'So we need a meaningful, on the spot punishment for transgressions,' furthered Larry King. 'Short and sharp!'

'Yep! Any ideas?'

There was a long quiet. Aah, the sounds of silence. Okay Larry.

'Hmm!' thought Larry aloud, playing devil's advocate. 'What about a single point penalty for each misdemeanour. A player takes longer than 25 seconds, then plain and simple, he's given a point penalty. This punishes him, and also rewards the player offended.'

'Sounds interesting!' remarked Justin. 'What about linecall questioning?'

'No questioning allowed!' interjected Tyrone, shattering the minds of the council. You could have heard a church mouse breathe!

'You can't be serious,' answered Justin, feigning surprise, suppressing a smile toying with his lips.

'Sure I am. It sucks! I guess I've lost more matches questioning linecalls, than better players kicking my ass!'

'What do you mean?' asked Justin, wearing a face of mock horror.

'If the facility exists, I use it to pressure the umpire. You guys know that if an umpire overrules, the fucker's never gonna change his mind. And if he goes with the linesman, it's two against one. So there's no way you can change the minds of those idiots. Sure, you question so they favour you next time. But mostly it unravels *my* mind. So, I'm all for it, I agree with Hoss. Open your mug to question a call and you're docked a penalty point. Open it again to complain about the penalty point and you're zapped another. No warnings, but no accumulation of points. Plain and simple.'

'I like it,' commented Larry King. 'Those in favour?'

All eight members raised their hands.

'Since we're entering an era of a new Code of Conduct,' continued Justin, 'I recommend a review of Tyrone's banning from tennis. As we have already said, such action can only hurt the game.'

All members except Larry King shuffled in their seats. Tyrone wore a sheepish smile.

'Rescinding his banning would make us look like fools,' responded the chairman.

'Not if we reduced the banning to two months, say, over the winter!' appeased Larry King. 'After all, if we announce the new Code of Conduct at the same time, it will take off some heat.'

'All those in favour?'

All eight members raised their hands.

'Thanks, Hoss. Ever thought of an acting career?' joked Justin, shaking his hand in private.

'If you direct! That was brilliant. To think they now believe *they* came up with the idea! I really didn't think it would work.'

On the morning of the Wimbledon championships, Justin woke with a warm feeling of contentment in his heart.

Wimbledon! The premier championships of the world, and I'm a part of it.

'Damn! My bloody car's been nicked!' cried Justin with utter dismay. *And all because of those bloody sphincter stinkers, making me park it here in the golf course car park.*

'Shit a brick!' he cursed with sudden alarm. 'I haven't organised to be chauffeured to Wimbledon!'

He hitched a lift to his stringer in Finchley Road, picked up his rackets, then lugged his voluminous hernia-afflicting tennis bag to catch the tube from Golders Green.

The station looked deserted. Justin waited and waited.

'Hey, look here, mate! There's a bleeding strike on the go. No public transport today.'

That's all I need! groaned Justin. *Will I ever get past the first round at Wimbledon?*

He walked up Golders Green Road, beside himself with worry.

Wimbledon's miles south, with the city of London between! What the hell am I going to do? puzzled an anxious Justin, inhaling a deep breath and sighing heavily.

Out of the corner of his eye he caught a glimpse of a parked car, sporting a sign, 'TODDY'S DRIVING SCHOOL'.

'Hmm!'

Justin quickly looked around and spotted a hairdressing salon across the road.

'A black wig with curls, please?'

'My pleasure, Mr Forrester,' blushed the assistant. After rummaging around she presented a hairpiece. 'Will this do, Mr Forrester?'

'Just fine!' replied Justin, paying the star struck lady.

He ran across the road and entered the shop behind the parked learner-driver car.

'May I have a driving lesson, please?' he enquired.

'A refresher, or a course?'

'How long's the refresher?'

'Half an hour!' the man answered in pompous tone. 'Good value for your money!'

'I'll take three. But *now*, please.'

The man looked a touch surprised. 'Bit rusty, eh!'

'Uh huh!'

'Now let me see. Aah, you're in luck. Lucy's free. Lucy?' called the man at the desk. 'She'll take you through your paces. You'll be as good as the best!'

Justin and Lucy climbed into a turquoise Honda Accord. Justin stepped on the pedal.

'You can drive!' exclaimed Lucy.

'Yep! I just need a ride to Wimbledon.'

'Oh yes, the tube strike. A nuisance, isn't it?'

Entering Church Road, a snake of cars lay ahead of them.

'Look, I'm getting out here. Are you a tennis fan?'

'Why, of course! Who isn't, with Justin Forrester about to win Wimbledon!'

Justin smiled.

'Here's something for you,' he said, handing her a £50 note and a Centre Court ticket. 'Maybe you'll see me again, someday soon!'

Justin alighted. He opened his bag, scrounged around, retrieved and donned the wig and a pair of Ray-Ban sun-glasses. Disguised, he hurried down Church Road, unnoticed, and into the All England Lawn Tennis & Croquet Club grounds.

Homecoming! thought Justin, his competitive juices flowing freely after breathing the smell of newly cut grass.

He easily won his first ever Wimbledon match against the right-handed Hamilton twin, Tugboat.

'Grass is for cows!' cried the dirtkickers, lamenting their anathema to the turf. On a day the London press labelled 'BLACK MONDAY', one by one grass-courters weeded the feet of clay from the lawn, and led the resigned herd *en masse* to the slaughterhouse. In two weeks, tennis had transformed from the artistry of Paris to the blood and thunder of Wimbledon, a game so alien to the peaceful mentality of Southern England. Aah, but the Americans brought it to Wimbledon! Alas, the Brits had not won since. Not yet, anyway!

'Grass is for cows? Not this grass! Good gosh, no!' echoed the game's ruling triumvirate, marching on, spearheaded by the bionic bull, Boris

Bauer.

Justin's next visit to Wimbledon started early.

No way will I risk missing a match at Wimbledon, not a match to be played on Centre Court!

He arrived at the All England Lawn Tennis & Croquet Club only to find the gates still locked.

'Excuse me, please!' said Justin, trying to enter the Wimbledon grounds.

'The gates are not open, sir,' informed the official. 'You must wait.'

Justin patiently waited one and a half minutes, amused at the club's allegiance to the letter of the law.

'Your pass please?'

'Oops!' spluttered Justin. He searched through his tennis bag, to no avail.

'I'm sorry, sir. You cannot enter without a pass.'

Justin looked at this man in bewilderment. 'Don't you know who I am?'

'I'm sorry, sir,' said the official, tilting his nose. 'But nobody can enter without a pass!'

Hmm! Wimbledon rules sure are for everybody! discovered Justin. *And I've as much chance of conning this bugger as The Championships going Day-Glo!*

Much to their delight, he bided his time talking to the fans, some who had queued for three days in the hope of catching a glimpse of him playing.

Tyrone bounced past with his inimitable orangutan gait. 'Hey, Pale Wog! Forget your pass?'

'Uh huh.'

'I'll sort you out,' he answered, urging Justin to walk further down the road.

Justin complied, and 10 minutes later, Tyrone's pass came hurtling over the fence. Such team work boded well for the tournament, since the dynamic duo had teamed up for the doubles! They also proceeded through the single's draw to a semifinal encounter.

Suffering that ignominious loss of my French Open crown, I'm more determined than ever to win the greatest tennis prize, Wimbledon, vowed Justin.

The Brits were determined that he should win, too! Each day at the All England Lawn Tennis & Croquet Club, screaming fans transformed the regal and hallowed grounds into a pop concert. Forrestermania stormed Wimbledon. From hordes of worshipping teenyboppers to little old ladies, they hunted and haunted him, following their Pied Piper, though there were rock and movie stars milling around. A combination of his skill and a personality shrouded in mystique made him the object of cult worship. They wanted his autograph! They wanted to touch him! They wanted him!

'Whilst you're in the Club grounds, we insist that you have police protection,' instructed a Wimbledon official.

Every match Justin played, and won, the masses grew, and each time another policeman expanded the bubble of security surrounding him.

After Justin and the defending champion took the Centre Court for their match, Tyrone Summers, without a flicker on his face, withdrew a golf club from his tennis bag, a five iron, walked to the baseline, and instead of serving, placed a golf ball on the ground and readied to tee off.

The stadium howled with mirth. All except the Andy-capped groundsman clad in a tweed jacket. This very worried man hurried onto Centre Court to protect his beloved grass.

Tyrone's face broke into a huge smile. He swapped the golf club for his Wilson Hammer and settled down to play.

'Time!' called the umpire.

Tyrone looked at his watch. 'Five past two!'

In such spirits, a match unfolded to grace the special place of Wimbledon. The World Champion versus the defending champion, the two gladiators of the game served a sumptuous spread for the tennis gods watching from the Elysian fields to feast on. Point and counter-point, they fought a cat and mouse match that sparkled with wit and nimble footwork.

With Justin serving at 6-7 and 15-30 in the fifth set, the sun dipped beneath the roof of the arena, casting a gilt-edged twilight on the tennis court of the gods, magnifying the two combatants in lengthening shadows on the lawn, imbuing a golden occasion with heightened drama. Suddenly, a big point.

About to serve, a flicker of movement caught Justin's attention.

Oh! A butterfly!

He stooped to the baseline, collected it on the strings of his racket, walked over and deposited it next to the lineslady behind him.

On return, he served from the Roller-end and ran up to the net, making an airshot, a complete miss!

Damn! Must have lost sight of the ball against that white panther! moaned Justin, referring to the Slazenger motif on the forest green canvas backdrop.

'Fifteen-forty.'

Shit! Down double match point! Pull your thumb out! So close to a bloody Wimbledon final! Revel in the battle.

Justin took a deep breath, and drew a bead on where to serve. He imparted vicious slice, hit wide to the deuce court, the ball pirouetting away from the left-hander's two-handed backhand past the wheelchair brigade, residing under the scoreboard. Tyrone erred.

Take that and die, you tyrant! the impassive Justin vociferated inside.

Most observers interpreted a tame unforced error, but Justin knew better. Over the fortnight, the Centre Court changes like a chameleon, from the slick green carpet of the first day to a worn brown surface, playing like a higher bouncing hardcourt, except by the outside edge of the service box, where the unused grass retains some sap. Justin used this to his advantage. The ball spun away from Tyrone, hardly rising, and with his limited reach on the two-hander, he hit the ball late, causing it to fade wide of the sideline.

One point to go. The bugger's got to be expecting another fast serve, surmised Justin. *Probably out wide.*

He tossed the ball up and delivered a three-quarter pace serve spinning out of the shadow and into the sun, swerving into the body. Nothing special, but nothing weak. The surprise caught Tyrone who returned the ball tamely into the net.

Aah! The sanctuary of deuce! sighed Justin, the crisis temporarily stayed.

Now turn the screws on him, urged Justin.

He lifted his game to a higher realm, daring Tyrone to raise the stakes. But the American had no ace to offer.

Out went the defending champion. For him, victory against Justin seemed like a hazy, heat mirage on a desert horizon. Always in sight, but out of grasp. For Justin, the final, a chance for Wimbledon glory in an eagerly awaited rematch against Boris Bauer.

The Wimbledon final. My chance for Wimbledon glory. My chance for a rematch against Boris Bauer. One match to go! Justin beamed inside, careful not to show any outward sign of emotion. *Relax now, I'm doomed tomorrow. There'll be plenty of time to smile after the final.*

'What will this do for tennis in Swaziland?' a reporter asked Justin at a press conference.

'Not much, I guess!' replied Justin, shrugging his shoulders.

'How many tennis players where you came from in Africa?'

'A couple of hundred hackers, I suppose!'

'Will your parents come over?'

'I don't think so.' Justin thought, *They'll probably be at the dam where*

206

my dream started all those years ago.

'Good luck for Sunday. We're holding thumbs.'

'Thanks.'

London buzzed. A Wimbledon champion for Britain? Not since Fred Perry in 1936 could the homeland boast a Wimbledon men's singles champion. Since then, the title had often gone to the colonies, but that was not the same, was it?

First, another engagement on Centre Court beckoned Justin. His unlikely tandem with Tyrone Summers won the men's doubles, Justin's first Wimbledon championship. A crowning moment for him as he stood in the Royal Box. A clowning moment for the inimitable Tyrone who deigned to place the cup upside down on his head and pull a tongue!

That Saturday evening, Justin entered his house via the golf course and went upstairs to his bedroom. On entering, he heard the sound of rushing water.

Outlined against the shower door was the unmistakable body of Heidi. A tightening emanated from his groin.

He flung back the shower door.

'Phew! Justin, you gave me a fright!' cried Heidi, holding her hand to her heart.

Justin said nothing. He gazed at her with lust. Her long blonde hair, the athletic contoured body, all wet, and a mound of soft blonde pubic hair reminding him what lay in the cleft between her long shapely legs.

Justin stepped into the shower and joined Heidi.

'Well done, darling!' he said, embracing the Wimbledon ladies' champion and kissing her lips, congratulating at first, then passionately, while the warm spray of water showered on his back.

As their lips pressed and tongues entwined, Heidi's hands deftly undid the buttons on Justin's drenched shirt, peeling it away to reveal his wiry muscled chest. She put her arms around him, squeezed her naked breasts against him, then looked up with flirtatious blue eyes. Justin obliged.

He reached behind her, grabbed a cake of perfumed soap, then gently caressed the nape of her neck, running it down her back to the mounds of her bottom. Then he titillated her front, rubbing the cake of soap over her chest, tenderly over each breast, down the smooth skin of her flat tummy and into her pubic hair. He dropped the soap and smiled, lathering her groin. Still Heidi's cheeky blue eyes coaxed him on.

As Justin knelt, the water spray washed away the soap down Heidi's long legs. He parted them slightly, edged closer and kissed her lips through a torrent of warm water. Justin felt her hands press the back of his head against her. He aroused her with his tongue, sensuously massaging to arouse her sexual desire.

He rose.

'You're ready!' he smiled satisfyingly.

'So are you!' laughed Heidi, unbuckling Justin's pants to reveal a startled penis.

Grabbing a bum cheek in each hand, Justin lifted Heidi onto him. She wrapped her strong legs round his hips and sank down on him, catching her breath, then clung onto his rippling shoulders.

'After our tennis careers, we can join the circus!' chuckled Justin.

Heidi closed her eyes and flung her head back. Her silky hair falling away, her full milky-coloured breasts bouncing, the spray splashing off Justin's shoulders into her face. She was wet. She was animal.

Her beauty ignited a sexual rage in Justin. In concert to the increasing moans of his partner, Justin spasmodically thrust deep inside her, rising in tempo so violently, he slipped out as she cried her passion, and ejaculated on her stomach, washing away in the warm water.

Heidi pulled herself forwards and looked deep into Justin's eyes.

'You horny animal,' she smiled mischievously. 'You need some of this!'

Her hand reached behind him and quickly turned on the cold tap. A blast of icy water tore into Justin's back.

'Aah!' Justin shouted, before sneakily turning round, and still carrying Heidi, held her under the cold water. 'You need to cool off, too!'

'Okay, I give up. Peace!' she shrieked.

Dripping with water, Justin carried Heidi to his bed and flopped down on the mattress. They lay there and embraced and kissed and sighed.

After a moment of quietness, Justin asked Heidi, 'What's it like to win Wimbledon?'

So to the last day, the blue riband of tennis, the men's singles final.

Justin woke on the morning of the first Sunday in July with a warm flutter in his heart.

I'm to play the final this afternoon! it suddenly dawned on him. *At last! The most important match of my life in the most treasured tournament, Wimbledon!*

Converging on the All England Lawn Tennis & Croquet Club in a chauffeured limousine, Justin noticed a billboard, 'BLACK MARKET TICKET FOR FINALS – £5,000'. Justin was to take on the expectant

English crowd and Boris Bauer, in the tennis shootout of the century.

I will not disappoint! thought Justin, determinedly. *But much more, I will expunge the bitter taste of that loss to Boris Bauer in Australia!*

Justin noticed, too, the London Daily News billboard, 'JUSTIN FORRESTER'S DIVORCE – THE INSIDE STORY'. He smiled to himself. He recalled the 'CHAMPIONS CELEBRATE WITH ORGY' headline that led to his intricate plot to bury his gutter press nemesis.

Parsen, you bastard! Get ready to fry!

In the locker-room, Justin underwent his pre-match ritual alone, stretching and making a final check on his equipment. Lastly, he combed his hair. For victory or defeat?

'Ready Justin?' called an official.

'Uh huh.'

'Boris?'

It's here! My moment has arrived, thought Justin, his heart excited and warm at the prospect. He thrived on competition, and the stiffer it was in the best of tournaments, the more he hankered after it.

The two adversaries made their way from the locker-room to the infamous waiting-room, but not before passing the famous archway inscribed, 'If you can meet with Triumph and Disaster and treat those two Impostors just the same'.

Then? chuckled Justin. *Not possible! It's just not the way with a tennis player!*

Outside on the Centre Court, a party excitement intoxicated the crowd. A Brit in a Wimbledon men's singles final! A great air of expectancy!

The waiting-room exuded tension. It seeped out of the cracks in the walls and the mood smouldered like a place of waiting before being taken to execution. In the taut silence Justin could hear his own heartbeat thudding in anticipation.

A court steward called the protagonists, and ushered them through the frosted glass doors and onto the hallowed Centre Court, to face the executioner. One would go to heaven, the other to hell.

The sun shone, hardly a cloud in the sky with only the smallest hint of a breeze. The crowd hushed and then broke into rapturous applause. They came, not only to see Justin, but to have his body and soul.

I love it! exclaimed Justin, the sound permeating his being, running all the way down his back.

He flourished on applause. It pumped adrenalin into him. It excited him, roused him to play his best. In return, the applause would grow and grow to an orgasmic crescendo, nurturing his tennis into another realm, feeding off each other. Such was the erotic love affair between Justin, his tennis and his fans.

But Boris Bauer, the robotic giant, soon reduced their passion to the passivity of a plastic blow-up doll. With the suddenness of air expelling out of Hot Lips Deluxe, the party atmosphere transformed to a sombre funeral. The extraordinary power Justin had faced head-on in Australia, increased on the fast grass.

It was testimony to Justin's talent that he garnered as many games as he did. He dug deep into his seemingly endless well of talent, but in the end the clear-cut story of the match told of power destroying artistry.

I'm too busy trying to get into a rally to stay alive, I've no time to use my tactics, my feints, complained Justin. He looked at the man facing him on the other side. Black tear-drop lines inscribed from the corners of his eyes to cut the glare. *He looks weird!*

With huge serves crushing into the green canvas sheets between ducking linejudges, the first set went to Boris Bauer 6-2, and the second 6-3.

Damn this Boris Bauer! Two sets to love down! lamented a devastated Justin, biting his lip. *I've come back before. I'll do it again!*

But never against the ferocity of Bauer power. Playing Boris Bauer, Justin hunted an elephant with a pea-shooter. Never one to give up, he ran the gauntlet of his marvellous mental and physical attributes, but when Boris served at 5-4 and 40-love, his bubbling well of genius ran dry. Only then did the reality dawn.

My game's too lightweight, vulnerable like a dandelion in a high wind, admitted a despondent Justin.

Boris Bauer became only the fifth man player, the first since Björn Borg, to win Wimbledon without the loss of a set, extending his empire of Australia and France to include Britain.

At first, the shell-shocked spectators offered Boris Bauer muted applause, desperately trying to pick up the pieces. England wept in commiseration with Justin, their dream of a Wimbledon title just that, a dream.

For Justin, his Wimbledon dream slipped into the guise of a nightmare. He sat in that lonely loser's chair, an empty black hollow where he heard the echoes of his anguish. The television eye intruded, sparing not one speck of his face.

Everyone's staring at me, disappointed! felt Justin. But none more so than he.

The risks are high in tennis. Only success feeds a champion's insatiable desire to prove his worth. Defeat for Justin, then, was a famine.

Now I have to suffer the presentation ceremony, a public crowning of my loss under the microscopic eye of the world. Shit, I wish I could disappear, run away from everything, escape from my mind! Coming second, is the pits. It's worse than losing early in a tournament, because the world remembers the runner-up's loss the most.

Justin received his silver salver with Royal words of sympathy. Then it was the turn of Boris Bauer to hold up the coveted Wimbledon trophy, pictures of his success winging across the globe to a billion people, who gatecrashed The Great English Garden Party via the biggest annual television broadcast in the world.

Justin looked up from the grass and caught a glimpse of the golden cup.

I wish that were me holding that trophy, yearned an envious Justin, choking back a lump in his throat. *Now I have to face the knockers in the grill room. Always the questions, questions, questions!*

His eyes dry, his face impassive, his body quiet, Justin walked patiently through the photographers, towards the glass doors and straight to the press conference room, intent on getting his ordeal over with. Few people understand how much a champion dislikes facing the rapid-fire questions of inquisitive strangers, so soon after a painful loss.

'Perhaps a British tennis player will never win The Championships again,' a reporter remarked.

Justin did not respond, but thought, *A Swazi will!*

'Is winning the doubles atonement for today?'

Justin shook his head.

'Are you finished? On the scrapheap?' asked Ted Parsen spitefully.

'Not likely! I lost a tennis match!' answered Justin, bewildered that after building him into a god, and believing him to be unbeatable, the press viewed him as a spent force after two losses during the year.

'*Lost!* You mean humiliated! Ever been so frightened?' sneered Ted Parsen.

'Sure!' replied Justin, irritated with this incessant interrogation. Laden with sarcastic wit, 'Once, when I was a kid we had this tame elephant that I would bath once a week. I would sit down on a retaining wall and use a broom and a bucket. Then one day when I was washing his rear end the elephant promptly sat on me and I went right up its bum hole and I couldn't get out. I was shit scared. Don't you think that is more frightening than losing a tennis match?'

'Well, uh, perhaps,' Ted Parsen replied sheepishly. Then, lured into the spider's parlour, 'How did you get out?'

'I woke up!' Justin answered with a deadpan face.

Ted Parsen slunk from the press conference room, and the venom slithered out of Justin's replies. He braved a barrage of questions from reporters who suddenly knew the answer to his predicament with Boris Bauer.

'Have you the ability to match his power?'

'Nope! I'm not as strong. I rely on speed of foot. Reflexes. My mind.'

'Then will you consider weight training?'

'Maybe I should,' Justin answered, knowing he would not. *My lean and wiry body has developed naturally, honed through the isotonic exercise of playing tennis, responding with the perfect body for tennis. Bulking up will interfere with my flexibility and nerve-ends, and diminish my huge asset, speed.*

'What of diet? What do you eat?'

'I'm a steak and potatoes man.'

'Would you ever, say, try pasta?'

'Nope!'

'Why don't you have a coach?'

'I have a coach,' answered Justin, trying to keep calm.

'A travelling coach?' asked the reporter.

Justin uniquely travelled alone when all other players surrounded themselves with a life-support system.

'I learned the game by myself. *I* am my coach. I know my game best.'

'Are you a dying breed?'

'No,' Justin answered with resignation. 'Tennis styles are cyclical, almost evolutionary. Racket technology has presently tipped the balance in favour of power away from skill, but the definitive tennis champion *has* to be multi-talented. Ultimate victory comes from the mind!' Justin wore a wry smile and said, 'Perhaps if we still played with wooden rackets ...'

'What now?'

'There'll always be another Wimbledon. I'll be back,' answered Justin, swallowing the bitterness of deep disappointment.

A day before, the world toasted Justin as a hero, beyond reproach. Now he defended against accusations by those who suddenly knew better.

Justin hurried back to his home in Hampstead, and being yesterday's news, entered for the first time in weeks through the front door.

He locked the door and sat in the darkening lounge, vegetating like a recluse, wallowing in his ignominious defeat.

I have to be single-minded. Tunnel visioned! he resolved. But deep inside he wrestled with a gnawing conflict. *Heidi!*

Shit! Why does life have to be so brutal! I'm so fond of her, but ... Justin inhaled a deep breath. *Single-minded! Tunnel visioned! To beat Boris Bauer I'll have to extract every ounce of flesh, every drop of blood, every fibre of my being. I must be totally dedicated. Eat, breathe and sleep tennis.*

Justin knew it, but fought to face it. He grabbed a cushion, hunched over it and brooded over his dilemma, the torment building. Finally it burst. He stood up and threw the cushion against the wall.

'Damn it! I love you, Heidi. Why? Why? Why?'

To escape, Justin squeezed the power button on the television remote control. The BBC 'Match of the Day' highlights of the men's singles final approached its end. Justin took one look at Boris Bauer holding the Wimbledon trophy and made his decision.

Wimbledon! he coveted.

He walked upstairs, dragging his racket against the balusters, playing a mournful xylophone tune. Entering his bedroom, the presence of Heidi caught him by surprise.

I thought I was alone!

She lay on his bed, seductively dressed in lace lingerie. Heidi rose and came towards Justin, her face mourning his loss.

'I'm sorry, darling,' she whispered, pressing herself against him.

'Don't, Heidi,' Justin resisted, dislodging her hands from his chest and clutching them in his hands. He looked into her eyes. They were wide and searching. 'Heidi, …,' he started, his voice tightening with strain, 'I'm going for a walk on the Heath. When I come back I want to be alone. It's over. I can't see you again.'

'Justin, Don't leave me. I don't want to be alone again! I'll give up tennis to be with you,' cried a desperate Heidi.

'You know that's impossible, you're too pedigree a champion. Besides, I *have* to be alone.'

'But—'

'Shh,' hushed Justin, putting a finger to her lips. 'Don't say anything. I don't want this, but it has to be. You're a champion. You should understand. I pray someday you will.'

Justin embraced and kissed Heidi, then without another word turned to leave. Walking out of his bedroom, her stunned eyes haunted him.

Damn it! Get out of my mind! commanded Justin, steeling himself against their mutual wishes, *I have to do this!*

He ran from his house to Hampstead Heath, to escape from his anguish with Heidi, to solve his anguish with Boris Bauer.

Loping the vast expanse of lawns, a hunger pang twitched in his stomach, an acorn at first, which grew and grew until he was ravenous. Out of his misery emerged resolve. Getting so close, only to lose, deepened Justin's mania to win.

'I'm going to beat that Boris Bauer, if it's the last thing I ever do,' shouted Justin, clenching his fist to the sky. 'I'll beat him at the US

Open!' he vowed of the greatest tournament for redemption. 'I will *not* give up my title!'

§

'Guilty of libel!' declared the High Court judge. 'You prey on the misfortunes of others, and when none is obtainable you stoop to fabricating wicked stories. Your kind is a curse to society, your slander despicable, and will *not* be tolerated. Judgement is awarded in favour of Mr Justin Forrester. The *London Daily News* is hereby ordered to pay damages to the order of £2.8 million. Let this serve notice to others who are so quick to create misery for others.'

§

'Ladies and gentlemen, please welcome my guests on tonight's number one television show, IMPOSTORS, which will discern traitor from truth.'

The audience applauded.

'On my left, Justin Forrester, world class tennis player with a flip side to his sporting career, a passion for wildlife,' introduced the host.

'A year ago, Justin told a press conference, and I quote, 'I hunt the hunter!' So tonight, opposing his impassioned plea against hunting, the self-proclaimed best hunter in the world, from Texas, Mr JR Carter.'

'I'll start with you, JR. Are you a threat to the preservation of wildlife in Africa?'

'No way!' answered the balding, rotund, larger than life JR Carter, sporting ivory tusk trinkets around his red neck. 'Pottin' one tusker's hardly goin' to do nothin'. It'll help them locals get rid of a pest to them crops. These critters eat a mighty plenty.'

'That's true, folks!' announced the host. 'Our research indicates an elephant consumes the equivalent of three of me every day! A herd can devastate a plantation like a swarm of locusts. How do you respond, Justin?'

'It's true. They do eat a lot. But I imagine JR here consumes twice as much as I do. Surely that's no reason to take a potshot at him. Unless, of course, he was hunting *my* elephants!'

'But are they destructive?'

'I'd say *he* is.'

'The elephants?'

'Nope! They may appear so, if you don't understand the ways of the wild, the balance of nature. But by uprooting trees, they lower foliage for other animals to reach, allow grasses and shrubs to take root and sunlight

214

to reach the ground. The fallen trees retard soil erosion. And importantly, elephants reforest their 'destruction' by—'

'Bullshit!' sneered JR.

'Yep! You're right! Seeds pass right through their digestive system, ideally placed for germination, in a ball of dung!'

The audience laughed.

Justin continued, 'Then dung beetles disperse and bury the growing and fertilised seeds in the soil. Nature is perfectly balanced. Without the elephant, there would be a domino-like extinction of many species of animals.'

'Look at me square in the eye, boy, and tell me you don't shoot elephants,' challenged JR.

'Now, now, JR, let's—'

'You tell me boy, because I know your kind,' shot JR Carter, climbing onto high moral ground. 'You shoot a plenty more elephants than I do, you lucky son of a gun.'

Strained silence.

'Is that true?' asked the IMPOSTORS's host, suspicious.

'Uh huh.'

The audience murmured loudly.

'You bloody hypocrite, pokin' your nose into the hunting business!' shouted JR belligerently.

'Mr Forrester, can you squirm your way out of this?'

'Ideally, there should be no need to cull elephants. But the human population explosion has squeezed wildlife tracts into small islands in a sea of people, islands so small, they are no longer balanced ecological systems. Man has upset the balance. In most African countries the elephant is dying out, but in Tamboti our herds are flourishing, so I *have* to cull for their own survival.'

'How do you cull?'

'Using a helicopter, we isolate a family herd to a pre-selected site, to avoid stressing other herds. Then I dart them with scoline, immobilising them. When a whole group is drugged—'

'You kill an entire family?' asked a shocked host.

'Lucky son of a gun!' retorted JR Carter.

'We *have* to. Culling individuals destroys their incredibly strong and intricate family relationships. As in hunting and poaching, it would mentally ravage the remaining elephants.'

'And all I pot is one!' sneered JR Carter.

'The cull?' asked the host, steering the interview.

Justin continued, 'When deeply drugged, a ground crew moves in and shoots them in the brain. It's all over very quickly.'

'Why aren't the elephants shipped to other sites?'

'Some are. Our 'Genesis Resurrection' operation restores elephants to areas barren of them for 150 years! Using the famed methods Dr Ian Player devised when relocating rhino in Zululand, we drug them with a narcotic and relocate to sister parks throughout Africa.'

'Why don't you do this with all excess elephants instead of culling?' asked the host, surprised.

'It costs a packet to relocate. Despite all the money I make in tennis it is still not enough to prevent culling.'

'I'll pay you, boy. Good dollars for—'

'We tag our relocated ellies,' interrupted Justin, his patience dwindling, 'and monitor them on a VDU via satellite. Soon we're going to implement an 'Adopt an Elephant' programme. People visiting zoos can sponsor a particular elephant in the wild. Follow it on a TV screen. Look after it!'

'What of JR's assertion that elephants destroy crops?'

'He's right. With the human population explosion and encroachment on wild areas, many tribes do see them as a nuisance, so they accept a pittance to have them hunted. When relocating elephants, we have a moral obligation to look after them. We use satellite monitoring and provide solar-powered electric fences. But education is the key—'

'Bullshit! You can't educate them savages!'

Justin ignored the interruption. 'We've set up community projects to teach the value of wildlife. Once they understand the immense worth of an elephant, as hunters and poachers do, they will covet them as they do their cattle.'

'Value?'

'Yep. Through tourism. Africa has an amazing array of animals that attract millions of tourists every year. The funds generated are enormous, but we need to get the local communities involved so that they can benefit. Not handouts, but through the wide ranging jobs that tourism creates.'

'But no hunting even though it brings in money?'

'No blood money!' swore Justin, his eyes turning icy. 'Not in *my* park.'

'Listen, boy. I pay good dollars for each kill. You and me, there's no difference.'

Justin stared coldly at JR Carter and spoke in a deliberate tone, 'There's a world of difference. You love it, don't you? Killing thrills you. I hurt inside. I cry every time. You're not a hunter. A tracker takes you to the right spot and you pull a trigger. You're just a *bloody murderer!*'

'I'm the world's best!' shouted JR Carter. 'I've stared down a barrel at six tons of beef hurtlin' at me, boy. Don't tell me I ain't no hunter. That takes guts. You're a bunch of cowards who pot from a whirlybird.'

Justin's hands gripped the arms of his chair, his knuckles turning white with the effort of remaining quiet. He had hoped not to slide into a slanging match with JR Carter, but it was difficult to resist.

'Tell us what it's like, JR?' asked the host.

'I've potted them all,' boasted JR Carter. 'Lion, leopard, cheetah, buffalo, rhino. But nothin' beats starin' down the barrel at a giant tusker. Man against beast. Equal odds. That's a thrill!'

You're nothing without a tracker! Nothing!

'Having done them all, what's left for ol' JR?' asked the host.

JR Carter looked intently at Justin. 'I want to shoot a tusker in *your* park. I hear you got some big 'uns down there.'

'I'll hunt you down, JR!' warned Justin

'And what you goin' to do pretty boy?' challenged JR.

With his piercing blue eyes focusing intently on JR Carter, Justin spat, 'Revenge!'

§

When a player pockets the first three Grand Slam titles of the year, the tennis world turns into a frenzy of speculation. The media shadows the pretender, haunting with incessant questions. 'Can you achieve the Grand Slam?' This pressure, more than the opposition, eventually leads to the demise of this gargantuan dream. But this occasion was different. Boris Bauer was nowhere to be found!

The world bristled with intrigue. What was the motive for shielding him from the public eye? How did he ever get match practice?

'Have you seen Boris Bauer?' the perplexed press plagued Justin.

'Nope!' he answered. *But Justin speculated, Maybe his mentor is expanding the Boris Bauer bubble of fascination to bursting point before signing up long term commercial opportunities.*

As expected, the US Open featured one theme, Grand Slam. Would Boris Bauer become only the sixth player in tennis history to achieve the coveted Grand Slam? It seemed he would. He was unstoppable.

Love one down in the third set of his second round match against Boris Bauer, Tugboat, the right-handed Hamilton twin, had not won a game. As Justin had jokingly suggested before the match, Tugboat surreptitiously swapped places with his left-handed brother during a change-over. Then pretending to be Tugboat and about to serve right-handed, Terrier suddenly stopped.

'Oh, what the heck! I might as well play left-handed!'

The crowd's chuckle turned to wide-eyed surprise.

'Fifteen-love.'

'Thirty-love.'

'Forty-love.'

'Game Hamilton. One-all.'

That was the last game the Hamilton tandem won!

Relentlessly, Boris Bauer steamrolled a path to the final, annihilating Tyrone Summers *en route*. How could anyone stop him? He had beaten everyone so convincingly in his simulated practice runs. Only Justin had the chance to stop Boris Bauer annexing the Grand Slam. A chance? Only because the two again renewed acquaintance in a Grand Slam tournament final. But what chance? A scalpel versus a sledgehammer!

Scheduled to start at 4.00 p.m., the US Open final bridges the transformation from daylight to night-time, exacting extraordinary adjustment from the eyes to pick up the flight of the ball. The eye has to adapt constantly to increasing darkness and the brain is caught not knowing whether to use day or night vision.

As the warm-up began, Boris Bauer donned a pair of photochromic spectacles.

'*Acht!* The glasses vill stabilise the change,' lectured Otto Weiner, wagging his finger. 'In the beginning they vill shade the light, then gradually allow more light in as night arrives. He vill not experience any stressful change.'

Boris Bauer did not need the photochromic glasses. Whereas on clay the rallies are long, making it difficult to hit winners, and on grass bad bounces affect the purity of timing, Flushing Meadows's hardcourts revealed his best tennis. He stared into the barrel of tennis history and never blinked. Before the lights switched on, Boris Bauer led 6-2 6-2 5-2 and 40-love. Grand Slam point!

Shit! This is bloody embarrassing. The match can't finish in daylight, felt a helpless Justin.

It did. The invincible Boris Bauer sewed up the match in just over an hour with another of the most awesome and terrifying displays of concussive power ever seen on a tennis court. Sheer *tour de force!*

His momentous scaling of the Grand Slam peaks, the brevity of his victories, his complete strangulation of the game, confirmed beyond all doubt his stature as a giant among giants. Within a year, Boris Bauer lived a legend, reserving his place in the Tennis Hall of Fame.

'Boris, first Australia, then France and Wimbledon, now the United States of America, all in the same year. The Grand Slam! A player for all seasons,' praised the president of the International Tennis Federation.

'Please accept this commemorative trophy for your stupendous achievement.'

The president presented Boris with a golden globe of the world resting in the palms of a pair of hands, diamonds studding each country of the Grand Slam quartet. Boris Bauer indeed had the world in the palm of his hands. What could he do for an encore? A back-to-back Grand Slam?

Whilst Flushing Meadows gave him a standing ovation, Justin looked on from afar.

I've abdicated my throne with my worst ever defeat, Justin grumbled bitterly, but trying hard to conceal his pain, not wanting to colour the sweet taste of this grand occasion. *Before the Aussie Open, I was king of tennis. And to think for a fleeting moment I entertained the preposterous idea of a Grand Slam. Now this bugger annexes the Grand Slam empire, and all I can feed on is the meagre scraps he leaves behind.*

As Justin left Flushing Meadows that day, his body still warm, he caught a glimpse of a stall selling memorabilia advertising, '20% off all Forrester items'. Justin smiled ruefully and sped off into the night.

In the inner sanctum of his Greenwich citadel, Amos Creighton contemplated the mega-dollar commercial offers streaming in.

'Cashing in, I could command $200 million, cut my losses, indeed make a handsome profit should the Grand Plan fail,' calculated Creighton. 'But sponsorship will drain BB, run the risk of him losing and burst his bubble of invincibility. People will get too close. ... Too risky. No, I've shrewdly bet on a piece of raw material. It's all or nothing. I want complete domination!'

My tennis is just inferior to his, resigned Justin. *He's strong like an ox, but I'm sinewy. I've got resilient strength. I feel I could outlast him, only I don't get a chance. I'll have to improve,* he decided, determined to restore the balance of power in his favour.

Justin telephoned Tyrone Summers.

'I want to do an exhibition tour across the States and Europe in the winter. Care to co-star?' Justin offered Tyrone a role which, due to his two month banning and consequential loss of match practice, he could not refuse.

'I'll whip your backside!'

'That's all you'll see!'

'I'll be there!'

§

Davis Cup! exclaimed Justin. *That's my only glimmer of hope for the year.*

After Britain destroyed Germany in their semifinal at Munich's Olympiahalle, enthusiasm for tennis renewed again. Britain was host to the final against the United States of America, the most successful country of this prestigious men's team competition.

Behind banners of the Union Jack and the Stars and Stripes, the two teams marched into the ornate wine red and gold decorated Royal Albert Hall to the sounds of their national anthems sounded by the imposing 10,000-pipe organ. The pomp and pageantry and the unique atmosphere of this grand venue instilled a feeling of something special in Justin.

A Davis Cup tie has five rubbers. On day one, players contest two singles, followed the next day by a doubles match, and capped on the third day by the reverse singles.

The ominously improved Byron Belvedere lost in four sets to Tyrone Summers in the opening singles, pressuring Justin to beat Dayack Sassoon, number two player for the United States of America.

Justin went on court against the sensation from American tennis, the leading whippersnapper of a brat pack snapping at the heels of the ruling party. Thousands of fans stomped their feet and waved Union Jacks.

Wow! exclaimed Justin, gazing in awe at the tiers of boxes rising steeply from the court, which rained popping champagne corks from affluent spectators attired in tails and tuxedos, who dined on sumptuous cuisine, relishing a quick kill. *It's like the bloody Colosseum and they've thrown one of us to the lions!*

The lion was not Justin! The pressure of expectation bore on him, whilst Dayack played with the knowledge that nobody expected him to win this match, swinging with gay abandon, defying the importance of the occasion. He was all arms and legs, motorised by the cocky orangutan walk of a greasy-haired, leather-jacketed sixties know-it-all. His tall daddy-long-legs body, an art of plumbing works come to life, covered the court in two strides and wielded his racket with orgiastic grunts, echoed naturally, by a laboured shriek as he gave birth to flashing winners. He break-danced to the first set, 6-0!

Shit! I didn't win a bloody game! grieved Justin.

Shouldering the expectations of his country in the high pressure cooker of a Davis Cup final, shards of panic pierced his heart. *What can I do? ... Hmm! Remember that story Coach once told me.*

'Rod Laver faced a barrage of winners from Arthur Ashe at Wimbledon one year,' rambled Charlie Morris. 'Rod could do nothing, but surmised that Arthur would *have* to come back to earth. If not, he would be a worthy winner. The Rocket won that match! So the best first reaction, is no reaction.'

I'll be patient!

Finding himself in that unenviable cul-de-sac of a 6-0 first set, Dayack Sassoon started to play like he was protecting a lead, playing not to lose. Games went with serve until 4-all. Inexplicably, Justin faced an avalanche of uninhibited service returns and lost his serve.

'Game to the United States of America. They lead by five games to four in the second set, and by one set to love,' announced the umpire.

Damn! Damn! Damn! I can't read his bloody game, reflected Justin at the change-over, worried that the match would have to go to a fifth set if he were to lose the second. *He's flashy. An entertainer,* thought Justin, studying the garish, Day-Glo suit and showbiz flair of theatrical bows and kisses blown to the fans. *That's for sure! I wonder how strong he'll be in a crisis? Has he got true champion grit? ... Dayack Sassoon! What do I know about the bugger? Hoss beat him last year at the US Open. Of course, Dayack blew the match!*

Suddenly, Justin felt a lot happier. Keep the ball in play and give him rope to hang himself.

Dayack Sassoon served for the second set.

An ace.

'Fifteen-love.'

A double fault.

'Fifteen-all.'

An ace.

'Thirty-fifteen.'

A double fault.

'Thirty-all.'

Justin had not touched a ball.

I'll be a son of a gun! He's got the collywobbles! A dribbler, shit scared to play a rally. Just going for broke. Please give me a ball so I can make you play it!

Dayack obliged. A rally. Justin hit one a little short, tormenting the grunter. He declined. Another invitation, this time RSVP'd. Justin floated a ball high and wide to Dayack's forehand volley, giving him all the time in the world to think. The shaky volley hit the tape, stuttered, but fell in for a dead netcord.

The Royal Albert Hall sighed in dismay.

'Forty-thirty.'

Shit! Why did it come to this? Set point down, before he's vulnerable. But that's okay. He's nervous, consoled Justin, having peeled off Dayack's game face and seen his soft spot underneath. *That netcord will prey on his mind. He won the point, but not the way he would have liked to. Now his volley is softened.*

Dayack missed the first serve.

Aah! The enigma of the mind game, ruminated Justin.

Whilst nervous twitches rattled jewellery in the Royal Albert Hall, Justin felt almost calm about his quandary.

Dayack threw caution to the wind, charging in to the net behind his second serve. Brave? No! He dreaded a rally that might expose his vulnerable nerve, his acute inability to guts out a crisis. Rather get to the net and hit a winner or be passed!

Unfortunately for him, Dayack's opponent possessed an instinctive feel for the game, an acute sensitivity to the pulse of the mind. Instead of going for the pass, Justin risked all, again floating a ball high and wide to Dayack's forehand side. To the crowd it all happened instantaneously, but to Dayack, the millisecond seemed an eternity as he waited for the floater to approach him.

Time for the nerves to tighten the muscles and asphyxiate the bugger's mind into mental paralysis, chuckled Justin.

Not having the nerve to punch his volley, Dayack swung a high risk drive-volley. It sailed out.

The impetuousness of youth, they would say. Justin knew differently. *He went belly up! Not got the nerve to be a champion tennis player!*

It was a glaring error in a match that tolerated none. Dayack groaned like a trapeze artist missing his catch. Suddenly the grunt lulled mute. His tissue-paper heart devastated, his coat-hanger shoulders carrying a world of stultifying self-doubt, he looked to his entourage, the life-support system from which he syphoned psychological sustenance, as if to say, 'Help me! What can I do?'

A clear body language sign of defeat, thought Justin. *That's why I'll never pump my arms, or wag my finger or shout 'Yeah!' on winning points. Sure they're all positive signs outwardly conveyed to inhibit the opponent. That's all fine if you're winning, you don't need to assert then. But what if you're losing, a time in need of strength. These buggers suddenly go dumb, a clear change of mood, a dead giveaway for me. Better I give away nothing! My tennis will speak for itself.*

The Brit broke serve and won the set on a tiebreaker. Dayack Sassoon's confidence ebbed, the missed shot preying on his mind. For 20 minutes the tall string bean groped hopelessly in a stupor.

He's gugalug! A drunk giraffe, chuckled Justin.

In this state of weakness, Justin savagely attacked and picked the third set carcass clean, 6-0.

Without the pressure of leading, Dayack recovered with verve.

But at 4-all, another test of nerve, Dayack succumbed and lost his serve.

'Game, Great Britain. They lead by five games to four, and by two sets to one.'

A game away from the match! Come on, Justin!

The game was long and hard and close. The upper crust twirled their diamond worry beads. Justin gritted to match point.

He sized up the situation. Finish this match now! *Overall he's played better tennis than me, but I've mastered the big points. I can't risk that continuing,* cautioned Justin, who waited for crucial moments like a champion middle distance runner hanging on the shoulders of the leader, toying with ebb and flow tactics, until the final bend, then digging deep into his reserves, mental and physical, to kick for the line.

Hmm! His favourite shot has been down the line, surmised Justin. *If he is what I think he is, and I tempt the bugger to go down the line, I bet he'll select the play insinuated by the path and speed of the incoming ball rather than the shot that'll tactically pressure me most. I hope so! Here goes!*

Justin served a three-quarter pace serve kicking wide to Dayack's backhand, tantalising him to go down the line. He raced in fast, blanketing his right. The ball came straight to his racket and he gently volleyed the ball into a great chasm of empty court for a winner. The match was Justin's.

Britain and the United States of America stood at one rubber apiece.

'On paper, we pan out equal in singles, so the doubles will be the key,' Justin counselled Byron Belvedere.

Britain lost the doubles! The whole country went into mourning. To win the Davis Cup final they would have to win both remaining rubbers. How could that be possible? How could Byron Belvedere, the pre-Justin wimp of British tennis, a man with no guts, win the most vital match in Britain's Davis Cup history?

One thing the British had not considered was the extraordinary spillover effect a body overhaul can have in strengthening the mind. Byron Belvedere heeded Justin's advice at the Barcelona Olympic Games, and transformed into a lean, mean, machine. This single, albeit major improvement, reaped a few extra victories, injecting confidence, a catalyst for further success. Mentally tough? No! But in this Davis Cup Final he benefitted from Justin's shrewd brain. Unlike normal tournament play, which subjects an individual to a stringent test of the self, where the answer to victory seems palpable to all but the blinded player, Davis Cup tennis is team tennis and allows on-court coaching.

At a critical juncture of Byron's match with Dayack Sassoon, Justin offered his sole advice to the Brit.

'Believe it or not, this cocky bugger is a nervous player. Keep the ball in play and he'll beat himself.'

Byron complied and reaped a most famous victory for his country.

'Thanks, old chap!' Byron said to Justin. 'Winning feels so gooood!'

The score stood at two matches each. Only Tyrone Summers stood in the way of ending decades of Davis Cup drought for Britain.

Again, Justin Forrester and Tyrone Summers locked horns in a gem. At 4-all and 30-all in the fifth and final set, a 'big point' in tennis, the British fans sat absolutely on the edge of their seats, screaming their jitters away, flooding them down onto the court.

Damn, I'm all shaky inside! fretted Justin, feeling the crowd's anxieties.

The one-on-one nature of tennis, where two athletes compete tit-for-tat in a small area, is conducive to reducing grown men to shuddering blobs of nerves. But it is the fine-motor skill of tennis that magnifies the nerves for all to see. Suddenly the easiest of shots is akin to threading a needle in a car travelling on a bumpy gravel road.

Choking is mental but a metabolic change occurs, causing physical symptoms.

Shit! My legs feel tight and heavy, like lead, panicked Justin, his heart fluttering in his chest. He wiped his sticky palms on his shorts, and frightened with nerves, complained, *I can't breathe. I feel exhausted!*

Come on, Justin! I can't let my team down. Okay, so I'm choking. Admit it! … There, I said it! Now, stuff what other people think. I'll show them I'm tough, he urged himself.

Like all great champions, Justin knew the panacea for nerves. *Run, Justin! Run!*

Facing Tyrone's serve, he pattered his feet on the ground until they blurred, slowly disentangling the constricting web of nerves.

Tyrone coughed, then tossed up the ball, but it hardly left his hand, as if tacky and would not prise loose. He caught the ball to try again.

Shit a brick! Terror's nervous too! discovered Justin. *Ha ha! His fingers tightened and would not let go of the ball! A sure sign of nerves!*

It gave Justin a mental booster, injecting a spur to exploit.

Don't poke at the ball and hope Terror'll make a mistake. Hit out and play aggressively, decided Justin, cloaking his nerves with a strong, aggressive attitude so the tightness would melt away. *Terror will least expect that!*

A glint of steel in his eyes, Justin drew a bead on Tyrone's weak delivery and pummelled a fierce return past him. Tyrone froze like a buck caught in the glare of headlights, glued to the baseline.

Gotcha! I was right! exclaimed Justin with unfettered joy.

224

He broke serve and held to win his match, and with Byron Belvedere, the Davis Cup for Britain. The Brits went wild, stamping their feet and singing God Save the Queen in a spirited display of national fervour.

At the presentation, while Justin and Byron stood next to the biggest trophy in tennis, the crowd hailed its heroes. In that ostentatious tub donated by Dwight Davis at the turn of the century, Britain marinaded her victory in champagne, forgiving Justin for losing at Wimbledon. The British tennis party resumed.

A great victory for Justin, but deep inside his gut, a festering sore bothered him.

Boris Bauer is number one, admitted Justin. *I'm clearly number two, but I'll never step away! I've got to beat that Boris Bauer if I'm to win Wimbledon.*

To that end, he and Tyrone Summers criss-crossed the Northern Hemisphere on their FIRE ON ICE exhibition tour.

The tour had a secondary purpose. It provided the acid test for Justin's proposed Code of Conduct and ET, his 'electronic tennis', an automatic linecalling system and timer countdown to enforce the maximum 25 second period between points. It kept Tyrone Summers in check. It worked!

No ordinary exhibitions, these! They were blood and guts displays, each player pushing the other to search for that little bit extra, striving for the apogee of their tennis talents, all for one purpose.

'Scudface, meet your Scudbuster,' Tyrone Summers declared at the conclusion of their tour.

CHAPTER 11

Whilst Justin circumnavigated a pothole route to the final of the Australian Open, Boris Bauer touched his racket on the draw and parted his way, leaving a bloody trail *en route*, demolishing Tyrone Summers in the semifinals.

Shit a brick! How does he beat Terror so easily, especially after the last two months? wondered Justin, bewildered.

He and Tyrone had honed their games immeasurably on their FIRE ON ICE exhibition tour, injecting a confidence booster in their maniacal obsession to beat Boris Bauer.

Maybe his game's too similar to Boris Bauer's. So often in tennis the slightly lesser of two similar styles ends up on the wrong side of a comprehensive thrashing. That's it! speculated Justin, consoled.

Justin had lost only four times the previous year, three to Boris Bauer and once by default. But for a man bent on cresting a sport that allowed only one king, it was a bad year. He erased it from memory. A new year, a new beginning.

Today, Justin Forrester challenged Boris Bauer for the Australian Open and he would have it no other way.

Boris Bauer, I want you! he coveted.

During the warm-up, Boris Bauer wore earmuffs.

'By muffling sound, BB's eyes will focus very quickly on the ball in the same manner a blind person develops acute sense of hearing,' expounded Professor Von Trapp. 'This sharpens concentration for a fast start. That's essential. When BB removes the earmuffs at the beginning of the match, he will hear twice as well!'

Across the net, Justin's dreaded nemesis appeared quite different from the menacing man in black of last year. His attire and equipment, right down to the racket handle and strings, shone luminous yellow in colour, the same shade as a tennis ball.

'The more I watch this game,' elaborated Professor Von Trapp, 'the more I'm convinced the top players have several uncanny edges, particularly information processing by the brain. They pick the direction of flight off the ball the instant it leaves the opponent's racket. Coupled with remarkable anticipation, this gives them an unbeatable edge. Justin Forrester is a past master at this. We must blunt his edge!'

'An' dressin' 'im like a bloody canary fairy's gonna do that, mate?'

challenged Bob Wallace.

Lurking in the shadows, Vich menacingly fondled his Donnay Allwood racket, itching to pluck the centre main string.

'Yes! The yellow ball will lose itself in a yellow background, hiding its point of contact, making it inordinately difficult for Forrester to instantaneously pick the direction of flight. In this game of fast reactions, that split second delay will be a vital loss to him. His timing will go awry!'

Professor Von Trapp hit the bull's-eye. The nightmare of last year haunted Justin with horror. He lost the first two sets 6-1 6-1.

My timing's buggered. I'm late on every ball, he lamented, unsure why. *Doesn't he let up? Doesn't he ever have a bad day?*

Justin lost the opening game of the third set, Boris Bauer serving four consecutive aces. He walked from side to side, not once making contact with the ball, a spare part in the yellow peril show. Defeat stared him straight in the eyes.

All my training, flushed down the loo! This bugger's immovable! bemoaned Justin. *Come on! Rise to the challenge! Break through!*

Justin dug deep into his new resources. His eye acclimatizing to the camouflage of the yellow background, he held serve twice to be down, 2-3.

During the change-over a sudden wind storm blew up. Paper cups swirled haphazardly through the stadium air and Akubras rolled across the court like tumbleweeds.

Hubba hubba! exclaimed Justin, sitting under his beach umbrella. *Mary Poppins, eat your heart out!*

The sky grew dark, punctuated by snarling tongues of forked lightning, followed by a deluge.

'Ladies and gentlemen,' announced the umpire, cowering from the danger above, 'due to the rain there will be a short interruption of play.'

The futuristic Flinders Park stadium revealed its trump card, a retractable roof. The 700 ton covering crawled together in two parts like a stage curtain, meeting in the middle.

After a 25 minute interruption, the players returned to court, warmed up, took the old balls out and continued the match. Incredibly, in the midst of an electric storm, unlike any other Grand Slam event, the Australian Open resumed life as an indoor tournament.

Justin won his serve to level the third set at 3-all. Then Boris Bauer changed sides.

'It's not a change-over,' the umpire announced.

Boris stopped dead in his tracks, looking surprised, sure that after the first game players changed sides.

'The score is 3-all,' informed the umpire.

Boris stood, terribly confused. At the counsel of the umpire, he retreated to his side to serve.

To everyone's surprise, Boris made two unforced errors to go down love-30. Then a Rosewallian sliced backhand pass down the line by Justin rekindled Australian memories of their golden era of tennis.

'Love-40.'

The crowd leant forward, excited at the sudden prospect.

One break point against Boris Bauer is as rare as a flicker of emotion on the robot's face, reflected Justin, excited. *A triple break point!*

Boris Bauer delivered a first serve fault. Justin returned the second serve deep to his backhand, and with his timing awry, Boris hit it wide.

'Game Forrester. He leads, four games to three,' announced the umpire.

Could it be true? It stunned Justin and the crowd. The Bauer serve, broken for the first time. Suddenly a small flicker of hope.

What did I do? asked a puzzled Justin, searching desperately for understanding of the secret formula so he could repeat it.

He held serve and broke Boris Bauer again to take the third set.

'Set Forrester, six games to three. Bauer leads two sets to one.'

He's lost his timing! He's human! chuckled Justin, towelling down at the change-over. *Ha ha! The roof's caved in on his game. ... Shit! That's it! The closed roof has thrown his timing into a loop. The indoor conditions have changed the complexion of the match, and the bugger hasn't adjusted. And if anything, I'm playing even better!*

So Justin should. For two months, he and Tyrone had dared each other to search the limits of their talent in the indoor arenas of the snow-bound Northern Hemisphere on their FIRE ON ICE tour. This ample practice coupled with his intuitive brain enabled him to adapt effortlessly to the indoor conditions.

Boris Bauer, on the other hand, had contested all his simulated matches under the outdoor conditions expected at a Grand Slam tournament. The closing of the roof threw a wrench into the gears of his game and his trained brain, inflexible to deviate from his practised pre-packaged mode, struggled to adapt.

Great! The roof stays! exclaimed an excited Justin, aware of the policy to keep it closed, once initiated.

He surged ahead 4-1 while Boris Bauer's game sputtered to the mournful chirp of a few magpies trapped inside the closed roof.

But time is a great healer. Slowly but surely, Justin felt the tumblers of Boris Bauer's game click into place, adapting to the conditions. The match took on a new dimension with this change of momentum as both raced for the critical fourth set.

Damn it! I must close out this set! panicked Justin. *He's never lost one before today. Anything can happen in a fifth set!*

The next three games went with serve, giving Justin a 5-3 lead with his serve to come.

A do or die game, fretted Justin. *Boris is back. I can feel him closing in, breathing down my neck. I've got to win it!*

But with the carrot so close, the desperation to win the set so suffocating, Justin lost his way and it all slipped away. A glimmer of hope tragically missed.

Boris broke serve, switched to turbo-mode and won the set 7-5, successfully defending his Australian Open title.

Boris Bauer lost a set! The world speculated that his contemporaries had caught up to him.

Justin secretly doubted. *He was a shadow of his normal self.*

Creighton knew the truth, too. A black mood pervaded the Team BB camp.

'How could you let a girl upstage you?' Creighton shouted in an emergency Team BB meeting.

He alluded to Steffi Graf and her win in the first ladies' final at Flinders Park. After beating Chris Evert in a rain-interrupted match, requiring a first ever indoor Grand Slam final, Steffi explained, 'That's my secret, Chris. I was practising all day indoors!' She went on to achieve her Golden Grand Slam.

'Make sure you prepare him adequately next year,' ordered Creighton

After the meeting, Creighton took Vich aside.

'This Forrester is too dangerous. Perhaps we've underestimated him,' cautioned the megalomaniac in Creighton. 'He nearly loused up my Grand Plan.'

He changed the subject of his concern to Boris Bauer. 'BB is not programmed to deal with losing a set. You are lucky Forrester choked. Do something to him,' ordered Creighton.

If Vich could express joy, then a moment of glee flickered across his face as he fondled his weapon.

'He's too public a figure for that! I want no attention drawn to Team BB,' cautioned Creighton. 'Something subtle! Don't foul up!'

§

The leopard competes with his father for prey. It is time to leave home. The young male uses scent to mark out new territory. Following deep and powerful

instincts, he employs the same tactics to kill as his mother, without ever having witnessed it done. The first kill is his rite of passage.

Having marked out his territory, the leopard remorselessly defends his space to the full. Even family members will pay the ultimate penalty for failing to heed the territorial imperative.

§

Sitting on the patio of Spaniards pub on a wintry London afternoon, Justin stared pensively into his passion fruit drink, mulling over his predicament with Boris Bauer.

Surely his desire to win must be waning, hoped Justin, despite knowing a champion never tires of winning. *That's if the bugger has any desires!*

Evident in the Championship Rolls, the unwritten laws of tennis deny a player from winning and winning. Not Boris Bauer! At least Justin pulled a set from the wreckage. But what emotional wreckage it was!

'A penny for your thoughts?'

Justin glanced up to see a pretty brunette shrouded in a fur coat.

'Mind if I join you?' she asked, taking the liberty to sit down, and extending her hand.

'Imitation?' Justin asked of the coat.

'Yes!'

'Then I don't mind.'

'Tracy. I know you, of course.'

'Now isn't this better than shivering out in the cold?' enticed Tracy.

Justin and the sultry temptress climbed into a hot, bubbly Jacuzzi. Whilst Justin tenderly soaped her voluptuous breasts, he grew to peep out from under the bubbled water. Tracy turned over on all fours, pouted her bum in the air, and glanced round with her alluring brown eyes.

'Make love to me,' she yearned in her husky voice.

Justin placed a hand on each of her firm cheeks, parted them, and in the cleft below invited a warm, moist vagina. Tracy gently guided him. On each thrust forward, Justin felt her hand stroke his testicles, coaxing him to clutch on to her bum and ride a wave of passion. The heat rising, Justin drew his lover to him and embraced her, fondling her full breasts. Bodies entwined, they writhed to orgasmic fruition.

Panting, Justin subsided back into the steamy whirlpool of warm water, drawing Tracy onto him. Parting her long, smooth hair, he kissed the nape of her neck and whispered in her ear, 'More in bed?'

The following morning, Justin woke, shocked to find Tracy in his bed.

Damn it! Who is she? he asked himself, not knowing her surname or a thing about her. *The highs and lows of the tour bug me. Last night I was lonely, and she satisfied me. But I don't want this, to wake up and find a strange woman in my bed!*

Justin dressed and packed a gaggle of suitcases for the tour. 'Tracy,' Justin called, waking her. He spelled out his plans to a sleepy face. 'Listen, I have to map out some travel arrangements. I'm leaving on tour later today. Mrs Clark will be in this morning. She'll get you something to eat, if you want.'

Then turning to leave, feeling revulsion at this one night stand and at a loss for words, Justin walked out.

He rejoined the tour on its yo-yo jerk around the world. Always a favourite stop was the Monte Carlo tournament.

After his semifinal match with Tugboat Hamilton, the short, stocky player with the tenacity of his nickname, Justin entered the clubhouse.

'A letter for you, Justin.'

He opened it and unfolded a single sheet of paper. An arrangement of letters cut from newspaper and glued on the sheet, baffled Justin.

PLAY RG AND DIE

Justin read and reread the letter, but remained utterly confused. *RG. What's RG? What a weird letter! RG ... Roland Garros? Play Roland Garros and die? One usually does! No need to tell me! ... Who sent this?*

Justin went to the tournament director's office.

'Where'd this letter come from?'

'It's all rather strange. I found it lying here on my desk marked Justin Forrester, as you can see,' the official commented, pointing to the brown envelope with Justin's name pasted on in newsprint. 'Anything wrong?'

'No,' replied Justin, shrugging it off and crumpling up the letter, throwing it into a wastepaper basket.

The following day, on a cool, sunny spring afternoon, Justin successfully defended his Monte Carlo title against Sern Stenmark.

During the next two weeks, Justin broke from the tour, preferring to train with his team-mates for an upcoming Davis Cup tie at the picturesque Foro Italico in Rome, Italy.

From the first ball in his opening rubber against local idol, Paulo Pinetti, thousands of fanatical partisan Romans baited and taunted

Justin. He felt like an ancient Christian thrown to the lions.

After taking a 3-0 lead, a missile struck his back and clanged to the ground.

Keep calm! Don't show a flicker of emotion! counselled Justin.

He picked up the coin, and looking neither left nor right, walked up to the umpire's chair and deposited the coin, calmly returning to play. Moments later another coin struck him. He repeated his ritual. It happened a third time. The umpire frantically called for good behaviour, on deaf ears. They barracked Justin, goading his façade to crack, but he simply refused to sniff the bait, steeling the fortitude of the eerie marble statue gods that gazed at the mayhem from the corners of the stadium. Then they tired of rattling him.

Now I've got you! exclaimed Justin gleefully, revelling in the Roma atmosphere, using it to his advantage.

Like Caesar before him, Justin came, saw and conquered, but no such luck for Byron Belvedere.

The British team of Justin, Byron and Jasper Ogilvy retired to their hotel for a pep talk.

'My room will be fine,' offered Justin.

'I postulate the doubles will be the decider, chaps,' Byron stated the obvious.

'Not necessarily,' comforted Justin. 'Remember the Royal Albert Hall last year?'

'Dare I forget. But—'

'No buts, Byron,' said Justin firmly. 'We can both do it. We've tasted the exotic flavour of tennis, Italian style. The shock is over. Let's turn it to our advantage. Feed off the atmosphere. Remember, their players are under enormous pressure.'

The informal meeting continued, while Justin idly flipped through his fan mail.

Suddenly, Byron broke off in mid-sentence. 'Justin, dare I say you've seen a ghost. You're the whitest chap I've ever seen! You look like an albino!'

Justin shrugged off his comments with a laugh.

'What's in that letter?' asked Byron.

'Nothing. Nothing much,' he concealed. *What the hell is going on here?* Justin asked himself, rereading the letter in his hands.

JF DEAD AT RG

Is someone following me? Someone want me dead? wondered Justin uneasily.

Justin took these thoughts onto court at the Foro Italico, engineering a dismal loss in the doubles.

'Care to share your bother?' Byron plucked up courage to ask Justin as they left the Foro Italico.

'Mmm?' said Justin, lost in thought.

'Is anything the matter?'

'Nope! Everything's fine,' replied Justin shortly. *Don't burden him. He has to win his singles match tomorrow to keep the tie alive.*

Returning from the tennis courts, as Justin began his ascent up the hotel stairs, avoiding the lift as usual, in the lobby below, he caught a glimpse of a familiar face.

Is it? Justin questioned. *Hmm … I think so!*

He hurried down stairs.

'Tracy,' Justin called, delighted. 'What brings you here?'

'Hello, Justin,' Tracy smiled warmly with her large brown eyes. 'I'm on business.'

'Forgive me. I don't even know what you do,' pleaded Justin, still repulsed by that one night stand.

'*Haute couture.* I'm in fashion design, the Santini range. You know, Tracy Santini!'

'You shouldn't design, you should model them!'

'I did once,' laughed Tracy. 'You still on the tour?'

'As always. Davis Cup.'

'Justin, shall we dine together?'

'I'm afraid I can't. I have to be with the team. An after dinner mint, say nine o'clock in my room?'

'Tracy, am I glad to see you!'

'Me too, you sexy hunk,' she whispered, slithering up Justin's body, nibbling his ear.

'No, there's something else,' said Justin, resisting her advances. 'I don't quite know what to make of it. I've been getting these weird letters. Here, let me show you.'

Justin jumped out of bed, retrieved the latest letter and showed Tracy.

'That's the fifth one. Obviously all by the same person. I don't know what to make of them, but they've got me shit scared!'

'It's the price of fame. Aren't all celebrities harassed by this sort of thing?'

'A first for me!'

'I'm sure it's harmless,' Tracy said soothingly.

Britain scraped through the tie against Italy, but with an amazing turnabout in scores. Byron Belvedere won his rubber in three straight sets, Justin struggled in five.

'Ted Parsen, of—'

'... the *London Daily News!*' responded Justin wearily. *Shit! The sphincter stinker! Is he back again?*

'Was your performance marred by having a lady in your room? It's against team rules!'

'Usually it improves!' Justin answered with a smile. 'But not with my mother-in-law!'

'Tracy, how long are you in Italy?'

'Three weeks.'

'Good. I'll be back before then for the Italian Open. I'll look you up.'

Both in Madrid and Hamburg, threatening letters haunted Justin. Frighteningly, they became more specific, more sinister.

ROLAND GARROS – COURT CENTRAL
A BULLET NAMED JUSTIN FORRESTER

Back at the Foro Italico for the Italian Open, they continued to plague Justin.

'Go to the police,' urged Tracy.

'What can they do? I'm in and out one country like a yo-yo. There's no way the police will be of much help.'

'Then what *are* you going to do?'

'I'm not sure!' responded an exasperated Justin, slamming down the latest letter.

'Are you going to play in Paris?'

Justin sat on the edge of his bed, shoulders slumped forwards, slowly shaking his head. 'I *have* to. How can I forgo playing the French Open?' He turned to Tracy. 'But how can I *play?*' cried a distraught Justin, contemplating his future at the next Grand Slam tournament, only two weeks away. For that he needed little reminding.

ROLAND GARROS
TWO WEEKS TO GO – PREPARE TO DIE

Justin hugged Tracy, drawing comfort from her.

'Will you come with me? To Paris?'

'Of course!'

Justin rushed to London with one idea in mind. Entering his intended destination, he glanced up to a revolving sign, 'New Scotland Yard'.

'We're dealing with an erotomaniac,' declared a detective.

'Huh?'

'Yes. He or she is one of a growing band of semi-delusional people, who target celebrities – usually someone unobtainable – for their aggressive or sexual intentions. They believe in a common destiny. It consumes them to the point where they become fixated with the star.'

'What sort of cases have you had?' asked Justin.

'All sorts,' replied the detective, shaking his head. 'A woman falsely claiming to be a star's wife and moving into his house! A film star getting over 5,000 letters from a stalker in one year. The price of fame, sir!'

Words Justin did not want to hear. 'How serious is the threat?'

'Very serious. But you're in luck, sir.'

'What do you mean?' Justin asked eagerly.

'Those who write letters containing outright threats, obscenities, sexual advances, or sheer vituperation, are among the least likely to confront a celebrity in person.'

'Then who does?'

'People with romantic delusions or other fantasies of personal intimacy expressing a desire for a meeting.'

'What profile do you draw from these letters?' asked Justin.

'Nothing is watertight, but most who badger stars with inappropriate letters, phone calls or contrived meetings, are men,' expounded the detective. 'But …,' he started, then paused.

'But what?' asked an anxious Justin, determined to know everything about this new type of foe.

'On the other hand, most pick famous women as the objects of their unwanted attentions.'

'What would you suggest as a plan of attack?' enquired Justin anxiously.

'Treat it seriously,' replied the detective, looking concerned. 'But the truth, sir, is that most erotomaniacs are never more than onlookers. If you're here in London we can assign you a tag, but I'm afraid Paris is out of our jurisdiction. I would suggest a personal bodyguard to be on the safe side.'

When Justin returned to his house in Hampstead, the discovery of another ominous-looking envelope lying on his bed pierced his heart like a dagger.

'Shit! Shit! Shit!' he cried, unnerved. 'How'd they get in here?' he questioned, furious that his unseen enemy had stripped his privacy bare. He could deal with anyone face to face, but this coward irked him. 'This isn't happening!' he screamed, not wanting to open the letter, but knowing he had to.

ROLAND GARROS
THE TIME IS NIGH, GET READY TO DIE
QUARTER-FINALS

Justin spent that night tossing and turning in bed, sweating his decision to play the French Open.

In the end he decided, *I have to play, it's the French Open! I can't miss a Grand Slam tournament. If I don't play, this maniac will continue to hound me. I must face it!*

Justin flew to Paris and met Tracy.

'Thank goodness you're here,' sighed Justin, hugging her at Charles-de-Gaulle airport.

'As long as you need me,' she comforted.

Once the tournament began, the assassination-threatening letters suddenly ceased. But the eerie silence served to heighten tension in Justin.

'Face me, damn you!' he shouted on return to the hotel after his second round win.

'Hush, Justin. Try to relax,' soothed Tracy.

'It's easy for you to say.'

'I know,' she consoled. 'But I think you know I'm right.' Justin acquiesced, flopped into her arms and murmured softly into her bosom, 'Hold me tight!'

Outwardly, Justin shunned the whole affair, trying to live a normal existence. After all, there was a Grand Slam tournament to be won. But deep inside, the threat ate at him like a cancer. He felt defenceless.

If only I didn't know the day of the quarter-finals, it would be easier. But I do! Wednesday of the second week!

The tension grew day by day, awaiting his appointment with death.

A nervous and edgy Justin took the court with Manolo Gonzales, surveying the crowd like a hawk.

It's so open, I feel vulnerable, naked. I can't hide in the camouflage of the bush like in Africa, thought Justin uneasily. *I'm like the proverbial sitting duck!*

He played like a lame duck too. Manolo won in three straight sets. As Justin shook hands with the Spaniard, his mind was still elsewhere, covering for the hollow in his back. He walked off court, then suddenly grew mad at himself.

'Damn it! Damn it! Damn it!' he shouted. *That blimmin' maniac has bamboozled me out of this match. Sure Manolo could have beaten me, but my opponent today was not on court!*

A bitter Justin met Tracy and left Roland Garros.

'I can't believe it came to this. Nothing happened, but I've lost in a Grand Slam tournament. It was all a bloody hoax!' griped Justin. He vowed, 'I swear if I lay my hands on that swine, I'll kill him!'

'Better lose a match than your life!'

'Damn it!'

Justin walked arm in arm with Tracy into his hotel room. He broke out in a cold sweat. On his side of the bed, lay another foreboding letter.

'Ignore it, Justin,' implored Tracy. 'It's over now.'

Justin visibly shook, his sweaty hands struggling to open the brown envelope.

A PRACTICE RUN
FOR REAL AT WIMBLEDON

§

'Pyramid water? Ya crazy, mate!'

'Believe me,' assured Romany Fatignon, holding up a compressed cardboard pyramid. 'Water placed under a pyramid of the correct dimensions and aligned to the four cardinal points, converts into a magic potion!'

'Bullshit!'

Undeterred, the nutritionist carried on. 'The power of pyramids is legendary, particularly their preservation powers. That's why batteries last longer and razor blades stay sharper when stored under a pyramid. As for water, they impart tremendous electro-magnetic energy into the polar molecules. I've even taken to wearing one on my head!'

'Cork it, pyramid head!'

'Hmmph!'

Boris Bauer swigged back pyramid water at each change-over throughout the French Open championships, and won with contemptuous ease, beating Tyrone Summers in the final for the loss of one game!

§

Back in London, Justin came to terms with the torment.

Just a cruel hoax. It'll never get to me again. I must focus all my energies on Wimbledon and beat that Boris Bauer, urged an inspired Justin.

Boasting a few extra days of unplanned grass court practice, courtesy of his early loss in Paris, Justin dedicated himself to training and worked like a terrier.

Then the rain came down.

'Just what we need,' Justin griped to his practice partner, Byron Belvedere.

'Let's play indoors at Queens,' suggested Byron.

'Uh huh. See you there this afternoon,' replied Justin. 'I must get these rackets restrung.'

Justin turned his new royal blue 500 SL into Ingram Avenue, then slammed on his brakes. Something had caught his eye.

Not the gutter press, this time! No, it's …

Eager to observe more closely, his vision blurred by the rain, he edged nearer, parking six houses away, shielding behind another car.

Shit a brick! I was right! That is Boris Bauer's mentor! exclaimed Justin, detecting with his eagle eyes.

Vich walked from a parked car, up Justin's driveway, to the front door.

What the hell is he doing here? wondered Justin, his heart pounding. Suddenly a monstrous thought struck him. *Is he the erotomaniac? … Nope! Surely that bugger can't have the hots for me!* he chuckled. *What then?*

Justin observed intently from afar. Vich rang the doorbell. The front door opened and Tracy appeared.

Careful, Tracy! Justin advised under his breath, his body tensing, ready to rush to her rescue. *Hey, what's this?*

An animated discussion exchanged between Vich and Tracy, concluded with him handing over a parcel. A knot tightened in Justin's stomach and he felt sick.

As Vich left, Justin ducked below the dashboard. He waited a few moments, then drove round to the golf course and entered the house by the back door. Stealth gained from stalking in the bushveld took him to his bedroom without detection. Tracy stood, busy at the dressing-table.

'Hi Tracy!' Justin greeted, entering the room.

'Justin!' she started, turning round, holding her hand to her heart. 'You gave me a fright! I didn't expect you back so early.'

'It's raining,' Justin answered, trying to detect what Tracy shielded on the dressing-table behind her. Unsuccessful, he thought, *I'll bide my time.* 'Look, I've arranged to play indoors at Queens with Byron, but I must get these rackets strung. Please, Tracy, please can you do me a favour and take them in?'

'Yes, of course, Justin,' she replied, standing her ground.

'Thanks. Some rackets will be ready, so you can pick those up, too. I'm sorry, but I can't let Byron down. You know how punctual I like to be.'

'My pleasure.'

'Thanks a million. My stringer is somewhere in Finchley Road. I'll fetch my address book from the study,' Justin said, giving Tracy just enough time to wrest herself from a sticky situation, without escaping with the evidence.

Two minutes later Justin returned, handed Tracy a piece of paper, and began to repack his tennis bag, including the last of his strung rackets.

'Bye. See you later,' said Tracy, kissing Justin on the cheek.

'I'll be back about six this evening.'

Justin peered from his third storey bedroom window to make sure Tracy had gone. Then he quickly telephoned his stringer.

'Jack, this is Justin.'

'Aah, Justin. Your rackets are ready.'

'A big favour, please?' begged Justin.

'For you, anything. Just name it.'

'A lady by the name of Tracy will be delivering and collecting my rackets. At all costs keep her delayed. Do anything. Rackets not ready. Whatever!'

'Gee, Justin. You got a problem?'

'Perhaps. One other thing, don't let her smell a rat.'

'Well, it's not my line of business, but I've always wanted to let down some tyres!'

'I need an hour, hour and a half. Thanks Jack. I owe you.'

Justin stood before the dressing-table and deliberated a second.

Please, Tracy, pleaded Justin, hoping his suspicions would be unfounded.

His pulse quickening, he opened the drawer, recovered the parcel and prised it open.

Damn it, Tracy! Justin cursed, his heart sinking.

Inside glared an ominous-looking stub-nosed Smith & Wesson .38 revolver and money, lots of it. He searched through her belongings, found her passport and flipped through its contents.

Monte Carlo, Rome, Madrid, Hamburg, Rome, London, Paris. She's done the bloody tour! discovered Justin with alarm. *Followed me everywhere!*

He rummaged through her suitcase and found the final evidence he had hoped not to uncover. Scissors, glue, brown envelopes, and traces of newspaper cuttings.

Why Tracy? Why? And what's the connection with Boris Bauer? As if I don't have enough trouble with him. What's going on?

'Hmmph!'

Four and a half months earlier, Vich intruded in a plush Kensington apartment in London at three o'clock in the morning. A feminine body stirred in her slumber.

'Wake up, whore!' Vich growled, switching the light on.

The girl under the cosy blankets shrieked at the sight of Vich, sat up in bed and pulled the covers up over her bosom.

'Don't hurt me!' she cried, cowering away from him. 'If it's money you want, take all I have.'

Her hand reached over and opened her bedside table drawer. She made a grab for a pistol but Vich kicked out and rammed the drawer shut with his heavy foot, crunching her hand. She screamed.

A Vich glare quietened her.

'Now listen good. I know your type. Whore!' spat Vich.

'No! I'm in fashion design. Tracy Santini.'

'Whore!' spat Vich, slapping her face. 'You infected the boss with the clap. It's driving him crazy. He wants you dead!'

'No, please, please,' cried a desperate Tracy. 'It's impossible. Madame Stella was scrupulous. She checked us regularly.'

'Quiet!' ordered Vich. He tossed a copy of medical records at Tracy. 'You saw Dr Genois.'

The blood drained from Tracy's face and she stared at him with stunned eyes.

'Smile, whore! You're worth more to me alive. I have a job for you. Screw up and the fashion world knows where you came from.'

Bloody hell! The gun! She's going to kill me! the realization shook Justin.

A plethora of thoughts flashed through the Forrester brain, Justin

240

seeking a solution.

Gotcha!

'Dare I say I've been to hell and back,' gasped Byron after their workout at Queens. 'It mystifies me how Boris beats you. Just not cricket!'

Justin stayed quiet.

'I'm jolly glad we stopped earlier than scheduled. I'm pooped, old chap!'

'We'll make up for it tomorrow. I must go. Bye.'

Justin went home via Scotland Yard. He entered his bedroom. Tracy sat on the bed, revolver in hand. Justin had left the package open, intent on bringing the issue to a head.

A long moment of silence strained the atmosphere.

'Why, Tracy?' Justin searched, his heart torn.

Tracy shook her head slightly before answering. 'You wouldn't understand.'

'Try me. You owe me that.'

'Don't Justin. Leave it.'

'Tracy, we could've had something. You meant a lot to me. You don't know how this hurts.'

'Stop it!' cried Tracy, her eyes glistened with tears. 'You don't understand. I *have* to.'

'What?' asked Justin, incredulous. 'What do you mean you *have* to? You're still going through with it?'

Her silence gave Justin his answer.

'Kill me?'

'No!'

'What then?'

Tracy's face dripped with tears, distraught. Justin edged closer.

'Justin, don't. Stay back. I warn you, I'm a good shot,' she cried.

Still he edged closer. Tracy raised her .38 revolver.

'Stop!' she screamed.

Suddenly a deafening report boomed from the exploding gun. Justin flinched, then grimaced in the stunned aftermath of the shot. A profusion of thoughts ran through his mind. Had he swapped the bullets with blanks? He had! Had she discovered the swap? She had not!

'Justin!' Tracy shouted, dropping the gun. She rushed forward to embrace him, sobbing hysterically.

'Why, Tracy? Please tell me?'

'I can't. You'll find out.'

Her response utterly confused Justin. It made no sense. His inner turmoil dissipated when four Scotland Yard detectives burst through the door.

'Awright, mate? Did it work?'

Justin nodded. He went to an air vent, took out a video camera, ejected a tape and handed it to the detective in charge.

'Come on, Delilah. There's a place for you to cool off for a long, long time.'

Justin sat on his bed, dazed. As the detectives handcuffed and led Tracy away, her face left a lasting impression on him. She looked desperate to tell him something. It haunted him.

CHAPTER 12

The rain in London,
Falls mainly on Wimbledon!

Strawberries and cream washed down with champagne, on tea lawns under sunny skies. But in time-honoured Swimbledon tradition, the weather had other ideas. Chilly winds to prompt an Eskimo to pack an anorak and ankle warmers, blew igloo weather in from the north. Leaden skies with large, bulbous, graphite clouds wept so much, the famed Beeb boob, 'There has been no rain since it last rained!' seemed to make sense! It rained, and rained, and rained!

And the few times the clouds disappeared, another kind of storm erupted at Wimbledon. Illuminated by the lightning, orchestrated by the thunder, Boris Bauer whipped up a tornado on the hallowed grass of the Centre Court.

§

'Gentlemen,' Creighton addressed Team BB, before giving Robin Wallenborg a cursory nod, 'the threat of Forrester is not over. Professor Von Trapp will elaborate a plan to extract the ultimate tennis from BB.'

'If you cast your mind back a couple of years, to when Justin Forrester became World Champion,' expounded Professor Von Trapp, 'he played sensational tennis for two sets against Tyrone Summers, losing just one game if I remember correctly. Then his game suddenly fell apart and the match became a dogfight. What he experienced in those first two sets, I believe tennis players call, Mr Wallace …?'

'Zonin', mate! That Forrester bugger played in the bloody zone, awright.'

'Yes,' said the professor, 'Forrester's play that day was equivalent to anything BB has played, and—'

'*Meine Güte!* BB comprehensively vins simulated matches against Forrester on that day!' retorted Otto Weiner.

'That's true,' agreed Professor Von Trapp. 'But Summers didn't put Forrester under any pressure. It's impossible for us to know how much better he *could* have played.'

'So a zoned Forrester is a threat to the boy?' asked a concerned Creighton.

'Perhaps. We don't know. It would help if BB *also* played in the zone,' said Professor Von Trapp. He expounded, 'In peak performance parlance we call it 'whole-brain experience'. You see, the brain divides into two halves, the left and right hemispheres, each controlling the other half of the body. Importantly, each half has decidedly different functions. The left-brain is rational and self-analytical, drawing conclusions based on logic. The right-brain is opposite. It suspends judgement, gaining insight based on intuition from a holistic view. Intriguingly, the brain can exist in either state or a mixture of the two.'

'Explain y'self, mate,' demanded Bob Wallace.

'Ideally, activities such as mathematics or keeping track of time use the left-brain, and creative drawing the right-brain.'

'Didn't think those art farts 'ad a brain,' responded Bob Wallace. 'Drawin' is a right-brain activity?'

'Well, spatial awareness is, yes,' answered the professor. 'Tests have shown that a person with a damaged right-brain can still answer abstruse mathematical problems, but finds walking through a room containing furniture a spatial nightmare!'

'Where does tennis fit in?' queried the Australian impatiently.

'That's a very interesting question. Tennis analysts believe zoning is a right-brain activity and—'

'That's fair dinkum, mate,' agreed Bob Wallace. 'When ya're zoned, ut's like those art farts. Floatin' blotto in a can o' piss. Time passes you by. You're in dreamland, a bloody wet dream! An' ut's bloody true, ya *do* see things as a whole. Ya don't question, mate, ya just do ut!'

'And what if you're not zoned?' asked Professor Von Trapp.

'Ya lug punish your game. Where's my bloody backswing goin'? Why'd the ball go in the net? I should've bent my bloody knees!'

'What is the result?' asked Professor Von Trapp.

'Ya play like a mug, mate. Come a gutzer!'

'That correlates with research,' agreed Professor Von Trapp. 'It appears that our modern lifestyle, which constantly requires logical decisions, forces us to exist in the self-critical state of mind of the left-brain. When suddenly asked to perform a right-brain activity such as drawing, most of us get frustrated and give up.'

The professor turned the subject to tennis. 'It appears that a zoned tennis player *does* shift from being exclusively left-brain. But unlike other analysts, I do not believe zoning is a total shift to the right-brain, but a harmonious use of both hemispheres, called whole-brain.'

'Doesn't this bung a blue on what we just said, mate?' challenged Bob Wallace.

'Not really. You see, in tennis, time and space go hand in hand. We cannot have one without the other. The timing of a return of serve requires a harmonious spatial adjustment to be effective. *Ipso facto*, a zoned tennis player is in whole-brain, performing in the right hemisphere whilst being served subconsciously by the functions of the left.'

'Hooly-dooly! 'Ow do ya get into this state?' asked Bob Wallace, suddenly interested.

'Most tennis players zone a couple of times a year, if not for the whole match, then for part of it. None have intentionally switched it on, although most champions naturally raise the level of their games in a crisis. The chase, the motivation to win, so consumes their minds, it quietens their critical left-brain. Forrester often exhibits this quality. He plays at the instinctive level when under pressure.'

'A can o' piss does ut for me!' beamed Bob Wallace.

'Getting zoned is not the only problem. As difficult as zoning is, snapping out of it comes readily.'

'That's fair dinkum,' agreed the Australian. 'Ya only 'ave to start thinkin' how the sun shines out ya backside, when, wham bang, and ya're playin' like a bloody mug!'

'Yes, you analyse with your left-brain. Question your fine play once and you open the door to slide back into left-brain. Make a mistake and it criticizes. Suddenly the floodgates open, until you're playing entirely with your left-brain, and badly. A classic example was Forrester's sudden decline in the ATP Tour World Championships. When Summers told Forrester to slow down, he shrewdly brought to his opponent's attention how quickly he won the first two sets, and—'

'And time is left-brain!' exclaimed Bob Wallace, getting the picture.

'Yes. It immediately set Forrester thinking about how well he was playing. The shift back to left-brain was dramatic.'

'Can ya switch on this wet dream?' asked an impatient Bob Wallace.

'Perhaps! I have an idea, but it's untested.'

§

'Justin! A mansion in London, a game park in Africa, and surely millions of dollars in the bank. You're a flame that pretty women flock to. Titles all round the world. What more do you want?'

'I'd give up the lot, just to win Wimbledon. There's no place I'd rather be, no title I'd rather win, than Wimbledon!' yearned Justin.

Wimbledon! Grass! The sensual feelings of this special place stoked his fires of competitiveness. He even declined to play doubles, preferring to be away from the claustrophobic confines of the club to conserve his energy, focusing his mind on one thing, Wimbledon.

Rain. Rain. Rain. The courts swamped into a morass. Not since 1922, when Wimbledon moved from Worple Road to its present location, had the courts played so badly. Back then, to speed up the move, they shipped in truckloads of sod from the coast, and after many days of rain, shrimps hatched from eggs in the turf and players found them wriggling in the courts.

I'll volley! decided Justin. *To avoid bad bounces, I'll play with the dictum that grass is not meant for a tennis ball, and get to the net to volley.*

A year ago, Justin Forrester had played his first Wimbledon final. Afterwards he wished he could go back to bed, wake up and start all over again. Now he could.

Would he become Britain's first Wimbledon men's singles champion since Fred Perry in the thirties? Not on this day! Nor would Boris Bauer retain his Wimbledon title. The fickle British weather beat them both, the Rolex scoreboard reading, 'RAIN BEAT JF & BB'.

Umbrellas unfurled like flowers blooming in spring, injecting a much needed rainbow of colour to contrast the cold, dank and dismal day. Rain delays are awful. People huddle around for hours, waiting. Above all, it is most disconcerting for the players. It is not unheard of for a Wimbledon match to take place over three days on three different courts. And always, it is the waiting, waiting, waiting, the ebb and flow of nervous energy, which becomes the biggest enemy. By the time the players get back on court, they can be drained of fight.

Whilst the ladies contested their singles final, also held over until this Monday because of rain, instead of fine-tuning his game on a tennis court, Boris Bauer sat in the locker-room and fed his mind, using a 'virtual reality' system of mental visualisation.

Wearing a headset containing tiny TV screens and a suit housing sensors that monitored the position of the body, head and eyes, Boris Bauer emerged into a three-dimensional world of virtual reality. Otto Weiner had programmed the high-speed computer connected to the headset with realistic images of Justin Forrester playing tennis at its zenith. Justin would bang a vicious serve into play, but Boris felt and saw himself returning the ball for an outright winner.

'Visual images get through to the muscles faster than verbal information. They serve as a blueprint for response,' elucidated Professor Von Trapp. 'Importantly, they stimulate the creative hemisphere of the brain.'

'What's that fly shit on 'is racket?' asked Bob Wallace.

Whilst the two protagonists sat in the bare waiting-room just off

Centre Court, awaiting their call, Boris Bauer stared into the pattern stencilled onto his racket strings. Instead of the normal company logo, it bore an unusual symmetrical pattern of concentric circles radiating from the centre.

'Tennis players don't know it,' explained Professor Von Trapp, 'but tinkering with their strings to straighten them after a point is a spatial exercise, and can mildly shift them into whole-brain. It helps them to relax before focusing all energies on—'

'The doily, mate?'

'The pattern is a mandala. By staring into its vortex, the mind becomes so spaced out by the spatial pattern, it frustrates the left-brain, which acquiesces to the power of the right-brain. BB will shift into whole-brain and automatically play in the zone.'

For Justin, on court, it was *déjà vu,* a nightmare recurring like a stuck record. While the rain dampened Justin's powder, Boris Bauer played a gargantuan game, scaling the heights of tennis nirvana. He was zoned, a man possessed of supreme skills, his racket fissioning the ball into a laser beam, shooting off the lines like greased lightning.

'Please ladies and gentlemen, no use of flash photography!' announced the umpire.

To a person, the crowd wished victory for Justin. Boris Bauer had won six Grand Slam titles in a row, equalling the record of Don Budge. Eventually the tennis world grew tired of one man taking all the honours. Besides, this was Britain, and Justin was their boy. Sadly, for them, the greatest tennis arena in the world became a morgue.

Justin salvaged precious little from the damaging fallout of the first set. He fought gallantly to arrest the onslaught at 1-all, but the dyke broke and the blitzkrieg swept in.

Down 1-2, Justin sat at the change-over and draped a green Wimbledon towel over his legs to protect against the cold, although he wished he could put it over his head and hide from this horrible nightmare. Meanwhile, Boris Bauer stared into the mandala on his racket strings.

'That should lock him into whole-brain,' rejoiced Professor Von Trapp.

It did. Against Boris Bauer, it never rained, it poured. His game remorselessly bludgeoned the more lightly built Justin into the hallowed turf, meagrely rationing Justin three break points in the whole match.

On the first, the ball hit a hole and bounced over his head. The second, a big serve almost took off his face, before he saw the ball. The last, the final insult, the ball hit the court with the aplomb of a soft-boiled egg and rolled like a carpet bowl into the hands of a ballboy.

Shit! You can't volley when returning serve!

Boris Bauer allowed Justin only a shadow of his pre-final form. The world caved in from under his feet. His island turned into a fragile sand castle and the incoming tide inexorably washed it away. In the end, extruded through the wringer, rung dry of skill and will, Justin died.

The chair umpire observed his last rites, announcing the score, 6-1 6-2 6-1, to the reigning monarch.

Sitting in that lonely loser's chair, feeling naked in front of the world, his champion's aura stripped bare, Justin donned his track suit top and swathed his head and shoulders in a towel. A lone bugler sounded the haunting 'Taps'.

The loss devastated him. Justin yearned to win Wimbledon, utterly coveted the title. But each time one man shattered his dream. For most, the abiding memory of Wimbledon was rain, but for Justin, Boris Bauer.

Later, in the dead of night on Hampstead Heath, a sad and forlorn figure, walked aimlessly in the Boris Bauer wilderness, brooding over this difficult and painful loss. The débâcle rankled, eating away at his stomach like acid. He sat under a tree and sobbed his heart out.

§

Justin picked up the phone and struggled to decipher a garbled message from a frantic Zola, induna of Tamboti.

'JR Carter!' exclaimed Justin, his heart leaping into his throat.

He immediately packed a modicum of belongings and boarded the first flight to Africa.

As Justin screeched into Tamboti camp, JR Carter, dressed in hunting gear and brandishing his Ruger rifle, came out to greet him.

'This wog of yours squeals like a stuffed—'

'Shut up, Carter! Get ready. We're going elephant hunting!'

Justin packed his Winchester and the unlikely couple set off in an open back four-wheel drive Land Rover, in search of elephant.

'Find me a big 'un, boy.'

Justin said nothing. He fumed inside.

Scouring a dirt-track hedged by tall grass, they confronted a black rhino without its horn. In a desperate measure to preserve the near extinct species, the park's management cut off its anterior horn.

Without one to gouge from its face, the rhino is of little use to those bloody poachers! thought Justin, sadly remembering his drastic decision to remedy their extinction.

'Tired of them. I want a big tusker. And when I've potted 'im, you'll oblige me, boy. Take a picture of me sittin' on top of the beast to show them fellows back home.'

Justin searched for a trail. After an hour of driving in the bushveld, he spotted fresh dung. He stopped the Land Rover, stepped out of the vehicle and poked his finger into the dung to test its temperature.

Still 10 minutes by car!

The Land Rover descended into the valley, across the Tamboti river and detoured round a hill. Again Justin stopped the vehicle, this time walking up to an uprooted umbrella thorn. He tested the freshness of sap, reading the book of nature.

They're pretty close, thought Justin. He shouted to JR Carter, 'Wait here!'

Like his feral kind, Justin vanished into some thick riverine bush, then ascended part way up the hill to gain a better perspective.

The elephant herd lay 300 metres ahead, concealed from the Land Rover by the bush. Some sparred for sport, sending the cold crack of ivory across the bushveld. Groups fed side by side, answering one another's rumblings, and a mother aided her distressed calf. Another movement caught Justin's attention. Much closer, towered a bull elephant in musth, oozing testosterone!

'There's a bull not far ahead,' Justin informed JR Carter on returning to the vehicle.

'That should tickle the ticker,' he sniggered, gleefully unloading his rifle, fondling the 458 Magnum cartridge, then reloading. 'This ounce of lead's got the name 'Bull's Eye' marked on it.'

That elephant's history against that calibre. 'You say you're a hunter?' Justin asked without conviction.

'The best,' boasted the rotund JR Carter. 'Now get me to that tusker.'

Justin drove ahead. Suddenly it burst into view, towering menacingly not 50 paces away. More than three metres tall, six tons of beast glared at them. Its huge ears outspread, its trunk raised like a lance, the surprised elephant trumpeted, its massive feet pounding the dust.

'Get outta here,' screamed a terrified JR Carter, frantically training his rifle on the bull.

Justin quickly steered the Texan's aim away from the elephant.

'Don't be a fool. We're too far away,' reproached Justin.

He swiftly slammed the gear lever into reverse. Having stirred the ire of the elephant, he edged back slowly. Just then, the Land Rover sputtered, ebbing lifeless.

'What's it, boy?' asked JR Carter absently, so engrossed in his find, he failed to notice the dead Land Rover.

'Oops! Out of fuel. Fancy that!'

JR Carter had not heard.

'Get me starin' into his face, boy,' the agitated Texan ordered.

Justin remained quiet and motionless.

'What's it, boy? You scared?' asked JR Carter, suddenly turning round.

Justin glared at the pudgy man with his icy blue eyes and mimicked JR Carter, 'And what you goin' to do pretty boy?' The pretty boy answered in a deliberate tone, 'Revenge!'

'Don't fuck around with me, boy!' threatened JR Carter, pressing his Ruger barrel into Justin's gut.

Justin looked to his right, ahead of the Land Rover at the menacing-looking bull, then back to JR Carter.

'Now the odds are equal!' he told JR Carter. 'Man against beast. Dumbo, meet your match!'

In a flash, Justin jumped out of the Land Rover, ducked below the door level of the vehicle, out of rifle sight, stalked round to the other side and vanished into the riverine bush.

In the background he heard, 'Get back here, you son of a bitch! Hey, boy! Get back here! Don't fuck around!'

The sounds grew dimmer as Justin tracked his way back to camp on foot in the darkening evening. The following morning he boarded a flight back to London.

§

A zoned Boris Bauer, pepped up with carbo-loading and fizzing with electro-magnetic pyramid water, played frightening tennis at the US Open. This did not enthuse the tennis world. They grew tired of exhibition tennis, tired of Boris Bauer. They wanted more, they wanted a match.

'DRUGS!' screamed newspaper headlines. How else could he attain such gargantuan levels of performance?

Such rampant rumours called for Boris Bauer to undergo a drug test. Despite standing for an hour next to a tap of running water to encourage his own, Boris struggled to contribute sufficient urine to test for anabolic steroids, masking agents and recreational drugs.

'Sir, we cannot wait all day. He must drink this.'

Vich held the large glass of water up to the light, peering at it with suspicious eyes. Eventually he relented, 'Hmmph!'

Boris Bauer drank and urinated.

'Wow! To think nobody can get near to Boris Bauer and here I'm holding his wee!' exclaimed an excited attendant, so excited she trembled, sending the vial of dubious contents crashing to the floor!

An irate Vich stormed out of the drug testing centre.

'You crass idiot!' Creighton reproached Vich. 'He's clean. Now they'll speculate. Make sure he doesn't even *smell* a cup of coffee!'

'ET works wonderfully well! How did you come upon this idea?' a reporter asked Justin at a press conference.

The brand new 24,000 seater Flushing Meadows stadium incorporated ET, Justin's 'electronic tennis', boasting an automatic linecalling system to eliminate on-court altercations, and a timer countdown between points to improve the flow of the game.

Once a point ended, an electronic counter, stationed at the umpire's chair, flashed a green light and reset to 25 seconds. The receiver had 15 seconds to get ready for play. Then the light changed to amber and the server could serve at will. But if 25 seconds elapsed, a beeper sounded and a red light flashed, and the server automatically lost the point.

'Well, after the catastrophe at last year's French Open, I knew tennis was in dire need of overhauling linecalling. The new Code of Conduct worked well, but was always a potential bomb with human emotions on the line.'

'Enter ET?'

'Yep. The best way to eliminate human error is to eliminate humans. We decided to electrify the chair and short-circuit disputes using ET.'

'We being?'

'Tyrone Summers and I checked it out on our FIRE ON ICE exhibition tour.'

'Tyrone? That's surprising!' remarked a reporter.

'Who better to test the efficacy of a linecalling system than Tyrone!' smiled Justin.

'Was he agreeable?'

'Certainly. Unknown to himself, this bugger's been crying out for a consistent application of the rules. He needs a barrier, to know where he stands. Otherwise he's up the creek without a paddle.'

'Ted Parsen of the *London Daily News*. Aren't you devious? Trying to quieten the wild boys to your advantage!'

'On the contrary, buggers like Tyrone Summers play better with their traps shut,' Justin said coldly. 'You should try it sometime!'

Justin reached the semifinals of the US Open. To observers, nothing appeared unduly different, but Justin knew otherwise. The inner-fire quelled, he fought more with himself than with his opponents. On Super Saturday, that opponent was Tyrone Summers.

'I'll let my racket do the talking,' Tyrone boasted, wary of the new Code of Conduct.

'Which racket?' wondered the crowd. 'The one in his hand or the racket that spews from his rat-a-tat mouth!'

'I have to control my temper to beat players like Pale Wog and Scudface. But plebs, they still bug the shit out of me!'

Tyrone's racket spoke eloquently. Whatever Justin conjured, Tyrone popped up elsewhere like a Jack-in-the-box. When Justin lost the first two sets against him and slipped 5-2 down in the third, the match seemed all over.

Five-two down. Shit! cursed Justin.

But suddenly, on the very brink of extinction, his love of the chase stoked the fire in his heart.

It's only one break of serve. Guts it out!

As so often happens in tennis, he converted the 5-2 deficit into a 7-5 victory, with the 'domino principle'. He won his serve, then with all the pressure on Tyrone, broke serve, and held his for 5-all. Tyrone, peeved at his inability to take the set offered on a platter and fearing the sudden surge against him, faltered again for Justin to serve out the set.

'Set, Forrester, 7-5,' announced the umpire.

Tyrone pouted and seethed inside, but said nothing. That would mean points lost. Points he could ill afford to lose against Justin Forrester.

Terror must be puncturing tooth marks on his tongue! chuckled Justin, proud of ET.

He was positively angelic. Well, almost! For just one moment he was torn between act and thought, eventually whacking a defenceless courtside pot plant with his racket to vent his anger. Then he looked at ET and mumbled laconically, 'Go home!'

Justin slipped the noose, and with an unexpected new lease of life, rampaged through the fourth set to square the match at two sets all.

In the fifth set, the two waged a battle royal as only they could, stretching each other's boundaries to draw the match level at 9-9 in the final set tiebreaker, at nine o'clock at night.

Tyrone coughed. But just when the odds favoured Justin in this nerve-jangling climax, he had nothing left to give. He looked jaded, and ragged edges tarnished his game. The dramatic, instinctive, death-defying feats that made him invincible in a fifth set, vanished. His touch, so important for one whose strokes were more intuitive than contrived, deserted him. He tried desperately, but from memory, not passion. It was not enough. There was no way back for Justin. Tyrone Summers exacted sweet revenge for many a defeat, and beat Justin for the first time.

'You've lost to Tyrone Summers. Are you finished?' a reporter asked.

'Losing to him?' Justin questioned, incredulous. 'I think not! My game constantly tests the edge, so sometimes it'll fail. But he's a great player, and today he was better than me. I'll learn from this. A loss is cathartic. It'll teach me new tricks.'

'Who'll win tomorrow?'

I hate a question like this, Justin thought to himself. *The obvious answer is Boris Bauer, but it fuels criticism of me being a sore loser.*

'Boris Bauer, for sure,' he spoke the truth, knowing that Tyrone would have done the same.

'Has Boris Bauer taken drugs?'

'It's not for me to speculate, but I'd hardly think so. Tennis is squeaky clean,' Justin lauded the sport. 'I don't know of any drug that can help us. There are too many variables in the game. A drug enhancing one area will affect performance elsewhere. If you bulk up, you lose flexibility.'

'Would *you* take drugs?' quizzed a reporter.

Justin paused. The press circled him like a horde of vultures.

'If I'm the has-been you say I am, maybe I should!' Justin fired a cynical barb at the press.

'Would you?' the reporter asked again, impatient for a scandalous reply.

By speaking his true feelings on a subject everybody tiptoed on eggshells, Justin offered the assembled media a field-day. Like a thousand terriers scratching away for a bone, the polyglot media, mainly pudgy men with paunches, drooled, their microphones and pencils poised to record any nuance or stray remark that might sell a story.

'Drugs! You make it sound so sensational. There's no big deal. I bet most of you have drunk enough coffee today to fail a drug test. Maybe they should institute a drug testing programme for the press!' attacked an irritable Justin.

'What of the unfair advantage?'

'What of it? Everyone's trying to get an edge to improve performance. *You* demand that! Some people carbo-load. Do you care about that?'

'What about the danger aspect?'

'I hope the dangerous press will be eliminated!' Justin uttered another barb. 'Taking drugs is no more dangerous than driving a car. Yet we all still drive and accept a quota of deaths. Do you pester a bugger for driving a car? No! Most of you smoke. That's a drug. *You* care about danger? Pah!'

'What about the ethics?'

'Ethics!' exclaimed Justin, raising his tone of voice. '*Taking* the drugs is not unethical. They're widely available prescription drugs, not illegal substances. We all take them for medical reasons. What is unethical is breaking the rule. But do you care about that? A player stalls past 25 seconds. That's cheating. Do you write about it? No! It's not sensational. But shroud the offence in the emotive word 'drugs' and you have a scoop, a chance to crucify someone. Talk about ethics!'

'In a nutshell, are you for or against drugs?' asked a reporter, hoping to get Justin out on a limb.

'Of course I'm against drugs! But for vastly different reasons from you. I wouldn't take drugs because of the unknown side-effects. That's why I would never smoke, and why I won't allow you to smoke whilst I'm giving a press conference. And breaking the rules *is* cheating, and I will *never* cheat. Accepting coaching from the sideline is also cheating. I treat them both the same. But you don't care about these things. … Oh, why do I bother talking to you!'

Justin got up and left.

The following day the newspapers were awash with gossip stories, painting Justin the supreme ingrate, the spoiled star incarnate, a drug addict.

SOURPUSS FORRESTER GIVES
SUMMERS NO CHANCE

JUSTIN ON DRUGS – THE INSIDE STORY

Justin saw the billboards, but did not bother reading the stories. Nor did he watch the US Open final.

The outcome is a forgone conclusion!

He was right. Tyrone's epic match with Justin proved a pyrrhic victory. He exhausted himself, without a drop left to offer. Boris Bauer killed him with his power play, serving a basket full of aces.

'Where's the next one going,' asked Tyrone wryly. 'Do *you* even know?'

Tyrone could only smile and joke at his inevitable fate. Boris Bauer was grand, indeed. He captured a back-to-back Grand Slam, another unique slice of history for a man who had carved an indelible mark in the record books and annals of the sport. Here was a Caesar. Whence comes such another? Such was the remote chance the tennis world would ever see his like again. The world looked on in awe at the immensity of his achievement, but no longer with much enthusiasm for the man.

A year ago Creighton commanded a potential fortune in Boris Bauer, but declined to cash in, risking all for the ultimate power he sought. Since then, the stampede to sign up Boris Bauer for commercial contracts had reduced to a trickle. Now the tap ran dry. The price plummeted.

For Creighton, it had been a case of all or nothing. But he had good reason to risk all. Boris Bauer was invincible.

§

Justin anguished. He was one of a special breed, a champion, driven by the lust to win. He knew he had to beat Boris Bauer, but his insuperable rival blocked his every move.

Without direction, he returned to the never-ending tour of tennis. What looks glitzy and glamorous to the outsider, is a grind. Money, parties, exotic locations. Sure! But a champion sees little of the world outside the white rectangles bisected by a net. His day quickly degenerates into a wasteland of loneliness. It has to be that way or he would not be a champion. Ivan Lendl once characterised his lot, 'My life as a champion is only more glamorous sounding than my life as a dog!'

The tour is a session of group therapy, where egos are massaged or stung, depending on whether one wins or loses. Only the top dozen or so players win more matches than they lose. For the rest, the sport is an ego-deflating drill. What once nurtured Justin's soul, now stole it.

I've got no energy! groaned Justin listlessly on a tour of Basel, Sydney and Tokyo, losing each time.

Players who once quaked at the prospect of a duel, now queued to take a shot at him, hellbent on playing the match of their lives to take the scalp of Justin Forrester.

At each stop, he faced the questions. Irritated with the prying press, stung by telling the truth, Justin doled out neutral platitudes and inoffensive cliches – 'I take it one match at a time!' – or simply ignored the inane questions – 'How old are you?' or 'What tension do you string your rackets?'

On a speedboat ferrying players from the Hotel Inter Continental along the Seine to the Open de Paris indoor tournament, a jaded Justin pensively stared into the water, plummeting to the nadir of his life. He had lost his idealism, energy and purpose. His creative muse evaporated.

This is so boring. What's the big deal? I lose, so what.

Such an uncharacteristic shrug of the shoulders to what once existed as his life and death struggle, suddenly struck a chord of concern in Justin. *That's not me! Until I can give of my best, I'm out of tennis!*

Justin took one look at the horde of vultures that gathered at the Palais Omnisports and screamed, 'Leave me alone!'

He walked out of the tournament.

With his career like a ship with a broken rudder, heading to a destination unknown, Justin derailed off the tour and returned to Hampstead. He shut himself up in his mansion, disconnected the telephone and vegetated, mired in stagnancy, forlornly licking his wounds.

In this weakened, vulnerable state, the media beat a path to his house like a pack of wild dogs. They staked outside his home, jostling for elevated vantage points, sharpening their pencils and filing their fangs, itching to air the dirty laundry to the heartless public, without first visiting the washtub. Justin ignored them.

After a couple of weeks, a brick crashing through a window woke Justin from his stupor. He picked himself up off the bed, trudged to the landing and stuck his head out of the broken window.

'Justin! Where the devil have you been?' demanded Albert Heathcote, shocked at his unkempt appearance, the dark shadows under his eyes.

'What do you want?'

'The Davis Cup final is in three weeks. We need you for practice.'

Justin walked down to the front door.

'I'm unavailable,' declined Justin.

'Don't play games with me, you pompous … Uh, look, you're our key player. You will play—'

'Cut the apron strings, Heathcote!' snapped Justin, turning to close the door.

'Wait! Let's calm down and be reasonable.'

'That would be a first!'

'Okay. Let's take it step by step. You don't want to play,' said Heathcote slowly, buying time, 'What do you want? We'll give you anything. Just name it.'

'Listen carefully. I'll say this only once. It has got nothing to do with you or the team or anyone else, … not yet! But there is *nothing* that will make me play. It's time you learned to get on without me.'

It's pointless to play the Davis Cup final, thought Justin. *I haven't touched a racket in weeks. I've no desire to play. Not only would playing embarrass me, my team and my country, but I cannot show the media how I feel. They'll crucify me, putting more pressure on me. My friends will understand. This will tell me who they are.*

Somehow, Ted Parsen got wind of the story and made a meal of it.

FORRESTER TURNS HIS BACK ON BRITAIN

Nobody believed Parsen at first. He had Justin engaged, married to and divorced from Heidi Schültz in a scandalous affair that stretched his credibility with the public once too often.

Justin sent a telegram to the British team, wishing them luck for their final against Germany. But to win in tennis requires more than luck. They lost. Now the media lacerated him with savage accusations.

JUSTIN FORRESTER, THE COLDEST, MOST SELF-CENTRED, RUTHLESS CHAMPION KNOWN TO TENNIS.

AIDS FEAR!

JUSTIN TO FATHER A LOVE CHILD!

Why ruin a good story with the facts! thought Justin, disbelievingly, then dismissed them.

They hardly mattered to him. His problem lay internally. He brooded over the impending Australian Open and a heart-wrenching decision.

I promised Terror I'd play doubles with him, and I pride myself in honouring commitments. But I'm just not ready to play singles, Justin decided. *If I cannot put in my best, I'd rather not play. It's not my style.*

'I've a hunch why you ain't playing singles,' Tyrone informed Justin in Australia. 'But I ain't letting you off the hook. We're gonna play doubles. When we win, the scent of victory will spur you on like a furburger. I need you, Pale Wog. We *have* to defuse that Scudface.'

Justin smiled, thankful for Tyrone's intentions, but dubious of their success.

The media hounded him.

'Why aren't you playing singles?'

Justin tried a mild-mannered defence, but tension lined his face. Gone was the fresh face of the kid who took the tennis world by storm in that sweet summer a couple of years ago. It had lost its boyish exuberance.

'Are you suffering from burnout?'

'You know, …' Justin started.

His speech bled into silence. He stared blankly into the distance, lost in a world of his own. The studio strained, waiting patiently. Seconds ticked by. Silence.

The interviewer who asked about burnout shuffled in his seat, embarrassed. 'Uh, Justin?'

'Yep!' he answered, snapping out of his trance.

'You were saying?'

Justin looked dazed and confused. 'I forget.'

'Go to commercials!' ordered control.

Justin and Tyrone won the doubles.

So what! thought Justin, measuring his self-worth in singles only. *So you need quick reflexes, but doubles requires little of the inner mettle that is so indispensable for the make-up of a single's champion. It means nothing!*

Having honoured his obligation to Tyrone Summers, feeling desperate to leave Australia and return home to Hampstead to shield away from the prying world, he boarded a Qantas jumbo at Tullamarine, destined for England.

Slumped in his bucket seat, on one of a thousand flights journeyed through his tennis career, Justin clenched his fist, and lay his forehead on it.

What is it, Justin? he cried to himself. *Time once healed my wounds, resolved defeat into strength. Now, nothing! Only emptiness!*

On the verge of tears, to escape embarrassment, he made a beeline for the toilet, but his tear-blurred vision sent him slap-bang into a woman returning from the ladies' room. They crumpled in a heap in the aisle.

His woe temporarily forgotten, Justin felt a spare part standing in the toilet. Instead, his thoughts turned to the woman he bumped.

Hmm! Kind of pretty. Very pretty! thought Justin. Then he cautioned, *Watch it! No more Tracy incidents. They're bad for my tennis!*

Whilst returning to his seat, Justin wrestled with his heart, but immediately on seeing the leggy lady with long auburn hair and deep blue eyes, he detoured his mind. *To hell with my tennis!*

'I'm sorry again. Mind if I sit next to you?' asked Justin.

The lady hesitated. 'I don't think—'

'Let me get you a drink. It's the least I can do.'

Still the lady hesitated.

'Please!'

'Okay, Justin,' she relaxed with a smile.

Huh? How does she know me? wondered Justin, the recognition of him by seeming strangers never ceasing to amaze him.

'Robin,' she held out her hand. 'Robin Wallenborg.'

'Where're you from?' Justin queried her Scandinavian accent.

'Stockholm. Sweden.'

'But we're headed for London.'

'I had to leave quickly. I'll take a connecting flight.'

'And I thought all Swedish women were blondes!'

Both laughed.

Hubba hubba! gasped Justin, absorbing her beauty.

Sapphire eyes burned brightly in a hearth of black eyelashes, the classical nose, cheek bones poised high, red rose lips bled on virginal snow, smooth as porcelain, alight with fire cascading down a slender neck giving way to a femininely accentuated body. Deep inside smouldered a woman, sophisticated in style, polished in poise, graceful in manner, captivatingly beautiful.

Justin inhaled a deep breath of the alluring sweet fragrance that was Robin's presence, then talking Strine to distract his enchantment, asked, 'What ya been doin' down under, mate?'

'Oh, a little of this, a little of that,' laughed Robin. 'You, mate? Not playin' singles! Hard yakker, eh?'

'You watch tennis?'

'A little of this, a little of that,' answered Robin evasively. 'I've seen you. I like your style. Fast and balletic, poetry in motion.'

'Hmm! Let's change the subject. What work *do* you do?' persisted Justin.

A stewardess interrupted Robin's hesitation, serving the couple with delectable cuisine.

Savouring the tangy, fruity taste of his exotic mango and lychee salad, Justin fondly reminisced, 'What I miss most on tour is climbing up a lychee tree and pigging out. Hanging bloated from a branch like an ant's nest. ... That's life!'

'Really! I thought it'd be your wildlife!'

'Me and wildlife!' expressed a surprised Justin. 'What more do you know?'

'I sponsor an elephant on your 'Adopt An Elephant' programme. It's a wonderful idea. Often I go to the Skansen zoo in Stockholm and feed my ellie. Well, watch him on a TV screen!'

'Wow!' exclaimed Justin, his eyes lighting up. 'Are you for real? You really like animals?'

Robin smiled and nodded.

Justin immersed himself in stories of his youth, living in the African bushveld. His woe forgotten, he waxed lyrical …

'Sorry Robin. Got carried away there!'

She smiled. 'It sounds beautiful. One reads of Africa, the wild, but you bring it alive!'

Justin paused for a moment, then face beaming, invited Robin, 'Come with me to Africa! Experience my treasure in Tamboti.'

Robin withdrew back into her seat and took a deep breath before resisting, 'No thank you!'

'Why not?'

'I can't!'

'Of course you—'

'Justin!' Robin spoke sharply.

He stopped, surprised at her reticence.

Checking in at Heathrow, Justin searched deep into Robin's eyes. He spoke softly, 'Surely this is not the end of the road for us?'

She said nothing.

'May I look you up, sometime?'

Robin hesitated a moment, then nodded and scribbled on a piece of paper.

'It's my number in Stockholm. Call.'

No sooner had Justin returned to his home in Hampstead, when the telephone attracted him like a magnet. He stared into it, then at the piece of paper in his hand. He dialled the Stockholm number, but there was no reply. Over the next three hours, he nearly developed a blister, punching the number pad in front of him.

'Hello, Robin Wallenborg speaking,' panted a voice through the receiver.

'Hi, Robin. Justin.'

'Hello, Justin,' giggled Robin. 'I've only just walked in.'

'I know. I think I've worn out your answering machine tape! I *had* to hear your voice,' Justin pined. He paused a moment, then said, 'Robin, I need you.'

She stayed silent.

'Are you there?'

'I'm here, Justin.'

'Look, if you don't want—'

'I'd love to be with you, Justin, but …,' hesitated Robin. Again, she went silent.

'But?'

'I must warn you up front that I'm under contract with Amos Creighton.'

'Who's Amos Creighton?' asked a bemused Justin.

'He's the driving force behind Boris Bauer!'

Shit a brick! Images of Tracy Santini flashed through Justin's mind. How do I get myself tangled up with Boris Bauer's women?

It was his turn to be silent.

'Justin?'

'Yes! Mmm … I can manage, if it's okay with you.'

'That's the only reason I've hesitated. This can put us both in an awkward position. I believe we should have a ground rule that prohibits discussing anything to do with Boris Bauer.'

'Right now tennis is the furthest thing from my mind. I'll see you, tonight!'

§

Returning from the show, 'ASPECTS OF LOVE', walking hand in hand across Hampstead Heath extension, Justin confided, 'Robin, the last three weeks with you have been some of the happiest moments in my life.'

Robin smiled. They stopped and turned to face each other, standing alone on a carpet of snow under a moonlit sky like two skaters in the spotlight on ice.

'Me being older,' started Robin, toying with a button on Justin's coat, then searching in his eyes. 'Does this not worry you?'

'Love, love changes everything!'

Breathing mists of love, they embraced and kissed, warmly and passionately.

Justin was in love. The empty house, where for weeks he heard the echoes of his footsteps, bubbled with laughter shared with Robin. She filled the void in his life. He had purpose again, a reason to live and to enjoy. But no tennis!

Mmm! A home life, sighed Justin, swigging back a mouthful of milk delivered to his door, enjoying the simple things life had to offer away from the gypsy life of the tour. *Hmm! That shrub needs pruning!*

But all changed on a brief holiday in early spring. Monte Carlo!

A favourite haunt of Justin's, one place in the world where the public did not treat him as an oddity. So many rich and famous people abounded, that sports and showbiz stars walked through the streets without people giving them a second glance.

Justin emerged from the shower to confront Robin lying on the bed, suggestively toying with a racket between her thighs. He did not take the bait.

'It's not like you, darling. What's the matter? Lately you seem agitated. Is it me?' she asked, concerned, lying on the bed of their holiday apartment.

'No, of course it's not you,' said Justin with a smile.

He walked to a window that offered a bird's-eye view over a bay bobbing with multi-million dollar yachts. Below, he gazed at the exclusive Monte Carlo Country Club with its palm trees and scented gardens. Whilst members feasted on lobster and caviar and vintage champagne, his fellow professionals ran and slid, stopped and turned, retrieving a little yellow ball in the never-ending story of the tennis tour.

Justin said pensively, 'My racket should be used out there, not to titillate you!'

Robin joined Justin, put an arm round him and absorbed the idyllic setting of the country club.

'If you don't enjoy tennis any more, why don't you give up?' she asked gently.

'I can't, Robin. I haven't won Wimbledon!' rasped Justin, sounding like a thirsty man crawling in a desert, jinxed by a mirage.

'Is that so bad? Tennis is really just a game!'

An incredulous Justin looked at Robin.

'It's everything! It's my dream. If you give up your dream you wither away and die. I know! Besides, I'd sooner not have started a tennis career if I knew I wouldn't win Wimbledon. I *have* to win. Every fibre of my being desperately wants to win Wimbledon.'

'Then play tennis again,' countered Robin, so simple in her outlook.

For Justin it was not that simple. 'I *want* to play again. I haven't told you, but these pangs are welling up inside me. It's like a drug. I need to go out there and compete again.'

'But?'

'Boris Bauer! To win Wimbledon I have to beat him, and I don't know how,' Justin replied with utter exasperation. 'And I *want* to beat him. I *need* to beat him. But I'm scared. Tennis is my passion. If I lose to him again, I'll go mad! … I have to find a way to beat Boris Bauer and win Wimbledon!'

Robin withdrew like a tortoise into its shell. 'Justin,' she spoke firmly, 'I can't talk about Boris Bauer.'

'I know. I know. I'd never expect you to. This is between him and me.'

A month of inner torment festered in Justin. He had clearly thawed his winter of discontent. But this locked him in a crucible. He *had* to win Wimbledon. But to do so he had to beat Boris Bauer. And he did not know how.

'Robin, I need to go home. Home to Africa. I have to see Charlie Morris. Please come with me?'

CHAPTER 13

To gain inspiration, Justin paid homage to his humble roots, the acorn that returned trappings of wealth and fame, but also the problem of Boris Bauer.

The simple way of life in Africa will clear my mind. Coach will know what to do! Justin consoled himself.

Suddenly he felt a little better, comforted by the warmth of home, the solid rock of his shadow-mentor, Charlie Morris.

Justin drove to Sand River Dam. With the sun scorching down, he gazed out across the vast expanse of water, up the tributary where he used to canoe. It was quiet.

Nothing's changed, observed Justin warmly. *Life has stood still for 15 years. It's so beautiful here.*

Only the people had aged.

'Mum,' Justin hugged his mother affectionately. There was less of her to embrace, her buxom bosom seemingly melted in the hot African sun and sunk to her bottom, making her positively pear-shaped. But still good old Mum.

'Dad,' Justin shook his hand before embracing him.

'Hello, boy. When're you gonna give up this tennis thing and come back and getta proper job?'

Dad hasn't changed!

Then there was Charlie Morris. Older, but still sprightly under his straw basher. Justin found him at the Mhlume Tennis Club.

'It bothers me, Coach! I'm fast and fit, my strokes are good, and I'm hungry. I feel I've played my best tennis against him, but each time he bulldozes me off the court!' Then Justin humbly asked, 'I need help. I cannot do it on my own!'

Coach assumed a pensive mood. Justin hung on to every moment of silence, hoping for a reward in profound advice, a key to the hidden treasure. The sounds of silence ticked by.

'We have a TV set now,' Charlie Morris said slowly, looking up from under his straw basher. 'I've seen him play, this Boris fellow.'

The old man looked away to the left, gazing into the distance, as if deciphering an incoming message. Then he addressed Justin. 'You can't beat him, son! His game is too brutal!'

What? a shocked Justin cried out inside, the words cutting right through him, as cruel as his defeats by Boris Bauer. *I believe in you Coach. Why do you say that? ... No!* rejected Justin, shaking his head. *To believe that, would be to kill my dream!*

But despite the odds looking bleak, a good teacher will always offer a route out of the maze, a message of hope.

'Take heart, son,' said Charlie, advising, 'Never give up hope. What chance had David against Goliath? Never give up hope!'

A pall of gloom fogged Justin's mind, clouding Charlie Morris's advice. Justin remained silent. All he heard were the cutting words, 'You can't beat him, son!'

'Would you like a knock?' asked Charlie Morris. 'Maybe I can still teach you a trick or two!'

'Huh? ... Sure, but I don't have a racket.'

'Hmm. I'll see what I can do.'

Charlie Morris entered the quaint clubhouse. Scrounging around in his bag, he found an old racket.

'There you are, son. That should do!'

Justin looked at the racket and his eyes brightened.

My Dunlop Maxply! he exclaimed, rubbing his thumb over his bloodstained initials carved into the laminated wood. *The same racket Dad won in a regatta all those years ago. The racket that gave birth to my love for tennis.*

'You've kept it all this time?' asked Justin, his face lighting up.

Charlie Morris smiled.

'It looks like a relic from the ark,' Justin laughed, lovingly fondling the timber. He put his nose to it and sniffed deeply. 'Now *that's* a racket! They don't make them like this anymore!'

'They don't make too many like that lady friend of yours. She gets *my* nod,' smiled Charlie with a glint in his eye.

Without his tennis gear, Justin played barefoot, trading the ball backwards and forwards with Charlie Morris. Not wanting to blast the elderly man off the court, he coaxed the ball with feel, gently swishing it with perfect timing and gifted touch. His heart beat a nostalgic trip back to the old days when he tried to knock the life out of his split pole tennis wall, to when he developed his game.

Those crazy days, Justin reminisced fondly. *Swing your ground strokes! Punch your volleys! Throw your serve! ... Running like a madman after a scruffy old ball ... weaving a web of spins ... winning Wimbledon against the greats, Budge, Laver and, of course, Borg.*

'Thanks, Coach,' acknowledged Justin when they finished. 'Look after her for me, will you?' he asked, handing back the racket. 'Tennis has never been quite the same since the demise of wooden rackets!'

Wooden rackets! An idea tapped him on the shoulder, but he unwittingly shrugged it off.

§

Justin took Robin to his pride of Africa, Tamboti. They packed a bottle green Land Rover and headed north from Tshaneni, entering Justin's heritage at four o'clock in the afternoon. From the border gate they headed west, following a sun painting the Tamboti river liquid gold.

Justin stopped the four-wheel drive and pointed in the distance to an acacia tree.

'The fastest animal in the world!' he spoke softly to Robin.

In the shade, lay four cheetahs, their inactivity belying their dazzling speed.

The dirt track headed through the river and wound itself up a large hill to a spot nestling on the river side, Tamboti Camp.

'Come and see Africa,' an excited Justin beckoned Robin the minute he braked the Land Rover to a halt.

He grabbed her hand and eagerly pulled her to the stone wall edge of the plateau on which the camp overlooked Tamboti river.

Below, grew a dense thicket of riverine bush, its lifeblood stained scarlet by the setting sun, meandering and nourishing the paradise. Across the river, stretched a panoramic African savannah as far as the eye could see, imbued with the golden hues of dusk, sustaining a living mosaic of wildlife.

The long necks of a group of giraffe popped out of the terrain, in characteristic guard position, nibbling foliage out of the cluster of thorns of acacia trees, each looking in a different direction to scan the widest possible area. Not far below, elephants wallowed in shaded pools along the river. And, of course, impala scattered everywhere.

'It's so beautiful. So peaceful. Africa's Garden of Eden,' whispered Robin, conscious of her voice in the African silence. 'One imagines lions savagely attacking the poor old antelope. And grisly beasts in a dog-eat-dog kind of world. But it's so tranquil here.'

Justin smiled. 'Those impala have as much chance of being eaten by a lion as you have of being killed by a car. It's no more cruel here. But let me assure you this is also no playground,' warned Justin, always aware of the nervous excitement of the savagery that *could* take place.

Hmm! I remember many years ago at dawn, catching a glimpse of the furtive shadow of that spotted hyena darting in and out of a herd of wildebeest, locating its prey, then ripping a half-expelled foetus from its mother's belly. Wow! ... But then such actions stimulate gregarious instincts amongst the wildebeest, helping to regularise their breeding cycle, so ensuring their survival!

'Everything works according to the laws of the jungle in a perfect balance!' he declared.

They breathed in exotic fragrances of wild flowers and dry veld grass and watched the sinking sun draw the veil of night across the sky on Justin's Tamboti.

'Is there any food around here?' asked Robin. 'I'm famished.'

The two unpacked their belongings into their thatched rondavel and showered before setting off to the camp diner. They entered a verandah decorated with traditional African curios. In the corner, a log fire crackled and glowed in the crisp autumn evening while rustic smells of timber and thatch and meat grilling on an open fire, permeated the bushveld air.

'There's no choice of food,' Justin warned Robin. 'You take what you get.'

'I'm so ravenous I could eat a buffalo!' joked Robin.

'Hi, Zola. What's on the menu tonight?'

'Mr Justin,' beamed the African cook with a mouth full of ivories gleaming in the log fire light, 'for you, buffalo steaks!'

Robin's heart sank into her empty stomach. 'He's joking!' She looked to Justin for confirmation.

Justin laughed. 'No, but you'll like it.'

'Tuck into these Kudu kebabs, ma'am. I go skin the buffalo,' teased Zola.

Justin and Robin dined on Tamboti cuisine, buffalo grills and marula pie, food from the park.

'This is too delicious for me to ask what's in it,' Robin commented, tucking into another slice of pie.

Satiated, they walked out to the verandah and leant against the stone wall that overlooked the river. Stars illuminated like sparkling diamonds in the pitch black African night sky, and the moon cast a romantic glow, reflecting eerily in the water below.

Justin looked into Robin's eyes, cherishing her breathtaking beauty in the moonlight.

'Robin, this is where I belong once my tennis career is over. If you're willing to share it with me, I'd like to marry you,' he proposed, offering a resplendent diamond solitaire ring from the black panther's lair in Paris.

Robin threw her arms round Justin's neck and kissed him in delight.

'I love you, Justin. Of course I'll marry you.'

'But Robin,' he cautioned, 'life here is like nothing you've ever experienced before.'

'So far I'm liking it more than you can imagine,' she said radiantly.

After spending an hour in the African night, punctuated only by the sounds of the wild, Justin and Robin retired to their thatched rondavel.

Justin sighed and flopped down on the double bed.

'Is the thought of married life such a strain?' Robin teased, slipping into a turquoise satin negligée.

Justin smiled. 'I'm just winding down, I guess. This place allows me to.'

'Let me help you,' said Robin, unbuttoning Justin's khaki shirt and unbuckling his belt. 'Down to your underpants, please!'

'How disappointing!'

'Just so I don't get distracted!'

Robin massaged Justin, starting at the neck, releasing the tension that had knotted through years of life on the tennis circuit. Justin groaned with oohs and aahs while Robin's expert fingers explored each and every muscle, plying the taut fibres until they relaxed, her long autumn hair tickling his tanned skin.

'Mmm! It's sore, but invigorating!' sighed Justin.

'Masochist!'

Slowly she worked her way down Justin's wiry, sinewy, muscled body, missing out his bum, and continuing with his thighs, right down to the ends of his toes, purging him of tension.

Robin placed her hands inside his underpants, folded them over his bum and gently removed them down his legs.

'I was wondering—'

'Shhh!' Robin hushed, putting her finger to her lips.

She kneaded his bum cheeks as if they were two lumps of dough, pressing her thumbs deep into the muscle. Slowly her hands slipped off the mountains, down the crevice until they found his testicles. In quietness she tenderly stroked them, tickling until they tightened. Justin groaned with delight, shifting to get comfortable as he grew underneath.

'Turn over,' Robin whispered.

Justin enthusiastically complied.

'Hmm. Frisky!' Robin giggled, seeing Justin's erect penis.

Robin climbed onto the bed next to Justin. Kneeling, she crouched over his groin. Then slowly, agonizingly slowly, she caressed the underside of his penis as it lay large on his belly.

Justin closed his eyes. A tingling sensation kindled and he groaned. Then he felt her hands take him, clutching him tight and massaging in long strokes. His breathing quickened. He sensed her coming closer, lowering her face on him. Suddenly he went warm as a moist tongue ventured and titillated, then soft lips covered him and delicately caressed, kissing him tenderly.

'Robin!' Justin cried out between short breaths.

He opened his eyes. Silhouetted through her negligée against the dim candlelight, he saw a seductive sprinkling of pubic hair. He searched his way under her negligée, ran his hand up her thigh and touched her. He rubbed her clitoris, stimulating her until she was open and moist.

The heat of passion flourished in Justin until it reached fever pitch.

I can't take it anymore!

He sat up and flung Robin back on the bed, her long chestnut hair radiating out on the soft pillow. He knelt over her, erect with lust.

'Come in me, you animal,' aroused Robin.

Justin pounced on her with wild desire while Robin clasped round her prey with love. The two writhed with passion, smothering each other with kisses, tongues entwining between deep, panting breaths, bodies sintered, glowing in the candlelight. Driven by a sexual drive naturally attracting male and female into the involuntary but enjoyable bond of passion that drives all other desires into submission, each sought and gave, their sexual tension rising to a point of no return, climaxing in the throes of animal groans.

Then they were silent, except their heavy breathing, slowly subsiding as they lay, still coupled and in each other's arms, glistening with perspiration. They said nothing, absorbing the stillness, reflecting on their love, purring their contentment. It was quiet.

Suddenly an almighty roar split the silence. Robin jumped in fright, disentangling from Justin, then quickly sought comfort in his arms.

'What's that?' she cried.

'Relax. It's just a lion roaring *his* contentment.'

'You mean—'

'No. He … oh, there's a few of them,' observed Justin, the roar turning into a chorus, filling the night. 'They've made a kill.'

'But it's so close!'

'It just sounds close in the night air. Let's go and see,' suggested Justin, rising from the bed and walking outside.

'Justin!' cried out Robin, nervous about what 'just sounds close' meant.

'They're probably across the river near that koppie. There's nothing to worry about,' Justin reassured, despite the heavens vibrating. He called to Robin, 'Come.'

She joined him. The two stood naked out on the edge of the precipice, overlooking the moonlit river. Justin took Robin in his arms and they hugged and purred whilst the lions roared in the distance.

'Tell me about a lion kill,' whispered Robin.

Expansive, almost lyrical, Justin told his African fables.

§

A herd of wildebeest and zebra dots the plain across Tamboti river. The sad-looking wildebeest appear greedy, gorging their meals with single-minded passion, but this is not so. Feeding buries their noses in the long grass, lowers the eyes, and the sound of their incessant chewing dims their hearing. With their sensory faculties severely diminished, they are at the mercy of concealed lions waiting for just such moments of inattention, to pounce. Having taken in their meals with haste, they raise their heads and regurgitate into the mouth for lengthy mastication before swallowing again. Now they can smell if danger lurks.

This finely developed sense of smell is complemented by the acute hearing of zebra, who mingle with the wildebeest. Zebra wisely sense lions prefer the ruminators. Besides, their stripes blur in motion, providing them with excellent camouflage, leaving the wildebeest vulnerable in an attack.

It is the lot of herbivores to eat, and avoid being eaten!

Lions! King of the beasts! Head of the predatorial hierarchy. They form prides and adhere to social structures to enhance their efficiency, hunting in open grassland and in woodland.

The pride divides into two teams. The catchers carefully move downwind into a line of ambush, and hide behind cover. The chasers stalk up along the river, circling behind the herd. They try to get as close as possible. A zebra looks up. The lions check, stand dead still, looking down their noses with intense concentration. The herd, scattered only moments ago, converges in formation, heads up, sniffing the air, bellowing nervously and gazing fixedly at the spot where the lions hide. A stench of fear taints the air. The grim game of life and death is about to begin.

A gust of wind. The faintest scent unleashes terror and confusion. Suddenly a strange clamour splits the silence and amazingly transforms the peaceful scene. Pandemonium! Cries mingle with the thunderous pounding of hooves in a cloud of dust. In the panic, the catchers are quick to exploit. They ambush, fixing on the weak or the sick, ensuring selective breeding. A lioness spots a straggler, a wildebeest lost in the wild flight. She charges, accelerating with graceful fluidity, intercepting, pouncing from below, her massive paws raking into the flesh of the shoulders, her fangs intent on the jugular. A brief falter and the wildebeest breaks free, stunned. They face head-on. Sensing the futility of flight, the wildebeest gambles its last. It charges the lioness! The predator retreats a few paces, falls on her back, and with lightning speed strikes from underneath, clamping shut the mouth of the wildebeest. The sheer weight of the

270

lioness brings her prey crashing to the ground. She will not let go now and her prey suffocates to death.

The lions unite with joy and much affection. But they are also strict in discipline. The job of the male lion is to protect the territory, securing a safe haven for the females to hunt and breed, ensuring the survival of the species. He eats first, then nobly and authoritatively roars his contentment, echoing across the dark plains. The others join in, calling the cubs who have watched from afar.

The pride glutted with freshly digested meat, zebras and wildebeest soon graze peacefully nearby. Now and then they raise their heads to glance at their carnivorous neighbours, reassuring themselves that they are still there!

The game of life and death is sudden and brief, wild and savage, but naturally beautiful.

§

'What's that?' asked Robin with a jump, quickly burying herself in Justin's arms.

A shrill cackling laugh pierced the still air.

'Hyenas. They're scavenging off the kill.'

They stood there, quietly absorbing the activities of the night. 'You showed me your expertise tonight,' said Justin, smiling, 'now I'll show you mine.'

'Now?'

'Yes, a dawn ride down the Tamboti river. Come, let's go.'

Justin and Robin headed upstream in the Land Rover, accompanied by Zola.

'This looks a suitable landing spot.'

Justin stopped the four-wheel drive and unloaded a kayak. 'Justin? You're, you're not serious about riding down river in that!' said Robin, wide-eyed.

'Uh huh. You want to live the rest of your life here with me, you might as well get used to it. Or change your mind now.'

'But—'

'We're going into winter,' Justin assured her. 'The river is calm.'

He gave Zola his keys to the Land Rover in exchange for a Winchester Magnum.

'Park it down by the river opposite the camp.'

Zola disappeared.

'Is that necessary?' Robin asked nervously, pointing to the rifle slung over his shoulder.

'Just a precaution,' he nodded. From Justin's neck hung another shooting weapon, a Nikon 3.

'I thought you said a dawn ride,' said Robin wryly, perturbed about the lack of light.

They climbed into the kayak and set off down the Tamboti river. 'Stick your knees into the side for balance and enjoy the ride. I'll do the rest.'

Justin let the kayak flow with the slowly meandering river, gently guiding where necessary. The sky was still dark, a time when nature displayed her richest colours. Stars sparkled through branches overhanging the river and the moody glow of the moon smouldered. It was eerie. Only the sounds of the wild broke the stillness.

The peaceful atmosphere intoxicated Robin. Absorbing the tranquillity of the bush at night melted away her anxiety.

'Justin?' whispered Robin with sudden alarm. She grew rigid.

So did Justin.

Shit! What is it? I've never seen anything like it!

Ahead of them, a strange Loch Ness-looking monster waved around the top of the moonlit water. Justin steered the kayak to a low overhanging branch and grabbed onto it, keeping his perilously close distance. Placing his other hand on walnut rifle stock, his heart pumped adrenalin through his veins, but he remained dead still and silent, eyes focused intently on the strange creature waving along the top of the water.

Uh oh!

Suddenly a monstrous beast emerged in full splendour from an almighty explosion of water. Robin froze, Justin relaxed. His fear of the unknown quickly dissipating, he sat back and marvelled at the enormous elephant in front of him, large white tusks gleaming in the moonlight. The giant had submerged into the deep water and used his trunk like a periscope for air. The large male casually walked out of the river on the opposite side, and in seconds, its outline disappeared from sight.

So large, yet so elusive! marvelled Justin.

Robin buried her head in her hands.

Ha ha! Justin chuckled inside, but quickly regained his composure. *Watch it! It is at relaxed moments like these when danger suddenly pounces!*

Half an hour went by without incident. Justin knew every nook and cranny of this river. They came upon an area he eagerly awaited.

'Zola tells me he spotted a pair of leopards here recently,' whispered Justin, eager to sight the predator he felt akin to.

He trained his eye on every fork of the trees they passed and his keen senses assimilated every nuance the bush had to offer, but without reward.

Robin's hand reached back and poked Justin in the leg. She pointed in the distance. Foliage moved on the water's edge.

Leopard!

Justin steered the kayak to the opposite side, and moored it. He climbed out, putting his hand up to signal Robin to stay. She wore a look of horror at the thought.

Rifle in hand, he stalked a few paces down the river's edge, and found a sycamore fig trunk that offered enough slant to couple with Justin's rifle into a tripod.

Something different about them, Justin observed with keen eyes. Could it be …?

He started trembling, then rebuked himself. While a rasping, sawing sound emanated from the erotic creatures of the night, Justin took aim and squeezed. Click!

Gotcha! he exclaimed, overjoyed at a chance in a lifetime to capture leopards mating on film.

Justin stealthily tracked back to Robin and climbed in the kayak. He was ecstatic, overjoyed with his luck, and it showed. Robin smiled in return, happy for him.

Enthralled, they stayed and observed the leopards until they, too, disappeared into the bush.

As their kayak ambled down river, light glimmered on the horizon, the rising sun sparkling a morning freshness in the air. The curtain of dawn drew open, ending most of the wild's activities.

'Robin,' started Justin, his heart bursting with contentment, 'I get excited winning a big final, but this equals that. I thrive here.'

'I think I could get addicted, too!' glowed his fiancé.

Silhouetted against the rising sun, Justin spotted a fish eagle perched on a dead tree.

'Look, Robin, she's going to fly off. Maybe take a dive,' he said, possessing a sixth sense, an uncanny feeling about the wild.

Spreading her broad black wings from chestnut body, the bird suddenly launched, glided down to the river, crashed her talons into the golden water, seizing a barbel, then rose majestically into the air, triumphantly calling with her white head thrown back. Kow, kow, kowkowkow. The evocative call of Africa.

'How did you know?' asked Robin, intrigued.

'They usually precede flying with a dropping!' smiled Justin.

Robin reached out behind her and held his hand.

'There's so much peace here. No greed, no grudges. Life just goes on. The cycle is so perfect, so balanced … Utopia!' raved Justin, gazing into the dawn. 'But that balance is on a knife edge. The over-population of Africa has encroached so much, there's a real danger of losing all this. Then we're in trouble!'

Robin listened intently to her fiancé, aware of his deep-rooted love for the wild.

'A North American Indian, some bugger by the name of Chief Seathl, once said, 'What is man without the beasts? If all the beasts were gone, man would die from a great loneliness of spirit. For whatever happens to the beast also happens to man. All things are connected. Whatever befalls the earth, befalls the sons of the earth.' … I read somewhere that scientists believe the HIV virus originated from the sooty mangabey monkey in Central Africa. Wouldn't it be ironic if the ol' chief was right, and AIDS or some other virus is nature's way of getting back at man! Maybe all things are connected!'

'Justin, that's a terrible thought,' said Robin, shocked.

'Very!' agreed Justin, believing it could be the stark truth.

He took Robin's hand, held it to his chest and purred, 'My heart beats for Africa. I spend my happiest hours here watching wild animals. There's been a symbiosis between the two great passions in my life, tennis and wildlife. I feel I owe much of my tennis success to the wild, things I have learned here, cues I have taken from nature. I want to pay it back.'

Meandering halfway round Tamboti Hill, Justin brought Robin's attention to a rising spiral of vultures describing circles in the morning sky.

'Now that the sun is up, they're soaring on hot air currents.'

'Are they after the remains of the lion kill?'

Justin beamed, pleased with her progress. He nodded affirmation. 'They're like a beacon for the wild, guiding all other scavengers to the kill. Us too!'

'Us?' Robin asked, wearing another of her horror faces.

'Yep! Let's go.'

Justin navigated the kayak across the river and anchored it on shore.

'We'll go round behind the koppie, and keep downwind.'

'From what?'

'Lions.'

Robin stopped dead in her tracks, shaking her head. 'Haven't we done enough for today?' she begged.

'Come. You'll love it,' said Justin, taking her hand and coaxing her feet from their quicksand.

Nearing the koppie, Justin pointed to scratch markings on an acacia tree.

'They sharpened their claws here. I suspect they … Come, let's climb.'

From their vantage point halfway up the koppie, they saw vultures, wings not fully unfurled, claws extended, swooping down like parachutists to join a clamorous throng of spotted hyenas, jackals and other vultures. In utter confusion, the heaving mass desperately scavenged the last remaining morsels of wildebeest flesh, before the inedible remains decomposed and returned to earth to complete and renew the great energy cycle.

Justin tapped Robin's shoulder and pointed to a spot a stone's throw away. A pride of lions lay under a tree, the adults satiated, licking their blood-smudged whiskers clean in anticipation of a day's rest, shaded from the heat of the sun, building energy for the night-time hunt.

'How can those animals stay so close to the lions?' asked Robin, pointing to a herd of wildebeest seemingly nonchalant about the purveyors of death.

'For the same reason we can. The lions have just eaten. They're not hungry. Provided they're not disturbed, it's quite safe. A lion with a distended belly can walk right through a herd of zebra or wildebeest. The herd will part a way and make a path, hardly flinching.'

'Remarkable!' exclaimed Robin. 'Much the same way champions are aloof and command respect, but suddenly gobble opponents up on court when hungry!'

'Well.'

'Oh, look!' Robin bubbled with excitement.

She saw five lion cubs frolicking in the long grass. They bounced and pawed and mischievously stalked the adults' swishing tails. One toyed with the hoof of the dead wildebeest, now ground and polished in the dust, rather like a kitten attacks a ball of wool.

An adult male yawned. So did Justin.

'Should we join him?'

Robin looked quizzically at Justin, one eyebrow raised in alarm, awaiting his next surprise.

'I mean in bed. Let's go and get some shut-eye.'

Justin and Robin spent a week in these idyllic surrounds, absorbing the exquisite joys of solitude in the African veld. More and more, Robin grew accustomed to nature's way of life.

'Now that I've been here, I'll never be the same again,' said Robin. 'The tranquillity and the splendour and the rhythm of this magic place seeps into your soul.'

Nature has a miraculous way of healing. She poured balm onto Justin's wounds, curing his winter of discontent. But now a feeling gnawed inside.

I have to leave, leave the vast open spaces, for the claustrophobic hotel life of a tennis player, decided Justin. *I have to return to tennis, to pursue my dream. Wimbledon!*

As the Land Rover sputtered its way along the dirt track, a sadness pervaded, a shared feeling of leaving a loved one. Just then, a baboon sitting alone in the middle of the track, decided to hitch a ride to its troop up ahead.

'Why, the lazy bum!' exclaimed Robin.

On cue the baboon raised its tail, mooned its red bum at her, plopped a dropping on the bonnet, and jumped off to join its troop.

'Spending a penny! The cheek of it!' Robin complained indignantly.

'That's his fare for the ride!' chuckled Justin.

He stepped on the pedal, then screeched on the brakes to roll the dropping off the bonnet. The tension broken, Justin and Robin suddenly found themselves in a happier mood, leaving Tamboti. They consoled themselves that their absence from this African Odyssey would be temporary.

'In a sense, darling, you never leave Africa of old, for the experience is indelible. When you have lived in Africa, you have lived.'

CHAPTER 14

The closer the SAA Boeing 747 approached London, the more Robin grew tense.

'What's eating you, darling?' asked a concerned Justin.

'I don't relish resuming work with Creighton.'

'*What?*' an incredulous Justin asked in raised tone. 'You can't be serious! You're not going back to *him!*'

'I *have* to, Justin. I'm under contract until the end of the US Open,' defended Robin.

'Oh no!'

'Justin, I put my father in a wheelchair. My contract with Creighton is my only hope of getting him out!'

'What's he paying you?'

Robin paused before answering, 'Around 28 million kronor.'

'Huh? That's crazy!' exclaimed Justin, mystified. 'That's close to $5 million!'

'It's true.'

'I believe you. But with all respect, why the hell is Creighton paying you so much? What's it all about?'

'I'm not sure. After Boris wins the US Open—'

'*If* he wins!' Justin interrupted.

'Whatever, but until then, I'm duty bound to fulfil my obligation.'

'I'll buy you out.'

'I cannot accept!'

'Bullshit!'

'It's something I have to do on my own. I—'

'But Robin, that means you'll be working *against* me!' exclaimed a shocked Justin.

Robin took a deep breath, looking despondent.

'We're going to be married,' Justin reminded her. 'I won't tolerate that.'

'Justin, I *have* to. You don't understand. Amos Creighton is not a man to be crossed. I can't say more than that!'

Justin recognised the look on Robin's face, the same haunted look Tracy wore as the police led her away. She wanted to tell him something, but could not.

'I'm scared, Justin. Please hold me,' Robin yearned, snuggling up to him.

Something's fishy, suspected Justin. *Five million dollars! What is going on*

As the tyres puffed smoke on Heathrow tarmac, Robin informed Justin that she was taking a connecting flight to Stockholm.

'I'll need a week to tie up ends in Sweden. Then I'll go straight to Paris. I can only see you after the French Open.'

'I understand,' Justin reassured Robin. *The hell I do! But she's got some problem, and I won't exacerbate it.*

'My contract stipulates no outside contact during Grand Slam tournaments,' she told him. Looking into his eyes and wiping away a tear, she whispered, 'I'll be pulling for you in my heart!'

'I'm not playing Roland Garros,' Justin surprised her. 'There's too little time. I have to shape up for Wimbledon. Find a way to beat this Boris Bauer!'

They parted.

No sooner had Robin entered her apartment when a loud knock interrupted her unpacking. Her heart gave a joyful start.

'Oh, Justin …,' she began, opening the door. 'You haven't followed me here, you love sick—'

Robin breathed in sharply, startled.

'Hmmph!'

Vich towered in the doorway. He barged in.

'I beg your pardon, you can't—'

'Quiet!' ordered Vich. 'Listen good. No more Forrester!'

'What I do in my spare time—'

Vich plucked the main string of his Donnay Allwood, and in an instant pushed Robin up against a wall, pricking her throat with the large blade. Her blue eyes stared at him in terror.

'Dump Forrester or die!'

Justin walked from his house, up Winnington Road, to Hampstead Heath and leisurely strolled the rolling lawns on a sweltering summer afternoon.

Phew! It seems hotter here than Africa!

He sat on the grass, leaning against a tree.

How do I beat Boris Bauer? I can't believe such a one-dimensional player is unbeatable. Sure he's powerful, but he's a machine! A robot! … On a straight run, he's better than me. But a natural player with flair must ultimately beat a cyborg. I have no option but to beat him tactically!

Justin picked a long stem of grass, chewed on one end and gazed into the distance, searching for an answer.

What has happened before, when a seemingly unbeatable player has crashed? Justin questioned, his mind paging through tennis history.

Suddenly it struck him like a Boris Bauer ace.

'Ashe versus Connors!' Justin cried out aloud, then looked around sheepishly to see if anyone heard. He was alone.

Jimmy Connors, the defending champion and overwhelming favourite, entered the 1975 Wimbledon final with a brutal display of tennis. But Arthur Ashe concocted an ingenious plan to defuse the power. He threw in junk shots, plays that offered Connors no pace to feed off, and the plan worked like a charm.

It's not my style, Justin commented to himself. *But then nor was it Ashe's.*

Justin nourished the embryo of his plan. *Hmm! ... Feed Boris Bauer junk. Off-paced balls. Surprise with fast shots. Totally mix up the rhythm. It'll take a lot of touch play, loads of control. I wish we still used wooden rackets!* mused Justin, thinking back to his knock with Charlie Morris and the wonderful control timber gave him.

'Wooden rackets!' Justin cried out aloud, hitting himself with a clenched fist. *Why, the son of a gun! Coach did offer me advice. The wily old bugger! He saw it all along. He said I couldn't beat Boris Bauer, and he's right! I can't, not the way I normally play. David killed Goliath with a slingshot. Justin Forrester will beat Boris Bauer with a wooden racket!*

He ran all the way home with spring in his step. He had a plan.

The next day, Justin frantically searched for and located Jack Mulligan, a master craftsman retrenched by the demise of the wooden racket.

'Can you still make them?' asked Justin anxiously.

'Still make them? You can't forget to make love! Wooden rackets ... that was a craft! You never forget a craft. None of this modern day racket!'

'I'll need about 50.'

The old man's eyes lit up. He was reborn.

'I still make the odd one. Nostalgia, you know! You may have those right away.'

Justin booked the grass courts at Cumberland Lawn Tennis Club, and practised like a madman, reminiscent of his youth spent bashing a ball against a split pole wall on a dust clearing in the African bush, also with a wooden racket! Slowly, the tumblers clicked into place, the subtleties, the spins, the innuendos, tennis as an art, not a war. He recaptured his zest for the game, working back into form in a race against time.

Each night at home, Justin avidly followed the events of the French

Open championship. Not through fascination with the tennis, but he itched to know when Robin would return to London so he could share his plan.

Tyrone Summers bit the dust early and joined Justin for practice at Cumberland Lawn Tennis Club.

'You're fucking mad! How do you expect to play with a carpet-beater?' sniggered Tyrone.

Justin remained quiet. He knew people would attack him with a barrage of questions. 'Playing with a wooden racket! Are you mad?' 'How do you expect to match the power of high tech widebodies?' 'Why? Why? Why?'

I'll answer them with my results, thought Justin, particularly if I play and beat Boris Bauer!

Come on, Boris, lose! Justin urged, hoping for Robin's early return.

But Boris Bauer did not oblige. He swept into the final where he beat the old clay court master, Manolo Gonzales, 6-3 7-5 6-4. The giant stood just two tournaments away from achieving Amos Creighton's dream.

Flight 237 spewed out Team BB minus Robin Wallenborg. 'Where is she?' asked a worried Justin.

'I'm afraid Mr Forrester, I haven't a clue!' replied the lady at customer services. 'She did not board the flight, nor has she booked on any other.'

Two days passed without a word. A worried Justin returned from Cumberland Lawn Tennis Club and switched on his answering machine. A whispered message from a distraught Robin, shocked him.

'It's me. Bassett's Wood in Essex. Help! And hurry!'

Shit! I must rescue her! decided Justin in a flash, heart pounding, mind searching its data bank.

He telephoned Tyrone. 'Robin's in trouble. She needs me, so I can't make it for practice. Byron Belvedere would be willing—'

'Want some help?' Justin's long-time nemesis offered. 'Anything to intercept Scudface! Besides, you've left me stranded with nothing else to do!'

'Thanks. I'll pick you up.'

They raced off in a rallycross to Essex, Justin at the wheel, Tyrone reading a map.

'Know where north is?'

Eventually they stumbled on the road to Danbury, drove through the village, and into farmland, finally to Bassett's Wood.

What's Boris Bauer doing out here? Justin wondered of the estate secluded by a high stone wall. *What's Amos Creighton hiding?*

'Shit! There's a guard at the entrance,' discovered Tyrone with horror. 'Bustin' in ain't gonna be stealing from Grandma's cookie jar! This is fucking Fort Knox!'

'Let's case the joint.'

They walked 200 metres alongside the stone wall.

'Give me a hand, Terror. Hope there're no electric wires on top of the wall.'

'Remember I'm earthin' you!' warned Tyrone, cupping his hands for Justin, who stepped on and scaled up the wall. 'What can you see?'

'Hubba hubba! I see Wimbledon! There's a bloody replica of the Centre Court stadium here!' relayed a staggered Justin, surveying the terrain. 'There're about six grass courts, and bubble domes, too. Probably for more courts. Shit! And a bloody mansion in front of them. I'm going over.'

Justin flung his legs over the wall. Still hanging by his hands, bracing for the drop, he looked down to discover two snarling Dobermans snapping their teeth at him.

'Uh oh!' he cried out.

Learning gymnastics on the spot, he flipped back like a seasoned gymnast on the pommel and quickly joined Tyrone on the outside. They scooted.

'What the fuck is Scudface hiding?' asked Tyrone.

'Buggered if I know. But I *have* to get Robin out.'

'Count me out. I ain't a bowl of Doberman din dins!'

'I've got an idea. We'll have to go back to, Chelmsford, I think it was. See a vet.'

'I like it already,' sniggered Tyrone, sensing something mischievous.

The two returned that evening, making a brief surveillance before effecting their plan.

'The lights are on in one dome,' Justin pointed out. 'I hope that means fewer people inside the mansion.'

'What if your fluff's in there?'

Justin shrugged his shoulders. 'Ready?'

Tyrone lifted him up again. This time Justin went over, prepared. He hurled some juicy steaks laced with a tranquilizing drug.

'Enjoy!' chuckled Justin.

Justin and Tyrone bolted round to the back wall, climbed over and scurried to the side of the mansion.

'Great. That window is still open,' observed Justin. 'I'm going up! Coming?'

'You bet!' responded Tyrone, not wanting to be outdone, his competitive spirit rising to the fore.

Reminiscent of his bunking days at boarding school, Justin shinnied up the drainpipe to the third floor. Tyrone followed. As Justin neared the open window, the rusty drainpipe prised loose from the gutter and swayed into the night air.

Shit! cursed Justin. *Now I'm a goner!*

He dived for the window sill, but the force split the drainpipe at a joint between him and Tyrone. Both froze, nervous that the noise would attract attention.

Justin slowly hauled himself up and through the window. He peered out to Tyrone, swaying aimlessly on a drainpipe going nowhere!

'Hey, Pale Wog!' Tyrone whispered. 'I'm a sitting duck!'

'I'll go and open that window,' consoled Justin, pointing down to the second storey.

He crept out of the room, tiptoed along the passage, then stopped, discovering light leaking from beneath a door. He bent down to peep through the keyhole. To his utter dismay, a moving body blocked his view. His worst fear realised, he watched mesmerised as the door handle turned. His heart thumped wildly in his chest. With no place to hide, he reacted swiftly.

Surprise attack is my best defence! Justin decided, bulldozing through the doorway, knocking the occupant to the floor.

'Justin!' shrieked Robin out of the wild skirmish, her hand on her heart.

'Robin!'

The sight of her knight in shining armour melted away her fear. Then overcome, she burst into tears and threw her arms around Justin.

'Darling, not now. Terror's hanging outside on a drainpipe. I must—'

'Terror? Tyrone Summers?' asked a bewildered Robin. 'What's *he* doing here?'

'I'll explain later. Is there anyone here?'

'I don't think so. They're at the tennis courts. But I can't be sure.'

'Let's hurry.'

Pulling Robin by the arm, Justin led the way, then suddenly realised he was running blindly.

'Second floor?' he asked.

'This way.'

They scurried down the stairs.

'It'll be directly under the room I came in,' Justin whispered. 'That one at the end of the passage.'

Robin stopped dead, as if she had seen a ghost.

'That's Creighton's inner sanctum! Nobody goes in there!'

'That doesn't matter now,' Justin answered, urging Robin on.

'But it'll be locked,' defended Robin, nearing the door. 'No one has a key except Creighton.'

Justin tried the door. 'Damn! What about the room below?'

Both froze. The door handle of Creighton's inner sanctum turned. Justin and Robin watched with wide eyes, then looked to each other, turned and began to scoot. But a voice stopped them in their tracks.

'Don't ask,' grinned Tyrone, holding up a set of lock picks.

Thunderous heart beats subsided when they heard the familiar voice. Usually it was the other way round!

'You wanna come in and see this joint!' lured Tyrone.

'Is Creighton routine?' Justin asked Robin.

'Like clockwork!'

'What time will they be back?'

'Ten o'clock.'

Justin looked at his Rolex. 'We've got 15 minutes. It'll be cutting it fine, but I'm dying to see what's behind Boris Bauer!'

The trio entered the inner sanctum. In the darkening English summer evening, Justin marched straight to a large oak desk. It was clean on top. He opened a drawer.

'Grand Plan,' Justin read, retrieving a dossier. He opened it and skimmed through the pages.

Three consecutive Grand Slams! Fifteen billion dollars! QE2! exclaimed Justin.

With the clarity of hindsight, he slotted the jigsaw pieces into place. *No wonder he didn't cash in on sponsorship.*

Shit! Justin's heart suddenly pounded. *That's* my *name! ... Justin Forrester favours down-the-line passes on break points by 3:2. I do?* Justin asked, surprised that Creighton knew more about him than he did.

In the eerie quietness, Justin heard the sound of a ticking grandfather clock. He looked at his watch.

Uh oh! he exclaimed with alarm, but his curiosity kept him paging through the thick dossier.

Tyrone Summers. Roland Drechsler. Manolo Gonzales. What does he say about him? Justin wondered, then chuckled as he read. *Unknown shot patterns. He's got that right!*

'Hey, Pale Wog!' Tyrone called in a stage whisper, rummaging through a body bag. 'This guy's wasted!'

Justin dropped the dossier on the large oak desk and joined Tyrone in the corner of the room.

'Bloody hell!' exclaimed Justin, before his face turned to despair.

'That's Bob Wallace, the famous Australian coach who mysteriously disappeared a few years back!'

A noise sounded down the passage. The trio looked at each other with wide eyes.

'Quick, let's split,' Justin commanded.

They rushed to the window.

'The drainpipe's buggered. It'll probably only survive the weight of one person. I hope! We'll have to go down one at a time,' Justin told Robin. 'You must go down by yourself. Wait at the bottom, up against the house.'

'Step on the juice, or the coroner will be doing overtime!' Tyrone urged.

'I'll hold Robin. You steady the drainpipe,' Justin organised.

Robin clambered onto the drainpipe and gingerly inched her way down whilst Justin and Tyrone nervously waited at the top, dreading the opening of the door. A minute turned into eternity!

'What the fuck are those things?' Tyrone asked, pointing to an Egyptian landscape on the floor.

'Pyramids,' whispered Justin. 'Apparently, if you align them in a certain direction you can make energised water, sharpen razor blades, lengthen the life of batteries, and so on. So I've read.'

Robin reached the bottom. Justin followed. Exiting the room, he caught a glint in Tyrone's eyes.

'You thinking what I'm thinking?' he asked.

'Pale Wog! There's hope for you yet!'

Tyrone quickly returned to the room and fractionally turned each pyramid out of alignment.

'Freak out, Scudface!' he said, his impish face jitterbugging with contagious convulsions of mischievous merriment.

The trio scurried to the wall undetected, climbed over and found sanctuary in Justin's 500 SL. All breathed a huge sigh of relief, their cloak and dagger operation over.

'You drive,' Justin told Tyrone. They headed straight to the police station in Chelmsford.

'Thanks, darling!' cried a relieved Robin, showering kisses on Justin, hugging him in the back seat of his Mercedes-Benz. 'Thanks to you, too, Tyrone,' she added, giving him a friendly pat on his shoulder. 'I don't know how you came into the picture.'

'Scudface! Anything to intercept that Scudface!'

'Why did Creighton keep you prisoner?' asked Justin.

'I don't know. He always treated me like an outcast. I don't think he likes women. Phew!' sighed Robin, catching her breath. 'I've been terrified. The others in Team BB disappeared one by one. After seeing Bob Wallace, I fear they're dead, too! Justin, this guy, Vich, Creighton's henchman, he threatened to kill me if I saw you again,' she faltered and burst into tears, the emotion too much.

'Hush, darling,' Justin soothed and comforted her. 'He won't come after us. They'd risk their whole operation for nothing because we've got nothing on them.'

Suddenly the reality dawned on Justin. He punched the seat in anger. 'Damn it! We've left the evidence behind!'

A deathly silence. Each understood their foolishness. Having detected their presence, Creighton would destroy all incriminating traces of the Grand Plan before the police arrived.

'We had enough to crucify Creighton. Now he lives,' bemoaned Tyrone, before spitting, 'Scudface!'

A cataclysm of utterances reverberated through the car.

'This bugger makes $15 billion if Boris Bauer gets three consecutive Grand Slams,' enlightened Justin. 'He's nearly there! I wouldn't mind if it was legit, but Creighton's a bloody murderer. We've *got* to stop him!'

'I'll do it. I'll beat Scudface at Wimbledon,' claimed Tyrone. He chuckled, 'No way *you* gonna beat him with your carpet-beater!'

'Carpet-beater?' Robin enquired.

'Yeah! Your Pale Wog's gonna try and beat Scudface with a wooden racket!' laughed Tyrone. 'He'll have to beat him over the head with it.'

'Is that true?' asked Robin, frowning.

'Uh huh,' responded an indignant Justin.

'Justin, I hate to say this, but Coach is right. I've seen Boris practising. He *can't* lose. These matches at Wimbledon and Roland Garros are a Sunday afternoon picnic for him. In practice he plays under conditions ten-fold more severe, and doesn't flinch!'

Justin disclosed his plan. 'I've tried everything. The only way to beat him is to confuse him. Play junk tennis and upset his rhythm. I can do that best with a wooden racket.'

'I go along with your plan. But not with a carpet-beater!' sniggered Tyrone, rubbing salt into the wound.

'Will it work?' asked Robin.

'I thought it would,' replied a hesitant Justin. 'But there's more pressure on me now. We *have* to stop this bugger at all costs. And on court, not in! If Boris Bauer wins Wimbledon and the US Open, Creighton'll have pulled the perfect caper without a hope of us screwing him. We need a magician on grass, something like Manolo on clay. If only I could wave my racket around like *his* wand and get those crazy spins.'

'Shit, it's hot! This rattletrap have air-conditioning?' asked Tyrone.

'Do umpires cause you spontaneous combustion? Next to the radio.'

Unaccustomed to the right-hand drive cars of Britain, Tyrone fumbled for the air-conditioning switch, but turned on the radio instead.

'This is the eleven o'clock news. Weather stations in Southern England have reported more record temperatures today. London registered 38 °C. A spokesperson for the Weather Bureau has predicted the drought will continue for many weeks ahead, and is the worst since the summer of 1976. Global warming—'

'Gotcha!' shouted Justin.

Tyrone jammed his foot on the brakes, hurtling the occupants forward.

'Borg … 1976 … Manolo! Manolo will be my slingshot!'

'What do you mean?' asked a puzzled Robin.

'Oh, nothing,' answered Justin. 'But Manolo's the one to beat Boris Bauer!'

'You forget, dummy, he can't play so well on grass,' countered Tyrone.

'But the drought!' bubbled Justin, so overexcited, he struggled to articulate his point. 'The drought. The courts will be brown and dusty. They'll play like clay. Manolo's the one to beat Boris Bauer at Wimbledon.'

'You're right. You're fucking right. Oops!'

When Björn Borg won Wimbledon in 1976 without the loss of a set, playing more from the baseline than any champion in memory, many believed his win to be a fluke because the courts, severely burned and dried out by the hot summer, played more like clay than fast grass. Borg, of course, confounded these critics, winning a record five successive Wimbledon titles under a diverse spectrum of weather conditions.

Justin contacted his Spanish friend, Manolo Gonzales, and related Creighton's insidious plot.

'We need you, Manolo. Terror and I will train you to beat Boris Bauer.'

'*Sí!*'

Justin immediately set to work on his plan of attack.

No shot patterns, he remembered from the Grand Plan. They must be concerned by Manolo's unpredictability. And with good reason! Boris Bauer only beat Manolo 6-3 7-5 6-4 in the recent French Open.

Justin researched through the latest World of Tennis annual, checking the results of Boris Bauer versus Manolo Gonzales. They confirmed his suspicions.

Manolo's pushed him more than anyone else!

Justin leapt into action. He obtained video tapes of Boris Bauer's matches against Manolo, Naresh and himself.

I'll be a son of a gun! It's there, right in front of my bloody eyes. He's vulnerable to returns floated to his feet, discovered Justin.

He received an IBM Match Facts fax from the ATP headquarters in Ponte Vedra Beach, detailing a complete analysis of the shot patterns Manolo used against Boris Bauer. Justin studied it. The stark reality of a computer printout eradicated all doubt.

Less than 50 percent success on shots returned low to his feet. Yep, it's a bit of a bugger for a giant to pick up shots off his shoelaces! And how can he hit with power, so low and close to the net? You're a genius, Manolo. Only you don't know it!

'What I don't understand ees, how come I lose on the clay, now you want me to ween on the grass?' Manolo asked Justin.

'You'll be seeded, so by the time you play him, the court will be a dust-bowl in this drought, and play like clay. On clay Boris Bauer stays back. But this is grass. He's programmed to serve and volley. His serves will bounce high. You'll have a fiesta floating them back to his feet!'

'*Sí!*'

Each day, Justin and Tyrone practised tirelessly with Manolo at Cumberland Lawn Tennis Club, training him to block service returns in his loosely strung racket and waft them low to the incoming server's feet. To emulate Boris Bauer, they served two metres in from the baseline, sharpening Manolo's reactions to those of a cat.

'Forrester. The name's Cooper,' a man introduced himself, interrupting a practice session at Cumberland Lawn Tennis Club.

They shook hands.

'I have a proposition,' said Cooper. 'I know you're aware of Creighton's Grand Plan. I entered his office while you scaled down the drainpipe.'

Justin's heart raced. 'I've nothing to say to you. Get out!' he ordered, marching Cooper up the stairs that led to the clubhouse.

'Wait! Wait!' cried out Cooper, before proceeding in a measured tone. 'I'm not one of them. On the contrary, I want Creighton stopped.'

Justin's ears pricked up. 'Oh? Tell me more!'

'I represent a syndicate of gamblers from the States who stand to lose a great deal if Creighton pulls off his cheap trick.'

'How do you plan to stop him?'

'I'm stumped!'

'But you were there!' exclaimed Justin, surprised.

'I had to vanish, too. It was ten o'clock. If you bothered to look behind you, we'd have met earlier. By the way, a neat trick, that, with the dogs. I'd been trying to break in for days. I must remember that next time.'

'What do you want from me?'

'To beat him. Beat Boris Bauer.'

Justin laughed.

'Ten million dollars is yours if you stop him here or in New York,' offered the agent.

'Mr Cooper! I'd *pay* $10 million to beat him. All the money in the world is not going to help. But believe me, I'll spill my guts trying.'

Cooper gave Justin a contact number and disappeared.

On the Monday before The Championships, the committee announced the seedings. Boris Bauer took pole position, followed on the grid by Justin and then Tyrone. It seeded Manolo number eight.

Strange buggers, seeding me two, thought Justin, now ranked third in the world.

Wimbledon reserves the right to deviate from the world rankings and seed how it sees fit. Justin was the runner-up for the last two years, and then, of course, there was the small matter that he was British!

Oh, what the hell! Seedings don't count. What matters is the draw!

The draw was made publicly at the club on the day following the announcement of the seedings, attended by anxious players and expectant press. Justin fretted nervously the whole day, praying for a favourable draw. His mood grew solemn. When he returned from a morning training session with Manolo, he could hardly bring himself to find out.

'Shit! Shit! Shit!' shouted Justin, swiping his racket at anything that dared to lie in his line of vision. 'Manolo's slotted in the same pocket of the draw as me! Why did it have to be like this?'

The draw impaled Justin's dream on the horns of a dilemma.

What do I do now? If Manolo and I get to the semifinals, I'm supposed to allow him through to the final to derail Creighton's Grand Plan, but how can I? That'll dash my hopes of winning Wimbledon. Damn! cursed Justin, agonizing with his conscience. *I've greater belief in myself beating Boris Bauer. I've never played him on clay. With the drought this year, I'd get to more balls and could tease him with what he doesn't like, now that I know,* argued the competitive side of Justin. *Besides, Manolo's not a great finals player. The occasion gets to him.*

But how can I? I expect other players to allow Manolo through the draw. How can I not do the same? Damn you, Wimbledon Committee! Why didn't you seed me number three where I belong? cursed Justin.

Seeded three, as the draw turned out he would slot into Tyrone's position in the draw, scheduled to meet Boris Bauer in the other semifinals. Then if Justin lost to Boris Bauer, the top seed would still have to contend with Manolo in the final.

Justin anguished the whole afternoon, grappling with his desire to win Wimbledon. In the end, his moral ethics won.

Manolo knows about the plan. I can't let him down now. I'll use the semis to prepare him, Justin decided.

A loud knocking on his front door woke him from his stupor.

'You've seen the draw, eh,' Tyrone commented with a long face. He rubbed salt into Justin's fresh wound. 'That's a tough one. I'd hate to be in your shoes.'

'Come in. Might as well go over it together,' suggested Justin morosely, leading the way into his lounge.

They poured over the draw laid out on a coffee table.

'I predict no potential problems for Manolo,' informed Justin. 'With Boris Bauer's stranglehold on the game, no one believes they can win the bloody title. Once they know Creighton's story, the buggers will allow Manolo through.'

'Until the semis,' reminded Tyrone.

Justin remained silent for a moment, then said resignedly, 'I've decided to let him through. The semis can be a dress rehearsal.'

'You're a big man, Justin,' praised Tyrone, to Justin's surprise. Then came the inevitable taunt. 'But it's easy being noble when you've got shit chance of getting to the semis with your carpet-beater!' laughed Tyrone.

Justin feigned annoyance.

'Pale Wog, I figure I owe you for conning those fuckers to rescind my banning, so I'm withdrawing from Wimbledon,' Tyrone announced.

'Don't be mad! Besides, what good …?'

The repercussions suddenly dawned on Justin. *If Terror withdraws, it's possible that all the seeds below him will shuffle up one position and move to new places in the draw. Wimbledon has done that before. Seeded eight, Manolo will become the seventh seed and move to the top half, freeing me from my dilemma.*

'You can't do that!' protested Justin. 'I won't have it. It's just not right.'

'It makes sense. I've got shit chance of beating Scudface. My game fits into his like, well, like a cock in a fur-lined rubber on a winter's day. He just fucks the living daylights out of me. With me gone, Manolo plays Scudface in the semis. You know he's gotta better chance beating him there, than in a final.'

'Uh huh.'

'You also know that if we beat Scudface once, it'll soften him. Make him beatable.'

'I'm well aware,' acknowledged Justin.

'By withdrawing, I'm buying my future.'

'I hear you, but I won't allow it. It's crazy!'

'Too late. I withdrew before coming here.'

Justin had mixed emotions. He was off the hook, but withdrawing from a Grand Slam tournament was not kosher, not Terror.

Only when Justin let Tyrone out the front door did he notice a limp.

'Hey, what's with you? Been pulling my leg?'

'Oh, that,' answered Tyrone, looking over his shoulder. 'Didn't I tell you? I pulled a hamstring in practice today. I'm outta tennis for three weeks. You'll have to double up training with Manolo.'

Tyrone left.

Why, the son of a gun! chuckled Justin, standing at his front door.

CHAPTER 15

'A wooden racket!' sneered Ted Parsen of the *London Daily News.* 'You expect to win Wimbledon, beat Boris Bauer with a wooden racket? You *are* barmy!'

Justin sat, silent.

'Will you use your Dunlop Maxply in the final, *if* you get there?' asked another reporter.

Justin nodded his head.

'Do you intend using a wooden racket after Wimbledon?'

Justin shook his head.

'Can you explain this madness?'

Justin stared at the reporter for a few moments before speaking in a measured tone. 'Boris Bauer *can* be beaten. But we've all barked up the wrong tree, trying to *match* his power.'

He then explained the method in his madness, hoping to interpose Creighton's mind via television, and confuse him. 'It'll take art, finesse, to defuse his might. A wooden racket is the ideal weapon to craft the plot.'

'But it's 15 percent slower than a high-tech widebody. Aren't you digging a hole for yourself?'

'On the contrary. It'll be to my advantage. I'm sacrificing power that doesn't work against Boris, but I'll gain control. I watched a tape the other day of the 1980 Wimbledon final. I reasoned that if McEnroe can ace Borg, the fastest player *I've* ever seen, then that's sufficient power for me!'

Day by day Justin waxed to his former standards, finding his old skills and form in as rich a measure as before.

Courtesy of walk-on characters, Tugboat, Jean-Pierre and Sern, Manolo Gonzales fandangoed through to the quarter-finals in protracted matches, designed to acclimatize the Spaniard to grass.

By Monday evening of the second week, the scam survived. Next opponent, Dayack Sassoon.

'I'm concerned about this bugger,' Justin told Tyrone. 'I don't know him well and since he's gagged the grunt, the bugger's playing better. He has the game to beat Manolo!'

They summoned Dayack to the golf course car park for a clandestine meeting.

'No way, man! I'm not suckering to you dudes. This is a plot to get me, man!' Dayack objected.

'You've got shit chance of beating Scudface,' informed Tyrone. 'He'll wipe you off court with that mop on top of your head!'

'Hey, man! You leave my dreads alone. And you leave Dayack Sassoon.'

He turned to depart.

'How much will it take, Dayack?' asked Justin shrewdly.

'Now you try to buy me! Man, Dayack Sassoon is not a piece of merchandise! It would take $5 million for me to tank. Get it man! I'm not for sale.'

'A million tomorrow, four after your match.'

'Hey man, don't you see so good? The price tag on this forehead says $10 million, man.'

'Five. Take it or leave it.'

'For you, Justin, Dayack Sassoon's on sale!'

Dayack left.

'What the fuck have you done?' asked a worried Tyrone. 'Where're you gonna get that lolly in a hurry?'

'I have a plan,' replied Justin. *I hope it works, or I'm $5 million down the tubes.*

Justin contacted Cooper from the gambling syndicate. 'I've an idea, Mr Cooper. But it needs a little sinking fund up front.'

Friday afternoon of the second week of Wimbledon, the men's singles semifinals.

'You ween your match, Justeen, and I ween mine. Then we spleet the prize,' Manolo joked.

'Let's do that!' smiled Justin, reading doubt in Manolo's mind.

A man born out of his time with the world passing him by, Manolo enjoyed playing more than winning. For him, the court was his canvas, the ball his paint. With his racket the artist virtuoso painted pictures to be savoured. But fate dealt Manolo a cruel hand in his chosen profession. Unlike Da Vinci or Van Gogh, tennis measured the Spaniard's talent more by result than aesthetic beauty. The primary goal in tennis is to win, the entertainment value a corollary bonus. Long after the biological clock humbles champions to mere mortals, the public remembers their results more than the stories they unfolded.

I've got to win my semi to take the pressure off him, exhorted Justin. *That way there's still the chance I can beat Boris in the final.*

He addressed Manolo, injecting confidence, 'Go out and pretend it's an exhibition. Remember, if you're in trouble, go low!'

Under a warm sun beating down from a rich blue, cloud-speckled sky, parasols replacing the umbrellas of last year, Justin played with *joie de vivre*, trouncing Roland Drechsler in the first semifinal. He had sailed to the championship round without the loss of a set.

He quickly showered, dressed in jeans and T-shirt, delayed his press conference, donned a pair of Ray-Ban sun-glasses and joined Robin, sitting on her left in the box reserved for relatives and friends.

She huddled close to Justin. 'They've just come on court. Am I glad you're here,' she whispered, before subtly pointing to a man in the row behind her. 'Vich!'

Strangely, at Wimbledon, the enemy camps always sit in the same box, suffering their lot together.

Justin shrugged him off. He whispered to her, 'Relax, darling, you're safe. He won't hurt you.'

Hmm! The corrida de toros! *The gifted matador versus the bionic bull in Boris Bauer!* thought Justin, excited.

'The court is playing just as we expected,' Justin told Robin. Over the fortnight, in the white-hot cauldron of the stadium, the court had changed like a chameleon from green to brown, becoming a dust-bowl, and played quite differently. 'Also, the balls are bouncing higher in the heat. It's playing like a fast clay court, if there's such a species. Ideal conditions for Manolo to weave his magic.'

'And Boris?'

'According to that dossier, they play on artificial grass. They change every two days to a court a little more worn, to acclimatize to the changes over the two weeks. But I doubt they prepared for *this* summer!'

'Justin, do you really think your plan will work, or are we getting our hopes up too high?' asked Robin, aware that nobody else at Wimbledon that afternoon doubted Boris Bauer would win.

Justin shrugged his shoulders. 'Naresh took more games off Boris than one would expect. He plays the same airy game as Manolo, although he has even less killer instinct. He injected doubt into Boris Bauer, a fortunate softening up. ... And the bugger's desire must be waning. You eat one chocolate cookie, it's delicious. So is the second and the third. But a dozen or so later, you start feeling ill. Still, it's touch and go. He seems indestructible. And Manolo can just as easily go walkabout! I wouldn't bet many pesetas.'

After the warm-up, Boris Bauer, attired in white, of course, Wimbledon rules, routinely removed his ear-muffs. He lowered his head like a ferocious bull, pawing at the ground, ready to charge.

'Ready? Play!' resonated the learned judge voice of the stately umpire.

Boris Bauer opened proceedings, winning his service game to love.

Then he rampaged through the next game without the loss of a point.

Robin sat with her hands clasped between her legs. 'What's the matter, Justin?'

'He's not doing what we planned,' answered a dismayed Justin. 'He's playing Boris the same way we all have. Damn!'

'Can't you do something?'

He shook his head. *That's what is so great about this crazy game of tennis. Players can be coached and prepared with the effort a chef puts into a cordon bleu banquet, but on court, the proof of the pudding is in the eating. The rules prohibit coaching during play, elevating the match to a test of the self, an ultimate examination of the inner being.* 'We've prepared Manolo to the hilt for this occasion. Now it's up to him.'

'Game Bauer. He leads by three games to love,' announced the umpire.

It seemed as if Manolo ran head first into the frenzied bulls in Pamplona's Fiesta de San Fermín. He had not won a point!

At the change-over, Boris Bauer put a yellow bottle to his mouth and meticulously sipped two mouthfuls of magic potion. First a sip, then he stared into the mandala pattern, then another sip.

'Playing Boris is like trying to hold back the sea during a spring high. Poor Manolo,' sympathised Robin, shaking her head.

'*This* is a key game,' Justin told Robin.

'So early?'

'I'm afraid so! If Manolo loses his serve, the set is history. Then Boris Bauer will steamroll.'

The game survived to deuce. Manolo served, attacked the net, but instead of volleying the return for a winner, he caught the ball in his fishnet racket, fading it short, down the centre. Boris Bauer ran forwards, desperately scooping it up, but Manolo pounced with a winning volley.

'Gotcha!' exclaimed Justin, clenching his fist. 'That's it. No angles. Hug the ground. Go low.'

Manolo repeated the sequence. He was on the board, 1-3.

'Phew! A little breathing space!'

Boris Bauer served and charged into the net. Manolo quickly moved forwards, took the high-bounding ball on the rise and deftly floated it back to Boris' feet. Boris Bauer netted.

'Love-fifteen,' called the umpire.

'Aah! *That's* the weakness! The broken hinge in his game!'

Manolo swirled the red cape and floated another return. This time, Boris Bauer picked up the ball, but with little venom. The matador raced in and clobbered it for a winner. The crowd uttered a huge, 'Aah!'

'Love-thirty.'

Justin grabbed hold of Robin's hand and squeezed it. '*This* is what we planned. Pray it continues.'

Boris won the next point with a service winner. The crowd groaned. 'Fifteen-thirty.'

'Justin?'

Again Manolo returned a floater to the feet of Boris Bauer, who netted.

'Fifteen-*forty!*' announced the umpire, emphasising the magnitude of the implication, injecting official drama into an already tense situation. A double break point for Manolo Gonzales.

'Don't block another one,' urged Justin, 'or the plan will wear thin and Boris will adapt.'

As if telepathy existed, Manolo usurped Boris's role as aggressor and blasted the ball past a man expecting a floater. It went for a winner.

'*Olé!*' Manolo cried out on execution.

'Game Gonzales. Bauer leads by three games to two,' announced the umpire.

The crowd cheered. 'When last did Boris Bauer lose his serve?' people whispered through the stadium. 'I haven't the foggiest!' echoed the replies.

Justin chuckled to himself. *At last year's Australian Open, in the fourth set. The only match Boris Bauer ever lost a set!*

'Another critical game,' Justin told Robin. 'Games are on service. Manolo can't afford to lose his. But if he wins, he levels at 3-all. That will pressure Boris.'

Manolo won his serve to thirty.

'Is this true, Justin? Is it happening?' asked Robin excitedly, clutching her seat.

'The match is far from over, darling. Save your excitement, just in case.'

Games went with serve, 4-all, then 5-all. Manolo matched Boris Bauer point for point. The excitement grew. Between points, the Wimbledon crowd shuffled in their seats, desperately stretching nerve-racked limbs.

'Manolo's keeping up, Justin. But why does the tennis look so, um, so, so feeble?' asked Robin, puzzled.

'He's playing junk shots. Shots which—'

'But if you know how to beat Boris, why haven't you tried this?'

'They're called junk shots, but they're not! It seems like he's doing nothing, but it's a deceptive art. Manolo strings his racket so loosely, it's like a fishnet. When he hits a ball, the strings hold it for an eternity, cushioning the power, then emerges tainted with Manolo wizardry. He shrewdly disguises each shot, subtly changing the pace or cleverly placing it to cause just that extra little stretch. He upsets your rhythm. The crafty bugger makes you go crazy. And there's little you can do. Playing his soft shots is as frustrating as writing on paper supported by a sponge. Funny, he's one of many Europeans who have played with similar magic. Santana ... Orantes ... Pietrangeli ... and who could ever forget Nastase!'

The plan was bewitchingly simple, but the occasion and opposition, monstrous. Though Justin conceived the plan, only Manolo Gonzales boasted the racket artistry to execute it. Would he have Justin's killer instinct to pull it off?

The set headed to a tiebreaker, the first of Boris Bauer's career. Suddenly the murmurous whispers of curiosity trebled to a buzz, spreading like a bush fire through the Wimbledon stadium. You could feel it in the air.

The tiebreaker points mounted to 5-all. The winner of the next point would garner set point.

'This set is absolutely crucial,' Justin told Robin, barely able to breathe. 'If Boris blows it, it'll be his first time in a losing situation. I'm not sure they've programmed him to handle it! If Manolo loses, it's over. Boris will grow wise to his ploys.'

'I can't watch!' Robin replied, burying her head in her hands.

'Hmmph!' echoed a grunt behind them.

Come on, Manolo. You can do it! implored Justin.

Manolo threw up the ball, served and raced in, piercing the volley. Boris Bauer bludgeoned the pass for an outright winner.

Damn it! cursed Justin. *That's the old way!*

'Six-five, Bauer,' announced the umpire.

'Oh, no!' Robin cried out from her buried head. She could not watch, but nor could she escape the umpire's bearing of bad news.

A groan of disappointment emanated from the crowd. Set point to Boris Bauer. Manolo possessed a beautiful game. But so often before in the heat of the battle, he snarled, not fangs, but the toothy grin of Bugs Bunny.

Boris Bauer served, Manolo chipped and ran in, hoisting an exquisite lob-volley over Boris's head. No ordinary Bugs Bunny this! No, this bunny ingeniously portrayed the rabbit in the magician's act of disappearing and reappearing when least expected.

The crowd stood to their feet as if Manolo had won the match, then quickly sat. They remembered it was only 6-all.

'Playing that bugger is like trying to catch a balloon in a gusty wind!' Justin told Robin with a smile. 'Believe me, I know!'

There followed an amazing tiebreaker, reminiscent of the famous fourth set of the 1980 men's singles final between Borg and McEnroe.

They matched each other point for point, Boris Bauer with his pre-programmed style of deforming the ball with force, Manolo with exquisite chicanery.

At 10-all, with Boris about to serve, in one of those delightful impromptu moments of Wimbledon, the telephone on the umpire's chair rang! The crowd murmured, aghast. What now? The umpire gingerly picked up the receiver.

'For me? I'm beesy. I call back, *sí!*' Manolo spontaneously declared with a toothy grin, bringing levity to a tense situation.

'Where's Terror and Hoss?' a suspicious Justin asked with a grin.

'They wouldn't!' responded Robin in disbelief.

Justin shrugged his shoulders, wondering how the *banderilleros* had obtained the hot line number to the umpire's chair to thrust another gaily decorated dart into the bull.

Still the tiebreaker went on and on, a lingering death for whom? The silence grew loud during points, broken by a few nervous coughs, while the shrieks and gasps of a Barcelonean bullring roared at winning points and lost opportunities. By a tiebreaker's very nature, every second point became a set point, of colossal importance.

At 14-all, Boris Bauer served. Suddenly, an unexpected intrusion.

'Foot-fault!' cried the linejudge.

A ballboy snapped out of his angelic kneeling pose, scurrying along the net to repossess the ball. The stadium hushed, eerily quiet.

Justin whispered to Robin, 'That foot-fault is a big sign of nerves.'

Boris Bauer served his second serve. Manolo defied the odds of tennis normality, returning with a winning topspin lob. Boris Bauer's face flushed red in the sun. He was a confused man.

'Fifteen-fourteen, Gonzales,' announced the umpire.

Justin squeezed Robin's hand tight. Now, even he, the coolest customer on court, could barely watch. 'I'm more nervous watching than playing. At least then you can move, you can run!'

The crowd hardly dared to breathe. Even the Spanish contingent lapsed into virgin territory for them, silence. All Wimbledon went quiet.

Manolo served, raced into the net and with the sleight of hand of a pickpocket, deftly caught the ball in his fishnet, delicately placing it over the net. Such exquisite artistry reaped a sigh followed by a roar from the Centre Court. They gave him a standing ovation out of sheer excitement.

'Game and set to Gonzales by seven games to six,' the umpire called the score.

Manolo bowed like a matador to the Spanish ensemble, who echoed back as one, *'Bravo! Bravo! Bravo!'* Then he looked to Justin and smiled his huge toothy grin. For Boris Bauer, the cunning Spaniard had spun a web of deceit, lured him into the parlour and strangled him. For the crowd, a web of charm, infectiously spreading through the spectators where it nourished. They turned to one another in helpless amazement, not quite sure whether to believe what they were witnessing.

Justin punched his hand, grabbed hold of Robin and hugged her.

'Calm down. Calm down,' he warned himself, remembering that in a tennis match, anything can happen. 'But this is unknown territory for Boris Bauer. It's the first time he's had to deal with losing. I'm not sure he knows how. He's a robot. Coming back in a match cannot be taught!'

Manolo held serve, and to the absolute astonishment of the crowd, broke Boris in the second game, bursting the bubble of Boris Bauer mystique. Manolo held serve again.

'Game Gonzales. He leads by three games to love, and by one set to love. New balls, please.'

The players sat down at the change-over. Manolo thought about the ease with which he was defusing the Bauer bomb. Such fare was paella and plonk for him. He gorged. Boris Bauer needed pyramid water. He swigged back vials of it, desperate for a shot in the arm.

The players changed ends.

'Hubba hubba! He forgot to change his racket,' an excited Justin told Robin. 'He *always* gets a new racket with each ball change. That's a tell-tale sign of a worried man!' he explained, brimming with mixed emotions of delight and disbelief. 'This isn't happening!'

Justin searched for a spectator with a camera armed with a telephoto lens.

'May I borrow it, please?' he whispered. Justin took the camera and trained it on BB. 'He's gone, Robin. Finished! The Bohemian Rhapsody has sputtered to an end. '

'What do you mean? How can you tell?' she asked, bouncing in her seat, itching to know.

'The eyes. The thousand yard stare. They're vacant, the dazed eyes of a buck locked in the jaws of a predator. Paralysed with fear.'

The two could hardly contain their joy. Through Justin's innate ability to read people, they knew it was over. Boris Bauer was a beaten man. But protocol forced them to sit in silence.

True to Justin's prediction, the muscle of Boris Bauer's game atrophied, disintegrating into fits and starts like a short-circuiting robot, his programmed data bank infected by the virus of Manolo's mad *mélange* of magic. With the sick man's cheeks sinking into a skeletal ghoul, Manolo took the second set 6-2, and jerking Boris into spasms like some mischievous puppeteer, led 4-1 in the third.

A great, great player, drained by the supremacy of his high standards, finally submitted, the bull's feet tied together, his head hung low, inviting the matador to thrust the sword. Manolo stood just two games away from skinning a hugely misunderstood champion in the greatest con-job of tennis history.

Justin felt a pull on his shoulder.

'Call off your Spanish fly-trap.'

'Huh?' Justin reacted, confused. He felt Robin's hand squeeze like a vice. She went rigid.

'Call him off and I'll make you a wealthy man.'

'I'm already a wealthy man,' answered Justin. 'I'm a professional tennis player!'

'I'm talking real money. Half a billion dollars.'

Shit a brick! exclaimed Justin, his heart pounding. *He's the notorious Amos Creighton!*

'Get lost!' spat Justin.

'A billion then, damn you, Forrester!' offered a desperate Creighton.

'Go and drown in your blood money. Watching you squirm is worth every cent,' Justin sneered his rejection.

A stressed Amos Creighton grew flustered, his dream garrotted by Catalan creativity.

'Do something!' he ordered Vich, who sat next to him.

'Fuck off!' growled Vich, fixing his glare, sending a *parte*, the customary black bordered funeral announcement of Czechoslovakia. 'You screwed up.'

'Stop him!' Creighton shouted, drawing attention from the crowd.

Vich refused to budge. A despairing Creighton reached into Vich's pocket, withdrew a 9 mm Beretta pistol and headed for the court in a reverse of Pat Cash's victory ascent. He clambered down the rows of spectators, trampling over them, the centre of attention.

Justin sprung into action, following the demented man's path.

'Stop!' Creighton screamed, running onto Centre Court, wildly waving the semi-automatic in his hand. 'Stop, you bastard!'

As Manolo emerged onto the court from the change-over, a shot rang out and he crumpled to the ground.

'Shit!' Justin panicked, desperately struggling to get down onto the court.

Amos Creighton went berserk, screaming unintelligible sounds at everyone. With Manolo prostrate on the grass, the madman turned his attention to Boris Bauer, shot at him, but missed, the bullet ricocheting off the netpost with a zing.

'Why? Why did you let me down?' he shouted at his robot.

Unmoved, Boris Bauer stood still, staring at Amos Creighton with vacuous eyes. Then he broke into a smile, destroying his master, as Karel Čapek wrote.

With bobbies converging on the madman, Justin eventually emerged onto Centre Court, and with ghostlike stealth, stalked up to Creighton. A gasp emanating from the stunned spectators, stopped him dead in his tracks. All watched in horror as Creighton raised the Beretta to his head, thrusting it into his frothing mouth. A loud explosion! The bullet ripped open his skull, spraying bloodied brains onto Justin. Undeterred, he raced to his friend who lay supine on the dry grass.

'Manolo?' he cried, seeing the Spaniard's blood-drenched shirt.

Manolo's face broke into a toothy grin. 'When een trouble, I go low!'

Sadly, instead of leaving the court with his head held high to the sounds of adoring applause, paramedics whisked Manolo off court laid on a stretcher, and took him to hospital.

Justin looked at Robin and gave her the thumbs up. *Manolo'll be fine, just gored. … Hmm! That Vich bugger's vanished!*

Justin turned round to look at Boris Bauer. He sat alone on his chair, staring into the distance.

The bugger must be hurting, thought Justin. *He was only a pawn in Creighton's lust for wealth.*

He walked over and put an arm round him.

An unintelligible sound rasped from Boris Bauer's throat. 'I'm free!' he said in his mother tongue. 'I'm free!'

That's the first time I've ever heard him speak! it dawned on Justin. Suddenly, Robin's words of a few months back haunted him. *Tennis is really just a game! … Perhaps!*

300

CHAPTER 16

Justin met Robin in the Player's Lounge and hugged her.

'Justin,' she sighed, relieved. 'I was so worried.'

'It's all over, darling. Creighton got what he deserved.'

'How's Manolo?'

'He'll be okay,' reassured a blood-spattered Justin. 'Come. Let's get out of here.'

Robin paused. 'Justin, what's going to happen to Boris?'

'Buggered if I know.'

'I think we should take care of him.'

'What do you mean?' asked Justin, bewildered.

'He should come home with us.'

'Are you *crazy?* Robin, I have a final to play on Sunday. A final *against* Boris Bauer!'

'I know, but he has no place to go. For all we know there could be dead bodies lying around at Creighton's house and—'

'He can stay at a hotel.'

'Justin,' said Robin, her voice rising. 'He's incapable of taking care of himself! I'm the only one left of Team BB who understands him.'

'Impossible! It's impossible for me to be near my opponent before a match. To have him living in my home is bizarre. I won't have it!'

Robin looked into Justin's eyes and spoke firmly. 'Darling, Boris was an innocent puppet in Creighton's scheme, as I was. In going after Creighton we destroyed Boris' life support. He won't be *able* to play on Sunday. Only if we take care of him will a victory over him be meaningful!'

Sunday morning, day of the final, Justin bounced downstairs on his way to breakfast. The doorbell rang.

'Manolo! How's your shoulder?'

'Justeen! They put me een thees straight jacket. I escape!' joked Manolo, no worse off in spirit despite his arm resting in a sling.

'Come in. Join us for breakfast?'

'*Sí!*'

As the two friends entered the sun-room, the sight of Boris Bauer staggered Manolo.

'Señor salami! I see a Boris Bauer. I go delirious. Maybe I go back to hospital!'

The tension defused, Robin fed them, Manolo on bacon and eggs,

Justin and Boris on pasta!

'Why you don't spin a coin and you both ween a Wimbledon? I be your umpire!' said Manolo with his toothy grin.

The Wimbledon final against Boris Bauer, pondered Justin. *My time has come!* 'Excuse me, please. I must be alone.'

Justin rose from the breakfast table and left the sun-room.

'Anytheeng I say?' a bemused Manolo asked Robin.

'Oh, no!' Robin shrugged off Justin's disappearance. 'There's no place for us now. It's something he has to do on his own.'

'*Sí!* Maybe *I* try, and I ween a beeg match!' said Manolo, smiling his toothy grin.

Justin went to his bedroom and checked on his tennis gear, all neatly packed the night before. This was his Gethsemane, his communion with the unseen gods of tennis. A time he relived the dream of last night. He always dreamt, vivid dreams of winning great matches at the big tournaments. A time his mind shut out all distraction, focusing his concentration on the task ahead with awesome tunnel vision.

He was ready! Justin drove his car to Wimbledon, Robin sitting next to him, Boris and Manolo in the back seat. The focused aura surrounding Justin cast a spell of total silence.

In contrast, when they arrived at the All England Lawn Tennis & Croquet Club, a party was in full swing, so jovial were the expectant spectators. The drama of Friday had reached breaking point. Now the pressure valve released a festive mood. They had seen a vulnerable Boris Bauer, so expected Justin to have a chance.

'Good luck, darling!' Robin offered.

Justin nodded and allowed just a peck on the cheek.

While Boris walked upstairs to the clubhouse, Manolo lowered his voice to tell Justin, 'Eef I had beat a Boris, the victory ees yours, Justeen! Your plan was perfeect.'

'I'm just sorry Creighton cheated you out of the chance to beat him. Would've been a stupendous victory!'

'You beat a Boris today, *si!* Eef you een a trouble, go low!' Manolo smiled. 'Good luck.'

'*Muchas gracias.*'

Justin headed to the locker-room. He stretched his muscles, checked his rackets again, and fiddled with this and that, all in a measured time, *his* way of dealing with the enormous pressure and the nerves of a Wimbledon final.

With military precision, the linejudges, clad in green blazers and khaki trousers or skirts, marched along the periphery of the court in single file, and one by one peeled off at their stations like jet aircraft in a manoeuvre, then all sat down, taking their cue from the netcord judge. The Centre Court waited in expectant anticipation.

Justin and Boris visited the infamous waiting chamber for a third time. They stood alone.

Boris plucked up the courage to speak to Justin. Looking deeply into his opponent's eyes he said in measured speech, 'I thank you, my friend. Because of you I'm free. ... After today, I want to play the tour, to be like you. Can you help me?'

Justin nodded.

Boris put out his hand. 'Let the best man win. Good luck!'

It was time. Justin Forrester and Boris Bauer walked out onto the famed Centre Court, bathed under glorious sunshine with hardly a suggestion of a breeze.

Eerie, felt Justin, tingling inside. *A nice eerie!*

They posed for the customary photographs in front of a battery of photographers, then started the warm-up, a lull before the storm.

Boris Bauer wore no earmuffs, no mascara tear-drop lines underscored his eyes, and his eyes were different. But Justin noticed none of this, so concentrated was his mind.

At precisely two o'clock, play commenced. Games went with serve to 2-all. At 30-all on Boris Bauer's serve, Justin blocked a return, floating a soap bubble to Boris's feet. It burst. Suddenly a break point. Justin's heart pounded.

It worked! he thought, looking at the wooden racket in his hand. He was amazed, despite the logic. *Coach, you wily old bugger!*

His mind wafted back to Creighton's citadel. 'Justin Forrester favours down-the-line passes on break points by 3:2.'

If that's the case, he's likely to serve wide to my backhand!

Justin leant to his backhand side. True to his expectations, Boris served a humdinger wide. Justin's mercurial speed positioned him perfectly, slightly beyond the ball, and with whipping topspin, he sent a raking crosscourt pass beyond a dumbfounded Boris Bauer.

'Game Forrester. He leads by three games to two,' announced the umpire, a hint of excitement in his voice.

The crowd erupted in applause. Justin had broken the Bauer serve!

He soon discovered Boris to be a vastly different player from last year.

Manolo's softened him, spread the cancer of doubt. He's ripe for the plucking, thought Justin. *And I no longer have to play this alien game. No more junk shots.*

He metamorphosed, broke out of his restrictive cocoon, and marshalled the full repertoire of his creative art of lawn tennis skills to a climax of unsurpassed majesty. He plundered the first set, 6-2. And then the second, also 6-2.

A buzz emanated from the crowd. They brimmed with excitement, but they knew to contain it, especially after Friday's drama.

Still Justin pressed with guile, sweeping inexorably towards his dream like a mighty tide. His ambition did not surpass his faith in his talents.

When he won his serve to lead 4-2, Justin started to giggle inside. He bubbled with the bounce of a baby impala finding its feet for the first time. He knew the championship was his.

Come on, concentrate. Don't start laughing! Justin urged, barely able to suppress his joy.

Fifteen-forty, break point for Justin. He crouched, feet frolicking on the hallowed ground, lightly pattering on the brown grass like a playful puppy. In an instant, they blurred like a cheetah in full flight, hunting its prey, for Justin a tennis ball.

'Game Forrester. He leads by five games to two, and by two sets to love!' announced the umpire in an excited voice.

One game to go! exclaimed Justin, clenching his fist.

From the Royal Box-end he served wide and came in, but Boris, defiant to die last, replied with an acutely angled crosscourt pass, not a shot normally exploited by a man only in possession of puissance.

The crowd groaned in agony. They did not want a match. They wanted a Wimbledon champion, English style!

'Good shot!' Justin acknowledged, clapping his hand against his racket, surprising even himself with his compliment.

Echoes of a bygone era. Such was the spirit in which they played this match, it swept the Centre Court in a great time machine back to the yesteryear of amateur tennis.

Justin dug deep into his reserves. He extracted a stabbing volley.

'Fifteen-all.'

Come on, Justin! he urged.

A trenchant smash.

'Thirty-fifteen.'

Brilliant! Two more points. Just two more points! cried Justin, the adrenalin pumping through his veins.

The rapturous crowd buzzed like a swarm of bees.

Justin served wide, returned crosscourt by Boris. Justin deftly muffled the power in a limp wrist, prising the ball off his shoelaces for a marvellous drop-volley. The ball landed like a snowflake, hugging the grass, then gently rolled away into the hands of a ballboy. A coup for courage. Championship point! Justin slapped himself on the thigh, a rare show of emotion.

'Forty-fifteen!' croaked the umpire, his voice straining.

The crowd went berserk, screaming, 'Justin! Justin! Justin!'

'Quiet please,' ordered the umpire, but to no avail. They stomped their feet in a drum roll of anticipation. A poignant moment in British tennis history.

Justin readied to serve. His heart raced. Suddenly, his face went white, his mind clouded and he froze.

Shit! How do I hold my racket? he panicked.

Still the crowd bayed. It took a special happening to transform the English crowd, genteelly raised on tea and cucumber sandwiches, into a howling mass screaming, 'Justin! Justin! Justin!'

'In the interest of both players, please keep quiet!' ordered the umpire, raising his voice.

Justin closed his eyes. He looked calm, but inside, butterflies strummed raptures of anguish on his taut tummy muscles. He could barely hold onto his trusty Maxply.

Revel in the battle, he told himself, steeling his mind out of the curse of fear. He stared at the Dunlop Maxply in his hands, the racket that sowed the seed for this blossoming moment, and said, *Just go through the motions. I've done it a million times before. Just hit and run in to the net. Have faith. ... Here goes!*

Justin looked across at Boris Bauer, then with all the courage he could muster, served. He struck the ball and ran. The ball split the line, exhaling a puff of white smoke. A scorching ace!

Justin bellowed a primal call and threw up his arms in ecstasy to the heavens, to the resounding euphoric noise that erupted through the stadium. Then he covered his face. He could not believe it. He was champion of Wimbledon!

He turned to Robin, blew her a kiss, then trotted up to the net, almost decided to jump over, but suddenly remembered how he fell flat on his face in his very first tournament win, the Mhlume Tennis Club championships in Swaziland.

Oh, what the heck! Justin said to himself, unable to contain his boyish insouciance.

He leapt over the net and put an arm round Boris Bauer, who reciprocated in kind. They walked back to the umpire's chair, arm in arm. Two great champions.

Justin sat on his chair. The light on court was molten, conducive to sentimental feelings of bliss and melancholy. There was relief, and there was joy, unbridled joy bursting in his heart, but there was also a touching moment, too. Remembering the past, how it all began and all the highs and lows that took him to this hour of triumph, he stared into the distance, and tears welled up in his eyes. A poignant moment.

The Wimbledon crowd were overcome, tears flowed freely and strangers embraced. The scoreboard wasted no time in reflecting, 'JUSTIN FORRESTER – GB : WIMBLEDON CHAMPION – CONGRATULATIONS!'

Justin took a deep breath, stood up and sought out Robin.

Come! he beckoned her.

After a few moments, she appeared at the entrance to the Centre Court, resplendent in a strapless red summer dress and French plait, radiant with love. She hesitated, then broke into a run, throwing herself into Justin's arms.

'Congratulations, darling!' she whispered in his ear.

He clutched her and kissed her in ecstasy. They hugged and kissed and kissed some more, not knowing what else to do!

With the pomp and pageantry only the British can lay on, the presentation ceremony began. First Boris Bauer went forward to receive his silver salver.

Then it was Justin's turn. The Wimbledon champion walked forward to the sound of tumultuous applause. First some royal words. Words that the whole world itched to know, words that went over Justin's head. Finally the prize, the greatest prize in tennis, the Challenge Cup. The game he loved crowned Justin king of Wimbledon.

Justin clutched the trophy in his hands, fondled it, perused it. He read the inscription, 'ALL ENGLAND LAWN TENNIS CLUB – SINGLE-HANDED CHAMPIONSHIP OF THE WORLD'. Engraved on it, were the immortal names Rod Laver and Björn Borg. Now Justin's name stood amongst the legends. He held the Challenge Cup aloft to the sunny sky, cradled in one hand, and it glittered like a golden sun. For British tennis and Justin, all was golden!

The crowd beckoned Justin to parade a victory lap of honour. He did, first holding his trophy up to a phalanx of photographers whose pictures would greet morning cuppas across the world. Then to the enthusiastic English crowd, presenting his trophy to all corners of the stadium, basking in an orgy of adulation.

In a mood reminiscent of the last night at the Proms, the exultant and joyous crowd stood to their feet, held hands, waved Union Jacks and swayed from side to side in time, singing, 'For he's a jolly good fellow!' in the most euphoric moment of emotional fervour and rampant chauvinism ever seen on the Centre Court. Suddenly they broke into the

Wimbledon Wave! Wimbledon Wave? 'Aah, but you see,' purists would one day etch into Wimbledon lore, 'it hiccuped at the Royal Box!'

For Justin, the giddy atmosphere intoxicated him. He wanted it to last forever, for there would never be another one. But nothing lasts forever. Exiting the court through an avenue of ballboys and ballgirls, Justin spontaneously looked over his shoulder and panned a Centre Court wrung dry of emotion, then he disappeared.

Behind him he heard a drill master command, 'Ballboys and ballgirls! Right to left, turn! Quick march! Well done!'

Justin climbed the stairs and entered the locker-room. His tennis friends warmly congratulated him. Tyrone, Larry, Byron, Tugboat and Terrier, and Manolo, a gigantic cog in Justin's wheel of fortune.

First the champion stretched down to avoid injury, then ran hot water into a tub, climbed in amongst large sponges, and marinaded in the bubbles of victory. He wallowed for an hour, coming to terms with all that had happened. A masterful victory, a tactical triumph for natural genius.

'A champion's true edge exists solely in the mind!'

Freshened, Justin walked into a raucous press conference. Bristling with anticipation, reporters jockeyed for space in the jammed interview room. On entry, they gave Justin a standing ovation and three cheers.

'How does it feel?'

'I can die a happy man, now,' beamed Justin.

'How does this compare with, say—'

'I've won many tournaments before and I thought the first Grand Slam in Paris would always be number one. But Wimbledon has shown me something else. I'm very excited, perhaps like never before.'

'You must have often dreamt of winning.'

'Yep!' answered Justin emphatically.

'How different was the reality?'

'I could touch it,' radiated Justin, 'feel the feeling.'

'What's it like to hold up that trophy?'

'It's a dream come true. The most wonderful feeling you can imagine! During those 10 minutes, so many things are swirling around in your head—'

'What things?'

'Joy! Excitement! The people who supported me. Is this for real? Life and its struggle. Now I've answered all questions.'

'Is there one special feeling you'll remember most?'

'Relief!'

Justin held up his hand to stem the questions. 'Before you ask anything else, I wish to make a statement.'

The reporters waited with bated breath.

'As you may know, it has been a lifelong dream of mine to win Wimbledon. Now I have. ... I've thought long and hard about this, grappled with my conscience for many lonely hours in the night, but eventually I came to this decision. As of now, I will no longer play competitive tennis. ... I still have to find a tuxedo for the Champions Dinner tonight, so you have 10 more minutes. Any questions?'

A funereal silence descended on the room. For once, the press was mute, absolutely stunned.

'None!' Justin commented. Shrugging his shoulders, he rose to leave.

But his golden silence was short-lived. All hell broke loose into an Indian market of questions fired by a polyglot gaggle of quacking reporters, panting after the big story.

'Why?' was the incredulous response from the press corps.

'I'm tired. Tired of the travelling. Tired of the inordinate pressures. You eat, breathe and sleep tennis. You dream about it at night. You stay in a hotel, you practise, you come back, order room service, you play your match, back to the hotel, room service again, you watch TV, you sleep, then it's the same all over again,' Justin elaborated in monotone. 'I feel much older than I am. In the last few years I've lived a lifetime. Now it's all over. It was a difficult decision, but I'm happy I made it.'

I'm also tired of you. Tired of the empty conversation, telling you what you want to hear. I can't breathe! gasped Justin, shaking his head. *All I wanted was to be a tennis player!*

'That can't be the real reason. What is?' asked a reporter.

The sport had lost a great champion, a phenomenon who brought talent, grace and dignity to the court, and many would wonder why. They would not accept Justin's reason for retiring.

Few people ever understand true champions, thought Justin, shaking his head. They don't know what's behind this façade, a mask I deliberately wear to protect from those who want more and more when there is nothing left. They think I'm indestructible, made of steel. But the human reality is the sacrifice, devoting my childhood totally to honing my skills to realise my single-minded quest to become the best tennis player in the world, the years of stress, internalising, masking my emotions. I cannot do it any more!

Justin ignored the question.

'This means you'll forgo your privilege, as defending champion, of opening proceedings on Centre Court at next year's championships?'

'Yep!' replied Justin. 'I now have a greater calling back home in Africa. I belong there.'

'Africa?'

'Life at the top in tennis is like a pressure cooker. I'm lucky I can decompress with my other interest, wildlife. There is a little corner of Africa calling me back home. I'm needed there. And I *want* to try something different.'

Home! thought Justin warmly. Home where I can be myself! I promised I'd be back. Now I'm going home!

'What will you miss most?'

'Hmm … the special feeling of winning … the applause, a little bit. Nothing else.'

'What won't you miss?'

'Booking out an entire restaurant, just to have a meal. Fans mobbing me when I walk down the street. All the people around me. They make me very, very tired. More than that, you won't want to know!'

'Is this just an intermission?'

'No. It's the final curtain call! When I see tennis from the other side, the madness, I'll *never* come back.'

There was a stunned silence. One of disbelief. Justin had realised all his boyhood fantasies. Now, on the verge of immortality, he turned his back on tennis and walked away from the game he loved.

'That's it?'

'I've been a lucky bugger. I've had a fun time. I will always love the game. I'll come back to Wimbledon,' Justin comforted. His eyes went vacant. 'But I will never play competitive tennis again.'

Again there was a stunned silence.

'How would you like to be remembered?'

'My record may not look as grand as past champions. But I've had to deal with Boris. He was immovable. I feel I've accomplished my goal. I'm tired now. But if people remember me as a great player, that's good enough for me. I think I'd like that.'

Justin rose to leave. An uncanny stillness pervaded the room. Palms were sweaty, a lump choked the throat. A pall hung over the British tennis party. It was as if Justin were a somewhat reluctant hero. He came into town, he conquered and sorted out the quandary of British tennis. That job done, he saddled up his horse and rode off into the sunset, following his heart into the bush to a cry out of Africa.

As Justin reached the exit, a pressman broke the silence.

'Ted Parsen of the *London Daily News*. What about British tennis? You've made yourself a little gold-mine here. How do you propose to pay us back?' shouted the reporter. 'How can you leave us in the woods? British tennis will go back to …?

The sphincter stinker! thought Justin, shaking his head slowly, almost in pity. *You want, want, want! You take so much, I have nothing left to give. You could have had it all!*

Justin ignored him, turned and left.

Thank goodness I can close the door on the chapter of press conferences and shed the clutches of the tabloid press. One battle I never won!

Behind him, a scuffle broke out in the press room.

Justin escorted Robin to the celebrity studded Champions Dinner at the plush Savoy Hotel in The Strand, where the tennis world toasted Heidi Schültz and himself as Wimbledon champions. They each made speeches.

Justin said little. So overcome with emotion, he merely shook his head in disbelief and uttered, 'All I can say, is that I won Wimbledon! What else can I say?'

Then it was time for the champion's traditional opening dance with the belle of the ball, Heidi Schültz.

'Keep your hands above her waist,' warned Robin with a mischievous grin.

Justin took the dance floor with Heidi to the tune of a waltz. She looked into his eyes.

'I know how much this means to you, Justin. I'm so happy for you,' Heidi said, planting a kiss on Justin's cheek before offering him back to Robin.

'Heidi, wait,' called Justin. 'I've someone I'd like you to meet.

'Matchmaking?'

'Uh huh! Just don't hold me responsible for your kids when they cry thwack, thwack, thwack!' laughed Justin. 'Heidi, meet Boris!'

While all around the world, fans watched and wondered in front of a tear-jerking montage of slow-motion Forrester to the accompaniment of Ol' Blue Eyes' rendition, 'I Did It My Way', Justin and Robin strutted their stuff through the night as sweethearts.

In the wee hours of the morning, an official tapped Justin on the shoulder and handed him a telegram. It read, 'CONGRATULATIONS, SON! – MUM, DAD AND COACH.'

THE END

www.ingramcontent.com/pod-product-compliance
Lightning Source LLC
Chambersburg PA
CBHW031249170626
46807CB00001B/54